T0088967

PENGUIN CLASSICS

MEDIEVAL WRITINGS ON
FEMALE SPIRITUALITY

Elizabeth Spearing holds a D.Phil. from the University of York. She has published articles on the *Amadis* cycle and on Aphra Behn, and she translated Julian of Norwich's *Revelations of Divine Love* for Penguin Classics. With A.C. Spearing (who wrote the introduction and notes to *Revelations*), she has collaborated on editions of Chaucer's *Reeve's Tale*, Shakespeare's *The Tempest*, and the anthology *Poetry in the Age of Chaucer*.

MEDIEVAL WRITINGS ON FEMALE SPIRITUALITY

———————

EDITED AND WITH AN
INTRODUCTION AND NOTES BY
ELIZABETH SPEARING

PENGUIN BOOKS

PENGUIN BOOKS
Published by the Penguin Group
Penguin Group (USA) Inc., 375 Hudson Street, New York, New York 10014, U.S.A.
Penguin Books Ltd, 80 Strand, London WC2R ORL, England
Penguin Books Australia Ltd, 250 Camberwell Road, Camberwell, Victoria 3124, Australia
Penguin Books Canada Ltd, 10 Alcorn Avenue, Toronto, Ontario, Canada M4V 3B2
Penguin Books India (P) Ltd, 11 Community Centre, Panchsheel Park, New Delhi – 110 017, India
Penguin Books (N.Z.) Ltd, Cnr Rosedale and Airborne Roads, Albany, Auckland, New Zealand
Penguin Books (South Africa) (Pty) Ltd, 24 Sturdee Avenue,
Rosebank, Johannesburg 2196, South Africa

Penguin Books Ltd, Registered Offices: 80 Strand, London WC2R ORL, England

First published in Penguin Books 2002

Acknowledgments for permission to reprint copyrighted
texts appear on pages 256–268.

LIBRARY OF CONGRESS CATALOGING IN PUBLICATION DATA
Medieval writings on female spirituality / edited with an introduction and
notes by Elizabeth Spearing.
p. cm.—(Penguin classics)
Includes bibliographical references (p.).
ISBN 0 14 04.3925 0 (pbk. : alk. paper)
1. Catholic women—Religious life. 2. Spiritual life—Catholic Church.
I. Spearing, Elizabeth. II. Series.
BX2353 .M43 2002
248'.082—dc21 2001058072

Set in Stempel Garamond

146119709

CONTENTS

INTRODUCTION

This volume offers a selection from some of the great variety of writing by and about religious women in the Middle Ages. The focus is on such writing in northern Europe, especially texts which were available in English, either because that was the language in which they were written or because English versions of them had been made. The choice of texts is deliberately wide—varied in period, purpose, and quality. It includes the visions of an aristocratic prophet, those of a narrow-minded and malicious nun, and a profoundly original exploration of the nature of God. When these women lived it was not normal for anyone who was reasonably rich, no matter how literate, to do their own writing—there would always be someone on hand to do it for them—nor were all the women in this selection literate. Some of the texts, it is true, present themselves as first-person writings by women themselves—whether poems, letters, meditations, or visions—but many are third-person accounts by men of the lives and practices of women regarded as holy.

Even in what may seem to be moments of the most direct self-expression, the writings are shaped by a variety of literary conventions. Some are poetic compositions, including letters, which draw on the tradition of courtliness. Some belong to the field of mysticism in its fullest sense—religious experience directed towards the soul's union with God in this life. Some are prophetic in ways that recall the prophets of the Old Testament and the Apocalypse. Some are visionary writings at a less exalted level, belonging to a tradition that goes back through the early centuries of Christianity to the Bible—visions of heaven and hell, and especially of purgatory, the only place from which spirits could reappear on earth to confirm the Church's teaching about the efficacy of prayer, comforting for laypeople and remunerative for the Church. Some are meditations on Christ's human life, from passionate imaginings of the Crucifixion to Margery Kempe seeing herself as a servant in St. Anne's household and caring for the Virgin in her childhood. Some are accounts by men of women's attempts to imitate Christ and purge sin through various kinds of bodily suffering; they often involve extreme kinds of self-mortification and seem bizarre by modern standards. Some will probably convince most readers of the authenticity of their strivings towards the transcendent. In others there are elements of fantasy and even comfortable self-deception: punishment is promised for enemies, heaven for friends and family. It is revealed to St. Bridget that her daughter would be more useful with her mother in Rome than with her husband in Sweden, and there are a number of instances of critics of a visionary coming to unpleasant ends after she has complained to God: " 'That jangling cleric is too proud of his learning to want me. But I shall give him a clout and he will really know that I am God.' And shortly after that he died of the palsy."[1]

From the beginnings of Christianity there had been deep suspicion of religious teaching by women. St. Paul's severe prohibitions were frequently repeated: *Let women keep silence in the churches; for it is not permitted them to speak, but to be subject* [1Cor 14:34], and *Nor I suffer not a woman to speak, but to be subject* [1Ti 2:12]. Many of the women in this collection lay claim to elevated religious insights, and yet they themselves and the men who write about them feel obliged to present them in terms of modesty and humility. Thus we are told that Mary of Oignies was "always modest and as simple as a dove in every way," and even Hildegard of Bingen, a great aristocratic lady who did not hesitate to denounce the leaders of the Church, felt obliged to describe herself as a "poor little creature." In the case of Margery Kempe, whose impact on others is a central theme of her book, hostility was aroused not just by her eccentricity but by the simple fact that she was a woman who dared to make public pronouncements about religious matters. Literacy was far less common among women than among men. Women who could read and write could usually do so only in the vernacular languages; very few learned Latin, the language of the Bible and the liturgy (Hildegard and Bridget were among the exceptions), and this meant that they were cut off from the world of learning and abstract thought and especially of theology. This put them at a great disadvantage but could also be an advantage to them. They could be more individual, more peculiar, and they could think in ways which were not bound by the rigid logic of scholasticism—and might more often be left alone to do so. Julian might not have got away with some of the things she wrote if she had been a man writing in Latin.

The survival and diffusion of texts before printing was dependent on a few people and local circumstances, and this was particularly likely to be true of women. Which women became well-known and widely-read must have depended not just on the value and interest of what they thought and experienced, but on which male clerics admired them and whether the women's teachings and ways of life were what the contemporary Church wanted to encourage. Bridget of Sweden, who lived in Rome for the last twenty-five years of her life, reiterated and expanded orthodox views; she had a direct connection with the papacy and was recognized and canonized soon after her death. However, though the Church could be very effective at promoting the works of women it approved, it could not always control the writing of such people as Marguerite Porete: she was not canonized, but burned at the stake. Our access to the women in this volume is through men; even texts that are almost certainly written by the woman herself owe their continued existence to a male scribe, and some exist because of a succession of men. For some women, a male cleric was not just the authorizer but the author of her text. Elizabeth of Spaalbeek had first to be recognized as peculiarly holy by senior churchmen in her area; at the bishop's request, a local abbot, her cousin, became her protector. This man did not just provide for her care; Elizabeth enacted a religious drama through the hours of the day and night, and her reverend cousin "presented" the performance to admiring visitors, selecting and interpreting her behaviour as he did so: "This reverend abbot . . . was with us during everything which I have described and was our informant and reliable expounder of the virgin's words,"[2] declares Philip, the monk from Clairvaux who wrote a Latin account of her life in which he also refers at intervals to "worthy men" who had added to his own first-hand knowledge. Before a medieval Englishwoman could read this account of Elizabeth's life, an unknown English cleric had to translate Philip's Latin, sometimes having trouble understanding it, cutting selectively as he went along.

The words of Hildegard of Bingen come to us more directly. She was not only highly literate, but she had an astonishing fluency in Latin for a woman of her era; however, she felt the need for male

(and clerical) authorization. In her fortieth year she felt great "pressure of pains to manifest what [she] had seen and heard" in visions,
and confided in her *magister*. "Astonished, he bade me write these
things down secretly, till he could see what they were and what
their source might be. Then, realizing that they came from God,
he indicated this to his abbot, and from that time on he worked at
this [writing down] with me. . . ." Further male approval gave her
more fame and influence: "When these occurrences were brought
up at an audience in Mainz Cathedral, everyone said they stemmed
from God. . . . Then my writings were brought to Pope Eugene
. . . he bade me commit whatever I saw or heard in my vision to
writing.[3]. . ."

The original transcriptions of the visions of St. Bridget seem to
have been firmly under her own control; the *Vita* written shortly
after her death describes the process in detail: " . . . the words that
were given her from God she wrote down in her mother tongue
with her own hand when she was well and she had us, her father
confessors, make a very faithful translation of them into Latin. She
then listened to the translation with her own writing, which she
herself had written, to make sure that not one word was added or
subtracted, but was exactly what she had heard and seen in the divine vision. But when she was too weak she would call her confessor and another scribe . . . whereupon with great devotion and fear
of God, and sometimes in tears, she spoke the words in her native
language in a kind of tense, ecstatic trance as if she were reading
from a book; and then the confessor dictated these words in Latin
to the scribe, and he wrote them down there in her presence. When
the words had been written down she listened very carefully and attentively."[4] As Bridget had begun Latin lessons with her sons in
Sweden and continued with her studies in Rome, she would have
been able to check the Latin translation.

Margery Kempe could not read or write, but she had access to
devotional works by hearing them read aloud, and she obviously
heard a great many sermons. She must have been something of an
Ancient Mariner, practicing an ever-expanding spoken account of
her physical and spiritual lives as she lived them to sympathetic
clerics: "And to this priest she confided her whole life, as near as
she could, from her young age, both her sins, her troubles, her trials, her contemplations, and also her revelations, and such grace as

God worked in her though his mercy.[5] . . ." In many such cases we might wonder in which direction the current of power was flowing, and might ask, as did a recent scholar, "Holy women and their confessors, or confessors and their holy women?"[6] Their gender meant that by definition these women were weak; many of them suffered from lengthy periods of illness, and yet they found ways to turn their weakness into strength. They were able to manipulate their families, their confessors, and other bystanders into serving them, they gained status and influence in their communities, they founded religious houses and reproved and advised people at every level of society. Hildegard and Bridget counselled emperors and popes; Christine the Astonishing, who had been a cowherd and chained as a lunatic, had only to cry, "Bring the convent to me, so that together we may praise Jesus for his great goodness in his miracles . . ." and "At once the nuns came running from every direction."[7]

The writings in this volume inevitably reflect a variety of developments in medieval piety. One of the most important of these, as far as women are concerned, has been summed up by Caroline Bynum in her remark that "bodiliness provides access to the sacred."[8] In the course of the Middle Ages there was a general shift in emphasis towards Christ's Humanity, God inhabiting a suffering human body, culminating in the mutilation of that body in the Passion and Crucifixion. Christ's pain, and the blood and water that flowed from his wounds, were the means by which it was possible for human beings to be saved. Given that medieval thought associated masculinity with mind and spirit and femininity with body, women, for all their inferiority and subordination, could be felt to have a special connection with Jesus in his Passion, and through their bodies they could hope to have special access to the sacredness associated with his body. This is the train of thought that underlies the intense focus on the bodies of holy women in the texts of the Douce manuscript (see below), the subtler focus on the body in Julian of Norwich's *Revelations*, and Margery Kempe's persistent weeping and other forms of bodily obstreperousness. The general link between female spirituality and the body of Christ is brought into especially sharp focus at a moment in Julian's *Revelations* when, seeing Christ on the cross and imagining his pain, she seems to hear a voice saying, "Look up to his Father in Heaven," but answers, "No, I cannot, for you are my Heaven," and proceeds to see the whole Trinity within the Humanity of Christ.[9] The celibate way of life adopted by medieval holy women in its various forms—as anchorites, nuns, and beguines and in less formal ways—was regarded as a way of escaping from the demands of the body, yet their writings are dominated by bodily practices and meditations.

Adopting celibacy obviously meant renouncing marriage. The biography of a holy woman often includes an admiring account of how she rejects her parents and their plans for her. Parents arranging just the marriage which a kind, sensible couple would choose for their daughter (as in the case of the rich young bridegroom who obviously loved and respected Mary of Oignies) are presented as cruel and unreasonable. And if a woman of special holiness does marry, she must distance herself from her husband (and any children she may have) to attain greater purity and spirituality. However, renunciation could include more than this. Medieval people, lay or clerical, did not see a family as the setting for a truly Christian life. To be closer to God, you had to distance yourself from your relatives. Encouraged by a celibate clergy, there was general awareness of such sayings of Jesus (now often forgotten) as, *If any man come to me, and hate not his father and mother and wife and children and brethren and sisters . . . he cannot be my disciple* [Lk 14:25, 26]. For women such as these, and a great many other people, earthly relationships gave way to the all-important heavenly one: God became Father, Mother, Spouse. "Unless their goodness and innate propensity to holiness commended them, her family relatives shared little of her affection," says the biographer of Christina of Markyate admiringly,[10] and St. Bridget prayed to God to "rip the thorn which is in my heart, which is bodily love for my husband or children or friends or relatives."[11] These women had human friends, relatives, and spiritual advisers, but more important were God, the Virgin, and any saints to whom they felt particularly close.

HILDEGARD OF BINGEN

Hildegard (1098–1179) would have been exceptional at any time but was quite extraordinary for a twelfth-century woman. The only playwright and only composer of her time (man or woman) to be known by name, the only woman to be an authorized exponent of

Christian doctrine and the only one to preach openly, she was also the author of remarkable scientific writings, a visionary, and a prophet. The tenth child of aristocratic parents who lived in the German Empire, in the archdiocese of Mainz, Hildegard was taken at the age of eight to be brought up by Jutta von Sponheim, whose small group of devout women expanded into a Benedictine community attached to the abbey of St. Disibod, with Jutta as abbess. Hildegard became a nun there at fourteen, eventually succeeding her teacher as abbess in 1136. Sometime between 1147 and 1152, she moved her community to nearby Rupertsberg, near Bingen, building a large convent there. Despite periods of sickness, often associated with moments of special stress in her personal and ecclesiastical life, she displayed extraordinary energy and determination and lived to an advanced age. She travelled widely in the Rhineland area and, aided by the confidence which came from her aristocratic rank, she influenced many powerful figures from the Emperor Frederick Barbarossa downwards. Her most important visionary work is the *Scivias* ("Know-the-Ways"); she was also an eloquent preacher and wrote copiously about the science of her time and about theology. These writings are all in Latin.

The texts in this volume are of two kinds: there are a number of extracts from the *Vita*, written with her collaboration, and from a letter to her last secretary describing her life and visions as she experienced them; and there are extracts from *Scivias* in which she gives accounts and interpretations of some of her visions. The visions are intensely dramatic and brilliantly coloured, sometimes reflecting, it has been suggested, the visual disturbances caused by migraine. They often possess a sharp-edged grotesqueness reminiscent of Romanesque sculpture and manuscript illuminations. The interpretations, too, are clear-cut and authoritative; they leave no room for further interpretation by the reader and in this are at the opposite extreme from the slow crystallizations of meaning in Julian of Norwich. There is little that is distinctively feminine about her visionary works; writing in a period before the development of the strongly emotional Christocentric devotion which had such appeal for later medieval women, she did not practice or recommend extreme asceticism, and presented herself as a prophet conveying God's word regardless of her own gender.

CHRISTINA OF MARKYATE

The life of Hildegard's almost exact English contemporary was written around 1160 by an anonymous monk of St. Albans Abbey who knew her well in her adult years and had heard from Christina herself about her early life. Though he wrote in Latin, while she would have spoken English and perhaps French, we often seem to be close to her own words and experiences. She was born in Huntingdon into a prosperous Anglo-Saxon family some thirty years after the Normans seized control of England. A childhood visit to the important Benedictine abbey of St. Albans in Hertfordshire moved her to make a vow of virginity—a means by which a medieval girl could hope to escape from the otherwise overwhelming power of the family. When she was about sixteen the worldly Norman bishop of Durham, a family friend, apparently tried to get her into his bed and then, made vindictive by her rejection of him, insisted that her parents should marry her to a young nobleman called Burthred. Christina was eventually forced into a betrothal.

The first extract in this volume, in which she dreams of quietness, flowers, and comfort from the Virgin Mary, occurs in the context of persecution by her parents and Burthred's attempts to force her to consummate a union regarded as binding. Cut off from religious friends, she has been beaten and shamed by her mother and has resisted efforts to make her drunk and attempts by her best friends to talk her round and of her husband to rape her. There follows an account of Christina's desperate escape on horseback from her cruel and powerful family and the persecution of senior clerics in order to become the virgin bride of Christ, which reads like a romantic elopement. (This dramatic phase of her life was later reflected in the inclusion in her personal prayer book, the famous illuminated manuscript called the *St. Albans Psalter*, of the French *Chanson d'Alexis,* a poem about a young man dedicated to virginity who flees his bride on their wedding night.)

In its next phase Christina's life was one of withdrawal from the world into solitude. One form of the ascetic life, dedicated to chastity, poverty, and obedience, was that of monks and nuns living in organized communities; another was solitary, the life of hermits and anchoresses, also under a recognized though less formal rule, but alone or in tiny groups. Christina now took refuge with an anchoress, Alfwen. While with her she had the vision described in extract (b), in which she was protected from angry bulls—a strongly sexual image—and loathsome toads. After two years, she moved to a tiny cell adjacent to that of Roger, an old hermit, with whom she shared her religious devotions. She was virtually entombed there for four more years, in such discomfort that she suffered from many illnesses. Extract (c) tells how Christ appeared to her in her cell and gave her a golden cross. Only two days later, Burthred came to Roger to say that the Virgin Mary had commanded him to release Christina from her marriage vow. Now Roger began to think of making Christina his successor in his hermitage; in extract (d) Mary appears to her and promises that this will happen. The archbishop of Canterbury himself then annulled Christina's "marriage," and in extract (e) we learn how she struggled against sexual temptation while staying with a cleric in whose charge the archbishop has put her, and how saints intervened to protect her. She was evidently highly sexed and irresistibly attractive to men, and this was no doubt part of the saintly charisma that spread her reputation beyond Markyate and made archbishops and abbots attempt to recruit her.

Christina cured a woman of the falling sickness but suffered from many maladies herself; these, and the miraculous means by which they are healed, are the subject of extract (f), along with her crowning by angels and the divine intervention that brought an end to her temptations. After this (about 1124) she first came into contact with Abbot Geoffrey of St. Albans, who subsequently became her admirer and patron; she converted him to genuine spirituality, and seemed to have miraculous knowledge of his activities and thoughts. About 1131 Christina made her formal profession as a nun at St. Albans. Extract (g) relates how Geoffrey's salvation was confirmed to her in a vision, and another vision revealed that her brother Gregory had found favour with the Virgin Mary while mortally sick. Christina three times received dream-like revelations that Geoffrey would be prevented from going abroad on dangerous political business. Her relationship with him aroused slanderous comment, and extract (h) explains how Christina appeared miraculously to a monk to disprove this and how a divine voice reassured her and her followers after a terrifying appearance by the devil as a headless body. The final extract concerns the appearances of a mysterious and handsome pilgrim, who turns out to be Christ himself. Shortly after this the only manuscript of Christina's life breaks off, and it is not known how much is missing. She lived for many more years; in 1145 Markyate priory was founded, with Christina as its head; in 1147 Geoffrey of St. Albans died; in 1155 there is record of a grant made to her by King Henry II; and she is thought to have died between then and 1166.

The extracts given here focus on the many visionary experiences that made Christina's life remarkable for the monk who wrote it. As he claimed, "These visions were not imaginary or dreams; she saw them with the true intuition enjoyed by the mystics."[12] The natural and the supernatural coexist, and so do sexuality and holiness: for all that she lived as an anchoress and a nun, there is a scarcely sublimated eroticism in Christina's relations with the male clerics who so much admired her and even with "the man whose beauty had only to be seen to be loved," the Christ who manifests himself to her at Christmas. This is a frequent and even normal element in medieval female devotion, but in the twelfth century it showed itself in an uncomplicated way, with an innocent joy that still resonates many centuries later.

HADEWIJCH AND MARGUERITE PORETE

Two of the writers included in this volume are best considered as a pair, because they were both beguines, and both not only great mystics, but great creative writers in their vernacular languages. Beguines were members of loosely organized, unenclosed lay sisterhoods, a way of life that originated in the Netherlands in the early thirteenth century and then spread rapidly through France and Germany (though apparently not England). They lived a communal semi-religious life, supporting themselves by their own work, but were not permanently bound by vows as nuns were: they could hold private property and could leave to get married. They aided the sick and the poor, but they also practiced contemplation, often of a visionary and ecstatic kind. Some of them expressed their religious insights in the vernacular languages, and at least three are now famous as writers: Mechthild of Magdeburg in German, Hadewijch in Dutch, and Marguerite Porete in French. Because the beguines were women speaking and writing about religious matters without being under strict ecclesiastical control, as their numbers grew they were held in increasing suspicion by the Church, and their way of life was condemned by the council of Vienne in 1312. By the middle of the fourteenth century the beguine movement, which had attracted many women and much attention, both admiring and suspicious, was in decline.

Hadewijch lived as a beguine in the first half of the thirteenth century, probably in or near Antwerp. At some time, as is indicated by Letter 29, she may have been head of a beguinage, but she was apparently driven out by opposition. Her biography is completely uncertain because the only documentary evidence is not literal but intensely literary. She is now regarded as one of the greatest Dutch poets of the Middle Ages, but her work was little known in her own time (in England it was completely unknown), and modern translations give little sense of the poetic quality of her writing, with its intricate ambiguity and paradox. Passionate love is its motive and theme—"Love is all!" she exclaims in Letter 25—a love that could be directed towards other women, as in that letter, but that had as its focus God in both his Humanity and his Divinity. In Vision 7 she describes suffering an agony of desire, and "such madness and fear beset my mind that it seemed to me that I did not content my Beloved, and that my Beloved did not fulfil my desire." An eagle appears, telling her, "If you wish to attain oneness, make yourself ready!" Hadewijch sees God as a child, as a man, and as the sacrament, and she enjoys an intensely erotic bodily union with him—he "took me entirely in his arms, and pressed me to him; and all my members felt his in full felicity, in accordance with the desire of my heart and my humanity"—until her ability to experience him fades and "I could no longer distinguish him within me." This moment of ecstasy, though, comes in her youth, and she learns that it is only the beginning of her mystical life, not its ultimate goal. As she writes in Vision 11, Love is to be "a heavy burden and disgrace"; and in Letter 1 she can even assert that God "has been more cruel to me than any devil ever was."

In her poems, Hadewijch writes in the tradition of *fine amour,* which goes back to the secular poetry of the troubadours. Love is a harsh discipline in which the lover is continually tested by suffering. There is no repose: the lover's life is a never-ending journey, an exile, "night in the daytime," madness, and yet this is the only way of living acceptable to the spiritual elite. In the poetry of the troubadours and their descendents, the lover is usually a knight in pursuit of a distant and haughty lady, and Hadewijch frequently adopts a male identity. "Love" (*Minne*) is God but is also "she," a seemingly cruel goddess who provokes insatiable desire. Her lyrics adopt traditional frameworks of the passing of the seasons or the knight setting out on a quest, and traditional gestures of hopeful beginning followed by despair, of farewell to love, of the contrast between the poet and happy lovers, but always as means of speaking about the soul's relation to God. Their most common image is of love as wandering in exile—the bitter relinquishment of normality and its satisfactions, to be dedicated to a power that is entirely arbitrary in its demands. Only when all hope of consolation is abandoned can the lover regain the union with God that gives meaning to life.

About Marguerite Porete we also know little before her last years, except that she lived in Hainaut around 1300. She seems to have begun as a beguine but later to have adopted a more wandering way of life. She probably wrote an early version of her allegorical poem in French verse and prose, the *Mirouer des simples âmes anienties* (*Mirror of Simple Annihilated Souls*), in the 1290s. Between 1296 and 1306 the poem was condemned as heretical by the bishop of Cambrai, and she was forbidden to allow its teaching to be circulated. Disregarding this ban, she sent it to three theologians to invite them to confirm its orthodoxy, adding for their benefit a further set of chapters (including the extract from chapter XXVII translated here), intended to help them understand it. She regarded them and most readers as her spiritual inferiors: even more than with Hadewijch, the tenor of her writing is esoteric and elitist, a form of courtly mysticism in which she sees herself as belonging to a spiritual aristocracy with God as its head. The three theologians approved the work as they saw it, though one said it was so exalted that he could not understand it. Marguerite then submitted it to the bishop of Châlons, presumably hoping that he would set aside the earlier condemnation. Instead, in 1308, she was arrested by the Dominican Inquisitor, William of Paris, a powerful man who was confessor to the king of France, Philip the Fair. The expectation was that a person accused of heresy would either defend or retract his or her teachings, but Marguerite would do neither—she simply refused to reply to her interrogators. She was kept in prison, and in 1310 a committee of theologians was invited to comment on propositions drawn from her book. One of them was that "the soul brought to Nothing takes leave of the Virtues, nor is she any longer in their bondage,"[13] an idea repeated in several forms in the excerpts in this volume, as when she writes that the soul in its third state renounces virtuous actions in order to sacrifice what she loves, "fulfilling the will of another so as to destroy her own will" (ch. XVII). Marguerite's concern was with the individual soul in its most exalted spiritual state of "annihilation"—total nothingness, total absorption on earth of the human will into the will of God—and it was alleged that she saw that superior soul as set above the Church's normal requirements, such as self-denial, asceticism, the pursuit of virtue, even God's gifts or consolations, from weeping to mystical ecstasy. For her, the institutional Church was "Holy Church the Little," by contrast with the true Church of annihilated souls.

The doctrines attributed to Marguerite Porete largely correspond to what is known as the "Heresy of the Free Spirit," the claim that those individuals inspired by the Holy Spirit have complete freedom of action on earth, because, as St. Paul writes in 2 Corinthians 3:17, "where the spirit of the Lord is, there is liberty." Such heretics, it was said, claimed not to be bound by the normal requirements of morality because they thought themselves incapable of sin. In all probability there was no such heresy, in the sense of an organized sect with a teaching programme hostile to the Church, there were only individual mystics like Marguerite, many of them women, whose use of language was daringly ambiguous. The Church, however, felt under threat from extreme ideas and constructed a heresy to account for this, a heresy denounced in 1312 at the council of Vienne, at which the beguines were also condemned.

Marguerite was caught up in this scare, and her obvious contempt for the ecclesiastics who were so much her spiritual inferiors that they could not understand her work cannot have helped. There was no powerful religious order or distinguished confessor to protect her, and she was again convicted and, as a relapsed heretic, was handed over to the secular court and immediately condemned to death. She was burned at the stake in the Place de Grève—the first heretic to be burned to death in the Paris inquisition. A contemporary chronicler reports that the spectators were moved to tears by her noble bearing as she endured this terrible end. Her book was burned at the same time, but it was already in circulation, and it was too late to stop it from continuing to be read. Only one French manuscript is known, but the *Mirror* was also translated into Latin, Italian, and English. The Middle English translation dates from about 1400. The translator, who calls himself "MN," did not know that his source was heretical or even that it was by a woman: he simply thought the *Mirror* an important work of speculative mysticism, though one that needed careful interpretation if it was to be kept within the bounds of orthodoxy. There are three manuscripts of the Middle English *Mirror*, and one of them also contains the only copy of the Short Text of Julian of Norwich's *Revelations*. All three manuscripts are associated with Carthusian monasteries, which were the focus of interest in contemplative practices and writings in late medieval England. MN may well have been a Carthusian monk. He wrote glosses on the more worrying parts of his French source, and he also had to deal with scribal errors in the manuscript and with his own unwillingness to believe that the author really intended some of her more startling statements, so he explains things away and sometimes writes what does not seem to make sense.

A detailed interpretation of the extracts from the Middle English *Mirror* translated here would be impossibly long, but it may be helpful to explain that the work is essentially a dialogue between Love and the Soul, with many interventions by other personified figures, Reason being the most prominent. Love is generally female in the French text but more often male in the English; he/she is the refined love of courtly poetry, possible only for those of high rank and exquisite sensibility, but is also God himself—"I am God, says Love, for Love is God and God is Love" (ch. IV). God, the transcendent being, is imagined as the distant beloved, the object of human love, but also as Love itself, that which makes human love possible. The Soul is God's lover, whose aim is to become perfectly identified with him, to be annihilated into him and thus to be deified. Ultimately the perfected Soul can make the startling claim: "I am the salvation of creatures and the glory of God" (ch. XIII). But the Soul is also Marguerite herself, the writer of this book as well as a character in it. In one sense, the book is about its own composition; it is always a work in progress, a work full of references to itself as a book. It is by Marguerite, but it is also something given to her by Love, the king greater than Alexander referred to in the prologue.

Reason is at a far lower level. She understands only literally and superficially, but her questions provide excuses for Love to expound her teachings more fully, for the benefit of those who are at a lower spiritual level than the Soul. Reason is Marguerite's own rational faculty, but she is also the guiding principle of the institutional Church, Holy Church the Little, the Church that Marguerite despised and that was going to put her to death. For Marguerite, though, the harsher discipline was that imposed by Love, and there is a kind of metaphysical masochism at the heart of her work, which emerges most clearly in the series of thought-experiments in the final extract here (ch. XXVII): nothing will satisfy her but total submission to a God who may after all reject her love. She is forced to accept that her book is no more than a fiction, that she cannot really engage in dialogue with Love; but with her final acceptance of disenchantment comes a release into freedom.

MANUSCRIPT DOUCE 114

This collection includes the lives of three women whose religious insights express themselves in physical behaviour that by modern standards is fascinatingly bizarre. The lives were originally composed in Latin by distinguished ecclesiastics. That of Christine, known as "the Astonishing," was written by Thomas of Cantimpré (who lived from around 1200 until after 1262), an Augustinian monk who, after meeting the holy woman Lutgard of Aywières in 1230, became a Dominican and devoted his life to spreading the fame of contemporary saints, most of them women. The life of Mary of Oignies is by Jacques de Vitry (c. 1170–1240), who became her confessor and after her death studied the practices of other holy women until he became bishop of Acre and finally a cardinal. The life of Elizabeth of Spaalbeek is by a Cistercian monk, Philip of Clairvaux. It has generally been thought that medieval religious devotion in England was comparatively sober and moderate, avoiding continental extremes. This makes it all the more surprising that all three of these lives were translated into Middle English, apparently around 1400. They are found together in a single manuscript, Douce 114, from which they are translated here.

CHRISTINE THE ASTONISHING

Thomas of Cantimpré's choice of Christine for one of his *Lives* of holy women has been called a lapse of judgement and the contents untrustworthy; more recently she has been seen as an exemplar of purgatorial cleansing, or a "fool for Christ's sake" [see I Cor 3:18–19]; a twentieth-century psychiatrist might have called her psychotic or schizophrenic. Her bizarre behaviour and Thomas's interpretation of it certainly proved interesting in the Middle Ages, as it survives in a number of manuscripts in Latin, Dutch, and English. Though astonishing, Christine was not as unusual as one might suppose. There seem to have been a number of people "possessed by the Spirit" in some way,[14] and even those possessed by a devil could be seen as having supernatural authority.

Christine, though her parents are described as having been "respectable," belonged to a family where she could be expected to spend her days watching over the family animals in the fields. Thomas says that this enables her to be particularly close to God, ascribing a sickness and her apparent death to the weakening effect of such contemplation. Despite her extraordinary resurrection during her own funeral, her sisters and the local community see her subsequent behaviour as madness, and she is treated as the insane were treated: she is chained up and neglected. Much of her behaviour does sound like accounts of diabolical possession, a frequent explanation for madness, but Thomas's account could be taken as showing how, after her journey into the next world, she is fulfilling the wishes of God by demonstrating how sin is punished in purgatory—she leaps into fiery ovens, plunges into icy water, hangs with the dead. Much of her behaviour could more easily be seen as holy: she flees to the wilderness, goes into trances in various extraordinary places and ways, she weeps and wails and sings, she has special insights into people's behaviour and the destination of their souls. Christine enjoys the company of nuns, is responsive to priests, and spends a considerable length of time with a recluse.

However, for many years her family try to confine her, until they are persuaded by miracles that she is especially holy. The local clergy also appear to be convinced of this but become uneasy about her public image when people begin to flock to their town and, as it says in chapter XIII, "Then men and women in religious orders in that town fear[ed] that the huge wonder of these marvels should be beyond man's comprehension, and prompt the beastly minds of men to wicked thoughts and deprive God's great deeds of their power, in that Christine fled from the presence of men, and climbed onto high things like a bird, and stayed in the water for a long time like a fish." So they prayed that God would make her more like other people—and this was successful, for after plunging into a baptismal font she became calmer, more socialized, and less embarrassing. It is possible that they felt simultaneously that God's great deeds should be truly valued and that they had an image problem on their hands. It has to be remembered when reading works which celebrate the lives and miracles of holy people that the local community and their clergy and religious houses stood to gain not only spiritually but also financially from the presence of such a figure in their midst, dead or alive. A well-known saint or relic could and did bring large numbers of pilgrims in search of help for their bodies and souls, and often a good holiday. Their money helped the local economy and Church coffers. There was great competition for the physical relics of saints and holy people, with a number of well-documented thefts.

Like other holy women, Christina became a preacher and a spiritual adviser. She even exerted considerable influence over Count Lewis of Looz, who treated her as a priest when he made his deathbed confession to her. A woman who three or four centuries later would have been burned as a witch, who nowadays might have been on medication, in an institution, or even living rough, in the Middle Ages moved from cows to castle, an honoured and valued member of the community.

MARY OF OIGNIES

Another beguine, the Blessed Mary of Oignies was born in 1176 in the diocese of Liège, remarkable for its spiritual energy in the Middle Ages—Christine the Astonishing and Elizabeth of Spaalbeek were from the same diocese. After her marriage at the age of fourteen, Mary's husband was persuaded to join her in a vow of chastity, and the young couple dedicated themselves and their money to a life of good works. They cared for lepers[15] in nearby Williambrouk where, although her husband disappears from the story at this point, we know that Mary inspired a number of like-minded women to join her. After some years so many devout admirers were coming to visit her that Mary sought greater seclusion in a house of Augustinian canons in Oignies, though she did not live an enclosed life but travelled about to teach the faith and comfort the sick and dying. Here, too, she was the centre of a group of men and women who admired and emulated her. Her fame reached Paris, where Jacques de Vitry was moved to go and see her, and then to remain with her as confessor and friend until her death in 1213, when he began writing her life while moving up the ecclesiastical hierarchy. The life is preceded by a prologue in which he extols the lives of beguines. Though it was strictly speaking his place to give her spiritual guidance, like the confessors of a number of other holy women, he seems to have been guided by her, calling her his spiritual mother; he revered her for the rest of his life and was buried near her at Oignies, where she had lived in the priory since 1207.

Jacques shows Mary as both practical and fervently spiritual. Like other holy women, she disciplines her flesh, fasting and making her body endure hardships; she prays, performs miracles, prophesies, and goes into ecstasies. Like many such women of her time, she is extreme in many of her practices. She makes her mouth bleed by eating hard black bread, she goes into an ecstasy which lasts for thirty-five days and during which she does not eat or speak; sometimes she cannot stop praying and genuflecting—once "she lashed herself with a sharp stick three hundred times each time she knelt, sacrificing and offering herself in a prolonged martyrdom." The whole of chapter V is devoted to her compunction and tears: when she considers Christ's suffering she weeps uncontrollably. Her power with God and the acceptability of her behaviour are shown when a priest teasingly reprimands her for weeping in church; she slips out, but her tears move God to justify her to the "man of bad judgement," who soaks himself and the altar with his own tears. This episode was known in England, as a priest who was having doubts about Margery Kempe's weeping read it and gave her a detailed account of it.[16]

One of the more spectacular episodes of Mary's life also gives an interesting insight into the way an adolescent crisis or the failure of a young person to conform to the life she was expected to lead was handled in Mary's lifetime. In chapter IX we are told about the strength of her prayer. Eileen Power writes of the extreme youth of some novices, who were occasionally put into convents when still almost babies,[17] and it is clear that girls could make their profession when still very young. They might well have had doubts when they reached puberty and a more thoughtful age. A "young virgin" in a Cistercian abbey begins to doubt her faith; she has "impure thoughts," makes "contemptuous remarks," becomes severely depressed, and makes several suicide attempts. Where a modern child would receive counselling, medication, psychiatric help, she is urged to confess her sins and to listen to holy exhortations, all to no avail. Her behaviour is read as diabolical possession. The meekness of her sister-nuns is remarked on in contrast to the fierce transgression of this adolescent: she hates what is good and shouts out blasphemies. She is finally taken to Mary, who has to fast, weep, and pray for forty days before the wailing fiend will leave the child; the dove is snatched from his jaws, conforms once more, confessing and taking communion, and she goes home to the abbey safe and sound. Holy women, including Mary, are frequently described by their male biographers as meek, modest, dove-like. Mary herself is sometimes referred to as Christ's dove; she covers her head and eyes with a veil and looks at the ground as she walks. In fact, in spite of every appearance of meekness—and usually poor health and physical weakness—these women must have had great strength of mind. To us they appear unusually determined; meekness of manner seems to have covered astonishing assertiveness. They are empowered by their faith and their visions.

In her last illness, while still only thirty-six, Mary virtually stops eating, unable to bear the taste of anything but consecrated wafers. After death her body is found to be so thin that her spine is sticking to her stomach, her bones show through her belly. It seems quite possible that both she and Elizabeth of Spaalbeek, who died in her early twenties, succumbed to anorexia.

The anonymous Middle English version follows the Latin original closely but omits the Prologue and Book III. The translation in this volume includes almost all of Book I and some of the beginning of Book II, stopping at Mary's death.

ELIZABETH OF SPAALBEEK

The Middle English version of the life of Elizabeth of Spaalbeek begins with male authority: the *compilour* quotes the Church father

St. Jerome on the difficulties of translation and is soon using the word *auctorité*. It is a paradox at the heart of this text that while conventional, patriarchal men appear to be in complete control, Elizabeth has made use of their structures to obtain power and to live a transgressive life. The narrator's voice is so strong and clear that the reader does not relate directly to what he is describing, but he only appears to be controlling a text, which is in fact dominated by its subject. The narrator is a constant presence, commenting, interpreting, wondering; to have such bizarre female behaviour carefully described by a conventional man produces an odd effect. And while Philip of Clairvaux controls her written life, her cousin, the abbot of Sint-Truiden, "a worschepful man . . . of grete auctorité," has taken over responsibility for her lived life. However, Elizabeth, an unmarried woman of twenty, has had special accommodation built for her; she has a *meynee*, her own household, devoted to her service. And she also has the constant and devoted attention of her immediate family. At the age of five, when younger sisters were probably being born, she had found in holiness a means of control, a source of power. Normally a female child in that situation would have received less attention herself and would have helped care for younger siblings. Elizabeth stood up against this loss of control and esteem, this loss of self. She not only retains her mother's attention and care as though still an infant (watched over constantly, put to bed, propped up on pillows, fed on little dishes of milk), but the younger sisters, instead of supplanting her and receiving her care, have become her servants. She also receives devoted fatherly care and admiration from various eminent and holy men: her cousin the abbot Sint-Truiden is an active guardian, and the abbot of St. Bernard's famous foundation at Clairvaux, who would have high status wherever he went, visits her and feeds her on sips of milk.

Elizabeth has gained this power and control, and is drawing pilgrims from far and wide, through performance. She lives a daily routine of performance art, which is at the same time religious ritual. She is actor, dancer, gymnast, and priest. She has been performing since she was five, presumably elaborating the routines as she grew up. Her behaviour must have developed partly in response to authoritative adults, and it includes audience participation: " . . . her fingers hold the picture so tightly that if anyone shakes moves or pulls it . . . her whole body is moved with the movement of the picture. . . ." Those watching must have been invited to try removing the picture or, at another point, to push her little finger so that her stiff body swayed over. The abbot-cousin who is presenting her may have been not just a spiritual director, but also a dramatic director. He is presenting a performance that he has helped to create. The narrator describes her rituals with reminders that he was part of an audience, and he keeps mentioning the reports of other people who had seen it. Elizabeth, like other women included in this volume, is circumventing the problem of women being forbidden to take on the priestly role: the watchers are both audience and congregation. She acts out Scripture, ". . . as if she were expounding what is written in the Gospel. . . ." Presumably all this continues to take place when no one is there—but is there ever no one there? A Mass is supposed to have at least one other person present besides the priest. Like the Mass, this is worship, holy ritual, and performance, with carefully chosen and draped garments and attendants to provide and remove holy objects at the right moment.

Much of Elizabeth's performance is violent and energetic, but there is emphasis on modesty, on seemliness. She is not revealing her body in an improper way, there is no vulgarity. Her whole demeanour is lady-like. Such a show could easily identify her with actors, but the writer keeps emphasizing propriety. It is clear that both physical energy and controlled movement are involved; she is strong and nimble, like a gymnast or a dancer. The words describing her are those used about romance heroines: she performs violent movements "ful honestly and fulle manerly"; she shows a "merueilous onest and schameful gladnesse of cheer" and "maydenly schamefastnes"; meanwhile, what she is representing is a man suffering at the hands of violent men, and what is being watched is someone actually harming herself: beating herself fiercely, stabbing her eyes until they bleed. Furious expenditure of energy is one of the features of anorexia nervosa: self-discipline in every sense of the word is not uncommon in devout women in the Middle Ages. Fasting was then, as now, a way to control your own life and to gain power over other people. At the same time, it was encouraged by the Church: the less you ate, the more you rejected your body and encouraged your spirit and the nearer you were to Heaven. Periods of fasting were an integral part of Christian life; it must have been just as easy for an adolescent to move on from that into anorexia as it is for a modern adolescent to move on from dieting. Reading the lives and seeing pictures of saints who had become pure and holy through fasting must have had some of the effect of modern role models of slimness. The description of one of Elizabeth's meals sounds very like a "Holy Anorexic":[18] ". . . her mother brought her a little milk in a little dish, . . . the abbot of Clairvaux . . . put a spoonful of it to her mouth, and she sipped three sips of it with apparent difficulty, and then she began to gag at it, as if she were being given food which she loathed. And then she was offered her drink . . . and when she had tasted it she would not drink it." The only food she seems to accept gladly is the consecrated wafer and that she does not appear to "eat."

The narrator frequently refers to Elizabeth as *mayden* and *virgyn*, and he emphasizes her physical purity. Yet in spite of such assurances, the text seems pervaded by a sense of unease. There is tension between private reclusion and public spectacle, clean and unclean, body and spirit, energy and weakness. This is partly the effect of the performance; men are watching women, watching some moments which should be intimate: putting a daughter and sister to bed, propping her up with pillows. If she is watched so constantly, what about bodily functions? And she is bleeding in many places; not only is the woollen cloth next to skin *defuyled* with blood, but her side, hands, and feet, and "hir pappys [breasts] were alle defuyled with blode rennynge fro hir eyen [eyes]." Furthermore, her room is almost consecrated ground, part of her chapel, from which it is separated only by a lattice. There is a central tension between the sacred and the profane.

BRIDGET OF SWEDEN

We know most about the women in this volume who were of highest social status and were successful and well-known before and after their deaths; the life of Bridget of Sweden is particularly well documented. She was born into an aristocratic family in a country where such families played an important part in government and in which "women of her background were accorded a status which extolled their co-operation and vigorous involvement in public as well as private enterprises.[19]. . ." Family interests and connections would have meant that she grew up among leading politicians, lawyers, and churchmen. Bridget was married to a rich and powerful man when she was thirteen, and though her daughter was to give the version of this event which was stereotypical in the *vitae* of female saints—she had been forced by her family, she would have preferred death to marriage, and she herself in pious widowhood is ashamed of her former sexual desire—her own words elsewhere suggest that she valued the institution of marriage and loved the husband to whom she was married for thirty years. Some of her maternal pronouncements are severe by modern standards, but Bridget clearly felt love and concern for her children. She is unusual among devout medieval writers in conveying a mother's trembling exhaustion after childbirth, her joy—all the greater as she feels the baby has been rescued from darkness, from the fear of limbo—and the tender vulnerability of the infant as it "stretched out looking for nourishment" and its mother ". . . with her cheek and her breast . . . warmed him with great joy and delight."[20]

After the death of her husband, Ulf, in 1344, Bridget lived in the Cistercian monastery of Alvastra, where Peter Olofsson became her confessor; he remained at her side for the rest of her life and became the main transcriber of her revelations, many of which she had received while at Alvastra. During the few years she spent there she issued prophetical denunciations of political and ecclesiastical leaders and undertook to establish a new religious order, the Brigittines, with double monasteries for men and women. The first woman to found a religious order, she wished to reform what she saw as the corrupt state of monasticism. In 1349 she received a vision in which she was called to go to Rome for the Holy Year of Jubilee in 1350 and to remain until the Pope and the Emperor were there at the same time: this meant that she lived there for the rest of her life. The papacy had left Rome for Avignon, where it was under French control; in its absence Rome was in decline and had lost its sacred character. Bridget helped St Catherine of Siena to persuade the last French pope, Gregory XI, to return to Rome in 1377 and restore order, but within a year Gregory died and the Great Schism began, a scandalous situation in which there were two popes, one in Rome and one in Avignon.

The *Liber Celestis* is one of a number of versions of the large collection of revelations which Bridget began to receive in the 1340s. They were highly influential throughout Europe, including England, where they were eagerly read and explicated before the end of the fourteenth century. It is a completely discontinuous work, and selection, from among more than 700 separate revelations ranging in length from a few lines to several pages, has to be arbitrary. I have brought together revelations from various parts of this manuscript so as to group them under distinct headings: those about the visionary experience itself, those concerning the lives of Christ and the Virgin, satires of the corruption of the times, and finally, a miscellany illustrating some other features of the collection. The selections are often representative: for example, besides the translated revelation on the corruption of the Franciscan friars, there is another, longer revelation on the corruption of the Dominicans. Although the revelations were received by Bridget and understood by her readers to be directly granted to her by God, Christ, and the Virgin Mary, it has been pointed out that they are in fact "a mosaic of reminiscences: of her readings of all kinds (Bible, Liturgy, Hymns to the Virgin, and the older Passion narratives)—and of the works of ecclesiastical art as she had meditated upon them."[21]

JULIAN OF NORWICH

We know nothing of the life of Julian of Norwich before 1373, when, in extreme sickness, she had the simple yet extraordinary religious experiences that led her to write the *Revelations of Divine Love*. Even her real name is unknown, "Julian" being taken from St. Julian's church, Norwich, to which she was later attached as an anchorite. She was probably born about 1343, and the presence of her mother and her parish priest at her sickbed suggest that she was still living at home and had not yet entered the religious life. As she describes herself, she was a young woman who was devout in a manner not uncommon in late-medieval England, and one with the leisure to dedicate herself to devotion, hence presumably from a prosperous family in Norwich, the flourishing major city of East Anglia. She longed to suffer in body for Christ's sake, even to the verge of death, and to share imaginatively in his Passion. Her wishes were granted, but the experiences that came to her were uncannier than the intense imaginings of Christ's human life and sufferings granted to other mystics such as Bridget of Sweden and Margery Kempe. At first she saw blood trickling down the face of a crucifix held before her by the priest, but alongside that a vision of God's sustaining love, in the form of "a little thing, the size of a hazel nut, lying in the palm of my hand" (Short Text ch. 4), which she was told was the whole of creation, so tiny and yet so lasting. The succeeding "showings," as she calls them, similarly mix relatively conventional visual imagery with far stranger manifestations of metaphysical truth. She explains that what was revealed to her came in three modes, "by bodily sight, and by words formed in my understanding, and by spiritual sight," and, unlike, say, Bridget of Sweden, who seems to feel no doubt about the absolute clarity of her visions and their significance, she is aware that her words must be insufficient to convey God's meaning, which is infinitely rich, complex, and beyond human understanding.

The excerpts translated here are taken from two different versions of Julian's *Revelations*. They begin with the first seven chapters of the Short Text. This is generally agreed to be earlier than the Long Text, and the traditional view is that it was written shortly after 1373. It describes the "showings" that came to her in that year and her initial, already deeply thoughtful probings of what they meant. Recent scholarship, however, suggests that the Short Text as we have it may have been composed after the rise and condemnation of the Lollard heresies, influential among women, had made it necessary for a woman visionary to stress as strongly as Julian does that she fully accepts ecclesiastical orthodoxy. Chapter 86 of the Long Text mentions a further revelation, received about 1388, teaching that God's meaning in all that he showed her was love; and it was possibly this insight that led her to write the Short Text. If so, the Long Text might well date from the fifteenth century, perhaps after 1413, the date given in the opening rubric of the Short Text. In any case, we have to suppose that the composition of the *Revelations* was an ongoing process, and one which, as she writes at the end of the Long Text, "is not yet completed," so that the teaching she has received is no more than "the beginning of an ABC" (ch. 51). For her, it was not just a matter of recording visionary experiences, but of pondering on them as they shifted and developed in her memory, and of exploring ever more deeply the further reaches of their meaning. It seems likely that Julian lived for some years after this: Margery Kempe visited her in 1415, and she is mentioned as alive in a will of 1416. The exact date of her death is unknown.

To comment briefly on the chapters translated here is an impossible task, for Julian is by far the greatest woman mystic of the Middle Ages—the wisest and most generous in her spirituality, the most modest in the claims she makes for herself, the one who can most

readily convince modern readers that she was really able to draw on
sources outside her own fantasies and her own reading. It is not by
accident that the visionary women who rapidly achieved sainthood,
such as Bridget of Sweden and Catherine of Siena, did so by adding
nothing of significance to what the Church was already teaching
(Catherine of Siena's God speaks to her in exactly the words of a
fourteenth-century theologian); Julian, far removed from the cen-
tres of ecclesiastical power, develops a speculative theology that,
while never asserting itself in opposition to the Church or question-
ing its doctrinal tenets, encourages deeper thought about what
God's love actually means for humanity and its future. What was
not shown to her assumed as great an importance as what was. She
writes, "I did not see sin" (Long Text ch. 27), and this absence of
the central and obsessive concern of much medieval religious writing gives her vision an extraordinary optimism. She does not under-
estimate the sufferings caused by sin, either to Christ or to
humanity, but what she is taught is that "Sin is befitting, but all shall
be well, and all shall be well, and all manner of things shall be well"
(ch. 27). But how can all be well, given that "one point of faith is
that many shall be damned" (ch. 32)? Julian is careful not to contra-
dict the Church's teaching, but she takes no pleasure in the thought
of hell, and her faith in God is such that she believes that he will
perform a "great deed . . . by which he will keep his word in all
things and shall make all well that is not well" (ch. 32). The logical
arguments of the theologians, lending themselves so readily to the
attribution of human anger and vindictiveness to God, give way to
this faith in his love for humanity and his power to do what is beyond human understanding.

Julian's faith is not without stress, and this reaches its height in
chapter 50 of the Long Text, in which she begs to be allowed to see
the truth about sin as God himself sees it. The following chapter,
the longest in either text, comes as a response to this plea, in the
form of a parable of a Lord and a Servant, a simple story in which
layer beneath layer of meaning is disclosed. What it ultimately reveals is that the fall of Adam and the incarnation of God as man are
in some sense not parallel events but the same event: to God,
damnation and salvation are not opposites. Julian's God is infinitely
tender in his identification with his children, and, as she puts it in
the insight for which she is most famous, he is our Mother as well as
our Father. The idea of God as mother was not new: it can be found

in the Bible and in monastic writings, and also in some of the other texts included in this volume. Hildegard writes that "God showed me his grace again, as . . . when a mother offers her weeping child milk . . . "; Hadewijch speaks of the soul being nursed with motherly care; Bridget explains that "this bird represents God, who brings forth every soul like a mother."[22] Julian develops the idea of God's motherhood more fully and with a stronger emotional charge than can be found elsewhere in the Middle Ages, in images of enwrapping, feeding, and cleaning taken from the daily life of medieval women. Her work repays many readings.

A REVELATION OF PURGATORY

Other accounts of spiritual experiences are included in this volume because the women who had them were remarkable; this one is included because the woman was not remarkable. Collections generally choose the best and most interesting passages from important texts. *A Revelation of Purgatory* (an account of a revelation which occurred in 1422) is an unimportant text and is given without cuts and without editorial tidying or clarifying because it offers a useful point of reference. Here we have the concerns, the attitudes, the words of a devout nun, but one whose ideas and language are limited—and probably representative of many women who spent their lives in medieval nunneries. To read this and then turn again to Julian of Norwich is to be struck with even greater wonder at the quality of her intelligence, the breadth of her thought and sympathy, the power of her imagination and language. It could also provide an explanation for Julian's choice of an anchor-hold attached to St. Julian's church rather than communal life just down the road in Carrow Abbey; she could listen sympathetically when Margery Kempe visited her but might have found it harder to live with this nun, who was probably from the Benedictine abbey of St. Mary in Winchester. While William of Wykeham was bishop of Winchester, he wrote to the then abbess of this house that it had come to his attention that some of her nuns ". . . will not bear or undergo the reproofs and corrections inflicted upon them by their superiors for their faults, but break out into vituperation and altercation with each other and in no way submit to these corrections; meanwhile other nuns of your house by detractions, conspiracies, confedera-

cies, leagues, obloquies, contradictions and other breaches of discipline and laxities [neglect the rule of St. Benedict]."[23]

The vision came "on the night of the feast of St. Lawrence." The
widely read collection of saints' lives known as the *Golden Legend*
includes a life of St. Lawrence, which could well have been in the
visionary's mind that day: it would give anyone nightmares about
tortures and fires. The saint is said to have been burned, clubbed,
beaten with scorpions, and whipped with lead before being burned
to death on a grill. We are also given details of five external (and
metaphorical) fires that he fought, then of three fires in his heart
and three more within him (faith, ardent love, and knowledge of
God). Words to do with fire, heat, and flames occur repeatedly.
Purgatory and its representation must also have been present in the
minds of everyone; it must often have filled some of the same space
that violence in film, video, and magazines do today. Good Christians were actually encouraged to fantasize about torture, including
torture of a sexual nature. There would have been sermons to listen
to and paintings on the church wall to look at while doing so: a representation of Christ in judgement, with the good being taken up to
bliss by angels on one side and the wicked down to the tortures of
Hell by devils on the other, was frequently painted on church walls.
And English people of this period had opportunities to see Lollards
being publicly burned to death. Many of the tortures in this vision
and the images used to describe them are from daily life, nasty but
unimaginative: the iron combs with which fiends rake the flesh of
the wicked were used for separating strands of wool or flax; burning hot iron hissing in cold water could be seen in any smithy; flesh
is said to melt like the tallow of a household candle; and a soul lies
there frying in the fire like a fish in oil.

The text reads as though it was taken down verbatim; the style is
that of vernacular speech, with simple, meandering syntax, frequent
use of conjunctions and limited vocabulary ("such torment then
that I could not describe it"). One can never forget the central situation: a devout woman is recounting her dreams to the man who is
not only her amanuensis but also her moral and spiritual guide.
"My dear father" is interpolated frequently among the recital of
horrors; it frames and mediates the trite and nasty discourse of purgatory, making the reader wonder about the priest's character and
his relationship with the nun, about the nature of affection and of
fatherhood in the circumstances. The cosiness of the phrase adds to

the nastiness of the revelation. And the revelation shifts the power ratio between the spiritual father and daughter. The priest is writing down what she says, and what she says includes commands for particular priests, knowledge of the fate of a particular soul, and detailed guidance to everyone of the kind which a priest himself might be expected to give. She also goes into great and unpleasant detail about the torments of those in holy orders—and they receive the worst tortures of all. She is in control of all her spiritual fathers, and it is she who performs the priestly functions of passing moral judgement and showing the way to heaven. We get an impression of complicit priests, narrow in their ideas, lacking in common sense, pleased with the importance of having a spiritual daughter who has revelations. The visionary's recital of beliefs and observances is glib and superficial; she shows no sign of spirituality and seems to treat observances almost like magic formulae or recipes—so many Masses of one kind, so many of another, and you will obtain the desired result. Protestations of inadequacy and humility were a normal part of women's writings in particular for many centuries: there is no indication that this woman felt humble or unworthy.

The fantasy must be very satisfying to the "dreamer." She assumes power not only over priests, but also over the soul of a religious sister, probably from the same convent, who has recently died. Seen in modern terms, this "Margaret" was a woman with a comfortable level of self-esteem who managed to enjoy the everyday pleasures available in her restricted circumstances. She adored her pet dog and cat, took pleasure in food and drink, she enjoyed a good gossip, a lie-in in the morning, and shopping. She sometimes swore, she had a tendency to envy others, and could lose her temper on occasion. As for the "lechery" she has to expiate, from what is said about nuns in the text, it probably consisted of fantasies and kissing visiting men rather too warmly. Unfortunately, these failings manage to include all the Seven Deadly Sins (Pride, Covetousness, Lust, Envy, Gluttony, Anger, and Sloth) and having taken religious vows, Margaret was especially bound to resist them, and confess and do penance when she failed to do so. The revelation is depressingly convincing as the sort of fantasy a limited person leading a limited life might indulge in. The dreamer is self-important, pettyminded, malicious. Someone she knew and disapproved of is suffering and turning to her for help. Margaret even appears wearing her worst clothes; she is suffering horribly for all the things which another nun or devout laywoman might have criticized in her, and she is very grateful to the visionary. The Virgin Mary herself not only makes it quite plain that it is the fantasizer who has released Margaret from her torments but promises that "those who have helped you out of your torment so quickly shall be richly rewarded."

MARGERY KEMPE

Though she herself was illiterate, the account of her life which Margery Kempe dictated was the first autobiography in English. However, just as we must not expect the lives written at the time to be like modern biography, so this book is not what we would expect of autobiography. The *Book* preserves the memory of individual incidents very vividly, but they are not linked into a sequential narrative. As Margery says in the Proem, "This book is not written in order, everything after another as it was done, but just as the matter came to this creature's mind when it was to be written down. . . ." It is also likely that she worked and reworked material in her head as she thought about it and as she related it to other people; many people are reworking an internal autobiography throughout their lives, and this is even more likely to happen in a culture where memories were not usually recorded in writing. Furthermore, it is clear from her *Book* that Margery was in the habit of recounting her physical and spiritual experiences to any priest who would listen sympathetically. Through such men she also had access to writings by and about other holy women—she mentions Bridget of Sweden and Mary of Oignies—and to other devotional writing. Sermons, which she clearly valued, would also be a source of knowledge of the Scriptures, saints' lives, and moral teaching. We cannot know what those who recorded her experiences contributed to the text, but her voice comes down to us with astonishing power and clarity. Margery must have wanted to be a saint. She perceives herself as someone who has a very special relationship with God and is writing her own *vita*, her life and her visions.

Margery was born in about 1373 in the prosperous East Anglian port of Lynn, now King's Lynn, in Norfolk. Her father was a burgess of considerable local eminence; among other positions he was mayor and a member of parliament. In a preface she describes herself as "set in great pomp and pride of the world . . . later drawn to our Lord by great poverty, sickness, shame, and great reproofs in diverse countries. . . ." She shows an obsessive concern with *worshep* (status or reputation), the goal of the urban patriciate from which she emerged; yet she is convinced that God calls her to behave in ways which could only be perceived as transgressive, and she cannot stop doing so, even though the responses of others cause her to suffer. Indeed, such behaviour could have had fatal consequences. In the early fifteenth century, Church and state combined in England to suppress the Lollard heresy, and though Margery's religious ideas were perfectly orthodox, she was accused of Lollardy and ran a real risk of execution. The atmosphere was not unlike that of the McCarthy period in the United States, when any form of independent behaviour or thought might be denounced as "Communist."

In her *Book* Margery passes over her childhood and begins, like Julian of Norwich, with a "bodily sickness" which marks a point of special intensity and change. In Margery's case this is childbirth—not the birth of the baby, of whom we hear nothing more, but the physical and above all the mental effects of the experience on the mother. She underwent a kind of madness from which she was rescued by an appearance of Jesus as a handsome man sitting at her bedside. She relapsed into worldly concerns, but after the failure of attempts to set herself up as a brewer and as a miller, she dedicated herself to a life of religious devotion. She was never entirely free from sexual temptation, but Jesus continued to intervene in her life, and in chapter 11, the first excerpt here, she persuaded her husband to allow her to live in chastity. The medieval Church set a far higher value on celibacy than on marriage, and a difficulty for Margery was that, though married, she wished to lead the untrammelled and impulsive life of the celibate holy women about whom she had learned. She wandered throughout England and, in chapters not included here, went to the Holy Land and various holy places in Western Europe. In chapters 17 and 18 she is in Norwich, where she visits Julian. The report of their conversation gives a convincing sense of the practical wisdom of the anchoress, filtered through some incomprehension on Margery's part. Chapter 22 provides an example of one of the many conversations Margery had with Jesus, in which he sets her on the same level as such favourite saints as St. Katherine and St. Margaret and promises that prayers by those who believe in her will be as effective as prayers to these saints. She will dance in heaven "with other holy maidens and virgins" because, though married, she is a maiden in soul. Chapter 35 finds her in Rome, dedicated to Christ's Humanity, and weeping aloud when she sees a little boy or a handsome man because she associates them with Jesus. But Jesus intends her for higher things and, despite her reluctance, insists that she must be married to his Father. This strange version of the Mystic Marriage provokes more tears, but it also leads to many "bodily comforts"—sweet smells, "sounds and melodies," "white things flying about her on all sides, as thickly . . . as specks in a sunbeam," and "the fire of love burning in her breast." These tokens are versions of the bodily symptoms experienced by the influential fourteenth-century mystic Richard Rolle as signs of God's presence. In the following chapter Christ assures her that if he were on earth, he "would not be ashamed of you as many other people are," and tells her that "you may boldly, when you are in bed, take me to you as your wedded husband."

Chapters 57 to 59 focus on Margery's violent bouts of weeping. Since these occurred in church and other public places they must have been extremely disruptive, yet she interprets them as signs of holiness and so does a priest, previously unknown to her, with whom she soon forms one of those relationships of mutual support so common between holy women and male clerics. He reads classic works of mysticism to her and, as she sees it, "receives a wealthy benefice" as his reward from God. She has sexual fantasies, which she interprets as God punishing her reluctance to hear about damnation as well as salvation. Later chapters tell of different kinds of punishment Margery receives through the hostile comments of others (something her conduct might have seemed designed to provoke), and through the penance involved in looking after her husband as he declined physically and mentally, a penance which also answers the prayer that her husband should live long enough to vindicate her behaviour as wife in the eyes of her critical neighbours. In the final excerpts given here, chapters 85 and 86, Margery is elaborately rewarded for her devotion with visions and ardent thanks from Christ himself.

SUGGESTIONS FOR FURTHER READING

GENERAL

Ancrene Wisse: Guide for Anchoresses, translated by Hugh White (London: Penguin, 1993).

Barratt, Alexandra, ed. *Women's Writing in Middle English* (London: Longman, 1992).

Beer, Frances. *Women and Mystical Experience in the Middle Ages* (Woodbridge: Boydell, 1992).

Bell, Rudolph M. *Holy Anorexia* (Chicago: University of Chicago Press, 1985).

Bestul, Thomas H. *Texts of the Passion: Latin Devotional Literature and Medieval Society* (Philadelphia: University of Pennsylvania Press, 1996).

Blamires, Alcuin, ed. *Women Defamed and Women Defended: An Anthology of Medieval Texts* (Oxford: Clarendon Press, 1992).

Bynum, Caroline Walker. *Jesus as Mother: Studies in the Spirituality of the High Middle Ages* (Berkeley: University of California Press, 1982).

———. *Holy Feast and Holy Fast: The Religious Significance of Food to Medieval Women* (Berkeley: University of California Press, 1987).

———. "Religious Women in the Later Middle Ages," in *Christian Spirituality: High Middle Ages and Reformation,* Jill Raitt, ed. (New York: Crossroad, 1987).

Dronke, Peter. *Women Writers of the Middle Ages* (Cambridge: Cambridge University Press, 1984).

Kieckhefer, Richard. *Unquiet Souls: Fourteenth-Century Saints and their Religious Milieu* (Chicago: University of Chicago Press, 1984).

McGinn, Bernard, ed. *Meister Eckhart and the Beguine Mystics: Hadewijch of Brabant, Mechthild of Magdeburg, and Marguerite Porete* (New York: Continuum, 1994).

———. *The Flowering of Mysticism: Men and Women in the New Mysticism (1200–1350)* (New York: Crossroad, 1998).

Milhaven, J. Giles. "A Medieval Lesson on Bodily Knowing: Women's Experience and Men's Thought," *Journal of the American Academy of Religion* 57 (1989).

Petroff, Elizabeth Alvilda. *Medieval Women's Visionary Literature* (New York: Oxford University Press, 1986).

———. *Body and Soul: Essays on Medieval Women and Mysticism* (New York: Oxford University Press, 1994).

Power, Eileen. *Medieval English Nunneries c. 1275–1535* (Cambridge: Cambridge University Press, 1922).

Sarum Missal, J. Wickham Legg, ed. (Oxford: Clarendon Press, 1969) [medieval liturgy in Latin].

Simons, Walter. "Reading a Saint's Body: Rapture and Bodily Movement in the *Vitae* of Thirteenth-Century Beguines," in *Framing Medieval Bodies*, Sarah Kay and Miri Rubin, eds. (Manchester: Manchester University Press, 1994).

Southern, R.W. *Western Society and the Church in the Middle Ages* (Harmondsworth: Penguin, 1970).

Voaden, Rosalynn, ed. *Prophets Abroad: The Reception of Continental Holy Women in Late-Medieval England* (Cambridge: D.S. Brewer, 1996).

Wiethaus, Ulrike, ed. *Maps of Flesh and Light: The Religious Experience of Medieval Women Mystics* (Syracuse: Syracuse University Press, 1992).

Zum Brunn, Emilie, and Georgette Epiney-Burgard, eds. *Women Mystics in Medieval Europe* (New York: Paragon, 1989).

HILDEGARD OF BINGEN

Flanagan, Sabina. *Hildegard of Bingen, 1098–1179: A Visionary Life* (London: Routledge, 1989).

Newman, Barbara. *Sister of Wisdom: St Hildegard's Theology of the Feminine* (Berkeley: University of California Press, 1987).

———, ed. *Voice of the Living Light: Hildegard of Bingen and Her World* (Berkeley: University of California Press, 1998).

CHRISTINA OF MARKYATE

Holdsworth, Christopher J. "Christina of Markyate," in *Medieval Women*, Derek Baker, ed. (Oxford: Basil Blackwell, 1978).

Camille, Michael. "Philological Iconoclasm: Edition and Image in the *Vie de St Alexis*," in *Medievalism and the Modernist Temper*, R. Howard Bloch and Stephen P. Nichols, eds. (Baltimore: Johns Hopkins University Press, 1996).

HADEWIJCH

Guest, Tanis. "Hadewijch and *Minne*," in *Poetry of the Netherlands in Its European Context, 1170–1930*, Theodoor Weevers, ed. (London: Athlone Press, 1960).

Murk Jansen, Saskia. "The Mystic Theology of the Thirteenth-Century Mystic, Hadewijch, and Its Literary Expression," in *The Medieval Mystical Tradition in England: Exeter Symposium V*, Marion Glasscoe, ed. (Cambridge: D.S. Brewer, 1992).

Newman, Barbara. "*La mystique courtoise*," in her *From Virile Woman to WomanChrist: Studies in Medieval Religion and Literature* (Philadelphia: University of Pennsylvania Press, 1995).

Petroff, Elizabeth Alvilda. "Gender, Knowledge, and Power in Hadewijch's *Strophische Gedichten*," in her *Body and Soul: Essays on Medieval Women and Mysticism* (New York: Oxford University Press, 1994).

MANUSCRIPT DOUCE 114

Horstmann, Carl, ed. "Prosalegenden: Die Legenden des MS Douce 114," *Anglia 8* (1885) [edition of the Middle English versions from which the *Lives* of Christine the Astonishing, Mary of Oignies, and Elizabeth of Spaalbeek are translated].

Kurtz, P. Deery. "Mary of Oignies, Christine the Marvellous, and Medieval Heresy," *Mystic Quarterly* 14 (1988).

MARY OF OIGNIES

The Life of Marie d'Oignies by Cardinal Jacques de Vitry, translated by Margot H. King [complete and from the original Latin; Prologue and Books I–III], and *The Supplement to Jacques de*

Vitry's Life of Marie d'Oignies, by Thomas de Cantimpré, translated by Hugh Feiss (Toronto: Peregrina, 1993).

ELIZABETH OF SPAALBEEK

Rodgers, Susan, and Joanna E. Ziegler. "Elisabeth of Spalbeek's Trance Dance of Faith: A Performance Theory Interpretation from Anthropological and Art Historical Perspectives," in *Performance and Transformation: New Approaches to Late Medieval Spirituality*, Mary A. Suydam and Joanna E. Ziegler, eds. (New York: St. Martin's Press, 1999).

Ross, Ellen M. *The Grief of God: Images of the Suffering Jesus in Late Medieval England* (New York: Oxford University Press, 1997), pp. 110–115.

Simons, Walter, and Joanna E. Ziegler. "Phenomenal Religion in the Thirteenth Century and Its Image: Elisabeth of Spalbeek and the Passion Cult," *Studies in Church History* 27 (1990).

MARGUERITE PORETE

Margaret Porette: The Mirror of Simple Souls, translated by Edmund Colledge et al. (Notre Dame: University of Notre Dame Press, 1999).

Finke, Laurie A. " 'More Than I Fynde Written': Dialogue and Power in the English Translation of *The Mirror of Simple Souls*," in *Performance and Transformation: New Approaches to Late Medieval Spirituality*, Mary A. Suydam and Joanna E. Ziegler, eds. (New York: St. Martin's Press, 1999).

Hollywood, Amy. *The Soul as Virgin Wife: Mechthild of Magdeburg, Marguerite Porete, and Meister Eckhart* (Notre Dame: University of Notre Dame Press, 1995).

Sargent, Michael G. "The Annihilation of Marguerite Porete," *Viator* 28 (1997).

———. "*Le Mirouer des simples âmes* and the English Mystical Tradition," in *Abendländische Mystik im Mittelalter*, Kurt Ruh, ed. (Stuttgart: J.B. Metzlersche Verlagsbuchhandlung, 1986).

Watson, Nicholas. "Misrepresenting the Untranslatable: Marguerite Porete and the *Mirouer des simples âmes*," *New Comparison* 12 (1991).

———. "Melting into God the English Way: Deification in the Middle English Version of Marguerite Porete's *Mirouer des simples âmes anienties*," in *Prophets Abroad: The Reception of Continental Holy Women in Late-Medieval England*, Rosalynn Voaden, ed. (Cambridge: D.S. Brewer, 1996).

BRIDGET OF SWEDEN

Sahlin, Claire L. "Gender and Prophetic Authority in Birgitta of Sweden's *Revelations*," in *Gender and Text in the Later Middle Ages*, Jane Chance, ed. (Gainsville: University Presses of Florida, 1996).

Ellis, Roger. " '*Flores ad fabricandam . . . coronam*': An Investigation into the Uses of the Revelations of St Bridget of Sweden in Fifteenth-Century England," *Medium Aevum* 51 (1982).

Morris, Bridget. *St Birgitta of Sweden* (Woodbridge, 1999) [includes a full bibliography].

Schmidtke, James A. " 'Saving' by Faint Praise: St. Birgitta of Sweden, Adam Easton and Medieval Antifeminism," *American Benedictine Review* 33 (1982).

JULIAN OF NORWICH

Aers, David, and Lynn Staley. *The Powers of the Holy: Religion, Politics, and Gender in Late Medieval English Culture* (University Park: Pennsylvania State University Press, 1996).

Baker, Denise N. *Julian of Norwich's Showings: From Vision to Book* (Princeton: Princeton University Press, 1994).

Jantzen, Grace. *Julian of Norwich: Mystic and Theologian* (London: SPCK, 1987).

McEntire, Sandra J., ed. *Julian of Norwich: A Book of Essays* (New York: Garland, 1992).

Watson, Nicholas. "The Composition of Julian of Norwich's *Revelation of Love*," *Speculum* 68 (1993).

———. "Yf wommen be double naturelly": Remaking 'Woman' in Julian of Norwich's *Revelation of Love*," *Exemplaria* 8 (1996).

A REVELATION OF PURGATORY

Federico, Sylvia. "Transgressive Teaching and Censorship in a Fifteenth-Century Vision of Purgatory," *Mystics Quarterly* 21 (1995).

MARGERY KEMPE

Atkinson, Clarissa W. *Mystic and Pilgrim: The Book and the World of Margery Kempe* (Ithaca: Cornell University Press, 1983).

The Book of Margery Kempe, Barry Windeatt, ed. (London: Longman, 2000) [Middle English original].

The Book of Margery Kempe, Lynn Staley, ed. (New York: Norton, 2001) [includes collection of critical essays].

McEntire, Sandra J., ed. *Margery Kempe: A Book of Essays* (New York: Garland, 1992).

Lochrie, Karma. *Margery Kempe and Translations of the Flesh* (Philadelphia: University of Pennsylvania Press, 1991).

Staley, Lynn. *Margery Kempe's Dissenting Fictions* (University Park: Pennsylvania State University Press, 1994).

ACKNOWLEDGMENTS AND A NOTE ON THE TEXTS

PREVIOUS TRANSLATIONS

Peter Dronke's translations of passages from the *Vita* and the letter to Guibert de Gembloux of Hildegard of Bingen are based on his own editions of the Latin sources. The present excerpts are taken from *Women Writers of the Middle Ages: A Critical Study of Texts from Perpetua (? 203) to Marguerite Porete (? 1310)*, by Peter Dronke, copyright © Cambridge University Press (1984), pp. 145–146, 150–151, 161, and 168–169; reprinted with the permission of Cambridge University Press.

The translations of *Scivias* derive from the text edited by Adelgundis Führkötter and Angela Carlevaris (Turnhout, 1978). Excerpts are taken from *Hildegard of Bingen: Scivias*, translated by Mother Columba Hart and Jane Bishop, copyright © 1990 by the Abbey of Regina Laudis: Benedictine Congregation Regina Laudis of the Strict Observance, Inc.; used with permission of Paulist Press.

C. H. Talbot's translation of *The Life of Christina of Markyate* is based on his own reconstruction of the damaged manuscript Cotton Tiberius E. 1. Excerpts here are reprinted from *The Life of Christina of Markyate: A Twelfth Century Recluse*, edited and translated by C. H. Talbot (copyright © Oxford University Press 1959), by permission of Oxford University Press.

The manuscripts of Hadewijch's works were rediscovered in 1838. The translations of the *Visions* are based on the edition by Jozef Van Mierlo (Louvain, 1924–1925) and those of the *Poems* and the *Letters* on Van Mierlo's editions (Antwerp, 1942 and 1947). Excerpts are taken from *Hadewijch: The Complete Works*, translated by Mother Columba Hart, copyright © 1980 by The Missionary Society of St. Paul the Apostle in the State of New York; used with permission of Paulist Press.

The excerpt from the Short Text of *Revelations of Divine Love*, by Julian of Norwich, is translated from an edition (*English Mystics of the Middle Ages*, edited by Barry Windeatt, Cambridge, 1994) of the single manuscript, British Library MS Add. 37790, a fifteenth-century anthology of late-medieval religious writings that includes the Middle English version of Marguerite Porete's *Mirror of Simple Souls*. The Long Text survives only in somewhat corrupt post-Reformation copies made by English recusants; the excerpts included are based on an edition (*Julian of Norwich: A Revelation of Love*, edited by Marion Glasscoe, revised edition, Exeter, 1993) of British Library Sloane MS 3705. Excerpts from both texts of *Revelations of Divine Love* are taken from *Julian of Norwich: Revelations of Divine Love (Short Text and Long Text)*, translated by Elizabeth Spearing, with an Introduction and Notes by A.C. Spearing (London, 1998), pp. 3–12, 55–57, 78–82, 85–88, 114–124, 136, 140–144, and 178–180. Translation copyright © Elizabeth Spearing, 1998. Introduction and Notes copyright © A. C. Spearing, 1998; reproduced by permission of Penguin Books, Ltd.

The cleric who gave *The Book of Margery Kempe* its final form seems to have done so in the late 1430s, and the last records of her as living are from 1438 and 1439. Extracts from the book were printed in the early sixteenth century, but the entire manuscript was not rediscovered until 1934. Windeatt's translation is based on this manuscript. Excerpts here are taken from *The Book of Margery Kempe*, translated by B. A. Windeatt (Harmondsworth, 1985), pp. 58–60, 74–75, 77–79, 86–88, 122–127, 175–185, 191–193, 219–221, and 247–255. Copyright © B.A. Windeatt, 1985; reproduced by permission of Penguin Books, Ltd.

NEW TRANSLATIONS

The following translations were made especially for this volume and were taken from Middle English texts.

The *Lives* of Christine the Astonishing, Mary of Oignies, and Elizabeth of Spaalbeek are from "Prosalegenden. Die legenden des ms. Douce 114," edited by C. Horstmann, *Anglia* 8 (1885), 102–196.

Excerpts from *The Mirror of Simple Souls* are from "Margaret Porete, *The Mirror of Simple Souls*: A Middle English Translation," edited by Marilyn Doiron, *Archivio Italiano per la Storia della Pietà* 5 (1968), 243–355. Doiron's edition is based chiefly on a manuscript of the first half of the fifteenth century, St. John's College, Cambridge, 71.

The excerpts from Bridget of Sweden are from *The Liber Celestis of St Bridget of Sweden*, edited by Roger Ellis, Vol. I, EETS No. 291 (Oxford, 1987). This is a Middle English version of the *Liber Celestis* (British Library MS Claudius B i); the manuscript and the version it contains date from the second decade of the fifteenth century—that is, about the time of Henry V's foundation of the Brigittine house of Mount Syon on the bank of the Thames at Sheen.

A Revelation of Purgatory is from *Yorkshire Writers*, edited by C. Horstmann, Vol. I (London, 1895) pp. 383–392, and (for the leaf missing from the Thornton MS) from *A Revelation of Purgatory by an Unknown, Fifteenth-Century Woman Visionary*, edited by Marta Powell Harley (Lewiston/Queenston, 1985). This work survives in three fifteenth-century manuscripts, two of them large anthologies. The present translation is based on the version in the mid-fifteenth-century Thornton manuscript in the Lincoln Cathedral Library, where it is found among other devotional writings and romances.

Where the translations derive from published sources, I have made use of the sometimes copious annotation supplied by the translators but have adapted the material to make it more suitable for the specific purposes of this collection.

THE BIBLE

"True translations of the whole Bible into the vernaculars were rare in the middle ages. Usually their place was taken by summaries of Old Testament history, collections of individual books of Scripture with glosses and comments, Bible-picture books with running captions, and poetic paraphrases."[1] None of the women represented in this book would have had a full, approved version of the Bible available to them in their own language. Medieval people, even scholars, often quoted from memory; this was even more likely to be true for women who were the authors of their texts. The words quoted may have been heard rather than read. The texts in this anthology contain numerous references to the Bible at every level from vague echo to direct quotation. Unless of special significance, only the latter have been annotated; simple references appear in square brackets in the text for prose, in the footnotes for poetry. The Douay translation of the Latin Vulgate is used; this does not always correspond to more familiar translations (and chapter and verse numbers will not always coincide exactly, especially in the Psalms), but it is closest to the Scriptures as these women and the men writing about them would have known them.

RELIGIOUS PRACTICE

Religious worship, practices, and life in institutions varied at different times and places during the four centuries in which these texts originated. Furthermore, liturgical "Hours" could be the result of dividing the hours of light and the hours of darkness, giving the "unequal" hours sometimes referred to by Chaucer. "Matins was at one o'clock" is therefore not a fact which can be given with any consistency or certainty. No attempt has been made to relate medieval to modern practice, and for the sake of simplicity and clarity, the past tense is used when describing medieval practice, although the practice of the contemporary Roman Catholic Church may be the same or similar.

ABBREVIATIONS

OLD TESTAMENT

Gen	Genesis
Ex	Exodus
2 Kin	2 Kings
2 Chr	2 Chronicles
Ps	Psalms
Prov	Proverbs
Eccl	Ecclesiastes
Song	Song of Solomon
Is	Isaiah
Jer	Jeremiah
Eze	Ezekiel
Joel	Joel

NEW TESTAMENT

Mt	Matthew
Mk	Mark
Lk	Luke
Jn	John
Acts	Acts
Rom	Romans
1 Cor	1 Corinthians
2 Cor	2 Corinthians
2 Th	2 Thessalonians
1 Ti	1 Timothy
1 Pet	1 Peter
Apoc	Apocalypse

MEDIEVAL WRITINGS ON
FEMALE SPIRITUALITY

Hildegard of Bingen

EXTRACTS FROM THE *VITA*

(a) Wisdom teaches in the light of love, and bids me tell how I was brought into this my gift of vision. . . . "Hear these words, human creature, and tell them not according to yourself but according to me, and, taught by me, speak of yourself like this"—In my first formation, when in my mother's womb God raised me up with the breath of life, he fixed this vision in my soul. For, in the eleven hundredth year after Christ's incarnation, the teaching of the apostles and the burning justice which he had set in Christians and spiritual people began to grow sluggish and irresolute. In that period I was born, and my parents, amid sighs, vowed me to God. And in the third year of my life I saw so great brightness that my soul trembled; yet because of my infant condition I could express nothing of it. But in my eighth year I was offered to God, given over to a spiritual way of life, and till my fifteenth I saw many things, speaking of a number of them in a simple way, so that those who heard me wondered from where they might have come or from whom they might be.

Then I too grew amazed at myself, that whenever I saw these things deep in my soul I still retained outer sight, and that I heard this said of no other human being. And, as best I could, I concealed the vision I saw in my soul. I was ignorant of much in the outer world, because of the frequent illness that I suffered, from the time of my mother's milk right up to now: it wore my body out and made my powers fail.

Exhausted by all this, I asked a nurse of mine if she saw anything save external objects. "Nothing," she answered, for she saw none of those others. Then, seized with great fear, I did not dare reveal it to anyone; yet nonetheless, speaking or composing, I used to make many affirmations about future events, and when I was fully perfused by this vision I would say many things that were unfathomable [*aliena*] to those who listened. But if the force of the vision—in which I made an exhibition of myself more childish than befitted my age—subsided a little, I blushed profusely and often wept, and many times I should gladly have kept silent, had I been allowed. And still, because of the fear I had of other people, I did not tell anyone *how* I saw. But a certain high-born woman, to whom I had been entrusted for education, noted this and disclosed it to a monk whom she knew.

. . . After her death, I kept seeing in this way till my fortieth year. Then in that same vision I was forced by a great pressure [*pressura*] of pains to manifest what I had seen and heard. But I was very much afraid, and blushed to utter what I had so long kept silent. However, at that time my veins and marrow became full of that strength which I had always lacked in my infancy and youth.

I intimated this to a monk who was my *magister*.[1] . . . Astonished, he bade me write these things down secretly, till he could see what they were and what their source might be. Then, realizing that they came from God, he indicated this to his abbot, and from that time on he worked at this [writing down] with me, with great eagerness.

In that same [experience of] vision I understood the writings of the prophets, the Gospels, the works of other holy men, and those of certain philosophers, without any human instruction, and I expounded certain things based on these, though I scarcely had literary understanding, inasmuch as a woman who was not learned had been my teacher.[2] But I also brought forth songs with their melody, in praise of God and the saints, without being taught by anyone, and I sang them too, even though I had never learnt either musical notation or any kind of singing.

When these occurrences were brought up and discussed at an audience in Mainz Cathedral, everyone said they stemmed from God, and from that gift of prophecy which the prophets of old had proclaimed. Then my writings were brought to Pope Eugene, when he was in Trier.[3] With joy he had them read out in the presence of many people, and read them for himself, and, with great trust in God's grace, sending me his blessing with a letter, he bade me commit whatever I saw or heard in my vision to writing, more comprehensively than hitherto.

(b) At one time, because of a dimming of my eyes, I could see no light; I was weighed down in body by such a weight that I could not get up, but lay there assailed by the most intense pains. I suffered in this way because I had not divulged the vision I had been shown, that with my girls [*cum puellis meis*] I should move from the Disibodenberg, where I had been vowed to God, to another place. I was afflicted till I named the place where I am now. At once I regained my sight and had things easier, though I still did not recover fully from my sickness. But my abbot, and the monks and the populace in that province, when they realized what the move implied—that we wanted to go from fertile fields and vineyards and the loveliness of that spot to parched places where there were no amenities—were all amazed. And they intrigued so that this should not come about: they were determined to oppose us. What is more, they said I was deluded by some vain fantasy. When I heard this, my heart was crushed and my body and veins dried up. Then, lying in bed for many days, I heard a mighty voice forbidding me to utter or to write anything more in that place about my vision.

Then a noble marchioness, who was known to us, approached the archbishop of Mainz and laid all this before him and before other wise counsellors. They said that no place could be hallowed except through good deeds, so that it seemed right that we should go ahead. And thus, by the archbishop's permission, with a vast escort of our kinsfolk and of other men, in reverence of God we came to the Rupertsberg. Then the ancient deceiver put me to the ordeal of great mockery, in that many people said: "What's all this—so many hidden truths revealed to this foolish, unlearned woman, even though there are many brave and wise men around? Surely this will come to nothing!" For many people wondered whether my revelation stemmed from God, or from the parchedness [*inaquositas*] of aerial spirits, that often seduced human beings.

So I stayed in that place with twenty girls of noble and wealthy parentage, and we found no habitation or inhabitant there, save for one old man and his wife and children. Such great misfortunes and such pressure of toil befell me, it was as if a storm cloud covered the sun—so that, sighing and weeping copiously, I said: "Oh, oh God confounds no one who trusts in him!" Then God showed me his grace again, as when the clouds recede and the sun bursts forth, or when a mother offers her weeping child milk, restoring its joy after tears.

Then in true vision I saw that these tribulations had come to me according to the exemplar of Moses, for when he led the children of

Israel from Egypt through the Red Sea into the desert, they, murmuring against God, caused great affliction to Moses too, even though God lit them on their way with wondrous signs. So God let me be oppressed in some measure by the common people, by my relatives, and by some of the women who had remained with me, when they lacked essential things (except inasmuch as, through God's grace, they were given to us as alms). For just as the children of Israel plagued Moses, so these people, shaking their heads over me, said: "What good is it for well-born and wealthy girls to pass from a place where they lacked nothing into such penury?" But we were waiting for the grace of God, who had shown us this spot, to come to our aid.

After the pressure of such grief, he rained that bounty upon us. For many, who had previously despised us and called us a parched useless thing, came from every side to help us, filling us with blessings. And many rich people buried their dead on our land, with due honour. . . .

Nonetheless, God did not want me to remain steadily in complete security: this he had shown me since infancy in all my concerns, sending me no carefree joy as regards this life, through which my mind could become overbearing. For when I was writing my book *Scivias*, I deeply cherished a nobly-born young girl, daughter of the marchioness I mentioned,[4] just as Paul cherished Timothy. She had bound herself to me in loving friendship in every way, and showed compassion for my illnesses, till I had finished the book. But then, because of her family's distinction, she hankered after an appointment of more repute: she wanted to be named abbess of some splendid church. She pursued this not for the sake of God but for worldly honour. When she had left me, going to another region far away from us, she soon afterwards lost her life and the renown of her appointment.

Some other noble girls, too, acted in similar fashion, separating themselves from me. Some of them later lived such irresponsible lives that many people said, their actions showed that they sinned against the Holy Spirit, and against the person who spoke from out of the Spirit. But I and those who loved me wondered why such great persecution came upon me, and why God did not bring me comfort, since I did not wish to persevere in sins but longed to perfect good works with his help. Amid all this I completed my book *Scivias*, as God willed.

(c) In vision I saw three towers, by means of which Wisdom opened
certain hidden things up for me. The first tower had three rooms. In
the first room were nobly-born girls together with some others,
who in burning love listened to God's words coming from my
mouth—they had a kind of ceaseless hunger for that. In the second
were some steadfast and wise women, who embraced God's truth in
their hearts and words, saying "Oh, how long will this remain with
us?" They never wearied of that. In the third room were brave
armed men from the common people, who advancing ardently towards us, were led to marvel at the miracles of the first two rooms,
and loved them with great longing. They came forward frequently,
in the way that common people seek the protection of a prince, to
guard them against their enemies, in a firm and mighty tower.

In the second tower there were also three rooms. Two of them
had become arid in dryness, and that dryness took the form of a
dense fog. And those who were in these rooms said with one voice:
"What are these things, and from where, which that woman utters
as if they were from God? It's hard for us to live differently from
our forefathers or the people of our time. So let's turn to those who
know us, since we cannot persevere in anything else." Thus they
turned back to the common people—they were of no use in this
tower, or in the first. . . . But in the third room of this tower were
common people who, with many kinds of love, cherished the words
of God that I brought forth from my true vision, and supported me
in my tribulations, even as the publicans clung to Christ.

The third tower had three ramparts. The first was wooden, the
second decked with flashing stones, the third was a hedge. But a
further building was hidden from me in my vision, so that I learnt
nothing about it at the time. Yet in the true light I heard that the future writing which will be set down concerning it will be mightier
and more excellent than the preceding ones.

EXTRACT FROM A LETTER TO
GUIBERT DE GEMBLOUX[5]

Then how could it be that I, poor little creature, should not know
myself? God works where he wills—to the glory of his name, not
that of earthbound man. But I am always filled with a trembling

fear, as I do not know for certain of any single capacity in me. Yet I stretch out my hands to God, so that, like a feather which lacks all weight and strength and flies through the wind, I may be borne up by him. And I cannot [see] perfectly the things that I see in my bodily condition and in my invisible soul—for in these two man is defective.

Since my infancy, however, when I was not yet strong in my bones and nerves and veins, I have always seen this vision in my soul, even till now, when I am more than seventy years old. And as God wills, in this vision my spirit mounts upwards, into the height of the firmament and into changing air, and dilates itself among different nations, even though they are in far-off regions and places remote from me. And because I see these things in such a manner, for this reason I also behold them in changing forms of clouds and other created things. But I hear them not with my physical ears, nor with my heart's thoughts, nor do I perceive them by bringing any of my five senses to bear—but only in my soul, my physical eyes open, so that I never suffer their failing in loss of consciousness [*extasis*]; no, I see these things wakefully, day and night. And I am constantly oppressed by illnesses, and so enmeshed in intense pains that they threaten to bring on my death; but so far God has stayed me.

The brightness that I see is not spatial, yet it is far, far more lucent than a cloud that envelops the sun. I cannot contemplate height or length or breadth in it, and I call it "the shadow of the living brightness." And as sun, moon and stars appear [mirrored] in water, so Scriptures, discourses, virtues, and some works of men take form for me and are reflected radiant in this brightness.

Whatever I have seen or learnt in this vision, I retain the memory of it for a long time, in such a way that, because I have at some time seen and heard it, I can remember it; and I see, hear, and know simultaneously, and learn what I know as if in a moment. But what I do not see I do not know, for I am not learned. And the things I write are those I see and hear through the vision, nor do I set down words other than those that I hear; I utter them in unpolished Latin, just as I hear them through the vision, for in it I am not taught to write as philosophers write. And the words I see and hear through the vision are not like words that come from human lips, but like a sparkling flame and a cloud moved in pure air. Moreover, I cannot know the form of this brightness in any way, just as I cannot gaze completely at the sphere of the sun.

And in that same brightness I sometimes, not often, see another light, which I call "the living light"; when and how I see it, I cannot express; and for the time I do see it, all sadness and all anguish is taken from me, so that then I have the air of an innocent young girl and not of a little old woman.

Yet because of the constant illness that I suffer, I at times weary of expressing the words and the visions that are shown me; nonetheless, when my soul, tasting, sees those things, I am transformed to act so differently that, as I said, I consign all pain and affliction to oblivion. And what I see and hear in the vision then, my soul drains as from a fountain—yet the fountain stays full and never drainable.

But my soul at no time lacks the brightness called "shadow of the living brightness". I see it as if I were gazing at a starless firmament within a lucent cloud. And there I see the things I often declare, and those which I give as answers to the people who ask me, out of the blaze of the living light.

EXTRACTS FROM SCIVIAS

(A) DECLARATION: THESE ARE TRUE VISIONS FLOWING FROM GOD

. . . It happened that, in the eleven hundred and forty-first year of the Incarnation of the Son of God, Jesus Christ, when I was forty-two years and seven months old, Heaven was opened and a fiery light of exceeding brilliance came and permeated my whole brain, and inflamed my whole heart and my whole breast, not like a burning but like a warming flame, as the sun warms anything its rays touch. And immediately I knew the meaning of the exposition of the Scriptures, namely the Psalter, the Gospel and the other catholic volumes of both the Old and the New Testaments, though I did not have the interpretation of the words of their texts or the division of the syllables or the knowledge of cases or tenses. But I had sensed in myself wonderfully the power and mystery of secret and admirable visions from my childhood—that is, from the age of five—up to that time, as I do now. This, however, I showed to no one except a few religious persons who were living in the same manner as I; but meanwhile, until the time when God by His grace wished it to be manifested, I concealed it in quiet silence. But the visions I saw I did not perceive in dreams, or sleep, or delirium, or by the eyes of the body, or by the ears of the outer self, or in hidden places; but I received them while awake and seeing with a pure mind and the eyes and ears of the inner self, in open places, as God willed it. How this might be is hard for mortal flesh to understand.

But when I had passed out of childhood and had reached the age of full maturity mentioned above, I heard a voice from Heaven saying, "I am the Living Light, Who illuminates the darkness. The person [Hildegard] whom I have chosen and whom I have miraculously stricken as I willed, I have placed among great wonders, beyond the measure of the ancient people who saw in Me many secrets; but I have laid her low on the earth, that she might not set herself up in arrogance of mind. The world has had in her no joy or lewdness or use in worldly things, for I have withdrawn her from impudent boldness, and she feels fear and is timid in her works. For she suffers in her inmost being and in the veins of her flesh; she is distressed in mind and sense and endures great pain of body, because no security has dwelt in her, but in all her undertakings she has judged herself guilty. For I have closed up the cracks in her heart that her mind may not exalt itself in pride or vainglory, but may feel fear and grief rather than joy and wantonness. Hence in My love she searched in her mind as to where she could find someone who would run in the path of salvation. And she found such a one and loved him [the monk Volmar of Disibodenberg], knowing that he was a faithful man, working like herself on another part of the work that leads to Me. And, holding fast to him, she worked with him in great zeal so that My hidden miracles might be revealed. And she did not seek to exalt herself above herself but with many sighs bowed to him whom she found in the ascent of humility and the intention of good will.

"O human, who receives these things meant to manifest what is hidden not in the disquiet of deception but in the purity of simplicity, write, therefore, the things you see and hear."

But I, though I saw and heard these things, refused to write for a long time through doubt and bad opinion and the diversity of human words, not with stubbornness but in the exercise of humility, until, laid low by the scourge of God, I fell upon a bed of sickness; then, compelled at last by many illnesses, and by the witness of a certain noble maiden of good conduct [the nun Richardis of Stade] and of that man whom I had secretly sought and found, as mentioned above, I set my hand to the writing. While I was doing it, I sensed, as I mentioned before, the deep profundity of scriptural exposition; and raising myself from illness by the strength I received, I brought this work to a close—though just barely—in ten years.

These visions took place and these words were written in the days of Henry, Archbishop of Mainz, and of Conrad, King of the Romans, and of Cuno, Abbot of Disibodenberg, under Pope Eugenius.

And I spoke and wrote these things not by the invention of my heart or that of any other person, but as by the secret mysteries of God I heard and received them in the heavenly places.

And again I heard a voice from Heaven saying to me, "Cry out therefore, and write thus!"

(B) Book I: Vision Four

[. . . Lament of the soul returning by God's grace from the path of error to Zion]

A pilgrim, where am I? In the shadow of death. And in what path am I journeying? In the path of error. And what consolation do I have? That which pilgrims have. For I should have had a tabernacle adorned with five square gems more brilliant than the sun and stars, for the sun and stars that set would not have shone in it, but the glory of angels; the topaz would have been its foundation and all the gems its structure, its staircases made of crystal and its courtyards paved with gold. For I should have been a companion of the angels, for I am a living breath, which God placed in dry mud; thus I should have known and felt God. But alas! When my tabernacle saw that it could turn its eyes into all the ways, it turned its attention toward the North; ah, ah! and there I was captured and robbed of my sight and the joy of knowledge, and my garment all torn. And so, driven from my inheritance, I was led into a strange place without beauty or honor, and there subjected to the worst slavery. Those who had taken me struck me and made me eat with swine and, sending me into a desert place, gave me bitter herbs dipped in honey to eat. Then, placing me on the rack, they afflicted me with many tortures. And stripping me of my garments and dealing me many wounds, they sent me out to be hunted, and got the worst poisonous creatures, scorpions and asps and other vermin, to hunt and capture me; and these spewed out their poison all over me so that I was made helpless. Therefore they mocked me, saying, "Where is your honor now?" Ah, and I trembled all over and with a great groan of woe said silently to myself, "Oh, where am I? Ah, from whence did I come here? And what comforter shall I seek in this captivity? How shall I break these chains? Oh, what eye can look on my wounds? and what nose can bear their noisome stench? and what hands will anoint them with oil? Ah, who will have mercy on my affliction?

"May Heaven graciously hear my cry, and earth tremble at my grief, and every living thing incline with pity toward my captivity. For the bitterest sorrow oppresses me, who am a pilgrim without comfort and without help. Oh, who will console me, since even my mother has abandoned me when I strayed from the path of salvation? Who will help me but God? But when I remember you, O mother Zion, in whom I should have dwelt, I see the bitter slavery to which I am subjected. And when I have called to memory the music of all sorts that dwells in you, I feel my wounds. And when I remember the joy and gladness of your glory, I am horrified by the poisons that pollute them. Oh, where shall I turn? and where shall I flee? My sorrows are without number; for if I continue in these evils, I shall become the companion of those whom I knew to my shame in the land of Babylon. And where are you, O mother Zion? Woe is me that I so unluckily drew back from you; if I had not known you, I would sorrow more lightly! But now I will flee from these evil comrades, for wicked Babylon has put me in a leaden dish and crushed me with heavy bludgeons so that I hardly breathe. And when I pour out my tears and groans to you, O my mother, wicked Babylon sends forth such a noise and roar of sounding waters that you cannot hear my voice. So with great care I will seek the narrow ways by which to escape my evil comrades and my unhappy captivity."

And when I had said these things, I went away by a narrow path and hid myself from sight of the North in a small cave, bitterly weeping for the loss of my mother, and also for all my sorrows and all my wounds. And so many tears did I shed, weeping and weeping, that my tears soaked all the pain and all the bruises of my wounds.

And behold! A most sweet fragrance touched my nostrils, like a gentle breath exhaled by my mother. Oh, what groans and tears I poured forth then, when I felt the presence of that small consolation! And in my joy I uttered such cries and shed such tears that the very mountain in whose cave I had hidden myself was shaken by it. And I said, "O mother, O mother Zion, what will become of me: And where is your noble daughter now? Oh, how long, how long have I been deprived of your maternal sweetness, in which with many delights you gently brought me up!" And I delighted in these tears as if I saw my mother.

But my enemies, hearing these cries of mine, said, "Where is she, whom up to now we kept with us as we liked, so that she completely carried out our will? Look how she is calling upon the dwellers in Heaven. Let us therefore use all our arts and guard her with such great zeal and care that she cannot escape us, for before she was completely subject to us. If we do this, she will follow us again."

But I came secretly out of the cave in which I had hidden and tried to go up to such a height that my enemies would be unable to find me. They, however, set in my way a sea of such raging heat that I could not pass over it. There was, indeed, a bridge, but so small and narrow a one that I could not cross by it. And on the shore of that sea appeared a mountain range so high that I could not make my way across it. And I said, "Oh, wretched woman that I am, what shall I do now? For a little while just now I felt the sweetness of my mother's presence, and I thought she was trying to call me to her; but ah! is she now leaving me again? Ah! where shall I turn? For if I return to my former captivity, my enemies will deride me more than before, because I tearfully cried out to my mother and for a little while felt her gentle sweetness, but now I am forsaken by her again."

But because of that sweetness which my mother had lately sent me, I was for the first time filled with such strength that I turned to the East and resumed my way along the narrow path. But the paths were so hedged in by thorns and thistles and such obstacles that I could scarcely take a step. However, with great labor and sweat I struggled through them at last, so worn out by my travail that I could scarcely breathe.

Thus, at last, I attained with the utmost fatigue to the summit of the mountain in which I had hidden before and turned downward

to the valley into which I had to descend; and behold! there in my
way were asps, scorpions, serpents and other like crawling things,
all hissing at me. Terrified I uttered the loudest of shrieks, crying,
"O mother, where are you? I would suffer less if I had not lately felt
the sweetness of your presence; for I am falling again into the captivity in which I lay just now. Where now is your help?" And then
I heard my mother's voice, saying to me: "O daughter, run! For the
Most Powerful Giver whom no one can resist has given you wings
to fly with. Therefore fly swiftly over all these obstacles!" And I,
comforted with great consolation, took wing and passed swiftly
over all those poisonous and deadly things.

And I came to a tabernacle, whose interior was all of the
strongest steel. And, in going in, I did works of brightness where I
had previously done works of darkness. And in that tabernacle I
placed at the north a column of unpolished steel, on which I hung
fans made of diverse feathers, which moved to and fro. And, finding
manna, I ate it. At the east I built a bulwark of square stones and,
lighting a fire within it, drank wine mixed with myrrh and unfer-
mented grape juice. At the south I built a tower of square stones, in
which I hung up red shields and placed trumpets of ivory in its win-
dows. And in the middle of this tower I poured out honey and
mixed it with other spices to make a precious unguent, from which
a great fragrance poured forth to fill the whole tabernacle. But at
the west I built nothing, for that side was turned toward the world.

And while I was absorbed in this work, my enemies seized their
quivers and attacked my tabernacle with their arrows, but I was so
absorbed in the work I was doing that I did not notice their madness until the gates of the tabernacle were full of arrows. But none
of the arrows could penetrate the door or the steel lining of the tabernacle, so that I also could not be injured by them. When they saw
this, they sent a tremendous flood of water to wash away both me
and my tabernacle, but their malice accomplished nothing. Where-
fore I boldly mocked them, saying, "The architect who built this
tabernacle was wiser and stronger than you. Collect your arrows
and put them down, for from now on they cannot make your will
triumph over me. See, what wounds have they given me? With what
great pain and labor I have waged many wars against you, and you
tried to put me to death, but you could not; for I was protected by
the strongest armor and brandished sharp swords against you and

thus vigorously defended myself from you. Retreat, therefore, retreat, for you will have me no longer."

(C) Book II: Vision One

THE REDEEMER
And I, a person not glowing with the strength of strong lions or taught by their inspiration, but a tender and fragile rib imbued with a mystical breath,[6] *saw a blazing fire, incomprehensible, inextinguishable, wholly living and wholly Life, with a flame in it the color of the sky, which burned ardently with a gentle breath, and which was as inseparably within the blazing fire as the viscera are within a human being. And I saw that the flame sparked and blazed up. And behold! The atmosphere suddenly rose up in a dark sphere of great magnitude, and that flame hovered over it and gave it one blow after another, which struck sparks from it, until that atmosphere was perfected and so Heaven and earth stood fully formed and resplendent. Then the same flame was in that fire, and that burning extended itself to a little clod of mud which lay at the bottom of the atmosphere, and warmed it so that it was made flesh and blood, and blew upon it until it rose up a living human. When this was done, the blazing fire, by means of that flame which burned ardently with a gentle breath, offered to the human a white flower, which hung in that flame as dew hangs on the grass. Its scent came to the human's nostrils, but he did not taste it with his mouth or touch it with his hands, and thus he turned away and fell into the thickest darkness, out of which he could not pull himself. And that darkness grew and expanded more and more in the atmosphere. But then three great stars, crowding together in their brilliance, appeared in the darkness, and then many others, both small and large, shining with great splendor, and then a gigantic star, radiant with wonderful brightness, which shot its rays toward the flame. And in the earth too appeared a radiance like the dawn, into which the flame was miraculously absorbed without being separated from the blazing fire. And thus in the radiance of that dawn the Supreme Will was enkindled.*

And as I was trying to ponder this enkindling of the Will more carefully, I was stopped by a secret seal on this vision, and I heard the voice from on high saying to me, "You may not see anything further regarding this mystery unless it is granted you by a miracle of faith."

And I saw a serene Man coming forth from this radiant dawn, Who poured out His brightness into the darkness; and it drove Him back with great force, so that He poured out the redness of blood and the whiteness of pallor into it, and struck the darkness such a strong blow that the person who was lying in it was touched by Him, took on a shining appearance and walked out of it upright. And so the serene Man Who had come out of that dawn shone more brightly than human tongue can tell, and made His way into the greatest height of inestimable glory, where He radiated in the plenitude of wonderful fruitfulness and fragrance. And I heard the voice saying to me from the aforementioned living fire: "O you who are wretched earth and, as a woman, untaught in all learning of earthly teachers and unable to read literature with philosophical understanding, you are nonetheless touched by My light, which kindles in you an inner fire like a burning sun; cry out and relate and write these My mysteries that you see and hear in mystical visions. So do not be timid, but say those things you understand in the Spirit as I speak them through you; so that those who should have shown My people righteousness, but who in their perversity refuse to speak openly of the justice they know, unwilling to abstain from the evil desires that cling to them like their masters and make them fly from the face of the Lord and blush to speak the truth, may be ashamed. Therefore, O diffident mind, who are taught inwardly by mystical inspiration, though because of Eve's transgression you are trodden on by the masculine sex, speak of that fiery work this sure vision has shown you.". . .

On God's omnipotence

This blazing fire that you see symbolizes the Omnipotent and Living God, Who in His most glorious serenity was never darkened by any iniquity; *incomprehensible,* because He cannot be divided by any division or known as He is by any part of any of His creatures' knowledge; *inextinguishable,* because He is that Fullness that no limit ever touched; *wholly living,* for there is nothing that is hidden from Him or that He does not know; *and wholly Life,* for everything that lives takes its life from Him. . . .

That the Word was and is indivisibly and eternally in the Father
You see that *that fire has a flame in it the color of the sky, which burns ardently with a gentle breath, and which is as inseparably within the blazing fire as the viscera are within a human being*; which is to say that before any creatures were made the Infinite Word was indivisibly in the Father; Which in course of time was to become incarnate in the ardor of charity, miraculously and without the stain or weight of sin, by the Holy Spirit's sweet freshness in the dawn of blessed virginity. But after He assumed flesh, the Word also remained inseparably in the Father; for as a person does not exist without the vital movements within his viscera, so the only Word of the Father could in no way be separated from Him. . . .

By the power of the Word of God every creature was raised up
And you see that *the flame sparks and blazes up.* This is to say that when every creature was raised through Him, the Word of God showed His power like a flash of flame; and when He became incarnate in the dawn and purity of virginity, it was as if He blazed up, so that from Him trickled every virtue of the knowledge of God, and Man lived again in the salvation of his soul.

God's incomprehensible power made the world and the different species
And the atmosphere suddenly rises up in a dark sphere of great magnitude. This is the material of Creation while still formless and imperfect, not yet full of creatures; it is a sphere, for it is under the incomprehensible power of God, which is never absent from it, and by the Supernal Will it rises up in God's great power in the twinkling of an eye. *And that flame hovers over it like a workman and gives it one blow after another, which strike sparks from it, until that atmosphere is perfected and so Heaven and earth stand full formed and resplendent.* For the Supernal Word, Who excels every creature, showed that they all are subject to Him and draw their strength from His power, when He brought forth from the universe the different kinds of creatures, shining in their miraculous awakening, as a smith makes forms out of bronze; until each creature was radiant with the loveliness of perfection, beautiful in the fullness of their arrangement in higher and lower ranks, the higher made radiant by the lower and the lower by the higher.

———

After the other creatures Man was created from earthly mud
*But then the same flame that is in that fire and that burning extends
itself to a little clod of mud, which lies at the bottom of the atmosphere*; this is to say that after the other creatures were created, the
Word of God, in the strong will of the Father and supernal love,
considered the poor fragile matter from which the weak frailty of
the human race, both bad and good, was to be produced, now lying
in heavy unconsciousness and not yet roused by the breath of life;
and warms it so that it is made flesh and blood, that is, poured fresh
warmth into it, for the earth is the fleshly material of humans, and
nourished it with moisture, as a mother gives milk to her children;
and blows upon it until it rises up a living human, for He aroused it
by supernal power and miraculously raised up a human being with
intelligence of body and mind.

Adam accepted obedience, but by the Devil's counsel did not obey
*When this is done, the blazing fire, by means of that flame which
burns ardently with a gentle breath, offers to the human a white
flower, which hangs in that flame as dew hangs on the grass.* For, after Adam was created, the Father in His lucid serenity gave to
Adam through His Word in the Holy Spirit the sweet precept of
obedience, which in fresh fruitfulness hung upon the Word; for the
sweet odor of sanctity trickled from the Father in the Holy Spirit
through the Word and brought forth fruit in greatest abundance, as
the dew falling on the grass makes it grow. *Its scent comes to the human's nostrils, but he does not taste it with his mouth or touch it
with his hands*; for he tried to know the wisdom of the Law with his
intelligence, as if with his nose, but did not perfectly digest it by
putting it in his mouth, or fulfil it in full blessedness by the work of
his hands. *And thus he turns away and falls into the thickest darkness, out of which he cannot pull himself.* For, by the Devil's counsel, he turned his back on the divine command and sank into the
gaping mouth of death, so that he did not seek God either by faith
or by works; and therefore, weighed down by sin, he could not rise
to true knowledge of God, until He came Who obeyed His Father
sinlessly and fully.

*And that darkness grows and expands more and more in the
atmosphere*; for the power of death in the world was constantly increased by the spread of wickedness, and human knowledge entan-
gled itself in many vices in the horror of bursting and stinking sin.

Abraham and Isaac and Jacob and the other prophets drove back
the darkness

But then three great stars, crowding together in their brilliance, ap-
pear in the darkness, and then many others, both small and large,
shining with great splendor. These are the three great luminaries
Abraham, Isaac and Jacob, symbolizing the Heavenly Trinity, embracing one another both by their works of faith and by their relationship in the flesh, and by their signs driving back the darkness in
the world; and, following them, the many other prophets both minor and major, radiant with many wonders.

The prophet John, glittering with miracles, foretold the Son of God

And then a gigantic star appears, radiant with wonderful brightness,
which shoots its rays toward the flame. This is the greatest prophet,
John the Baptist, who glittered with miracles in his faithful and
serene deeds, and pointed out by their means the true Word, the
true Son of God; for he did not yield to wickedness, but vigorously
and forcefully cast it out by works of justice.

At the Incarnation of the Word of God the great counsel was seen

And in the earth too appears a radiance like the dawn, into which
the flame is miraculously absorbed, without being separated from
the blazing fire. This is to say that God set a great splendor of light
in the place where He would bring forth His Word and, fully willing it, sent Him there, yet not so as to be divided from Him; but He
gave that profitable fruit and brought Him forth as a great fountain,
so that every faithful throat could drink and never more be dry.
And thus in the radiance of that dawn the Supreme Will is enkin-
dled; for in the bright and roseate serenity was seen the fruitfulness
of the great and venerable counsel, so that all the forerunners marvelled at it with bright joy. . . .

Christ by His death brought back His elect to their inheritance

And you see a serene Man coming forth from this radiant dawn,
Who pours out His brightness into the darkness; and it drives Him
back with great force, so that He pours out the redness of blood and
the whiteness of pallor into it, and strikes the darkness such a strong
blow that the person who is lying in it is touched by Him, takes on a
shining appearance and walks out of it upright. This is the Word of

God, imperishably incarnate in the purity of unstained virginity and born without pain, and yet not separated from the Father. How? While the Son of God was being born in the world from a mother, He was still in Heaven in the Father; and at this the angels suddenly trembled and sang the sweetest praises of rejoicing. And, living in the world without stain of sin, He sent out into the darkness of unbelief His clear and blessed teachings and salvation; but, rejected by the unbelieving people and led to His Passion, he poured out His beautiful blood and knew in His body the darkness of death. And thus conquering the Devil, he delivered from Hell his elect, who were held prostrate there, and by His redeeming touch brought them back to the inheritance they had lost in Adam. As they were returning to their inheritance timbrels and harps and all kinds of music burst forth, because Man, who had lain in perdition but now stood upright in blessedness, had been freed by heavenly power and escaped from death. . . .

The Son of God rising from the dead showed Man the way from death to life
And, as you see, *the serene Man Who has come out of that dawn shines more brightly than human tongue can tell,* which shows that the noble body of the Son of God, born of the sweet Virgin and three days in the tomb (to confirm that there are three Persons in one Divinity), was touched by the glory of the Father, received the Spirit and rose again to serene immortality, which no one can explain by thought or word. And the Father showed Him with His open wounds to the celestial choirs, saying, "This is My beloved Son, Whom I sent to die for the people." And so joy unmeasurable by the human mind arose in them, for criminal forgetfulness of God was brought low, and human reason, which had lain prostrate under the Devil's persuasion, was uplifted to the knowledge of God; for the way to truth was shown to Man by the Supreme Beatitude, and in it he was led from death to life. . . .

When Christ ascended to the Father His Bride was given many ornaments
And He makes His way into the greatest height of inestimable glory, where he radiates in the plenitude of wonderful fruitfulness and fragrance. This is to say that the Son of God ascended to the Father, Who with the Son and the Holy Spirit is the height of lofty and ex-

celling joy and gladness unspeakable; where that same Son glori-
ously appears to His faithful in the abundance of sanctity and
blessedness, so that they believe with pure and simple hearts that
He is true God and Man. And then indeed the new Bride of the
Lamb was set up with many ornaments, for she had to be orna-
mented with every kind of virtue for the mighty struggle of all the
faithful people, who are to fight against the crafty serpent.

But let the one who sees with watchful eyes and hears with at-
tentive ears welcome with a kiss My mystical words, which proceed
from Me Who am life.

(D) BOOK III: VISION ONE

God and Man

And I, a person taken up from among other people—though unworthy to be called a human, since I have transgressed God's law
and have been unjust when I should have been just, except that by
God's grace I am His creature and will be saved—I looked toward
the East. And there *I saw a single block of stone, immeasurably
broad and high and the color of iron, with a white cloud above it;
and above the cloud a royal throne, round in shape, on which One
was sitting, living and shining and marvellous in His glory, and so
bright that I could not behold Him clearly. He held to His breast
what looked like black and filthy mire, as big as a human heart, surrounded with precious stones and pearls.*

*And from this Shining One seated upon the throne extended a
great circle colored gold like the dawn, whose width I could not take
in; it circled about from the East to the North and to the West and to
the South, and back toward the East to the Shining One, and had no
end. And that circle was so high above the earth that I could not apprehend it; and it shone with a terrifying radiance the color of stone,
steel and fire, which extended everywhere, from the heights of
Heaven to the depth of the abyss, so that I could see no end to it.*

*And then I saw a great star, splendid and beautiful, come forth
from the One seated on the throne. And with that star came a great
multitude of shining sparks, which followed the star toward the
South, looking on the One seated on the throne like a stranger; they
turned away from Him and stared toward the North instead of contemplating Him. But, in the very act of turning away their gaze,
they were all extinguished and were changed into black cinders.*

And behold, a whirlwind arose from those cinders, which drove them away from the South, behind the One sitting on the throne, and carried them to the North, where they were precipitated into the abyss and vanished from my sight. But when they were extinguished, I saw the light, which was taken from them, immediately return to Him Who sat on the throne.

And I heard the One Who sat on the throne saying to me, "Write what you see and hear." And, from the inner knowledge of that vision, I replied, "I beseech you, my Lord, give me understanding, that by my account I may be able to make known these mystical things; forsake me not, but strengthen me by the daylight of Your justice, in which Your Son was manifested. Grant me to make known the divine counsel, which was ordained of old, as I can and should: how You willed Your Son to become incarnate and become a human being within Time; which You willed before all creation in Your rectitude and the fire of the Dove, the Holy Spirit, so that Your Son might rise from a Virgin in the splendid beauty of the sun and be clothed with true humanity, a man's form assumed for Man's sake."

And I heard Him say to me, "Oh, how beautiful are your eyes, which tell of divinity when the divine counsel dawns in them!" And again I answered from the inner knowledge of the vision, "To my own inner soul I seem as filthy ashes of ashes and transitory dust, trembling like a feather in the dark. But do not blot me out from the land of the living, for I labor at this vision with great toil. When I think of the worthlessness of my foolish bodily senses, I deem myself the least and lowest of creatures; I am not worthy to be called a human being, for I am exceedingly afraid and do not dare to recount Your mysteries. O good and kind Father, teach me what to say according to Your will! O reverend Father, sweet and full of grace, do not forsake me, but keep me in Your mercy!"

And again I heard the same One saying to me, "Now speak, as you have been taught! Though you are ashes, I will that you speak. Speak of the revelation of the bread, which is the Son of God, Who is life in the fire of love; Who raises up everyone dead in soul and body, forgives all repented sins in His serene clarity, and awakens holiness in a person and sets it growing. Thus God, the magnificent, glorious and incomprehensible, gave Him as a great intercessor by sending Him into the purity of the Virgin, who had no corruptible weakness in her virginity. No pollution of the flesh should or could have been in the mind of the Virgin; for when the Son of God came in silence into the dawn, which was the humble maiden, Death, the slayer and destroyer of the human race, was deceived without knowing it as if in a dream. Death went on securely, not realizing what life that sweet Virgin bore, for her virginity had been hidden from it. And that Virgin was poor in worldly goods, for the Divine Majesty willed to have her so. Now write about the true knowledge of the Creator in His goodness."

(E) BOOK III: VISION TWELVE

The New Heaven and the New Earth
After this I looked, and behold, all the elements and creatures were shaken by dire convulsions; fire and air and water burst forth, and the earth was made to move, lightning and thunder crashed and mountains and forests fell, and all that was mortal expired. And all the elements were purified, and whatever had been foul in them vanished and was no more seen. And I heard a voice resounding in a great cry throughout the world, saying, "O ye children of men who are lying in the earth, rise up one and all!"

And behold, all the human bones in whatever place in the earth they lay were brought together in one moment and covered with their flesh; and they all rose up with limbs and bodies intact, each in his or her gender, with the good glowing brightly and the bad manifest in blackness so that each one's deeds were openly seen. And some of them had been sealed with the sign of faith, but some had not; and some of those signed had a gold radiance about their faces, but others a shadow, which was their sign.

And suddenly from the East a great brilliance shone forth; and there, in a cloud, I saw the Son of Man, with the same appearance He had had in the world and with His wounds still open, coming with the angelic choirs. He sat upon a throne of flame, glowing but not burning, which floated on the great tempest which was purifying the world. And those who had been signed were taken up into the air to join Him as if by a whirlwind, to where I had previously seen that radiance which signifies the secrets of the Supernal Creator; and thus the good were separated from the bad. And, as the Gospel indicates, He blessed the just in a gentle voice and pointed them to the heavenly kingdom, and with a terrible voice condemned the unjust to the pains of Hell, as is written in the same place. Yet He made no inquiry or statement about their works except the words the Gospel declares would be made there; for each person's work, whether good or bad, showed clearly in him. But those who were not signed stood afar off in the northern region, with the Devil's band; and they did not come to this judgment, but saw all these things in the whirlwind, and awaited the end of the judgment while uttering bitter groans.

And when the judgment was ended, the lightnings and thunders and winds and tempests ceased, and the fleeting components of the elements vanished all at once, and there came an exceedingly great calm. And then the elect became more splendid than the splendor of the sun; and with great joy they made their way toward Heaven with the Son of God and the blessed armies of the angels. And at the same time the reprobate were forced with great howling toward the infernal regions with the Devil and his angels; and so Heaven received the elect, and Hell swallowed up the reprobate. And at once such great joy and praise arose in Heaven, and such great misery and howling in Hell, as were beyond human power to utter. And all the elements shone calm and resplendent, as if a black skin had been taken from them; so that fire no longer had its raging heat, or air density, or water turbulence, or earth shakiness. And the sun, moon and stars sparkled in the firmament like great ornaments, remaining fixed and not moving in orbit, so that they no longer distinguished day from night. And so there was no night, but day. And it was finished.

And again I heard the voice from Heaven, saying to me:

In the last days the world will be dissolved in disasters like a dying man

These mysteries manifest the last days, in which time will be transmuted into the eternity of perpetual light. For the last days will be troubled by many dangers, and the end of the world will be prefigured by many signs. For, as you see, *on that last day the whole world will be agitated by terrors and shaken by tempests, so that whatever is fleeting and mortal in it will be ended.* For the course of the world is now complete, and it cannot last longer, but will be consummated as God wills. For as a person who is to die is captured and laid low by many infirmities, and in the hour of his death suffers great pain in his dissolution, so too the greatest adversities will precede the end of the world and at last dissolve it in terror. For the elements will then display their terrors, because they will not be able to do so afterward.

All creation will be moved and purified of all that is mortal in it
And so, at this consummation, *the elements are unloosed by a sudden and unexpected movement*: all creatures are set into violent motion, fire bursts out, the air dissolves, water runs off, the earth is shaken, lightnings burn, thunders crash, mountains are broken, forests fall, and whatever in air or water or earth is mortal gives up its life. For the fire displaces all the air, and the water engulfs all the earth; and thus all things are purified, and whatever was foul in the world vanishes as if it had never been, as salt disappears when it is put into water.

The bodies of the dead will rise again in their wholeness and gender
And *when, as you saw, the divine command to rise again resounds, the bones of the dead, wherever they may be, are brought together in one moment and covered with their flesh.* They will not be hindered by anything; but if they were consumed by fire or water, or eaten by birds or beasts, they will be speedily restored. And so the earth will yield them up as salt is extracted from water; for My eye knows all things, and nothing can be hidden from Me. And so all people will rise again in the twinkling of an eye, *in soul and body, with no deformity or mutilation but intact in body and in gender; and the elect will shine with the brightness of their good works, but the reprobate will bear the blackness of their deeds of misery.* Thus their works will not there be concealed, but will appear in them openly.

The risen who are signed and unsigned
And some of them are sealed with the sign of faith, but some are not; and the consciences of some who have faith shine with the radiance of wisdom, but the consciences of others are murky from their neglect. And thus they are clearly distinguished; for the former have done the works of faith, but the latter have extinguished it in themselves. And those who do not have the sign of faith are those who

chose not to know the living and true God either in the old Law or in the new Grace.

The Son will come to the judgment in human form

And then the Son of God, in the human form He had at His Passion when He suffered by the will of the Father to save the human race, will come to judge it, surrounded by the celestial army; He will be in the brightness of eternal life, but in the cloud that hides celestial glory from the reprobate. For the Father vouchsafed to Him the judging of the visible things of the world, because He had lived visibly in the world; as He Himself shows in the Gospel, saying:

The Gospel on this subject

And He has given Him power to judge, because He is the Son of Man [Jn 5:27]. . . .

Christina of Markyate

EXTRACTS FROM *THE LIFE OF CHRISTINA OF MARKYATE*

(a) Amidst all these trials Christ, wishing to comfort His spouse, gave her consolation through His holy Mother. It happened in this way. One night whilst she was sleeping, it seemed to her that she was brought with some other women into a most beautiful church. At the altar stood a man clothed in priestly vestments, as if ready to celebrate Mass. Looking over his shoulder, he beckoned to Christina to come to him. And when she approached with trembling, he held out to her a branch of most beautiful leaves and flowers saying: "Receive this, my dear, and offer it to the lady." At the same he pointed out to her a lady like an empress sitting on a dais not far from the altar. Curtsying to her, she held out the branch which she had received. And the lady, taking the branch from Christina's hand, gave back to her a twig and said, "Take care of it for me"; and then added as a question: "How is it with you?" She said: "Ill, my lady: they all hold me up to ridicule and straiten me from all sides. Among those that suffer there is none like me. Hence I cannot stop crying and sobbing from morning till night." "Fear not", she said. "Go now, since I will deliver you from their hands and bring you to the brightness of day." So she withdrew, full of joy as it seemed to her, carrying in her right hand the little branch of blossoms. And where she had to go down, there lay Burthred prostrate on the ground swathed in a black cape with his face turned downwards. And as soon as he saw her passing by he stretched out his hand to seize her and hold her fast. But she, gathering her garments about her and clasping them close to her side, for they were white and flowing, passed him untouched. And as she escaped from him, he followed her with staring eyes, groaning horribly, and struck his head with repeated blows on the pavement to show his rage.

Meanwhile, the maiden looked closely in front of her, and saw an upper chamber, lofty and quiet, which could be reached only by a series of steps, steep and difficult for anyone wishing to climb. Christina had a great desire to climb up, but as she hesitated on account of its difficulty, the queen whom she had seen just a short time before helped her, and so she mounted to the upper chamber. And as she sat there enjoying the beauty of the place, behold, the aforesaid queen came and laid her head in her lap as if she wished to rest, with her face turned away. This turning away of her face was a source of disquiet to Christina and, not daring to speak, she said inwardly: "Oh, if only I were allowed to gaze upon your face." Straightway the empress turned her face towards her and said to her with winning kindness: "You may look now; and afterwards when I shall bring both you and Judith[1] also into my chamber, you can gaze to your full content." After this vision she awoke and found her pillow wet with tears, so that she was convinced that as the tears she dreamed she had shed were real, so were the rest of the things which she had dreamed. From that moment you could see she was completely changed, and the immense joy which filled her at the thought of her freedom was displayed for all to see in the cheerfulness of her countenance.

(b) . . . she had another vision there by which she was consoled. She saw herself standing on firm ground before a large and swampy meadow full of bulls with threatening horns and glaring eyes. And as they tried to lift their hooves from the swampy ground to attack her and tear her to pieces, their hooves were held fast in the ground so that they could not move. Whilst she gazed on this sight with astonishment, a voice was heard saying: "If you take a firm stand in the place where you are, you will have no cause to fear the ferocity of those beasts. But if you retreat one step, at that same moment you will fall into their power." She woke up, and interpreted the place as meaning her resolution to remain a virgin: the bulls were devils and wicked men. And taking great confidence, she was inspired with a deeper desire for holiness, and had less fear of the threats of her persecutors. In the meantime her concealment and her peaceful existence irritated the Devil: her reading and singing of the psalms by day and night were a torment to him. For although in her hiding-place she was hidden from men, she could never escape the notice of the demons. And so to terrify the reverend handmaid of

Christ toads invaded her cell to distract her attention by all kinds of ugliness from God's beauty. Their sudden appearance, with their big and terrible eyes, was most frightening, for they squatted here and there, arrogating the middle of the psalter which lay open on her lap at all hours of the day for her use. But when she refused to move and would not give up her singing of the psalms, they went away, which makes one think that they were devils, especially as they appeared unexpectedly; and as the cell was closed and locked on all sides it was not possible to see where they came from, or how they got in or out.

(c) . . . on the day of Our Lord's annunciation, whilst Christina was sitting on her stone and giving anxious thought to the senseless be-haviour of her persecutors, the fairest of the children of men came to her through the locked door, bearing in His right hand a cross of gold. At His appearance the maiden was terrified, but He put her fears at rest with this comforting assurance: "Fear not", He said: "for I have not come to increase your fears, but to give you confi-dence. Take this cross, therefore, and hold it firmly, slanting it nei-ther to right nor left. Always hold it straight, pointing upwards: and remember that I was the first to bear the same cross. All who wish to travel to Jerusalem must carry this cross." Having said this, He held out the cross to her, promising that after a short time He would take it back again from her. And then He vanished. When Christina recounted this experience to Roger, the man of God, he understood its meaning and began to weep for joy, saying: "Blessed be God, who succours His lowly ones at all times." And he said to the maiden in English: "Rejoice with me, *myn sunendaege dohter*", that is, my Sunday daughter, because just as much as Sunday excels the other days of the week in dignity so he loved Christina more than all the others whom he had begotten or nursed in Christ. "Re-joice with me," he said, "for by the grace of God your trials will soon be at an end. For the meaning is this: the cross which you have received as a token will shortly be taken from you." And it hap-pened as the man of God had foretold. . . .

(d) . . . once when she was at prayer and was shedding tears through her longing for heaven, she was suddenly rapt above the clouds even to heaven, where she saw the queen of heaven sitting on a throne and angels in brightness seated about her. Their brightness exceeded that of the sun by as much as the radiance of the sun exceeds that of the stars. Yet the light of the angels could not be compared to the light which surrounded her who was the mother of the Most High. What think you then was the brightness of her countenance which outshone all the rest? Yet as she gazed first at the angels and then at the mistress of the angels, by some marvellous power she was better able to see through the splendour that encompassed the mistress than through that which shone about the angels, though the weakness of human sight finds brighter things harder to bear. She saw her countenance therefore more clearly than that of the angels; and as she gazed upon her beauty the more fixedly and was the more filled with delight as she gazed, the queen turned to one of the angels standing by and said: "Ask Christina what she wants, because I will give her whatever she asks."

Now Christina was standing quite close to the queen and clearly heard her speaking to the angel. And falling downwards to the ground, she saw in one flash the whole wide world. But above all else she turned her eyes towards Roger's cell and chapel which she saw beneath her, shining brilliantly, and she said: "I wish to have that place to dwell in." "She shall certainly have it," replied the queen, "and even more would gladly be given if she wanted it." . . .

(e) Christina remained therefore with Roger in his hermitage until his death. But when he had gone to heaven, where he rested in peace after his many tribulations, it was imperative that Christina should go elsewhere to avoid the anger of the bishop of Lincoln. Therefore after she had first taken various hiding-places, the archbishop commended her to the charge of a certain cleric, a close friend of his, whose name I am under obligation not to divulge. He was at once a religious and a man of position in the world: and relying on this twofold status Christina felt the more safe in staying with him. And certainly at the beginning they had no feelings about each other, except chaste and spiritual affection. But the Devil, the enemy of chastity, not brooking this for long, took advantage of their close companionship and feeling of security to insinuate himself first stealthily and with guile, then later on, alas, to assault them more openly. And, loosing his fiery darts, he pressed his attacks so vigorously that he completely overcame the man's resistance. But he could not wrest consent from the maiden, though he assailed her flesh with incitements to pleasure and her mind with impure thoughts. He used the person she was lodging with to play her many evil tricks and wiles. Sometimes the wretched man, out of his senses with passion, came before her without any clothes on and behaved in so scandalous a manner that I cannot make it known, lest I pollute the wax by writing it, or the air by saying it. Sometimes he fell on his face at her feet, pleading with her to look pityingly upon him and have compassion on his wretchedness. But as he lay there she upbraided him for showing so little respect for his calling, and with harsh reproaches silenced his pleadings. And though she herself was struggling with this wretched passion, she wisely pretended that she was untouched by it. Whence he sometimes said that she was more like a man than a woman, though she, with her more masculine qualities, might more justifiably have called him a woman.

Would you like to know how manfully she behaved in so imminent a danger? She violently resisted the desires of her flesh, lest her own members should become the agents of wickedness against her. Long fastings, little food, and that only of raw herbs, a measure of water to drink, nights spent without sleep, harsh scourgings. And what was more effective than all these, . . . trials[2] which tore and tamed her lascivious body. She called upon God without ceasing not to allow her, who had taken a vow of virginity and had refused the marriage bed, to perish for ever. Only one thing brought her respite, the presence of her patron, for then her passion abated: for in his absence she used to be so inwardly inflamed that she thought the clothes which clung to her body might be set on fire. Had this occurred whilst she was in his presence, the maiden might well have been unable to control herself. One day as she was going to the monastery, the cleric, her evil genius, appeared to her in the form of an enormous wild, ugly, furry bear, trying to prevent her from entering the monastery, for nothing repelled his attacks so effectively as the prayers and tears of the lowly ascetic maiden. But as she proceeded on her way the earth opened a pit for her despairing foe.[3] . . . One result of this was that she was ill for a fortnight or more.

And yet the abandoned cleric did not cease from molesting the sick maiden with as much importunity as he had done when she was well. At last one night there appeared to him three saints, John the evangelist, Benedict the founder of monks, and Mary Magdalene, threatening him in his sleep. Of these Mary, for whom the priest had particular veneration, glared at him with piercing eyes,

and reproached him harshly for his wicked persecution of the chosen spouse of the most high king. And at the same time she threatened him that if he troubled her any further, he would not escape
the anger of almighty God and eternal damnation. Terrified at the
vision and awakened from sleep, he went to the maiden in a
changed mood and, revealing to her what he had seen and heard,
begged and obtained her pardon: afterwards he changed his way of
life. Nevertheless neither this nor anything else was able to cool the
maiden's passion. And so, after a long time had been spent in constant warring against her tireless adversary, disgusted with that
deadly lodging, she returned to the pleasant place in the wilderness
bestowed on her by the queen of heaven; and there day and night
she knelt in prayer, weeping, and lamenting, and begging to be freed
from temptation. Even in the wilderness she unwillingly felt its
stings. Then the Son of the Virgin looked kindly down upon the
low estate of His handmaid and granted her the consolation of an
unheard-of grace. For in the guise of a small child He came to the
arms of his sorely tried spouse and remained with her a whole day,
not only being felt but also seen. So the maiden took Him in her
hands, gave thanks, and pressed Him to her bosom. And with im-
measurable delight she held Him at one moment to her virginal
breast, at another she felt His presence within her even through the
barrier of her flesh. Who shall describe the abounding sweetness
with which the servant was filled by this condescension of her creator? From that moment the fire of lust was so completely extinguished that never afterwards could it be revived.

(f) Christina, moreover, who obtained cures for others from
heaven, suffered from grievous ailments which she had contracted
through the various trials which she had endured. And as time went
on new ones were added to the old. And as they were all incurable
(for everything known to human science had been tried in vain), she
was cured in the end, quite unexpectedly, by divine power. But first,
listen carefully how appropriately Christ cured her of only one
malady, and that the worst, through His Mother, and then how sub-
limely He cured her of all the rest altogether, by sending her a
crown from heaven to signify her virginal integrity. The malady,
which they call paralysis, attacked one half of her body, spreading
from her lower limbs to the top of her head. As the result of a recent illness the cheeks of the patient were already swollen and

inflamed. Her eyelids were contracted, her eyeball bloodshot, and underneath the eye you could see the skin flickering without stopping, as if there were a little bird inside it striking it with its wings. For this reason experienced physicians were sent to her and to the best of their power they practised their craft with medicines, bloodletting, and other kinds of treatment. But what they thought would bring relief had quite a contrary effect. Indeed the malady, which they ought to have cured, became on the contrary so irritated and inflamed, that she suffered from it for five whole days without ceasing, so that what her health had been in comparison with her sickness before treatment, now her sickness became in comparison with the maladies that followed. And that nothing should be lacking either in time for her perfection or in pain for her suffering, a certain old man sent her a tablet, which, dissolved in wine and drunk, would, he asserted, eradicate and expel that malady from her. But in order that the spouse of God should put her trust only in divine help, her final suffering was as much greater than all the rest as the second was greater than the first. So violent was it on the sixth day that at any moment she was expected to breathe her last. But on the following night, by the will of God (who rested on the seventh day), when she woke up, she found herself restored to health and, thanks be to God, to us. For no matter at what hour she was released from the prison of her flesh, who could doubt that her Spouse would come and lead her with Him to the nuptials? Feeling a movement of her eyelids, sight in her eye which had been blind, the swelling gone from her cheeks, and relief in the other limbs of her body, and hardly believing it through surprise, she called her maidens together and corroborated the fact with a lighted candle. On the following day, when they had come together, they began to talk about the sudden cure of their mistress.

Then one of them said that in the first watch of the night she had seen in a dream a woman of great authority, with a shining countenance, whose head was veiled in a snow-white coif, adorned across the breadth of it with gold embroidery and fringed on each end with gold. And when she had sat down before the patient's bed, she took out a small box in which she had brought an electuary[4] of unusual fragrance. While she was daintily preparing to give it to her, all of them with tears in their eyes warned her, saying: "Do not waste both your lozenge and your labour, lady, because we saw the woman you are trying to cure barely escape death after taking a similar electuary yesterday." But she took no notice of what they were saying, and, carrying out the errand on which she had come, gave the lozenge to the sick woman and cured her. The patient who was cured and the maiden who had seen the dream discussed both cure and vision with all the greater joy, because before their talk the one was unaware of the vision, the other of restoration to health. You see how easily and how appropriately God cured His virgin daughter with heavenly medicine through His virgin Mother, deeming anything employed by mortal man to be unworthy of His spouse.

It now remains to reveal how she was released from her many other maladies, for they were not few. Each one was worse than the paralysis. As they threatened to cut short her life at any moment, she had no wish to die until she had been professed. Furthermore, she had frequent visits from the heads of celebrated monasteries in distant parts of England and from across the sea, who wished to take her away with them and by her presence add importance and prestige to their places. Above all, the archbishop of York tried very hard to do her honour and to make her superior over the virgins whom he had gathered together under his name at York, and if not, send her over the sea to Marcigny or at least to Fontevrault.[5] But she preferred our monastery, both because the body of that celebrated martyr of Christ, Alban[6] rested there (whom she loved more than the other martyrs revered by her), and because Roger the hermit came from there and was there buried: also because, as you have learned by experience, she revered you more than all the pastors under Christ, and because there were in our community certain souls whom she cherished more than those of other monasteries, some of whom owed their monastic vocation to her. And it should be borne in mind that as our blessed patron St Alban had her from the Lord as co-operator in building up and furthering his community on earth, so he had her afterwards as sharer of his eternal bliss in heaven.

For these reasons she decided that she would make her profession in this monastery and would receive her consecration from the bishop. But inwardly she was much troubled, not knowing what she should do, nor what she should say, when the bishop inquired during the ceremony of consecration about her virginity. For she was mindful of the thoughts and stings of the flesh with which she had been troubled, and even though she was not conscious of having fallen either in deed or in desire, she was chary of asserting that she had escaped unscathed. At last she turned to the most chaste Mother of God with her whole heart, pleading with her and asking her to intercede for release from this uncertainty. Whilst she was thus occupied, she began to feel more confident about gaining permission, and she hoped it would come about the feast of the Assumption of the Mother of God. For this reason she had no peace of mind until the feast day actually arrived. The nearer it approached, the more anxiously did Christina complain about the delay. At last it came, but her hopes were not immediately fulfilled. The first day passed; so did the second; so in the same way passed six days of the festival. She was unwearying in her entreaties; indeed, her devotion and hope increased as the days went by.

On the seventh day, that is 21 August, about cock-crow and before the dawn, she got up and stood before her couch. The hour had passed at which it was usual to sing the nocturns. Thinking that this was due to the laziness of the nuns, she noticed that, contrary to custom, all of them were fast asleep, and the world about them was sunk in deep silence. Whilst the virgin was standing still in astonishment (o ineffable kindness of divine condescension), behold, there gathered round her youths of extraordinary beauty. There were several present, but she could see only three. Addressing her, they said: "Hail, virgin of Christ. The Lord of all, Jesus Christ Himself greets you." And when they had said this, they approached nearer and, standing round about her, placed on her head a crown which they had brought with them, adding: "This has been sent to you by the Son of the Most High King. And know that you are one of His own. You marvel at its beauty and the craftsmanship: but you would not marvel if you knew the art of the craftsman." It was, as she averred, whiter than snow and brighter than the sun, of a beauty that could not be described and of a material that could not be discovered. From the back and reaching down to her waist hung two white fillets, like those of a bishop's mitre. Thus crowned, Christina stood in the midst of the angels who had been sent to her from cock-crow until the day grew warm after the rising of the sun. Then, as the angels withdrew to heaven, she remained alone, knowing for certain from the heavenly crown that Christ had preserved her chaste in mind and body. Furthermore, she felt so strong in health that never afterwards did she feel the slightest twinge from those maladies which had afflicted her earlier on.

Disturbed by these events, the demon launched out into new warfare, so terrorizing the friend of Christ with horrible apparitions and unclean shapes that for many years afterwards, whenever she composed her weary limbs to rest, she dared not turn upon her side nor look about her. For it seemed to her that the Devil might stifle her or inveigle her by his wicked wiles into committing some unseemly wantonness. But when he was foiled in his unwearying attempts to debauch her mind, the poisonous serpent plotted to break her steadfastness by creating false rumours and spreading abroad unheard-of and incredible slanders through the bitter tongues of his agents. Everyone with a perverse mind, prompted by malice and goaded on by him who was always a liar, took pleasure in disseminating every imaginable evil of her, each one thinking himself to be the more admired, the more wittily he fabricated lying tales about Christina. The maiden of Christ, sustained in the midst of all this by her good conscience, committed herself to the loving care of her Redeemer, and submitted her case to the judgement of God. In order not to transgress our Lord's precept, she prayed for them that reviled her. The demon, seeing that all his schemes were nullified by Christina's faith, and that one possessed, as she was, by the love of God could not be turned aside by love of this world, to employ every stratagem in his bold and ruthless warfare assaulted her with the spirit of blasphemy. He was confident that if he could cloud her faith with the slightest darkness, [he would win the fight]. He came by stealth and put evil thoughts into her mind. He suggested horrible ideas about Christ, detestable notions about His Mother. But she would not listen. He attacked her, but was put to flight. He pressed his assaults, but was routed. Even so he would not be silenced; when put to flight, he would not disappear; when routed, he would not retreat. Taking new and more elaborate weapons of temptation, he assaulted the virgin all the more intensely, as his resentment grew to find a tender virgin more than a match for him. When she was all by herself in the chapel he molested her with such sordid apparitions, terrified her with such harsh threats that any other person would easily have gone out of his mind.

Harassed by these and other matters, the handmaid of Christ was inwardly disturbed and feared that God had abandoned her; she knew not what to do, where to turn, or where to go to avoid the machinations of the Devil. At length, pulling herself together and taking courage from the remembrance of past mercies, she entered the church and, bathed in tears as was her wont, placed herself in the loving presence of God. But when she recalled that God leaves no sin unpunished, she wondered whether these many and grievous ills might not have come upon her through her own fault: she fell prostrate on the ground, raising her mind to God and praying earnestly about it, for she was afraid that if help was not quickly forthcoming, she would be tempted beyond her strength, though God allows no man to be tempted beyond his strength. And behold, whilst she was praying and nothing distracted her attention, whilst she was rapt from earth to heaven, she heard (but with what ears I know not) the divine words: "Be not afraid of these horrible temptations, for the key of your heart is in my safe keeping, and I keep guard over your mind and the rest of your body. No one can enter except by my permission." Immediately she felt relief from all these trials, just as if she had never felt them at all; and during the rest of her life, as often as she was assailed by temptation or wearied with suffering, she remembered the key and as confirmation of Christ's promise to His handmaid she instantly experienced divine consolation.

(g) Henceforward the man devoted to good works[7] visited the place even more: he enjoyed the virgin's company, provided for the house, and became the supervisor of its material affairs. Whilst he centred his attention on providing the virgin with material assistance, she strove to enrich the man in virtue, pleading for him so earnestly with God in prayer that, whilst occupied in it, she became unaware of the man's presence. After receiving the Eucharist or even during the celebration of Mass (for she communicated at the table of Christ as often as the abbot celebrated the divine mysteries), she was so rapt that, unaware of earthly things, she gave herself to the contemplation of the countenance of her Creator. Knowing this, the abbot used to say: "Great is my glory in this, that though for the moment you are forgetful of me, you present me to Him, whose presence is so sweet that you fail to realize that I am present."

Now the handmaid of Christ, disciplining her mind by watching, her body by fasting, stormed God in prayer and would not cease until she was satisfied in her mind about the sure salvation of her beloved. God listens more attentively to the prayers of the pure in heart, and even before He is invoked says: "I hear". This He designed to show in a vision. For Christina saw herself in a kind of chamber, pleasing in its material, design, and atmosphere, with two venerable and very handsome personages clothed in white garments. Standing side by side, they differed neither in stature nor beauty. On their shoulders a dove far more beautiful than other doves seemed to rest. Outside she saw the abbot trying without success to gain entrance to her. Giving her a sign with his eyes and head, he humbly begged her to introduce him to the persons standing at her side in the divine presence. The virgin lost no time in coming to her friend's aid with her usual prayers. For with all the energy of which she was capable, with all the love she could pour out, with all the devotion she knew she pleaded with the Lord to have mercy on her beloved. Without delay, she saw the dove glide through the chamber with a fluttering of its wings and delight the eyes of the onlooker with its innocent gaze. When she saw this, God's servant took courage and would not stop pleading until she saw the man already mentioned either possessing the dove or being possessed by the dove: and when she came to herself, she understood clearly that the dove meant the grace of the Holy Spirit, and that the abbot, once filled with it, would be able to aspire only to things above. Filled with joy at this, she cherished him and venerated a fellow and companion of heavenly not earthly glory, and took him to her bosom in a closer bond of holy affection. For who shall describe the longings, the sighs, the tears they shed as they sat and discussed heavenly matters? Who shall put into words how they despised the transitory, how they yearned for the everlasting? Let this be left to someone else: my task is to describe quite simply the simple life of the virgin.

This same virgin had a brother, Gregory, a monk of St Albans, whom she cherished with extraordinary affection for the charm of his manners and the staunchness of his belief. Unless their goodness and innate propensity to holiness commended them, her family relatives shared little of her affection. This Gregory then, having with his abbot's permission stayed a short time with his sister, used to say Mass there. But as the day approached on which God had disposed to snatch him from the cares of this world, he was seized with that sickness which was to end his life. His sister, having great compassion on him (for she stood out above all others in those days in loving the good), had recourse to her usual remedy—prayer— and pleaded with God to reveal to her in His mercy what plans He had in mind for her brother. The result of her prayers was long in coming, but their constancy never flagged, even though her brother's flagging health seemed to forebode death. At this Christina grew more sad and for the sake of her brother moved Christ with floods of tears until she heard a voice from heaven saying these words: "Thou mayest be sure his lady loves him." And after a brief space the same voice added: "And she loves you also." Convinced therefore of his death, and no less convinced that her own passing was not far off she gave thanks to God both because she had deserved to be heard, but more because she had learned that both of them would be summoned by the queen of queens. So going to her brother, she intimated to him that he would be summoned by the Mistress of heaven. And she added: "If some noble and powerful lady in the world had called you to her service while you were in the world, you would have taken great care to appear gracious in her eyes. Now that the Mistress of heaven calls you, how much more should you fulfill her behests to the best of your ability while you can!" When Gregory heard this, believing that his death was near, he fortified himself with the sacraments of Christ so much the more composedly as he felt the more certain that he would die. And after he had received the viaticum,[8] and all those things which concern the burial had been decently arranged, he was borne unconscious to the church in the presence of the abbot and the community of St Albans, not without the tears of many mourners. Full of hope, he breathed forth his last and, what he had most hoped for earlier in life, both his sisters, Christina and Margaret, were present at his burial.

(h) In the monastery of Bermondsey[9] near the city of London there was a man venerable in his way of life, a true monk, living up to the meaning of his name Simon, who was sacrist[10] to that house and who on account of his holiness and the strictness of his life was a leading member of that community. This man had great respect for the virgin just mentioned: he cultivated her friendship, and spoke affectionately of her, since through being accepted into her familiar circle he had felt a greater outpouring of the Holy Spirit. He was so antagonistic to tale-bearers and detractors that he silenced them as soon as they opened their mouths to speak. But as he knew that God defends just causes, he decided that he would beg Him, who is the judge of thoughts and desires and the knower of all secrets, to reveal to him the truth about Christina. For this reason he afflicted his body with fasting, his mind with watching and tears: he slept on the bare ground and would accept no consolation until he received some answer from the Lord. For he considered it a crime to make false accusations against Christina, and he could not believe that he had been led astray in his affection for Christina. God therefore wished to put an end to his troubles and to show him, as a lover of the truth, the true state of affairs; and so one day whilst the same venerable man Simon was at the altar celebrating Mass, mindful of his prayer, he saw, with surprise, Christina standing near the altar. He was astonished at this for the virgin could not have come out of the cell and it was hardly possible that any woman would be allowed to approach the altar. Not without amazement he awaited the issue. Then she said: "Thou mayest be sure that my flesh is free from corruption." And when she had said this she vanished. Filled with gladness and hardly able to contain himself for joy, he finished the Mass in due course, though he was not able to put as quick an end to his affection for the virgin. Finding one of the monks of St Albans, who by chance had come to Bermondsey at that time, he sent a message to Abbot Geoffrey through that same monk telling him what he had seen, what he had heard, and what he knew about the case of Christina. And as that monk was one of those who slandered her, the Lord in His kindness and justice had arranged that through this message he should become aware of what he ought to feel about Christina; so that if he should spread false rumours about her in future, he should not be left in doubt that he was acting against his conscience, and that he would be visited with the heavy punishment due to tale-bearers. But the venerable Simon was quite unaware that the monk was such a one. And when the abbot received the message from Simon he gave thanks to God because He had mercifully revealed to others what he already knew himself.

Christina, incapable of being crushed by the cunning of the Devil, having already overcome it many times by her faith, wondered what new offering she could make to God in order to enlighten the abbot and put an end to the shamelessness of her detractors, whom she pitied. So the virgin, being endued with light which enlightened without consuming, proposed to offer a wax candle in the church as a gift every Sunday night. The proposal was endorsed by the sisters, who knew nothing of the reason for it. It was then Saturday. The Devil, irritated by the virgin's constancy,

which he could not inwardly disturb by any attempts of his own or
of his followers, tried to frighten her outwardly by assuming a
monstrous appearance. And so on the following night, that is, towards daybreak on Sunday, whilst Christina was in the monastery
and whilst the others were getting ready for Matins, they saw a
body without a head (for the Devil had lost his head, God) sitting in
the cloister near the entrance to the church. At this sight (for
women are timid creatures) they were terrified and all of them fell
on their faces at the feet of their mistress. You could see one trying
to bury herself in her bosom, another covering herself under her
veil, another clinging to her knees, another wishing to hide at her
feet, this one concealing herself under a bench, another lying on the
ground and trembling as if at the hour of death. To all there was one
way of escape; to touch, if possible, the garments of Christina. The
Devil, no less bold, burst into the church. At the sight of this mon-
ster the handmaid of Christ was somewhat afraid, but, taking her
courage in her hands, she turned to the Lord and, uttering prayers,
thrust out that monstrous phantom. But for some time afterwards a
more than ordinary horror swept over her. Deeply grieved at this,
she poured out prayers and laments to Him in whom she had
placed her trust, fearing that if she began to be afraid of the monstrous appearances of the Devil she was being abandoned by the
Lord. As she continued to pray on this matter, this answer was
given her: "Your prayers on such things are unnecessary: but the
prayers for your beloved friend, that he be enlightened with eternal
light, have been granted. All the same, the frightful images and the
envy of your detractors will, in a short time, be suppressed. For
though the Devil rages inwardly and sharpens the tongues of your
detractors outwardly, you must not cease to do good nor lose constancy in time of difficulty."

(i) It happened once that a certain pilgrim, quite unknown but of
reverend mien, came to the virgin Christina's cell. She welcomed
him hospitably as she did everyone, not asking him who he was nor
being told by him at that time who he was. So he went on his way,
leaving on her memory a deep impression. After a while he returned a second time: first he offered prayers to the Lord and then
he settled down to enjoy Christina's conversation. Whilst they were
talking, she felt a divine fervour which made her recognize him as
being far beyond ordinary men or man's deserts. Greatly delighted

at this, she urged him with kindly hospitality to take food. He sat down whilst she and her sister Margaret prepared the repast. Christina paid more attention to the man, whilst Margaret was busily moving about concerned with the preparations of the meal, so that if it had been possible to see Jesus sitting down you would recognize another Mary and another Martha.[11] And so, when the table was prepared, he raised bread to his mouth and seemed to eat. But if you had been present, you would have noticed that he tasted rather than ate. And when he was invited to taste a little of the fish that was set before him, he replied that there was no need to take more than would keep body and soul together. And whilst both sisters were admiring his well-shaped features, his handsome beard, his grave appearance, and his well-chosen words, they were filled with such spiritual joy that they felt they had before them an angel rather than a man, and, if their virginal modesty had allowed, they would have asked him to stay. But he, after imparting a blessing, and taking his leave of them, went on his way, still known to the sisters only by sight. On the other hand so deep an impression did his manner leave on their hearts, so much sweetness did he instill into them, that often when they were talking together they would say, with sighs that showed their feelings: "If only our pilgrim would return. If only we could enjoy his company once more. If only we could gaze upon him and learn more from his grave and beautiful example." With these yearnings for the man they often stimulated each other's desire. Christina, [thinking over] these things, prepared herself for the coming of the feast of Christmas, uncertain however where her yearnings would lead her. On the day preceding the vigil of the feast, she was confined to bed with an illness, and so strong was her weakness that she was unable to go to church on the vigil. Two monks, religiously inclined, hearing this decided to visit her out of courtesy. And whilst they were chanting the hours of the Christmas vigil to the sick virgin, she heard, and retained in her mind along with the rest the versicle of the hour of None,[12] that special joy of that singular feast: *Today ye shall know that the Lord will come and tomorrow ye shall see His glory.* Realizing the significance of the verse, she was so moved with joy that for the rest of the day and the following night thoughts of this kind kept running through her mind: "Oh, at what hour will the Lord come? How will He come? Who shall see Him when He comes? Who will deserve to see His glory? What will that glory be like? And how great? What and how great will be the joy of those who see it?" Fixing her mind on holy desires of this kind, confined as she was to bed with a severe illness, she prepared herself, with great joy for the hours of Matins. And as she heard the [anthem] proper to the feast, *Christ is born,* she understood that she had been invited to the joy of His birth. Her illness disappeared and she was filled with such spiritual happiness that her mind could dwell on nothing but divine things. And when the others sang the hymn *Te Deum laudamus,*[13] she looked up and felt as if she had been borne into the church of St Albans and stood on the steps of the lectern where the lessons of Matins are read out. And looking down on the choir, she saw a person in the middle of the choir looking approvingly at the reverent behaviour of the monks singing. His beauty exceeded the power and capacity of man to describe. On his head he bore a golden crown thickly encrusted with precious stones which seemed to excel any work of human skill. On the top was a cross of gold of marvellous craftsmanship, not so much man-made as divine. Hanging over his face, one on either side, were two bands or fillets attached to the crown, delicate and shining, and on the tops of the gems there were seen as it were drops of dew. In this guise appeared the man whose beauty had only to be seen to be loved, for He is the fairest of the children of men. And when she had gazed on this beauty, she felt herself rapt in some way to another world. But whether she saw these things in the body or out of the body (God is her witness), she never knew.[14] On the morrow of Christmas day, when the time for the procession was near, a message was brought to her that her beloved pilgrim had arrived. When she heard this, her joy was unbounded, and added fire to the flames of her desire. For she hoped to reap no little benefit by entertaining in the person of this pilgrim Him whose presence had brought her such sweet relief. She ordered the doors, therefore, [to be closed].

Therefore the pilgrim followed the procession of chanting virgins: his modesty in gait, his grave expression, his mature appearance, were closely observed, setting as it did the virgin's choir an example of grave deportment, as it says in Scripture: *I will give Thee thanks in the great congregation* [Ps 34:18]. In the procession and the Mass and the other parts of the service the pilgrim took part. And when they were over, the virgin of Christ, preceding the rest (for she could not have too much of her pilgrim), left the church so that she should be the first to greet him as he came out.

For there was no other place of exit except where Christina was. As he stayed awhile, the virgin became impatient with waiting. And when they had all come out, she said: "Where is the pilgrim?" "He is praying in the church", they answered. Impatient of delay, she sent some of the nuns to call him. But they returned to say that he could not be found anywhere. The virgin, rather surprised and disturbed, said: "Where is the key of the door?" "Here it is", said the one who had charge of it. "From the moment that Mass began no one could come out, since the door had been closed and I have guarded the key." Nor was there anyone else who had even seen him come out of the Church. Who else could we say he was, except an angel or the Lord Jesus? For He who appeared that night in such a guise showed Himself in some sort of way as He will be seen in glory. For this is how that glory appears to us in this present life, since we see it only through a glass. Hence God is said to dwell in darkness,[15] not that He dwells in darkness, but His light because of its brightness blinds us who are weighed down by the body. . . .

However, nothing is lacking to those who fear God nor to those who love Him in truth. *For, behold, thou hast loved truth: the uncertain and hidden things of thy wisdom thou hast made manifest to me* [Ps 50:]. Among these Thy handmaid Christina was pre-eminent, who the nearer she approached Thee in true love, the more clearly was she able to penetrate the hidden things of Thy wisdom with her pure heart. Hence Thou gavest her the power to know the secret thoughts of men, and to see those that were far off and deliberately concealed as if they were present. This was made manifest in what follows. One of her maidens was thinking of doing something or other secretly; and the handmaid of God, seated in another house, saw it through the walls and forbade her saying: "Do it not, do it not." The girl said: "What, mistress?" She said: "What you were thinking of then." "But I was not thinking of anything that is forbidden", said she. Then Christina called her to her and whispered in her ear what she had seen her thinking in her heart. On hearing it the girl blushed with shame, and proved that she spoke true. Then she besought and implored Christina for the sake of her good name not to tell anyone, because she would never be able to bear the shame of it if it were revealed.

On another occasion, as we were sitting at table with the maiden of Christ, the same girl placed food on the table for us to eat. And as we ate, Christina refused to touch it. And when we asked her to

take a little food with us, she summoned Godit, for that was her
name. Christina asked her, but quietly, out of respect for the guests,
if she had made the salad from ingredients which had been forbidden, for Christina had been emphatic that for a time she would eat
nothing from the garden next door because the owner, out of miser-
liness, had denied her a sprig of chervil when she had recently asked
for it. In the meantime she accepted the salad, but refused to taste of
the dish, and after the meal was over she proved the girl's guilt by
the testimony of those who saw her. And the girl admitted that
what they had eaten had been gathered in the forbidden garden.

Hadewijch

EXTRACTS FROM THE *LETTERS*

LETTER 1

. . . Learn to contemplate what God is: how he is Truth, present to
all things; and Goodness, overflowing with all wealth; and Totality,
replete with all virtues. It is for these three names that the *Sanctus* is
sung three times in heaven, for they comprehend in their one
essence all the virtues, whatever may be their particular works from
their three distinct attributes.

See how God has protected you with fatherliness, and what he
has given you, and what he has promised you. Behold how sublime
is the love of the Three Persons for one another, and show your
gratitude to God through love. Do this, if you wish to contemplate
what God is and to work in him, in his radiance, with fruition in
glory and manifestation in radiance, in order to enlighten all things
or to leave them in darkness, according to what they are.

It is because of what God is that it is right to leave him fruition
of himself in all the works of his radiance, *sicut in caelo et in terra*,
and never stop saying, both in actions and in words: *fiat volun-
tas tua*.[1]

O dear child, in proportion as his irresistible power is made
more clear in you, as his holy will is better perfected in you, and as
his radiant truth more fully appears in you, consent to be deprived
of sweet repose for the sake of this great totality of God! Illuminate
your mind and adorn yourself with virtues and just works; enlarge
your spirit by lofty desires toward God's totality; and dispose your
soul for the great fruition of omnipotent Love in the excessive
sweetness of our God!

Alas, dear child! although I speak of excessive sweetness, it is in
truth a thing I know nothing of, except in the wish of my heart—
that suffering has become sweet to me for the sake of his love. But
he has been more cruel to me than any devil ever was. For devils

could not stop me from loving God or loving anyone he charged me to help forward; but this he himself has snatched from me. What he is, he lives by, in his sweet self-enjoyment, and lets me thus wander far from this fruition, beneath the constant weight of non-fruition of Love, and in the darkness where I am destitute of all the joys of fruition that should have been my part.

Oh, how I am impoverished! Even what he had offered and given me as a pledge of the fruition of veritable love, he has now withdrawn—as, in part, you well know. Alas! God is my witness that I earnestly acknowledged him as my Lord and asked of him little more than he wished to give me. But what he offered I would gladly have accepted in fruition, if he had willed to raise me to it. At first this grieved me, and I let many things be offered to me before I would receive them. But now my lot is like his to whom something is offered in jest, and when he wishes to take it his hand is slapped, and he is told: "God's wrath on him who fancied it true!" And what he supposed he held is snatched from him.

LETTER 6

... We must be continually aware that noble service and suffering in exile are proper to man's condition; such was the share of Jesus Christ when he lived on earth as Man. We do not find it written anywhere that Christ ever, in his entire life, had recourse to his Father or his omnipotent Nature to obtain joy and repose. He never gave himself any satisfaction, but continually undertook new labors from the beginning of his life to the end. He said this himself to a certain person who is still living,[2] whom he also charged to live according to his example, and to whom he himself said that this was the true justice of Love: where Love is, there are always great labors and burdensome pains. Love, nevertheless, finds all pains sweet. ...

LETTER 8

In proportion as love grows between these two,[3] a fear also grows in this love. And this fear is of two kinds. The first fear is, one fears that he is unworthy, and that he cannot content such love. And this fear is the very noblest. Through it one grows the most, and through it one submits to Love. Through this fear one stands at the service of Love's commandments. This fear holds men in love and in the dispositions they most need. It maintains them in humility when it is needful that they be awakened so they become fearful.

For when they fear that they are not worthy of such great love, their humanity is shaken by a storm and forbids them all rest. For indeed to suffer pain through love makes a person courtly in speech, because he fears that all he says about Love will be of no account to her. This fear makes a man free, for he can no longer think of anything or feel anything except that he would gladly please Love. Thus this fear adorns the one who loves. It gives clarity to his thought, instructs his heart, purifies his conscience, gives wisdom to his intellect, confers unity on his memory, watches over his works and his words, and permits him not to fear any sort of death. All this is done by the fear that is afraid it does not content Love.

The second fear is, we fear that Love does not love us enough, because she binds us so painfully that we think Love continually oppresses us and helps us little, and that all the love is on our side. This unfaith is higher than any fidelity that is not abysmal,[4] I mean, than a fidelity that allows itself to rest peacefully without the full possession of Love, or than a fidelity that takes pleasure in what it has in the hand. This noble unfaith greatly enlarges consciousness. Even though anyone loves so violently that he fears he will lose his mind, and his heart feels oppression, and his veins continually stretch and rupture, and his soul melts—even if anyone loves Love so violently, nevertheless this noble unfaith can neither feel nor trust Love, so much does unfaith enlarge desire. And unfaith never allows desire any rest in any fidelity but, in the fear of not being loved enough, continually distrusts desire. So high is unfaith that it continually fears either that it does not love enough, or that it is not enough loved.

He who wishes to remedy this inadequacy must keep his heart ever vigilant, so as to maintain perfect fidelity in all things. And all pain for the sake of Love must be pleasing to him. He shall silence good answers he would have regretted to silence were it not for love. He shall be silent when he would gladly have spoken, and speak when he would gladly have fixed his thought on divine fruition, in order that no one blame the Beloved on account of his love. He ought rather to suffer woe beyond his strength than to fail on any point relating to the honor of Love.

Anger we must have nothing to do with, if we want the peace of veritable love—even if he whom we loved were the Devil in person! For if you love, you are bound to renounce everything and despise yourself as the last of all, in order to content Love according to her dignity. He who loves gladly lets himself be condemned without excusing himself, because he wishes to be freer in Love. And for Love's sake, he will gladly endure much. He who loves gladly lets himself be beaten in order to be formed. He who loves is glad to be rejected in order to be utterly free. He who loves gladly remains in aloneness, in order to love and to possess Love.

I cannot say much more to you now, because many things oppress me, some that you know well and some that you cannot know. Were it possible, I would gladly tell you. My heart is sick and suffering; that comes partly because my fidelity is still not abysmal. When Love wells up in my soul, I will tell you more about these things than I have yet said to you.

LETTER 11

O dear child! May God give you what my heart desires for you—that God may be loved by you worthily.

Yet I have never been able, dear child, to bear the thought that anyone prior to me should have loved him more than I. I do believe, however, that there were many who loved him as much and as ardently, and yet I cannot endure it that anyone should know or love him so intensely as I have done.

Since I was ten years old I have been so overwhelmed by intense love that I should have died, during the first two years when I began this, if God had not given me other forms of strength than people ordinarily receive, and if he had not renewed my nature with his own Being. For in this way he soon gave me reason, which was enlightened to some extent by many a beautiful disclosure; and I had from him many beautiful gifts, through which he let me feel his presence and revealed himself. And through all these tokens with which I met in the intimate exchange of love between him and me—for as it is the custom of friends between themselves to hide little and reveal much, what is most experienced is the close feeling of one another, when they relish, devour, drink, and swallow up each other—by these tokens that God, my Love, imparted to me in so many ways at the beginning of my life, he gave me such confidence in him that ever since that time it has usually been in my mind that no one loved him so intensely as I. But reason in the meantime made me understand that I was not the closest to him; nevertheless the chains of love that I felt never allowed me to feel or believe this. So that is how it is with me: I do not, finally, believe that he can be loved the most intensely by me, but I also do not believe there is any man living by whom God is loved so much. Sometimes Love so enlightens me that I know what is wanting in me—that I do not content my Beloved according to his sublimity; and sometimes the sweet nature of Love blinds me to such a degree that when I can taste and feel her it is enough for me; and sometimes I feel so rich in her presence that I myself acknowledge she contents me.

LETTER 13

. . . What satisfies Love best of all is that we be wholly destitute of all repose, whether in aliens,[5] or in friends, or even in Love herself. And this is a frightening life Love wants, that we must do without the satisfaction of Love in order to satisfy Love. They who are thus drawn and accepted by Love, and fettered by her, are the most in-debted to Love, and consequently they must continually stand subject to the great power of her strong nature, to content her. And that life is miserable beyond all that the human heart can bear. . . .

LETTER 18

. . . Now understand the deepest essence of your soul, what "soul" is. Soul is a being that can be beheld by God and by which, again, God can be beheld. Soul is also a being that wishes to content God; it maintains a worthy state of being as long as it has not fallen beneath anything that is alien to it and less than the soul's own dignity. If it maintains this worthy state, the soul is a bottomless abyss in which God suffices to himself; and his own self-sufficiency ever finds fruition to the full in this soul, as the soul, for its part, ever does in him. Soul is a way for the passage of God from his depths into his liberty; and God is a way for the passage of the soul into its liberty, that is, into his inmost depths, which cannot be touched except by the soul's abyss. And as long as God does not belong to the soul in his totality, he does not truly satisfy it.

The power of sight that is created as natural to the soul is charity. This power of sight has two eyes, love and reason. Reason cannot see God except in what he is not; love rests not except in what he is. Reason has its secure paths, by which it proceeds. Love experiences failure, but failure advances it more than reason. Reason advances toward what God is, by means of what God is not. Love sets aside what God is not and rejoices that it fails in what God is. Reason has more satisfaction than love, but love has more sweetness of bliss than reason. These two, however, are of great mutual help one to the other; for reason instructs love, and love enlightens reason. When reason abandons itself to love's wish, and love consents to be forced and held within the bounds of reason, they can accomplish a very great work. This no one can learn except by experience. For wisdom does not interfere here or try to penetrate this wonderful and fathomless longing, which is hidden from all things; that is only for the fruition of love. *In this joy the stranger shall not intermediate* [Prov 14:10]—or anyone outside of Love. To gain it the soul must be nursed with motherly care, in the joy of the blessedness of great love, and disciplined by the rod of fatherly mercy; moreover it must cling inseparably to God, read its judgments in his countenance, and thereby abide in peace. . . .

LETTER 19

> . . . He who wishes to taste veritable Love,
> Whether by random quest or sure attainment,
> Must keep to neither path nor way.
> He must wander in search of victory over Love,
> Both on the mountains and in the valleys,
> Devoid of consolation, in pain, in trouble;
> Beyond all the ways men can think of,
> That strong steed of Love bears him.
> For reason cannot understand
> How love, by Love, sees to the depths of the Beloved,
> Perceiving how Love lives freely in all things.
> Yes, when the soul has come to this liberty,
> The liberty that Love can give,
> It fears neither death nor life.
> The soul wants the whole of Love and wants nothing else.
> —I leave rhyme: What mind can say eludes me. . . .

LETTER 25

Greet Sara also in my behalf, whether I am anything to her or nothing.

Could I fully be all that in my love I wish to be for her, I would gladly do so; and I shall do so fully, however she may treat me. She has very largely forgotten my affliction, but I do not wish to blame or reproach her, seeing that Love leaves her at rest and does not reproach her, although Love ought ever anew to urge her to be busy with her noble Beloved. Now that she has other occupations and can look on quietly and tolerate my heart's affliction, she lets me suffer. She is well aware, however, that she should be a comfort to me, both in this life of exile and in the other life in bliss. There she will indeed be my comfort, although she now leaves me in the lurch.

And you, Emma and yourself—who can obtain more from me than any other person now living can, except Sara—are equally dear to me. But both of you turn too little to Love, who has so fearfully subdued me in the commotion of unappeased love. My heart, soul and senses have not a moment's rest, day or night; the flame burns constantly in the very marrow of my soul.

Tell Margriet to be on her guard against haughtiness, and to be sensible, and to attend to God each day; and that she apply herself to the attainment of perfection and prepare herself to live with us, where we shall one day be together; and she should neither live nor remain with aliens. It would be a great disloyalty if she deserted us, since she so much desires to satisfy us, and she is now close to us— indeed, very close—and we also so much desire her to be with us.

Once I heard a sermon in which Saint Augustine was spoken of. No sooner had I heard it than I became inwardly so on fire that it seemed to me everything on earth must be set ablaze by the flame I felt within me. Love is all!

LETTER 29
God be with you! and may he give you consolation with the veritable consolation of himself, with which he suffices to himself and to all creatures according to their being and their deserts. O sweet child, your sadness, dejection, and grief give me pain! And this I entreat you urgently, and exhort you, and counsel you, and command you as a mother commands her dear child, whom she loves for the supreme honor and sweetest dignity of Love, to cast away from you all alien grief, and to grieve for my sake as little as you can. What happens to me, whether I am wandering in the country or put in prison—however it turns out, it is the work of Love.

I know well, also, that I am not the cause of such grief to you; and I am close to you in heart, and trusted; and for me, you—after Sara—are the dearest person alive. Therefore I well understand that you cannot easily leave off grieving over my disgrace. But be aware, dear child, that this is an alien grief. Think about it yourself, if you believe with all your heart that I am loved by God, and he is doing his work in me, secretly or openly, and that he renews his old wonders in me, you must also be aware that these are doings of Love, and that this must lead aliens to wonder at me and abhor me. For they cannot work in the domain of Love, because they know neither her coming nor her going. And with these persons I have little shared their customs in their eating, drinking, or sleeping; I have not dressed up in their clothes, or colors, or outward magnificence. And from all the things that can gladden the human heart, from what it can obtain or receive, I never derived joy except for brief moments from the experience of the Love that conquers all.

But from its first awakening and upward turning, my enlightened reason (which, ever since God revealed himself in it, has enlightened me as to whatever in myself and in others was lacking in perfection) showed me and led me to the place where I am to have fruition of my Beloved in unity according to the worthiness of my ascent.

This place of Love, which enlightened reason showed me, was so far above human thought that I was obliged to understand I might no longer have joy or grief in anything, great or small, except in this, that I was a human being, and that I experienced Love with a loving heart; but that, since God is so great, I with my humanity may touch the Godhead without attaining fruition. . . .

EXTRACTS FROM THE *POEMS IN STANZAS*

POEM 6

. . . Love makes me wander outside myself.
Where shall I find something of Love
According to my heart's delight,
So that I may sweeten my pain?
Although I follow her, she flies;
Although I attend her school,
She will not agree with me in anything.
In a moment this becomes all too clear to me
Alas! I speak from heart's distress;
My misfortune is too great,
And for me, to do without Love is a death,
Since I cannot have fruition of her.

—

Since I ought to love totally,
Why did she not give me total love?
Yet according to my small desires
That would be small pleasure for me;
To win Love's favor, however,
I have brought all my understanding to nought;
I no longer know what to live on.
She knows well what I imply.
For I have so spent what is mine,
I have nothing to live on—or she must give it.
But even if she gave something, hunger would remain,
For I want the whole. . . .

POEM 9

To sing of Love is pleasant in every season,
Be it autumn, winter, spring, or summer,
And to plead our case against her power,
For no courageous man keeps out of her way.
But we lazy ones often say in anxiety:
"What, would she tyrannize thus over me?
I had rather share the lot of those
        Who manage to secure quiet,
        And remain at home! Why should I
        Sally forth to meet my doom?"

Ignoble persons of small perception
Fear the cost will be too high:
Therefore they withdraw from Love,
From whom all good would have come to them.
If they withdraw from Love's service,
They will be the conquerors, so they think.
But fidelity will show they are poor and make them known as they are,
        All naked before Love's magnificence;
        These are they who consumed everything they had,
        But without coercion from Love.

He who would gladly suffer sweet exile
(The roads to the land of high Love)
Would find his beloved and his country at the end;
Of this, Fidelity gives seal and pledge;
Many a yokel, however, is such a beggar
That he takes what lies nearest his hand,
        Remaining before Love unknown
        With his beggar's garment;

So he has not the form or badge of honor
By which Love recognizes what is hers.

A fine exterior, fine garments,
And fine language adorn the knight;
To suffer everything for Love without turning hostile
Is a fine exterior for him who has such ability;
His garments then are his acts,
Performed with new ardor, not with self-complacency,
And with regard for all the needs of strangers
    Rather than of his own friends:
    This is the colored apparel, best adorned
    With blazons of nobility, to the honor of high Love.

Veracious words and great expenditures
In public, and fair splendor at home,
Most give the knight honor and luster;
By these signs can he best be recognized.
So it is also with them who love,
If they are established in the truth
And if they arrange their inner life with fair splendor,
    As best pleases Love,
    And give their whole love for Love's sake:
    This gift is best pleasing to Love.

I speak of Love; and I counsel
Adorned splendor and noble deed.
That fidelity must pay back what Love consumed
Is small consolation for many a one
Who stands in the chains of Love,
In nonfruition and disgrace.
    "Love always rewards, even though she comes late."
    Here is my answer to that:
    They who follow her suffer
    From night in the daytime!

Who would be ever singing the praises of Love,
Since she gives night in the daytime?
Those she ought to clothe, honor, and nourish,
She robs of all their strength:
Anyone who would gladly pay the tribute of love.
She ought to teach according to all justice,
And under the seal of fidelity raise to the height
    Where the loved soul both encounters

      And, with the whole fruition of love,
      Honors and adorns the Beloved.

What seems to the loved soul the most beautiful encounter
Is that it should love the Beloved so fully
And so gain knowledge of the Beloved with love
That nothing else be known by it
Except: "I am love conquered by Love!"
But he who overcame Love was rather conquered
So that he might in love be brought to nought:
      In this lies the power that surpasses everything,
      That from which Love
      Was born from the beginning.

But we who are shallow, of frivolous mind,
Find the fears of Love harsh;
We are inconstant with small gains;
Therefore we are deprived of Love's clear truth
I know (although I know not all the joys
That one experiences in Love's wealth,
Still enlightened reason teaches all this)
      How to correspond with Love to the full.
      Reason does not reach this truth:
      No task too hard, and all is prepared anew.

They who early
Catch sight of Love's beauty,
And are quickly acquainted with her joy,
And take delight in it—
If things turn out well for them,
Will have, God knows,
A much better bargain in love
Than I have found so far.

POEM 17

      When the season is renewed,
      Although mountain and valley
      Are everywhere dark and colorless,
          The hazelnut tree is already in bloom
      While the lover of Love has a sad lot,
          He too shall grow in every way.

What use are joy or springtime to him
Who gladly took delight in Love

And never finds in the wide world
 One whom he can trust or rest in
To whom he can freely say: "Beloved, it is you
 Who can utterly satisfy me!"

What joy can surround
Him whom Love has thrown into close confinement,
When he wishes to journey through Love's immensity
 And enjoy it as a free man in all security?
More multitudinous than the stars of heaven
 Are the griefs of love.

The number of my griefs must be unuttered,
My cruel burdens must remain unweighed:
Nothing can be compared to them,
 So it is best to give up the attempt.
Though my share of griefs is small, I have borne it;
 I shudder that I exist.

How can life horrify and grieve
One who has given his all for all,
And in the darkness is driven the wrong way
 To a distance from which he envisages no return
And in a storm of despair is wholly crushed?
 What grief can compare with this pain?

O proud souls who stand as if on Love's side
And live freely under her protection,
Pity one who is disowned, whom Love overwhelms
 And pursues in a despairing exile!
Alas! let whoever can observe reason live free with reason
 My heart lives in despair.

For I saw a shining cloud rise
Over all the dark sky; and its form seemed so beautiful.
I fancied I would soon with full happiness
 Play freely in the sunlight:
But my joy was only a fancy!
 If I should die of it, who would blame me?

Then for me night fell over the daylight,
Oh, woe that I was ever born!
But if one gives his all in reliance on Love,
 Truly Love will compensate him with love

Although I am again under the lash,
    God consoles all noble souls.

In the beginning Love always contents us.
When Love first spoke to me of love,
O how with all that I was I greeted all that she is!
    But then she made me resemble the hazelnut trees
That bloom early in the dark season,
    And for whose fruit one must wait a long time.

Fortunate is he who can wait
Until Love gives him all in exchange for his all.
O God! what is patience to me?
    To wait, on the contrary, gives me greater joy,
For I have abandoned myself wholly to Love.
    But woe has treated me all too harshly.

This is all too hard for the lover:
To stray after Love without knowing where,
Be it in darkness or in daylight,
    In wrath or in lovingness: Were Love
To give her true consolation unmistakably,
    This would satisfy the exiled soul.

Oh, if my Beloved let me obtain what is lovable in love,
Love would not be completely exhausted by it,
And so there would be no joy but a delusion;
    And if this happened it would be a pity.
Oh may God make noble spirits understand
    What harm would come of it!

Oh, what I mean and have long meant,
God has indeed shown to noble souls,
To whom he has allotted the torments of love
    To give them fruition of Love's nature;
Before the All unites itself to the all,
    Sour bitterness must be tasted.

Love comes and consoles us; she goes away and knocks us down.
    This initiates our adventure.
But how one grasps the All with the all,
    Alien rustics will never know.

          —

POEM 21

When the flowers of summer are with us again,
We look forward to the fruit,
So also does the noble, valiant heart
That wishes to endure every storm of Love,
    And says with brave mind:
    "I greet you, Love, with undivided love,
    And I am brave and daring;
    I will yet conquer your power,
    Or I will lose myself in the attempt!"

What evil could ever befall a brave heart
That stakes everything on the conquest of Love?
This could never actually happen
If you, Love, gave all you should have given,
    Entirely as it might be;
    Alas, if your mountains were valleys,
    And we then could see
    Our journey toward you pressed to the end,
    All would be well with us!

He must march far who presses on to Love—
Through her broad width, her loftiest height, her deepest abyss.
In all storms he must explore the ways;
Then her wondrous wonder is known to him:
That is—to cross her desert plains,
    To journey onward and not stand still;
    To fly through and climb through the heights,
    And swim through the abyss,
    There from Love to receive love whole and entire.

Alas! sublime Love, though she seems so sweet
That her sweetness consumes all other sweetness,
Wounds heart and mind; yet he whom she stormily touches
Always desires new assaults,
    So that he shrinks from no difficulties,
    No pain, no anguish, no death,
    All the while he has no success in the service of Love.
    Oh may God, who brings this about, bless him!
    Noble heart was never cowardly.

I let Love be all that she is.
I cannot understand her fierce wonders;

Although I can recover from this in my own case,
She has greatly troubled man.
>   This disaster must be borne by one
>   Who addresses words of protest to her,
>   If he does not ward off her power by his power.
>   For he who has never fought against Love
>   Has never lived a free day.

I bid farewell to Love now and forever.
He who will may follow her court; as for me, I have had too much woe.
Since I first chose her, I expected to be the lady of her court;
I did everything with praise: I cannot hold out.
>   Now her rewards
>   Seem to me like the scorpion
>   That shows a beautiful appearance,
>   And afterwards strikes so cruelly.
>   Alas! What does such a show mean?

If in love I had good fortune (which ever fled from me
And during my whole life was not at hand),
I should still conquer and live in joy,
While I now stray in too cruel misery.
Were it possible, I'd gladly make an end of this!
>   I stray with courage and ardor
>   Where Love requires of me
>   To follow her without success,
>   And where, for me, she remains too unattainable.

May God give good success to all lovers, as is fitting.
Though I and many others have so little part in Love,
They who know her fully give all for all.
She gives herself wholly to whom she pleases.
>   He who was empowered always attained her.
>   What use is it for anyone to fear
>   What must invariably happen?
>   All her blows are good.
>   But it takes a warrior to keep up the fight!

To make any complaint against Love is now unheard of;
Her name is so love that, from her, men suffer everything.
I counsel them whom she now confuses to say nothing;
This state is unknown to him whom she does not so oppress
>   But let him who is high-minded and daring
>   Look to himself

And ward off blow with blow;
So shall he still see the day
When Love herself offers him reconciliation.

To him who dares to fight against her,
Love grants full pardon
And makes him perfectly free of her.
So we can well say: "Woe is me!
How dare we cling to our repose?"

POEM 28

Joyful now are the birds
That winter oppressed.
And joyful in a short time will be
(We must thank Love for that)
The proud hearts who too long
Have borne their pain.
Through confidence in Love.
Her power is so effective
That she will give them in reward
More than they can conceive.

He whose wish it is
To receive all love from high Love
Must seek her gladly,
No matter where,
And dare the worst death
If Love destines him for it,
Being always equally bold—
Whatever noble Love commands—
That he may not neglect it
But be ready to perform it.

Alas! What then will happen to him
Who lives according to Love's counsel?
For he shall find no one
Who understands his distress.
With unfriendly eyes
Men will show him a cruel look,
For no one will understand
What distress he suffers
Until he surmounts his distress
In the madness of love.

The madness of love
Is a rich fief;
Anyone who recognized this
Would not ask Love for anything else:
It can unite opposites
And reverse the paradox.
I am declaring the truth about this:
The madness of love makes bitter what was sweet,
It makes the stranger a kinsman,
And it makes the smallest the proudest.

The madness of love makes the strong weak
And the sick healthy.
It makes the sturdy man a cripple
And heals him who was wounded.
It instructs the ignorant person
About the broad way
Whereon many[6] inevitably lose themselves;
It teaches him everything
That can be learned
In high Love's school.

In high Love's school.
Is learned the madness of Love;
For it causes delirium
In a person formerly of good understanding.
To one who at first had misfortune,
It now gives success;
It makes him lord of all the property
Of which Love herself is Lady.
I am convinced of this,
And I will not change my mind.

To souls who have not reached such love,
I give this good counsel:
If they cannot do more,
Let them beg Love for amnesty,
And serve with faith,
According to the counsel of noble Love,
And think: "It can happen,
Love's power is so great!"
Only after his death
Is a man beyond cure.

———

High-minded is he
Who becomes so fully ruled by Love
That he can read
In Love's power her judgments on him.

POEM 34

In all seasons new and old,
If one is submissive to Love,
In the hot summer, the cold winter,
He will receive love from Love.
He shall satisfy with full service
        In encountering high Love;
So he speedily becomes love with Love;
        That is bound to happen.

Bitter and dark and desolate
Are Love's ways in the beginning of love;
Before anyone is perfect in Love's service,
He often becomes desperate:
Yet where he imagines losing, it is all gain,
        How can one experience this?
By sparing neither much nor little,
        But giving himself totally in love.

Many are in doubt about Love;
Love's labor seems to them too hard,
And at first they receive nothing in it.
They think: "Should you wander there?"
If their eyes clearly saw the reward
        That Love gives at the end,
I dare indeed say openly:
        They would wander in Love's exile.

In love no action is lost
That was ever performed for Love's sake;
Love always repays, late or soon;
Love is always the reward of love.
Love knows with love the courtly manners of Love;
        Her receiving is always giving;
Not least she gives by her adroitness
        Many a death in life.

It is very sweet to wander lost in love
Along the desolate ways Love makes us travel.

This remains well hidden from aliens;
But they who serve Love with truth
Shall in love walk with Love
    All round that kingdom where Love is Lady,
And united with her receive all that splendor
    And taste to the full her noble fidelity.

As for the tastes that fidelity gives in Love—
Whoever calls anything else happiness
Has always lived without happiness,
To my way of thinking.
For it is heavenly joy, free,
    To the full, devoid of nothing:
"You are all mine, Beloved, and I am all yours"—[7]
    There is no other way of saying it.

I can well keep silent about how it is
With those who have thus become one in love:
Neither to see nor to speak is my part;
For I do not know this in itself,
How the Beloved and the loved soul embrace each other
    And have fruition in giving themselves to each other.
What wonder is it that grief strikes me
    Because this has not yet fallen to my share?

That I was ever short of love
Causes me sadness; that is no wonder.
Rightly do I suffer pain for it,
That I ever descended so low.
For Love promised me all good,
    If I would conceive the high plan
Of working in the realm she assigned me,
    In her highest possible service.

That realm to which Love urges me on,
And the service she commands us to perform,
Is to exercise love and nothing else,
With all the service this entails.
He who truly understands this,
    How to work in every respect with fidelity,
Is the one whom Love completely fetters
    And completely unites to herself in love.

—

To this I summon all the perfect,
Who wish to content Love with love,
Thus to be in Love's service
In all her comings and in all her goings.
If she lifts them up, if she knocks them down,
    May it all be equally sweet to them;
So will they speedily become love with Love:
    In this way may God help us!

POEM 41

Although this new year has begun—
Both month and year together—
But little joyousness is gained by the fact,
For we lack clear days
And all the other joyousness
That makes young hearts happy.
But nothing equals the woe of one
Who desires Love and never tastes her to the full.

Alas! He who must journey into distant exile
Is wearied by the deeply worn roads;
He wanders after Love and suffers reverses;
His sad lot causes him woe,
In that he does not know enough about Love
To ascertain by clear evidence
What gives her pleasure or displeasure;
Truly he often experiences sorry days.

Alas, Love, your wrath or your favor
We cannot distinguish—
Your high will and our debt,
Why you come, or why you fly?
For you can give, in response to small service,
Your sweet splendors in great clarity;
But for small faults this seems withheld,
And then you give blows and bitter death.

Alas, Love, how shall we learn
The why of your comings and goings?
Where shall we stop your escape,
And the storms by which you strike us down?
And by what exertions will your sweet splendors
Remain for us in wise clarity?

So that we may not by baseness deprive ourselves,
It may be, of what would otherwise protect us!

Alas! On dark roads of misery
Love indeed lets us wander,
In many an assault, without safety,
Where she seems to us cruel and hostile;
And to some she gives, without suffering,
Her great and multiform joy:
For us these are truly strange manners,
But for connoisseurs of Love's free power, they are joy.

Alas, Love! In whatever you do,
Your departure seems to be wrath;
But he who is high-minded and wise
Had best follow you perfectly
In sweet, in bitter, in consolation, and in fear,
Until he fully knows what you will for him:
When you show him your will so clearly,
His woe is silenced in peace.

Oh! He who sets sail for afar must suffer
What adventure brings him.
So he who loves must strive anxiously
Before he lives perfectly to Love's contentment.
In every season he must seek
Nothing but her high will,
And be saddened or gladdened by nothing else,
Whatever happens to him besides.

Oh! If anyone thus totally loves the will of Love—
In mounting tumult, in lowly silence,
Through everything Love ever inflicts on him—
In him Love ever has her fullest contentment.
This is one of the strongest fortresses,
The fairest rampart ever man saw,
And the highest walls and the deepest moat,
In which to guard Love prisoner forever.

EXTRACTS FROM THE *VISIONS*

Vision 1

. . . And then he said: "Turn from me, and you will find the one
whom you have always sought, and for whom you have turned
away from all things of earth and heaven." And I turned from him,
and I saw standing before me a cross like crystal, clearer and whiter
than crystal. And through it a great space was visible. And placed in
front of this cross I saw a seat like a disk, which was more radiant to
see than the sun in its most radiant power; and beneath the disk
stood three pillars. The first pillar was like burning fire. The second
was like a precious stone that is called topaz; it has the nature of
gold and the brightness of the air, as well as the colors of all gems.
The third was like a precious stone that is called amethyst and has a
purple color like the rose and the violet. And in the middle under
the disk, a whirlpool revolved in such a frightful manner and was so
terrible to see that heaven and earth might have been astonished and
made fearful by it.

The seat that resembled a disk was eternity. The three pillars
were the three names under which the wretched ones who are far
from Love understand him. The pillar like fire is the name of the
Holy Spirit. The pillar like the topaz is the name of the Father. The
pillar like the amethyst is the name of the Son. The profound
whirlpool, which is so frightfully dark, is divine fruition in its hidden storms.

At this mighty place sat he whom I was seeking, and with whom
I had desired to be one in fruition. His appearance could not be described in any language. His head was grand and broad, with curly
hair, white in color, and crowned with a crown that is like a precious stone that is called sardonyx and has three colors: black,
white, and red. His eyes were marvelously unspeakable to see and
drew all things to him in Love. I cannot bear witness to it in words,
for the unspeakable great beauty and the sweetest sweetness of this
lofty and marvelous Countenance rendered me unable to find any
comparison for it or any metaphor. And my Beloved gave himself
to me, both in spiritual understanding of himself and in feeling. But
when I saw him, I fell at his feet, for I divined that I had been led
toward him the whole way, of which so much was still to be lived.

And he said to me: "Stand up! For you are standing in me, from all eternity, entirely free and without fall. For you have desired to be one with me, and in all respects you have done what you could to this end. And since you are so shaken by the storm of inquietude, because you possess testimony from me and from the obvious acts you have performed in all things where you believed you discerned my will, and because of your wise works, *I have sent you this Angel* [Apoc 22:16]—from the choir of Thrones—who is wise in leading those of good will to perfection. He found you so arrayed inwardly that he actually led you by all the ways, which he had wished merely to show to you, as to a child. He likewise gave you such exalted names that they have beautified you in my sight.

"Now I shall make known to you what I wish of you. I wish you for my sake to be prepared for every kind of affliction. I forbid you ever, even for the twinkling of an eye, to dare to strike back for any reason or take revenge for any cause. If you dare to do that in any way whatever, you will be the one who wishes to supplant my right, and who mars my greatness."

He continued: "Moreover *I give you a new commandment* [Jn 13:34]: If you wish to be like me in my Humanity, as you desire to possess me wholly in my Divinity and Humanity, you shall desire to be poor, miserable, and despised by all men; and all griefs will taste sweeter to you than all earthly pleasures; in no way let them sadden you. For they will be beyond human nature to carry. If you wish to follow Love, at the urging of your noble nature, which makes you desire me in my totality,[8] it will become so alien to you to live among persons, and you will be so despised and so unhappy, that you will not know where to lodge for a single night, and all persons will fall away from you and forsake you, and no one will be willing to wander about with you in your distress and your weakness, whatever the state in which you find yourself. You will still for a short time lead such a life of suffering, and I shall find my pleasure in it. For your hour has not yet come. . . ."

VISION 5

At Matins on the day of the Assumption,[9] I was taken up for a short while in the spirit: and I was shown the three highest heavens, after which the three highest Angels are named—the Thrones, the Cherubim, and the Seraphim. Then came to me the eagle from among *the four living creatures,* sweet Saint John the Evangelist,[10] and he said: "Come and behold the things I saw as man; all that I saw only in symbol, you have seen disclosed and entire, you have understood them, and you know what they are like." And in thinking about what Saint John had said to me here, I fell on my face in great woe, and my woe cried aloud: "*Ah, ah!* [Jer 1:6] Holy Friend and true Omnipotence, why do you let those who are ours wander off to alien things, and why do you not flow through them in our oneness? I have my whole will with you besides, and I love and hate with you, like you. For now—since you once again gave me assurance—I am no longer a Lucifer, like those who are now Lucifer and wish that good and grace be given them, when they offer entry neither in their lives, nor in their works, nor in their service; and they wish to get rid of their labor, and they wish to enjoy grace; and they exalt themselves and, because you show them a little of your goodness, they wish to have it as their right. And they fall from your heavenly honor; this you made known to me.

"In one thing I did wrong in the past, to the living and the dead, whom I with desire would have freed from purgatory and from hell as my right. But for this be you blessed: Without anger against me, you gave me four among the living and the dead who then belonged to hell. Your goodness was tolerant of my ignorance, and of my thoughtless desires, and of the unrestrained charity that you gave me in yourself for men. For I did not then know your perfect justice. I fell into this fault and was Lucifer because I did not know this, although on that account I did no evil in your eyes. This was the one thing because of which I fell among men, so that I remained unknown to them, and they were cruel to me. Through love I wished to snatch the living and the dead from all the debasement of despair and of wrongdoing, and I caused their pain to be lessened, and those dead in hell to be sent into purgatory, and those living in hell to be brought to the heavenly mode of life. Your goodness was tolerant of me in this and showed me that for this reason I had fallen in that way among those people.

"Then you took my self into yourself and gave me to know what you are, and that you hate and love in one same Being. Then I understood how I must hate and love wholly with you, and how I must be in all respects. Because I know this, I desire of you that you will make those who are ours all one with us."

And he who sat on the throne in heaven said to me: "These three thrones I am in Three Persons—Throne, Man; the Cherubim, the

Holy Spirit; and the Seraphim, in my fruition, in which I am all."
And he took me out of the spirit in that highest fruition of wonder
beyond reason; there I had fruition of him as I shall eternally.

The time was short, and when I came to myself he brought me
again into the spirit and spoke to me thus: "As you now have
fruition of this, you shall have fruition of it eternally."

And John said to me: "Go to your burden, and God shall renew
his old wonders in you."

And I came back into my pain again with many a great woe.

VISION 6

It was on a certain feast of the Epiphany:[11] I was then nineteen
years old, as was mentioned to me that day. Then it was my will to
go to our Lord; for at this time I experienced desires and an exceedingly strong longing—how God takes and gives with regard to persons who, lost in him and taken up in fruition, are conformed to his
will in all circumstances. On this day, because of my longing, I was
again strongly moved in Love. And then I was taken up in a spirit
and carried on to where a vast and awe-inspiring place was shown
me, and in this strong place stood a seat. And he who sat upon it
was invisible and incomprehensible in the dignity of the jurisdiction
he exercised on that height. To be seated in such a place is ununder-
standable to either heavenly or earthly beings. Above that high seat
in this lofty place, I saw a crown that surpassed all diadems. In its
great breadth it embraced all things beneath it, and beyond the
crown was nothing.

And an Angel came with a glowing censer, which glowed all red-
hot with fire and smoke. He knelt before the highest place of the
seat above which the crown hung, and he paid him honor and said:
"O unknown Power and great almighty Lord, receive herewith
honor and dignity from this maiden who resorts to you in your secret place: This place is unknown to all those who do not send you
such an enkindled offering with such sharp arrows as she sends you
with her new burning youth, for she has now ended her nineteenth
year, so people say. And it is she, Lord, who comes to seek you in
the spirit—who you are, in your incomprehensibility. For that mysterious life, which you with burning charity have aroused in her,
has led her to this place. Now reveal to her that you have drawn her
here, and transport her wholly within yourself."

And then I heard a Voice speaking to me; it was terrible and un-heard of. It spoke to me with imagery and said: "Behold who I am!"

And I saw him whom I sought. His Countenance revealed itself with such clarity that I recognized in it all the countenances and all the forms that ever existed and ever shall exist, wherefrom he received honor and service in all right. I saw why each one must receive his part in damnation and in blessing, and by what each one must be set in his place; and by what manner of acting some persons wander away from him and return to him again, finer and more beautiful than they were before; why still others seem always wandering and never came back—they remained standing entirely still, and almost devoid of consolation at all times. And others have remained in their place since childhood, have known themselves at their worth, and have held out to the end.

I recognized all these beings there in that Countenance.

In his right hand I saw the gifts of his blessing; and I saw in his hand heaven in its vastness opened, and all those who will be with him there eternally. In his left hand I saw the sword of the fearful stroke, with which he strikes all down to death. In this hand I saw hell and all its eternal company.

I saw his greatness oppressed under all. I saw his littleness exalted above all. I saw his hiddenness embracing and flowing through all things: I saw his breadth enclosed in all. I heard his reasoned understanding and perceived all reason with reason. I saw in his breast the entire fruition of his Nature in Love. In everything else I saw, I could understand that in the spirit.

But then wonder seized me because of all the riches I had seen in him, and through this wonder I came out of the spirit in which I had seen all that I sought; and as in this situation in all this rich enlightenment I recognized my awe-inspiring, my unspeakably sweet Beloved, I fell out of the spirit—from myself and all I had seen in him—and, wholly lost, fell upon the breast, the fruition, of his Nature, which is Love. There I remained, engulfed and lost, without any comprehension of other knowledge, or sight, or spiritual understanding, except to be one with him and to have fruition of this union. I remained in it less than half an hour.

Then I was called back again in a spirit, and again I recognized and understood all reasoning as before.

And once again it was said to me by him: "From now on you shall never more condemn or bless anyone except as I wish; and you shall give everyone his due, according to his worth. This is what I am, in fruition and in knowledge, and in entrancement for those who wish to content me according to my will. I direct you— to live in conformity with my Divinity and my Humanity—back again into the cruel world, where you must taste every kind of death—until you return hither in the full name of my fruition, in which you are baptized in my depths."

And with this I returned, woeful, to myself.

VISION 7

On a certain Pentecost[12] Sunday I had a vision at dawn. Matins were being sung in the church, and I was present. My heart and my veins and all my limbs trembled and quivered with eager desire and, as often occurred with me, such madness and fear beset my mind that it seemed to me I did not content my Beloved, and that my Beloved did not fulfill my desire, so that dying I must go mad, and going mad I must die. On that day my mind was beset so fearfully and so painfully by desirous love that all my separate limbs threatened to break, and all my separate veins were in travail. The longing in which I then was cannot be expressed by any language or any person I know; and everything I could say about it would be unheard-of to all those who never apprehended Love as something to work for with desire, and whom Love had never acknowledged as hers. I can say this about it: I desired to have full fruition of my Beloved, and to understand and taste him to the full. I desired that his Humanity should to the fullest extent be one in fruition with my humanity, and that mine then should hold its stand and be strong enough to enter into perfection until I content him, who is perfection itself, by purity and unity, and in all things to content him fully in every virtue. To that end I wished he might content me interiorly with his Godhead, in one spirit, and that for me he should be all that he is, without withholding anything from me. For above all the gifts that I ever longed for, I chose this gift: that I should give satisfaction in all great sufferings. For that is the most perfect satisfaction: to grow up in order to be God with God. For this demands suffering, pain, and misery, and living in great new grief of soul: but to let everything come and go without grief, and in this way to experience nothing else but sweet love, embraces, and kisses. In this sense I desired that God give himself to me, so that I might content him.

As my mind was thus beset with fear, I saw a great eagle flying toward me from the altar, and he said to me: "If you wish to attain oneness, make yourself ready!"

I fell on my knees and my heart beat fearfully, to worship the Beloved with oneness, according to his true dignity; that indeed was impossible for me, as I know well, and as God knows, always to my woe and to my grief.

But the eagle turned back and spoke: "Just and mighty Lord, now show your great power to unite your oneness in the manner of union with full possession!"

Then the eagle turned round again and said to me: "He who has come, comes again; and to whatever place he never came, he comes not."

Then he came from the altar, showing himself as a Child; and that Child was in the same form as he was in his first three years. He turned toward me, in his right hand took from the ciborium[13] his Body, and in his left hand took a chalice, which seemed to come from the altar, but I do not know where it came from.

With that he came in the form and clothing of a Man, as he was on the day when he gave us his Body for the first time;[14] looking like a Human Being and a Man, wonderful, and beautiful, and with glorious face, he came to me as humbly as anyone who wholly belongs to another. Then he gave himself to me in the shape of the Sacrament, in its outward form, as the custom is; and then he gave me to drink from the chalice, in form and taste, as the custom is. After that he came himself to me, took me entirely in his arms, and pressed me to him; and all my members felt his in full felicity, in accordance with the desire of my heart and my humanity. So I was outwardly satisfied and fully transported. Also then, for a short while, I had the strength to bear this; but soon, after a short time, I lost that manly beauty outwardly in the sight of his form. I saw him completely come to nought and so fade and all at once dissolve that I could no longer recognize or perceive him outside me, and I could no longer distinguish him within me. Then it was to me as if we were one without difference. It was thus: outwardly, to see, taste, and feel, as one can outwardly taste, see, and feel in the reception of the outward Sacrament. So can the Beloved, with the loved one, each wholly receive the other in all full satisfaction of the sight, the hearing, and the passing away of the one in the other.

After that I remained in a passing away in my Beloved, so that I wholly melted away in him and nothing any longer remained to me of myself; and I was changed and taken up in the spirit, and there it was shown me concerning such hours.

VISION 11

. . . I have hated many great wonderful deeds and experiences, because I wished to belong to Love alone, and because I could not believe that any human creature loved him so passionately as I—although I know it is a fact and indubitable, still I cannot believe it or feel it, so powerfully am I touched by Love.

In this wonderful way I belong to God alone in pure love, and to my saint in love, and then to all the saints, each one according to his dignity, and to men according to what each one loved and also according to what he was and still is. But in striving for this I have never experienced Love in any sort of way as repose; on the contrary, I found Love a heavy burden and disgrace. For I was a human creature, and Love is terrible and implacable, devouring and burning without regard for anything. The soul is contained in one little rivulet; her depth is quickly filled up; her dikes quickly burst. Thus with rapidity the Godhead has engulfed human nature wholly in itself.

I used to love the blessedness of the saints, but I never ceased to desire the repose in which God within them had fruition of himself; their quietude was many a time my inquietude; yes, truly, it was always forty pains against one single pleasure. I could not but know that they were smiled at, while I wept; that they boasted themselves fortunate, while I pitied myself; and that they were honored by God, and that God was honored because of them in every land, while I was an object of derision. All this, nevertheless, was my greatest repose, for he willed it—but this was such repose as comes to those who desire love and fruition, and who have in this desire such woe as I do. . . .

Christine the Astonishing

THE LIFE OF ST CHRISTINE THE ASTONISHING

Here begins the life of Saint Christine the Astonishing.

CHAPTER I: HOW SHE WAS BROUGHT UP

Christine, God's holy virgin, was begotten and born of a respectable father and mother in the town of Sint-Truiden[1] in Limburg. And when her father and mother died she was left with her two sisters. Then the sisters, wishing to regulate their lives in a religious manner, arranged between them that the eldest sister should devote herself to prayer, the middle sister to running the household, and the youngest, Christine, should guard their animals at pasture in the fields. And from the beginning Christ did not withhold his comfort from Christine, who was given the humblest and the meanest position; our Lord gave her the gift of inner sweetness and very often visited her with heavenly mysteries. She was unknown to all men but to God alone; the more secluded she was, the better she was known to God.

CHAPTER II: HOW CHRISTINE DIED

And after this she became sick in bodily strength from practising inner contemplation, and she died. Then the dead body was laid out and her sisters and friends watched over it, and in the morning it was carried to church. And while a Mass was being said for her soul, the body suddenly stirred on the bier and rose into the air, and then flew up like a bird and soared into the rafters of the church. And then everyone who was present fled, except her eldest sister, who remained motionless with fear. And Christine remained unmoving in the church roof until the Mass was over; then the invocations of the church priest made her come down. Truly, as some suppose, her subtle spirit loathed touching and smelling men's bodies. And then she went straight home with her sisters and ate her food. And then her close friends went to her and asked her what she had seen and what had happened to her.

CHAPTER III: HOW SHE WAS CONVEYED FROM HER BODY AND HOW SHE WAS BROUGHT BACK TO HER BODY AGAIN

"As soon as I was dead," she said, "ministers of light, God's angels, took my soul and led me to a hideous place full of men's souls; and the torments which I saw in that place were so great and so cruel that no tongue could describe them. And truly I saw many dead there that I knew before when they were alive. Feeling compassion and great pity for those poor wretched souls, I asked what manner of place that was—I thought that it was hell. And those who led me answered that the place was purgatory, where those who had been sinners in their lives suffered fitting punishment for their misdeeds. From there they led me to the torments of hell, and there, too, I recognized some that I had known when they were alive. After that I was taken to the throne of God's Majesty. And when I saw our Lord looking joyful and well disposed towards me, then I was extraordinarily happy, thinking that I would remain there from that time forth for evermore. Then our Lord answered my wish at once, 'Certainly, my love,' said he, 'you shall be with me here; but now I am going to give you a choice of two things: that is to say, whether you would rather stay here and live with me now, or return to your body, to endure there the sufferings of an immortal soul in a mortal body with no risk to yourself, and by your sufferings to deliver from purgatory all the souls there for which you felt compassion, and also through the example of your sufferings and your life to move men to repentance and penance and to forsake their sins and turn truly to me; and when all this is done, then you shall come to me again and be richly rewarded.' And I answered without hesitation that I would return to my body under the conditions that were given to me. Our Lord was very pleased with my answer and at once ordered that my soul should be restored to my body. And see how swiftly the angels did our Lord's bidding: for at the very time that the requiem Mass was being sung for me, when the first *Agnus dei*[2] was said, my soul stood before the throne of God's Majesty, and when the *Agnus dei* was said for the third time, those swift angels brought me back to my body. This was the manner of my going out and of my coming in, and I have returned from death to life for the amendment of men. Therefore, do not be troubled by those things which God shall ordain for me, for indeed, such things have never been seen in this world." Hearing this, her family and friends were very astonished and waited for what was to come with great wonder and fear.

CHAPTER IV: HOW SHE WAS CAPTURED BY HER FAMILY AND FRIENDS AND DELIVERED BY OUR LORD, AND FED FROM HER OWN MAIDENLY BREAST

After this, Christine felt a great loathing for people and fled from their presence into the wilderness, and into the trees, and to the tops of towers or churches or other high places; and her family and friends, supposing her mad and possessed by fiends, eventually managed with great difficulty to capture her and bind her with iron chains. And when she was bound like this she suffered much hardship and pain, but she suffered most from the smell of men, until one night she was helped by our Lord, and with her bonds and fetters undone, she ran quickly away and fled far through the wilderness into the woods, and there she lived as the birds do, in trees. And even when she needed food and was suffering greatly from hunger—for her body, though it was very light and subtle, could not do without food—she was quite unwilling to go home again, but wished to live in seclusion in the wilderness with our Lord. So she humbly prayed that he would look mercifully upon her anguish. And then, straight away, she looked down at the dry breasts of her virgin bosom and saw them dropping sweet milk, quite contrary to what happens naturally. This is an astonishing thing, unheard of since the incomparable and unparalleled virgin, Christ's mother. And so the virgin Christine was fed for nine weeks with milk from her own breasts. Meanwhile they were searching for her, and she was found and captured by her family and friends, and tied up as she had been before, but in vain.

CHAPTER V: HOW SHE WENT INTO THE WATERS

Christine was delivered by our Lord and came to the city of Liège. And she begged the priest of St Christopher's church that he would give her communion, beset as she was with many troubles. And when the priest promised that he would, but made an excuse and said that he was too busy to do so immediately, she would not wait, but went to another church and asked the priest for the body of our Lord Jesus Christ. And he gave her communion immediately after she had asked for it. Then she was moved by a violent impulse and fled from the city. The priest was amazed that she ran away so fast, and, with the other priest from St Christopher's, he followed her almost to the river Meuse, and they were glad, thinking that they might be able to stop her at the water's edge. But then they were astounded to see the woman before them in bodily form go into the deep streams of the water like a phantom and come up unharmed on the opposite bank.

CHAPTER VI: HOW SHE WAS TORTURED IN THE FIRE
Christine then began to do what our Lord had sent her back for. And she went into burning-hot ovens which were ready to bake bread in; and the burning and the heat tortured her as it would one of us, so that she screamed hideously with anguish; nevertheless, when she came out there was no injury or scorching to be seen on her skin. And when there was no furnace or oven for her, she threw herself into huge great fires in men's houses, or put in just her feet and hands, and held them there so long that if it had not been a miracle from God they would have been burnt to ashes. At other times she also went into cauldrons full of boiling-hot water, up to her breast or to her hips, depending on the height of the cauldrons, and she poured scalding-hot water over those parts of her body which were safely above the surface, and she screamed like a woman in labour; yet nevertheless, when she came out she was uninjured.

CHAPTER VII: HOW SHE WAS TORTURED IN WATER
She often remained for a long time under the waters of the river Meuse in frosty weather, to the extent that she remained in the water for six days or more. But her parish priest came and stood on the river bank and solemnly charged her in Christ's name to come out, and then she was forced to go home. Also, in winter-time, she walked bolt upright on the wheel of a water mill: standing like that, she should have been dashed down head-first, with her whole body following. And at other times she came floating with the water and fell with the water above the wheel, but nevertheless no injury could be seen on her body.

CHAPTER VIII: HOW SHE WAS TORTURED ON WHEELS
Also, like those who are tortured, she bent her legs and arms in the wheels in which thieves were customarily subjected to duress; and yet, when she came down, none of her limbs seemed to be broken.

She also went to the gallows and hung herself up with a noose among the hanged thieves, and she hung there for a day or two. And she very often went into dead men's graves and grieved there for the sins of man.

CHAPTER IX: HOW SHE WAS TORMENTED BY THORNS AND BRIARS, AND SHE WAS CHASED BY DOGS
At other times she rose up at about midnight and called out all the dogs of the town of Sint-Truiden and made them all bark, and ran fast in front of them like an animal, and they followed her, and drove and chased her through bushes and briars and thick thorns, so that no part of her body remained unwounded; yet nevertheless, when she had washed away the blood, there was no sign of any wound or injury. In the same way, she lacerated herself all over with briars and thorns, so that her whole body on both sides seemed to be covered in blood. This caused many people who saw her to marvel that there could be so much blood in one body. Yet truly, apart from all this bleeding, she often let much blood from her veins.

CHAPTER X: OF THE SUBTLETY OF HER BODY, AND HOW SHE WAS WHEN SHE PRAYED
Her body was so subtle and light that she could climb high and cling to the smallest twigs of trees like a bird. And when she wanted to pray, she felt compelled to escape into the tree-tops, or towers, or other high places, so that, away from other people, she could find rest for her spirit. And then, when she was praying and God's grace of contemplation came to her, just as she became warm and heated, all her limbs closed up together into a lump, nor could anything be seen of her except a round gobbet. And after her spiritual experience, when her bodily feelings returned to their natural state again, like a hedgehog the lumpen body returned to its own shape and stretched out the limbs that had previously taken on unseemly matter and form. And she often stood bolt upright on hedge-posts, and there she said her psalms; for it was distressing and painful for her to touch the earth while she was praying.

CHAPTER XI: HOW HER LEG WAS BROKEN AND SHE WAS CAPTURED AND THEN DELIVERED BY OUR LORD
Such behaviour as this embarrassed her sisters and friends greatly, for men thought she was possessed by fiends; and they made an

agreement with a very wicked and very strong man, and paid him to pursue and capture her and bind her with iron chains. And when that evil man had pursued her into the wilderness he could not capture her with his hands, but he managed to grab her at last and break her leg from behind. Then she was taken home, and her sisters paid a doctor to treat her broken leg. Then she was taken in a cart to Liège. And the doctor knew how strong she was and bound her firmly to a pillar in a cellar with walls all round it and he locked the door securely. Then he bound her leg with healing bandages. But when the doctor had gone, she pulled them off again—she thought it unworthy to have any doctor for her wounds but our Lord Jesus Christ. And almighty God did not betray her, for one night when the Holy Ghost descended upon her, the bonds that tied her were loosed, and, all healed and unharmed, she walked on the cellar floor and danced and blessed our Lord, for whom alone she had chosen to live and to die. Then, feeling in her spirit that she was enclosed and stuck in the cellar, she took a stone from the floor and in a state of spiritual elevation she pierced the wall; just as an arrow flies faster the harder the bow is drawn, so her spirit thrust directly upward along with her own body in its true fleshly state, as it is said, and flew out like a bird in the air.

CHAPTER XII: HOW OIL SPRANG FROM HER BREASTS, AND SO HER FAMILY AND FRIENDS LET HER GO

Nevertheless, her sisters and friends refused to stop pursuing her; for when she returned to a place where they could capture her they bound her shoulders tightly to a wooden stake and fed her like a dog with nothing but a little bread and water. But because Christ wanted to show in her a surpassing miracle of his power, he allowed her to be overcome and suffer tribulation for the time being. So her buttocks were badly chafed from the hard wood and her shoulders festered; and this made her so feeble and faint that she could not eat her bread, and no one there took pity on her wretched state. But our Lord was marvellously merciful to her, and wrought in her a noble miracle which had never been heard of before. For her maidenly breasts began to flow with a liquid which was the sweetest oil; and she took it and spread it on her bread to flavour it, and used it as a soup and as an ointment, anointing the wounds of her festering limbs with it. When her sisters and her friends saw that, they began to weep, and from then on they stopped struggling and using force against God's will as manifested in the miracles of Christine; they freed her from her bonds and knelt down, begging forgiveness for the wrong they had done her, and so they let her go.

CHAPTER XIII: HOW PEOPLE IN RELIGIOUS ORDERS MADE A GENERAL PRAYER FOR CHRISTINE

She was then free and did what she liked, and suffered tortures for man's sins, as has been said before. And many people came every day from far and near and from very distant countries to see the miracles and marvels of God in Christine. Then men and women in religious orders in that town were afraid that the huge wonder of these marvels would be beyond man's comprehension, and prompt the beastly minds of men to wicked thoughts and deprive God's great deeds of their power, because of the way that Christine fled from the presence of men, and climbed onto high things like a bird, and stayed in the water for a long time like a fish; so they besought our Lord with eager prayers to temper his miracles in Christine and make her more like other people. And God did not despise their prayers as they humbly wept.

CHAPTER XIV: HOW HER LIFE WAS MADE TO CONFORM TO THAT OF OTHER MEN

And so one day it happened that Christine, her spirit violently stirred, ran to a church in the town of Wellen, and finding the baptismal font uncovered, she plunged herself into it completely. And that, it is said, changed her so that from then on her way of life conformed more to that of other men, and she behaved more calmly afterwards and was better able to endure the touch of men and to live among them.

CHAPTER XV: HOW THE SPIRIT MOVED HER TO LIVE FROM CHARITY AND IN THE SAME WAY AS OTHER MEN

She often received the sacrament of the altar with great devotion, especially on Sundays, and that, she said, gave her bodily strength and the greatest spiritual joy. She had given up her own property for the love of Christ, and would not use her own rightful inheritance to obtain food or drink; she took food from the whole community, begging every day from door to door so as to take away the sins of those whose alms fed her. And she said that she was compelled by God's spirit to beg alms from wicked men so that they would come to loathe sin and do penance for their lives. For she said that truly nothing made God more merciful toward sinners than that they should take pity on their fellow Christians. For mercy and pity can only make for a good end on the last day. So as to show this with an example, we will illustrate what we have said with a deed of Christine's.

CHAPTER XVI: OF HIM WHO GAVE HER A DRINK

It happened one day that God made her intolerably thirsty, and she ran to the table of a very wicked man who was eating splendidly, and she asked him for a drink. Then, unusually for him, he felt sorry for her and gave her a little wine to drink. This made Christine say, contrary to the opinion of everyone who knew the man, that when he died he would need no further contrition or penance.

CHAPTER XVII: WHAT HAPPENED WHEN SHE ATE THE ALMS OF EVIL-DOERS; AND WHAT SHE ATE

And this was why, as we have said, she was obliged to eat the alms of wicked men. However, when she ate anything given to her as alms which had been wrongfully obtained, it seemed to her that she was eating the bowels of frogs and toads or the guts of adders. For while she was eating such alms she screamed like a woman in labour, and said, "Oh, Christ, what are you doing to me? Why do you torment me like this?" And beating her body and her breast, she said, "Oh, you wretched soul, what do you want? Why do you long for these foul things? Why are you eating this filth?" For it tortured her to eat anything unjustly obtained. And she also suffered just as much when any evil man denied her what she asked. Once it happened that she forcibly took away something which a wicked man denied her, and she said, "You may not want to give it now, but hereafter you will not be sorry that you did; and then what is no good to you now will do you a great deal of good." And when she needed a sleeve for her tunic or a hood for her cloak, she would ask for it from someone she met if the spirit told her to do so; and if they gave it to her, she thanked them; and if they refused, she took it against their will and sewed it on to her own clothes. Nor was she embarrassed if the sleeves and the gown did not match and were of different colours. She was dressed from head to foot in a white tunic and a white scapulary;[3] often the only thread which held them together was the bark of a certain tree called *tilia*,[4] or willow twigs or splinters of wood. She wore no shoes or stockings, but always went barefoot. And the food which she was accustomed to eat was foul garbage; dish-washings which should have been thrown away she boiled in water and ate with hard bran-bread which she softened first in water. And this was her food, after two or three days fasting.

CHAPTER XVIII: OF HOW CHRISTINE SORROWED AND LAMENTED FOR THOSE WHO WERE DAMNED AND REJOICED FOR THOSE WHO WERE SAVED

She took great pains to avoid admiration and praise, and said that those to whom God had given knowledge of his truth while they were alive received most torment in hell or purgatory for accepting such things. She always walked around sorrowing and lamenting because every day God truly revealed to her whether those who died were to be saved or [damned]. And when anyone died in that city whom she knew to be damned because of their sins, she wept and tormented herself and wrung and twisted her arms and fingers as if they were so soft and boneless that they were pliable. Indeed, that sorrow of hers was so unbearable to all who saw it that no man, no matter how hard-hearted, could see it without feeling great contrition for his own sins. And truly, for those who were going up to heaven and would be saved, she leapt and danced so much that it was a great marvel to see her so happy. Because of this, those who knew the power of her spirit could quickly tell from her joy or sorrow what was going to befall those in the city who died. . . .

CHAPTER XXIV: HOW CHRISTINE PROPHESIED A GREAT FAMINE

She also prophesied a long time in advance a great famine that came in about 1270. And Christine made many other prophecies, some of which are fulfilled and some of things we believe are yet to come. Another wonder also occurred: she was friendly and at home with the nuns of St Catherine's, outside Sint-Truiden, and now and then she used to sit with them and talk about Christ. Once her whole body was suddenly and unexpectedly seized by the spirit and began to whirl around like a teetotum or top that children play with, and the great speed of the whirling meant that no form or shape of the limbs of her body could be perceived. And when she had been spun round for so long that it seemed as if she would faint from the speed, she rested with all her limbs. And then there sounded from between her throat and her breast a marvellous melody which no man living could understand or had the skill to imitate. That song had within itself high and low notes and musical tones, and indeed the words of the melody, if they can be called words, ran together incomprehensibly. And meanwhile neither voice nor breath came out of her mouth or nose, but just between the breast and the throat there sounded a melody of angelic song. Meanwhile, all her limbs were at rest and her eyelids were closed as if she were asleep. Then shortly after that she gradually returned to herself, like a drunk person, and, truly drunk in spirit, she rose up and cried aloud, "Bring the convent to me, so that together we may praise Jesus for his great goodness in his miracles." At once the nuns came running from every direction and rejoiced in Christine's pleasure. Then she began *Te deum laudamus* and, with all the nuns accompanying her, she sang it to the end. And after that, when she had come completely to herself, and learned what she had done from what others said, she fled for shame and thought herself a fool.

CHAPTER XXV: HOW SHE REBUKED THE WORLD BECAUSE IT DID NOT ACKNOWLEDGE ITS CREATOR

Later, when she was herself again after being in the state just described, she said with great bitterness of heart, "Oh, miserable and wretched world, not to acknowledge your Maker; why do you not serve him? Why do you ignore his longsuffering and patience? If you saw his goodness, though a whole world denied it you would not be turned away from him, you would have to love him. But you, wretched world, have turned away; you have closed your eyes and refuse to understand." And as she said these words she cried out like a woman in labour, and twisted her limbs together and rolled about on the ground, crying out and lamenting and saying repeatedly that the world did not acknowledge its Creator.

CHAPTER XXVI: HOW SHE UNDERSTOOD HOLY WRIT THROUGH GOD'S TEACHING

After this she left her own house and her relatives and went to a castle called Looz, on the borders of Germany, where she lived for nine years with a woman called Jutta who was a recluse[5] and led a very holy life; and there our Lord did wonders through Christine. And this recluse told me many of the things which I have written; indeed I went to her from the distant provinces of France for that reason. And in this place Christine went to Matins every night; and when everyone else had left the church and the doors were locked she remained on the floor and sang a song of such great sweetness that it seemed angelic rather than human. The song was so marvellous to hear that it surpassed all the voices and instruments of musicians and minstrels, but it was quieter and very unlike the sweetness of that melody that had sounded between her throat and her breast. This song was in Latin and beautifully composed, with many harmonious phrases. She knew Latin completely, and thoroughly understood the meaning of Holy Scripture, though she had been illiterate all her life; and when she was asked theological questions about Holy Writ she would explain them very clearly to some of her friends in the spirit. But she would do this very seldom and greatly against her will, saying that it was for scholars to expound Holy Writ, and that such things were none of her business. Because of her enormous love of Christ she showed remarkable reverence for the clergy, especially priests, despite the fact that she had often been wronged by them. She reproved priests and clerks tactfully, privately and with great respect when they sinned, as their own spiritual fathers might have done, lest by their excesses they should bring Christ's good name into disrepute among the people.

CHAPTER XXVII: HOW MUCH SHE WAS ADMIRED BY EARL LEWIS

The very noble man Lewis, earl of Looz, hearing about Christine's holiness by widespread report, began to love her greatly and made use of her conversation and advice. Wherever he saw her he rose and went to meet her, calling her "mother." Indeed, if this earl did anything against justice or Holy Church or its ministers, she grieved for him like a mother for her son, and, going to him in his palace, she reproved him with motherly confidence, and she obtained from him whatever justice demanded in the way of recompense. . . .

CHAPTER XXXII: HOW SHE CONDUCTED HERSELF IN THE LAST YEAR OF HER LIFE

In the last year of her life she often lived in the wilderness and in solitude, returning however, though very seldom, for the good of men and when the spirit constrained her to get food. No man on earth could hold her back then when she wanted to go into the wilderness. And when she returned, no one greeted her and no one dared ask her anything. Truly, one evening she came home and passed through the middle of the house like a spirit on the earth, and it could hardly be told whether a spirit was passing or a body, for it seemed that she hardly touched the ground. Indeed, in the last year of her life the spirit had taken over her fleshly body almost entirely, to such an extent that men's minds and eyes could hardly catch sight of the shadow of her body without fear and terror of spirit. At that time, when she came home she often lived in St Catherine's Abbey at the town of Sint-Truiden. . . .

CHAPTER XXXIV: THE WAY SHE LIVED BEFORE HER DEATH
At the end of her life she ate very little and very seldom. She did not want to sit as she used to before, talking to nuns and monks, but after eating a little and refreshed by sleep, she went into the wilderness shortly before midnight. In those days no man ever saw laughter on her lips, but she was like someone who is out of his mind with excessive grief. She went around praying, lamenting, and mourning; and therefore some people believe that our Lord revealed more to her than before of the state and wickedness of the world. There was one thing over which she often grieved and lamented extraordinarily: that very nearly the whole of humanity was corrupted by abominable varieties of lechery, and therefore God in his wrath was about to take swift vengeance on nearly all Christendom. . . . After she first rose from death to life she lived for forty-two years, and she died in about the year our Lord 1224.

CHAPTER XXXVII: OF HER BURIAL, AND THE TRANSLATION OF HER BODY
She was buried outside the town of Sint-Truiden, in the abbey of St Catherine, and she rested there for seven years, until the time when the abbey building was transferred to a nearer and better place. Then, with all the people gathered together, the clergy and the nuns of the convent went to the tomb of the holy Christine. When they had opened it and laid the covering aside, everyone that was there felt the grace of so much sweetness that with a single thought and a single voice they all cried out together that Christine was marvellous throughout her life and glorious after her death. And truly, no one doubts the miracles which have been done there to those who visited her tomb with true faith. . . .

Mary of Oignies

FROM BOOK I

CHAPTER I: HER CHILDHOOD

In the bishopric of Liège in the town of Nivelles there lived a young maiden called Mary, glorious both for her life and her reputation. Her father and mother were citizens, and though they had abundance of riches and worldly goods, worldly goods never attracted Mary, even in early childhood. Almost from her mother's womb she turned to our Lord; she seldom or never played as other children do, nor did she spend her time with the sort of girls who entertain themselves with futile trivialities. She kept her soul safe from all vanity and worldly cravings, and by living as God ordains in her childhood, she prefigured her mature life. This meant that in her youth she often knelt by her bed and offered the prayers she had learnt to our Lord as the first fruits of her life.

As she grew from a little child, so she grew in mercy and pity, and she loved the monastic life as though with a natural piety; so much so that when some brothers of the Cistercian order walked past her father's house one day she looked up and noticed them, and followed them secretly, wondering at the habits they wore. And when there was nothing else she could do, she was so fascinated by them that she set her feet in the footsteps of the lay brothers or monks.

And when her mother and father wanted to dress her in bright, elegant clothes, as worldly people usually do, she was upset and put them aside, as if by nature she had St Peter's words about women imprinted on her mind: *Whose adorning let it not be the outward plaiting of the hair, or the wearing of gold, or the putting on of ap-*

parel [1 Pet 3:3]; and St Paul also says: *Not with plaited hair, or gold, or pearls, or costly attire* [1 Ti 2:9]. Because of this her father and mother laughed and mocked her, saying, "What kind of woman will our daughter be?"

CHAPTER II: HER MARRIAGE

Her parents resented Mary's righteous behaviour, and when she was fourteen years old they married her to a young man. Once she was away from her father and mother, she was fired with such intense religious passion and fought so hard to punish and subdue her body that often when she had toiled with her own hands for much of the night she followed this work with long hours of prayer, and in what was left of the night she slept a little when she needed to do so on a few planks which she had secretly hidden at the foot of her bed. And because she was not in a position to do what she liked with her own body, she secretly wore a very harsh rope beneath her shift, tied tightly round her waist. I do not say this to praise her excess, but to show her fervour. In this and many other things that she did through the privilege of grace, the wise reader must realise that the life of a few chosen people should not be considered a rule for everyone. Let us emulate her virtues, but only the specially chosen should copy her deeds. Indeed, though the body should be forced to serve the spirit, though we should bear on our flesh the wounds of our lord Jesus Christ, nevertheless, we know that the honour of the King favours law and justice, and sacrifice of stolen goods does not please our Lord. Necessities are not to be withheld from the poor flesh, though vices are to be avoided. And therefore we must rather admire than imitate the things that we read some saints have done through familiar and intimate counsel of the Holy Spirit.

CHAPTER III: HER RELATIONSHIP WITH HER HUSBAND AND HOW THEY GAVE UP A WORLDLY LIFE AND LIVED CHASTELY

When she had lived like this with her husband John for some time, our Lord beheld the lowliness of his handmaiden and graciously heard her prayers; John was inspired to become the caregiver of her who had been his wife. God made this chaste man his maiden's guardian so that she might be sustained by the person who cared for her, and gave her a steward so that she might serve our Lord more freely. And even earlier, out of a natural goodness, this same John had not opposed his wife's holy endeavours as other men usually do, but had tolerated them most admirably and felt compassion for her laborious efforts. He was visited by our Lord, for he devoted himself not only to a [celibate] and truly angelic life in his continence and chastity, but also to giving all that he had to poor men for the love of Christ and following his partner in her holy purposes and holy practices. The more he was separated from his wife in bodily affection, the more closely he was bound to her in the love of spiritual marriage. Because of this our Lord appeared to his maiden later in a vision and promised that in compensation for matrimony, he would give her again in heaven the companion who because of his love of chastity had denied himself the lust of the flesh on earth.

Therefore wretched lechers who befoul themselves out of wedlock with unlawful couplings should feel fear and shame: these two blessed young people abstained from lawful embraces for the love of God and overcame the fierce heat of burning youth through their religious fervour. Our Lord gave them places and names better than sons and daughters within his house and walls, and they deserved crowns as their prize; for, in a blessed kind of martyrdom in fire that did not burn, slaying their own lust where lust abounded, thirsting beside the water and hungering amidst food, they pierced their flesh with nails of the fear of God. Indeed, for the love of our Lord they degraded themselves completely and looked after lepers for a while at a place called Williambrouk.

CHAPTER IV: THE SCORN AND PERSECUTION OF THEIR RELATIVES

Devils saw and envied them, worldly people and relatives saw them and gnashed their teeth. The couple they had once honoured when they were rich were despised and treated with contempt when their love of Christ had made them poor. For God they were looked down on as scum, and they suffered many insults for the sake of our Lord. Fear not, Christ's maiden, to choose to go with your Christ towards the humiliating insults of the Cross and to reject all the joys of worldly honour. It is better to be considered the lowest of the low in the house of our Lord than to live in the halls and chambers of sinners. You have lost the favour of your relatives, but you have found favour with Christ. Have you lost your relatives' love? Certainly not, for it was your possessions they loved, not you. Flies are attracted by honey, wolves by carrion, and thieves by what they steal and not by the man that owns it.

CHAPTER V: HER COMPUNCTION[1] AND TEARS

Lord, you are very good to those who put their trust in you, you are true to those who await your will. For love of you, your maiden has rejected the kingdom of this world and all its honours, and indeed you have given her back a hundredfold in this world and everlasting life in the world to come. Let us consider the great jewels of virtue with which you have decked and adorned your dearest friend, just as a solemn vessel of solid gold is dignified with every precious stone; the great miracles with which you have honoured her who was rejected and despised by worldly people. The beginning of her conversion to you, the first fruits of her love, was your Cross and your Passion; she heard your praises and trembled, she beheld your works and was afraid. One day because of this, guided and inspired by you, she considered the gifts which you mercifully gave mankind in your incarnation, and so much gracious compunction, such plenteous tears were forced out by the weight of your cross in your Passion that they flowed copiously down onto the church floor and showed where she had walked. And so for a long time after this visitation she could not look at an image of the Cross, nor speak or hear others speak of Christ's Passion without falling into a swoon from the great longing in her heart. And so for a while, to temper her sorrow and hold back such abundant tears, she ceased to contemplate the manhood of Christ and raised her mind to the Godhead in his Majesty so that she might find comfort in his incapacity for suffering. But no matter how much she struggled to restrain her tears, she continued to weep more and more abundantly. For when she considered the greatness of Him who suffered such humiliation for our sake, her sorrow was constantly renewed and her soul refreshed by new tears and sweet compunction.

One day before Good Friday, near the time of Christ's Passion, when she had offered herself to our Lord with sobbing, sighing, and streams of tears, a priest of that church scolded her playfully, telling her that she should pray quietly and stop weeping. She was always modest and as meek as a dove in every way, and she tried her hardest to obey him. Then, realizing that it was beyond her power, she left the church inconspicuously and hid herself out of sight and away from everybody; and then by her tears she gained our Lord's promise that he would show this priest that it is not humanly possible to hold back the powerful stream of tears when a great blast blows and the water flows. And then the priest, while he was singing Mass on the same day, was so overcome by an abundance of tears that he was nearly suffocated in spirit. And the harder he tried to stop weeping, the more not only he himself, but the book and the altar cloths were soaked by his tears. So this man of bad judgement, this critic of Christ's maiden, learned from shameful experience what humility and compassion had failed to teach him in the first place. And after much sobbing and getting many words wrong as he went along, finally he just managed to get safely to the end of the Mass; this is vouched for by someone who was present and knew what was happening, and we can rely on his evidence. Long after the Mass was over, Christ's maiden returned and miraculously, just as though she had been there, she reproachfully told the priest what had happened. "Now," said she, "you have learned from experience that it is not possible for a man to hold back the fierce wind when a gale is blowing from the south."

Water flowed continually from her eyes by day and night, and the tears did not just wet her cheeks—to stop them falling to the ground where people would see them, she used the veils with which she covered her head to soak them up. She used many such linen cloths and needed to change them often, so that while one was getting wet, another might be drying. Compassionate people questioned her, wishing to know whether after fasting for so long, staying awake so frequently and weeping so often, she felt any aches and pains of the kind that are common when one is lightheaded. And she said, "These tears refresh me, they are what sustain me night and day; they do not hurt my head, but feed my mind; they do not torment me with pain, but light up the soul with brilliance; they do not empty the brain, but fill up the soul's will and soften it with a comforting balm, when they are not forced out with effort and violence but graciously offered and given by our Lord."

CHAPTER VI: HER CONFESSION
From her compunction let us now turn at once to her confession. As God is my witness, I could never perceive a single deadly sin in her whole way of living or relating to other people. And if it seemed to her that by chance she had committed any small venial sin, she revealed it to her priest with such great sorrow of heart, with so much shame and with such lengthy contrition, that sometimes the great anguish of her heart forced her to cry aloud like a woman in

childbirth; yes, even though she so avoided minor and venial sins that sometimes she could not find an inordinate thought in her heart in a full fortnight. And because the minds of good people find guilt in themselves where there is none, she often knelt at the priest's feet and, accusing herself, confessed with tears something about which we could hardly refrain from laughing, such as some childish words that she regretted, which, as she recalled, she had spoken vainly when she was young. But the truth is that once she had passed childhood she made a constant effort to guard her soul with such anxiety, her mind with such diligence and her heart with such great purity, always having before her mind Solomon's saying: *He that contemneth small things shall fall by little and little* [Eccl 19:1], that we could seldom or never perceive in her any idle word, immodest glance, unsuitable gesture, excessive laughter, or unseemly and ill-mannered behaviour. This was so even though sometimes abundant joy, when she could scarcely contain herself, forced her to express the rejoicing of her heart in outward bodily behaviour with a little outburst of happiness, whether expressing the cheerfulness of her heart in quiet laughter, or in her goodness receiving any of her friends with small, modest embraces, or kissing the hands or feet of some priest in entire devotion. And when she pulled herself together again after this softening of her feelings, she very strictly assessed all that she had done; if she could perceive that she had gone even a little too far, she confessed herself with remarkable contrition of heart and, punishing herself, she often feared when there was no reason for fear. And in this respect alone, seeking to excuse our laziness, we sometimes reproached her for confessing such small matters more often than we wished.

CHAPTER VII: HER PENANCE AND SATISFACTION

After her confession, let us go on to describe the great and amazing penances with which she punished her body, the great love and delight with which she embraced Christ's cross and tormented her own flesh. Let us look at the first lesson which our Lord Jesus Christ gives his pupils and the first teaching of the Gospel: *If any man will come after me, let him deny himself and take up his cross daily and follow me* [Lk 9:23]. She considered this often in her heart and strove diligently to follow Christ in these three steps or measures. She assuredly gave up not only other people's possessions, coveting nothing that belonged to anyone else, and not only her own possessions, renouncing everything, and not only her outer self, punishing her own body, but even her inner self, entirely renouncing her own desires and wishes. She denied herself, submitting in obedience to another man's will; she took up the cross, punishing her body with abstinence; and she followed Christ, humbly setting herself at nought.

She had such a strong liking for spiritual food that all fleshly pleasures were distasteful to her, so much so that once she remembered how she had been very sick and, because she really needed it, she was forced to eat meat and drink wine for a while, and afterwards her abhorrence of this pleasure was so great that her spirit could not rest until she had punished herself and made amends, torturing her flesh amazingly for her previous enjoyment, such as it was. In a spiritual fervour, loathing her flesh, she cut off great lumps of it and felt such shame that she buried them in the earth. And because she was so enflamed with the immense heat of love, she saw in her ecstasy of mind one of the Seraphim, a burning angel, standing beside her. And when the time came to wash her body after her death, the women found scars from the wounds and were very astonished; but they who had heard her confession knew why the scars were there.

Those who wonder and worship when they consider the worms crawling out of St Simeon's[2] wounds and how St Antony[3] burnt his feet in the fire, why should they not wonder at such a frail being, a woman with such strength, who, wounded with love and quickened by Christ's wounds, paid no attention to the wounds of her own body?

CHAPTER VIII: FASTING

Christ's maiden so surpassed others and excelled in the grace of fasting that on those days when it was proper for her to refresh her body she sat down to eat as though she were about to take medicine. She ate only once a day, and very little—in the evening in summer and at the first hour of the night in winter. She drank no wine, ate no meat and very rarely any fish, just small ones occasionally; her sustenance was the fruit of trees, green vegetables, and soup. And for a long time she only ate bread so black and sour that dogs would hardly have managed to eat it, bread so bitter and hard that it took the skin off the inside of her mouth and left bleeding wounds. But thinking of Christ's blood made this sweet to her, Christ's wounds healed hers, and the bitterness of hard bread was softened by heavenly bread. One day while she was eating she saw our old enemy the Devil suffering agonies of malice, and when he realised that there was nothing else he could do, he spoke contemptuously to her, saying, "Just look what a glutton you are, stuffing yourself with food!"

Indeed, eating often caused her discomfort because she fasted so much and for such long periods; her stomach ached and churned as though it were so cold and bloated that it found food repulsive. But she recognized the tricks and wiles of the Devil, knowing he would be eager to trouble someone he knew to be afraid of him and make her falter through too much abstinence. Therefore, whenever the venomous spirit was tormented by her eating, she forced herself to eat all the more and put him to scorn. For whether she ate or whether she fasted, it was all done for the glory of God. And indeed, for three consecutive years she fasted on bread and water from Holy Cross Day[4] until Easter, without any effect on her physical well-being or the amount of work she did with her hands. And when she refreshed her body in the evening or at night by taking a little bread and water in her cell within the church, holy angels stood and watched over her frugal supper from the moment she first asked blessing until the moment she returned thanks, and they moved up and down as though through a bright window. And their presence gave her such comfort and such joy of spirit that the spiritual sweetness surpassed any delicious taste.

St John the Evangelist, whom she loved with particular devotion, also sometimes came to her table while she was eating, and in his presence her physical appetite was so overcome by her devout longing that she could hardly eat at all. God certainly gave her spiritual rewards for the bodily delights which she had renounced for the love of Christ: for it is written: *Man liveth not by bread alone* [Lk 4:4]. Sometimes this spiritual food sustained her so that she fasted for eight days without eating or drinking, or sometimes eleven, that is from the Ascension of our Lord until Whitsun; and amazingly, her head never ached, nor did she stop working with her hands—she was as strong on the last day of her fast as on the first. And if she had wanted to eat on those days she could not have done so until her bodily senses, which were as if weakened by her spirit, came back to her; for while her soul was so overflowingly full of spiritual sustenance, it would not let her eat any bodily food.

Once, she rested peacefully with our Lord in sweet and blessed silence, eating no food, for thirty-five days; and on some days the only sentence she would speak was, "I want the body of our lord Jesus Christ." And when she had received the sacrament, she lived every day in silence with our Lord. She certainly felt at that time as though her spirit had left her body, as though it had been hidden in the body as in a clay vessel, and her body like a sheet of clay, wrapping and covering her spirit. In this way she was removed from the sensory world and swept up into ecstasy. After five weeks she came to herself again and opened her mouth to speak and to receive bodily food; and all those who stood around marvelled. A long time after this she became unable to bear the smell of meat, of frying food, or of wine, except when she drank the wine rinsed from the chalice after the sacrament, and then she was not distressed by the smell. Also, when she travelled through various towns to receive the sacrament of confirmation from a bishop, the smells which she could not bear before did not distress her at all.

CHAPTER IX: HER PRAYER
The more Mary's body wasted away with fasting, the more her spirit was freed and filled with prayer; the body was weakened by abstinence, and the soul gained strength in our Lord. Our Lord granted her such great gifts, especially the gift of prayer, that night and day her spirit seldom or never faltered, nor did it ever stop praying. She prayed unceasingly, either crying out to God quietly in her heart, or else expressing the longings of her heart in words. When she was working with her hands and spinning she had a psalter placed in front of her and lovingly recited psalms to our Lord as she sat there, fastening her heart to God as though with strong nails while doing so, to prevent it straying idly. And when she prayed for someone in particular, our Lord revealed his response and answered her spirit with a wonderful sensation; for she perceived each time by the elevation or depression of her spirits whether her prayer would be answered or not. Once, she prayed for the soul of a dead man, and the answer came to her, "Do not pray for him, for he has been condemned by God," and it is true that this man died in sin, mortally wounded in a tournament and damned forever.[5]

One day, when she was in her cell at the church at Oignies, she saw a multitude of hands before her as though in prayer; she marvelled at this, not knowing what it might mean, and was rather frightened and fled into the church. On another day she saw the same hands again when she was in her cell, and was frightened; but when she wanted to flee into the church, the hands grasped her and held her back. Then she went into the church and prayed to our Lord, asking him to tell her with certainly what those hands meant. And God answered that it was the souls who were suffering in purgatory asking to be helped by her prayers and the prayers of others, and this softened her sorrow like a precious ointment. Sometimes she gave up her customary prayers for the delight of contemplation, and sometimes she could not open her mouth or think of anything but God.

She was in the habit of visiting the church of St Mary at Oignies as a pilgrimage, or to pray, and there our Lady gave her great comfort; and the church was more than two miles from where she lived. And in the middle of a very harsh winter she walked barefoot through the frost to that church without doing herself any harm, and though she only had a servant girl with her and could not make out the path, which is very treacherous and thickly wooded, a light went before her to show her the way, and she never strayed from it. She had eaten nothing all day either, and she watched all night in the church; and in the morning when it was time for her to go home and she was not going to eat until the evening, she nevertheless went safely home again with no difficulty, supported on each side by holy angels. Sometimes, on the same path, when there were huge rain-clouds overhead and she had no garments to protect her from the rain, she looked up and saw obedient stars holding back the rain, and so she reached home again untouched by the wet weather.

On some occasions, when her soul was filled and pure, as it was at some times more than others, she could not stop praying. So she saluted our Lady by night and by day, genuflecting one thousand one hundred times and continuing with this amazing and unparalleled office of salutation for forty days continuously. On the first occasion, carried away by her passionate feelings, she genuflected six hundred times without pausing. On the second occasion she read out the entire psalter while standing and, genuflecting at each psalm, recited the salutation to our Lady, *Ave Maria*. However, on the third occasion she lashed herself with a sharp stick three hundred times each time she knelt, sacrificing and offering herself in a prolonged martyrdom to God and the Blessed Virgin Mary. And with the three final strokes, to intensify the effect of the others, she made her body bleed profusely, and then she just genuflected fifty times and so she ended her office. She did this not with her own bodily strength, but with the help of angels who supported and succoured her.

The strength of her prayer was so great that it not only succoured men, but tormented fiends, over which she had such power that she drew them to her as though by ropes; they were compelled to come to her by her burning prayers. Sometimes they gnashed their teeth at her, sometimes they made accusations and complaints about her and sometimes, too, they besought her humbly. And it is true that when any of her friends were struggling against temptation she was moved by the spirit of compassion and did not stop praying until the enemy was overcome and the person free.

. . . There was a young virgin in a Cistercian abbey wearing a nun's habit and serving our Lord among the sisters, and, seeing someone embarking on such a hard way of life, someone so weak because she was a woman and because she was young, that old serpent the Devil was all the more anxious to injure her. Since he knew the girl was meek and fearful, he attacked her with blasphemous and impure thoughts so that he could reduce her to despair through anxiety and excessive fear. Since she was so fearful and not used to such thoughts, when they first occurred to her she believed she had lost her faith and struggled against them for a long time in great distress of mind. At last, not telling anyone about her inner sickness so that remedies might have been found for her fears, she fell into something like despair.[6] The enemy had depressed her mind so much that she could say neither the Lord's Prayer nor the Creed, and she could not bring herself to confess her sins. And even if she was occasionally compelled by friendly persuasion or threats to confess some sins, nothing would make her ask forgiveness. She could not be present at the sacraments of Holy Church and she refused to receive communion. She was in such a state of mental distress that she often tried to commit suicide.[7] She despised God's word and the holy exhortations intended to restore her; she hated all that was good, and through her mouth the Devil uttered many blasphemous and contemptuous remarks. Her meek sisters offered many prayers for her to our merciful Lord, but they could not snatch his dove from the Devil's jaws, nor could this diabolic influence be readily cast out through fasting and prayer. It was not that the merciful heavenly Bridegroom despised the prayers of so many

holy virgins, but he had destined this most cruel evil to be overcome by his maiden; the power of her prayers was to pierce
through the Fiend's cheeks and draw the quarry from his jaws.

So when that young virgin was taken to Christ's maiden, she
who was so full of compassion and spiritual tenderness welcomed
her warmly, not only into her cell with generous hospitality, but
also into her heart with the spirit of love. She said many prayers to
our Lord for her, but the Devil thought he held her fast and would
not let her go. Then Mary sacrificed herself even more to our Lord,
and fasted with prayers and weeping for forty days, eating only two
or three times a week. Then indeed, when her fast was over, that
most hideous spirit left the virgin and was compelled to come to
Christ's maiden with disgrace, sorrow, and shame, heavily fettered
and punished by Christ's angel, so that it looked as though he had
been disembowelled and all his entrails were hanging round his
neck; for what our Lord works invisibly in the spirit he sometimes
reveals visibly through outward signs. Then the Fiend wailed and
entreated her to have mercy on him, and begged her as Christ's
friend to order him to do penance, saying he was obliged to do
whatever she ordered. Then she, who was never presumptuous and
never did anything without asking for advice, summoned a priest, a
close friend whom she trusted. This man advised her to send the
Fiend into a wilderness where he could harm no one until Judgement Day. Another man, very well known to both of them and in
their confidence, had come too; his ardent disposition made him
much more vehement, and when he heard this advice, he said, "No,
that traitor should not get off so lightly. Tell him to go down at
once into the depths of hell." And that is what she told him to do.
He fell, screaming, and in her spirit she heard the fiends yelling
when they saw such a great and mighty prince coming to join them.
Christ's maiden was amazed, and thanked God for his great favour
and goodness. And the virgin we have been talking about was released that very hour; she made her confession, received communion and went home again safe and sound, thanking God.

On other occasions, while Christ's maiden was resting in bed
after much watching, the Fiend appeared to her in various forms,
gnashing his teeth at her and cursing. "May you rest in torment
with us," said he. "May you rest in hell. Your rest tortures me as
much as your work and your prayers." And she smiled and crossed
herself and sent that grisly spirit on his way.

CHAPTER X: HER VIGILS AND HER SLEEP

This strong and wise woman thought that idleness was wicked and intolerable—for the days pass by, but they never return, so nothing can make up for the evil of wasted time, nor can lost days be restored like material things which are lost. So she was very careful to avoid idleness as far as possible, trying not to be unoccupied for any hour of the day or night. She seldom slept at night, knowing that in his mercy God provided us with sleep not as reward and recompense, but as a restorative for man's weak frailty. The truth is that when we are asleep we can earn no spiritual reward, for then we cannot exercise our freedom to judge and make moral choices. So she denied herself sleep as often as possible, serving our Lord during the watches of the night, and all the more devoutly because there was no noisy hustling and bustling around to distract her. The intensity of her abstinence made her dry and lean, and the love of God burned within her, making it easy for her to avoid dozing or sleeping; and the sweet songs of angels, which often accompanied her during the night watches, kept all sleep from her eyes while preserving her bodily health. And so, secluded from the company of men, she spent the nights in the company of a host of blessed spirits who made a marvellous sound, like a crowd of people, delighting her ears with their sweet and cheerful melody. It shook off sloth, it cleared her head, it comforted her mind with its amazing sweetness, it inspired devotion and inflamed desire. And the voices set her an example of praise and thanksgiving as they repeated again and again: *Sanctus, sanctus, sanctus dominus*—that is, "Holy, holy, holy Lord."

Let stupid, sinful women consider this, take heed and grieve for their sins. With their wanton and idle songs they kindle the fire of lechery just as though their breath were setting fire to coal. And so, cut off from the song of angels, they perish in their pride and vanity; their laughter is turned to weeping, their joy to sorrow and their songs into dismal shrieking. Our Lord has promised to replace their colourful girdles with hempen ropes, their sweet perfumes with disgusting smells and their curled and coloured hair with bald heads. Truly our Mary, despising merrymaking and the clamour of the Devil, deserved to be blessed and happy amid the joyful melody of the holy angels. She also guarded at night the precious relics of saints with which the church at Oignies is enriched and honoured; those relics passed the night with her in holiness, and, as though pleased with their guardian, they gladdened her spirit with amazing joy.[8] And in her last illness they felt compassion for her, comforted her, and asked God to help and reward her for her trouble and guardianship.

In spite of her frequent vigils she had a bed in her cell with a little straw, on which she only rested very occasionally, for often, sitting in the church and leaning her head against the wall, she was refreshed by a short sleep and then returned to the sweet labour of her vigils. However, the time she spent asleep was not entirely wasted, for while she slept her heart was awake:[9] Christ was tightly bound to her heart during her waking hours, and Christ filled her dreams. Just as a hungry man dreams of many different kinds of food, so she had always before her in dreams Him for whom she longed; where love is, there is the eye and where her treasure was, there was her heart also. As Christ says of himself: *Where I am, there also shall my minister be* [Jn 12:26]. God often disclosed many things to her while she slept and visited his maiden with many revelations so that the time she spent asleep did not pass in vain. Joseph and other saints received warnings in their sleep, and God promised through the prophet Joel: *Your old men shall dream dreams, and your young men shall see visions* [Joel 2:28].

Sometimes she was able to rest in her cell, but at other times, especially when a solemn feast day was approaching, she could manage to rest only in the church itself, in the presence of Christ,[10] and she had to remain in the church day and night, for above everything else she had to obey her guardian angel as a monk would an abbot. Sometimes when she was exhausted by too much fasting, this angel warned her that she must rest; and when she had rested a little, he raised her and led her back into the church. And once, with enormous encouragement from him and inspired with energy and strength, she clung so close to the church paving from Martinmas until Lent[11] that whether she was sitting or lying she could not bear so much as one little straw to come between herself and the bare ground. While she slept her pillow was either the bare ground or a log of wood before the altar steps. That very winter the cold and the frost were so intense that I remember while the priest was singing Mass the wine in the holy chalice turned rapidly and perceptibly into ice. Nevertheless, she did not feel the cold, and because her guardian angel held his hand under it, her head ached only a little. Woe to you that are indolent, sleeping in soft sheets and ivory beds, enjoying soft, silken things; you are dead and buried in the desires and pleasures of your flesh. You who spend your days amid the wealth of this world, you shall fall down in an instant to the depths of hell where you will lie on vermin and your blanket will be worms. Look how the ground cushioned Christ's maiden; because she served our Lord devoutly she was not hurt by its hardness; winter spared her so that she was not tormented by the cold; holy angels ministered to her, so that nothing caused her grievous suffering. Fond fools! The world will fight against you on God's behalf; his creation shall take up arms to avenge his enemies, and the creature who serves our Maker shall rise up against you.

CHAPTER XI: HER CLOTHES

She who was clothed in the fleece of the holy Lamb, she whose spirit was adorned with the bridal garment, she who had clothed herself inwardly with Christ, cared nothing for outward array. However, she never liked her clothes to look either ostentatiously filthy or studiously clean, but preferred them between the two extremes. She avoided both fine and filthy clothes equally, for the former suggest pleasure and worldly desires and the latter hypocrisy and the wish for public admiration. She knew, however, that our Lord not only praised St John the Baptist because his clothes were so rough but also said himself: *They that are clothed in soft garments are in the houses of kings* [Mt 11:8]; so she did not wear a linen smock next to her skin, but one of coarse sackcloth, the kind of fabric which is popularly called stamin. She also had a white woollen tunic and a mantle of the same colour, without any skins or fur, for she knew that our Lord covered the nakedness of our first father and mother after their fall not with precious cloth skilfully dyed but with leathern garments. She who burned with an inner fire was satisfied with the simplicity of these clothes and did not fear the cold, nor did she need material fire to drive away the chill of winter. And it was marvellous how when there was a harsh winter and a hard frost her spirit burned so fervently within her while she prayed that her body without was hot, so much so that sometimes the inside of her clothes was perfumed with her fragrant sweat. And sometimes her clothes smelled of incense while she was offering her prayers to our Lord with the censer of a pure heart.

What do you think of this, you extravagant women, full of pomp and pride, you who load your carcasses with layer upon layer of clothing and parade around like unnatural beasts with your long tails, disgracing yourselves by appearing with horns and tusks[12] and decorated like a temple? Moths gnaw at your stinking clothes while the sweet-smelling garments of this holy woman are treasured as relics. They are precious garments made holy by the cold because they never let the cold through, however thin they were; and because they are holy they are carefully treasured, venerated with pious affection by her devout disciples after her death.

CHAPTER XII: OF THE LABOUR OF HER HANDS
This wise woman knew well that when our first father and mother had sinned our Lord imposed a penance on them, and through them on their children: *In the sweat of thy face shalt thou eat bread* [Gen 3:19]. Therefore she laboured with her own hands for as long as she could—so that she might inflict a penance on her body, so that she might supply the needy with the necessities of life, and so that she might earn her living and clothe herself, as one who had given up everything for Christ's sake. Indeed, our Lord granted her such favour and such excellence in her work[13] that she far surpassed her fellow workers, so that by working hard she could almost support herself and another person by the fruit of her hands. She heeded the words of the apostle: *If any man will not work, neither let him eat* [2 Th 3:10]. Indeed, she considered every hour that she worked a pleasure, since she was aware that the unbegotten son of the King of Heaven, he who opens his hand and fills every beast with his blessing [Ps 144:16], was nurtured by the labour of Joseph's hands and that of a poor little working virgin. So she worked with her hands and ate her bread uncomplainingly and peacefully, as the apostle bids, for her strength was in silence and hope.

She was so anxious to avoid the noise and company of men and she so loved stillness and calm that she was once silent from Holy Cross Day until Easter, hardly speaking a single word. And our Lord finds such silence so acceptable that the Holy Ghost revealed that because of this above all else, God had promised she should pass to paradise without the pains of purgatory. This shows how great is the vice of loquacity and chattering, since silence and stillness please our Lord so much. And so she worked hard every day to increase the talents which she had been given, and every day she mounted higher up Jacob's ladder from virtue to virtue until she reached the last rung and attained a higher state, going beyond all perceptible things. Her sensual being was so absorbed in the abundance of her spirit that she could only labour for the food *which endureth unto life everlasting,* as the Gospel says [Jn 6:27], for she was entirely occupied and filled with Christ. And so she lived the life of a hermit; Christ freed his maiden from all manual labour and from then on she rested wholly in our Lord.

CHAPTER XIII: HER BEARING AND BEHAVIOUR

The way she carried herself outwardly demonstrated the nature of the mind within, and her modest demeanour could not hide the joy in her heart. Indeed, the gravity in her heart was tempered to a marvellous extent by her cheerful face, and the mirth in her mind was somewhat concealed by the innocent diffidence of her expression. Because St Paul says that women should pray with their heads covered [1 Cor 11:5], she wore the white veil which covered her head hanging over her eyes. She walked modestly, with a slow, easy pace, her head bent and her eyes looking at the ground. Her full heart made the grace of her soul shine out through her face, so that many were spiritually refreshed and moved to devotion and tears just from the way she looked; reading the unction of the Holy Ghost in her face as though in a book, they knew that she emanated divine power.

FROM BOOK II

CHAPTER II: THE SPIRIT OF THE FEAR OF GOD

. . . She would not allow herself to do many permissible things in case too much freedom somehow degenerated into behaviour which was against the law of God. In fact, this God-fearing spirit gave her such a love for poverty that she would barely tolerate necessities. And one day she decided to flee so that, unknown and despised among strangers, she might beg from door to door in order to follow Christ stripped of everything[14]—the mantle of all worldly goods like Joseph, the pitcher like the Samaritan woman, the fine cloth like St John the Evangelist.[15] She thought long and hard about Christ's poverty, that when he was born there was no room for him in the public market place so that he had nowhere to lay his head, that he had no money to pay his tribute, and that he had to eat food given as alms and be received in other men's lodgings. So one day she felt such a great longing for poverty that she took a satchel for alms and a little cup from which to drink while she ate: either water or soup if anyone gave her any. And in the end, in her old clothes, she could hardly be held back by the weeping and sobbing of her friends. But when she had said goodbye to her friends and Christ's poor maiden was about to set off like that with her satchel and cup, all the friends who loved her in Christ wept and grieved so much that she, kind and loving as she was, could not bear it. She was pulled in two directions: she wanted to flee and become a beggar with Christ; nevertheless she chose to stay for the sake of her brethren, to whom her absence seemed unbearable.

. . . criticism did not crush her, nor did praise make her proud. She was so humble that she always wanted to be as private as possible. Therefore, when she could not conceal the joy in her heart and the abundance of grace, she sometimes fled to neighbouring fields and bushes, so that by keeping out of sight she might hide the secrets she shared with God in the coffer of a clear conscience. However, she sometimes had to strengthen the faith of feeble folk—induced by the supplications of friends, sent especially to someone by God or moved by compassion. Then, modest and embarrassed, she explained a few of the many things she knew. And oh, how often she said to her friends, "Why are you asking me? I am not worthy to perceive the things you are asking me." How often she answered our Lord as though she were grumbling, "What has that got to do with me, Lord? Send whoever you like; I am not worthy to go and give your advice to others." And yet she could not withstand the urgings of the Holy Ghost but by telling certain things served to benefit other people. How many of her close friends she warned of impending danger! How often she revealed to friends the secret snares of evil spirits! How often she strengthened folk who were weak and wavering in their faith with the miracles of God's revelations! How often she warned people not to do things which were still only in their minds! How often she relieved with heavenly comfort folk who were falling into sin, who were nearly in a state of despair!

. . . Sometimes when we asked her whether she felt any titillations of vainglory from men's praise or God's revelations, she replied, "When compared with the true joy that I long for, all man's joy and praise is as nothing and of no account." . . .

CHAPTER IV: THE SPIRIT OF WISDOM

. . . It happened one day that because of the visit of some close friends while she was living at Oignies, she went to Williambrouk, and as she was going through Nivelles on her way home she began to think of the sins and abominable deeds often committed by secular people in that town. She was overcome by such indignation and disgust that she began to weep with sorrow, and when she was out of the town she asked her servant girl for a knife. And she wanted to cut the skin from her feet because they had walked through places in which evil people provoke their Creator with so many wrongs and beset him with so many evil deeds and sins. And then she not only grieved in her soul, but even more astonishingly, she felt pain in the feet on which she had been walking. At last she managed to find a little relief after she had beaten her feet against each other many times. . . .

CHAPTER XII: HER SICKNESS BEFORE HER DEATH

During this sickness her body suffered grievously, but her spirit was at ease. The saints who had often stood beside her when she was well visited her more often when she was sick, and Christ often appeared to her, looking at her with a compassionate expression; his blessed mother Mary was almost always at her side. Among the others, St Andrew the apostle often came to her, comforting her greatly and making her seem not to feel the pain of her sickness, and holy angels stood by her and served her devotedly. And so, when she was thirsty at night and was so weak that she could not rise or sit up by herself, two holy angels supported her and led her to a place where there was water; and when she had drunk they led her back and she went to bed without any difficulty. . . .

. . . During her sickness, when she could not eat any kind of food or even bear the taste of a little bread, she partook of Christ's body gladly and often; it seemed to melt into her soul immediately, and not only comforted her spirit, but quickly eased her bodily sickness. Indeed, when she received Christ's body during her illness, her face shone with beams of light as bright as the sun. And once, when we tried to see if she would eat an unconsecrated wafer, she was immediately disgusted by the taste of bread. When a very little of it touched her teeth she cried out, spat, and panted as though her breast was bursting. She cried for a long time with the pain and often washed her mouth out with water, but even when much of the night had passed she could hardly rest. . . .

CHAPTER XIII: HER DEATH

. . . on St John's Eve, at about the time when our Lord gave up the ghost on the cross, that is to say at about noon, she did indeed pass on to God. The sorrow of death never changed her glad expression or her joyful face; nor do I ever remember her looking happier or more alive when she was in health. Her face did not go brown or blue, as is usual in death; her countenance was angelic, white, and bright, with a dove-like simplicity. In her dying and after her death she moved many to religious devotion. There were also many who at her passing were sweetly softened by a plentiful flood of tears, and they felt that God was with them in their prayers, as it had previously been revealed by the Holy Ghost to a holy woman that those who came together at her passing would receive much comfort from our Lord.

When her holy body was washed after her death, she was found to be so small and thin from infirmity and fasting that her spine was stuck to her stomach and the bones of her back showed through the scant skin of her belly as through a linen cloth. . . .

. . . In the year of the Incarnation of Christ one thousand two hundred and thirteen, on the eve of the feast of St John the Baptist,[16] on a Sunday at about noon, Christ's precious pearl, Mary of Oignies, of about six and thirty years of age, was carried into the palace of the everlasting King, where there is life without death, day without night, truth without falsehood, joy without sorrow, trust without fear, rest without labour, everlastingness without end; where the heart does not suffer from distress, the body does not sicken with sorrow and the river of pleasure overflows all barriers with the spirit of complete freedom, where we shall know as we are known, when God shall be all in all and shall grant his kingdom to our lord Jesus Christ, who with the Father and the Holy Spirit lives and reigns without end. Amen.

Elizabeth of Spaalbeek

THE LIFE OF ST ELIZABETH OF SPAALBEEK

In the province of Liège, next to a famous abbey of Cistercian nuns called Herkenrode, six or seven miles from the city of Liège,[1] there lived a maiden called Elizabeth, in whom our merciful Lord has shown marvellous miracles of his blessed Passion that may move all Christian people to devotion. When I, father Philip of Clairvaux,[2] heard about these marvellous works of our Lord while I was visiting houses of our order in that area, I did not believe those who told me, until I visited her and saw for myself and understood that I had not heard the half of it. Therefore I shall describe a few of the many marvels, those which in my humble opinion and in the judgement of my conscience are the most noteworthy and the most marvellous, beginning with those which I undoubtedly saw with my own eyes, and then adding what I have heard from other trustworthy men.

Therefore let it be known that this maiden bears the signs of the wounds of our Lord Jesus Christ for all to see; that is to say that on her hands, her feet, and her side, without any doubt, imitation, or fraud, fresh wounds can very clearly be seen; they often bleed, especially on Fridays. The wounds on her hands and feet are round, the wound in her side is oval, as though made with a spear, and the others with nails. As well as these signs of five wounds, our Lord Jesus Christ, who is the spouse of virgins and most beautiful of all men, shows in a marvellous way through the person of this same virgin— the purest, singled out by the special quality of her love—a representation of his blessed Passion occurring each day at the seven canonical Hours: Matins, Prime, Terce, Sext, None, Vespers and Compline.[3]

WHAT SHE DOES FOR THE HOUR OF MATINS
Truly, at midnight she rises to manifest wonderfully the beginning of our Lord's Passion, that is to say, how he was seized and dragged

hither and thither most cruelly by the hands of wicked men. It must also be known that at both this Hour and other Hours she goes into a state of ecstasy before she rises from her bed, and remains in this same state of ecstasy for some time, as rigid as a statue of wood or stone, with no sensation, no movement and no breath, so that no part of her can be touched or moved, not so much as her little finger, unless her whole body is moved. After this ecstasy she comes to herself again, rises and quickly leaves her bed, and walks to and fro in her chamber with a seemly and wonderful gait, and it is believed that she is led by angels. Truly, such a weakness of body and limbs overcame her when she was no more than about five years old that even if the house she was in had burnt down around her she could not have gone out without help, and everyone who lives around there is sure of that. And this continual chastisement by the rod of God and mortifying of her own flesh from the innocent age of five until her present age of twenty is strong and infallible proof of pure and complete virginity. What I have just said is what I have been told, not what I have seen myself, nevertheless, I am including this incident as an addition to my account so that those who read or hear it may know that the inner impulses and the behaviour of this virgin which, as far as possible, will be described later, do not come from her own strength but from the power of God himself.

So, as I was saying, at midnight, after her ecstasy, she whose body was weak and feeble before arises with marvellous strength to endure labour and pain. And when she is up, dressed as she always is with a woollen tunic next to her skin and a white linen overgarment which trails a little on the ground, she walks in a very seemly way in her chamber, and unceasingly as she goes to and fro she strikes her own cheeks with both hands, and the strokes can be heard loud and clear. And in this way, instead of psalms, she accompanies the watches of the first Nocturn[4] as if with timbrels[5] and high-sounding cymbals. After that, in place of readings, she begins our Lord's Passion, how he was seized and dragged along with fearful cruelty. Then it is marvellous to see how she grasps her own clothes over her breast with her right hand and drags herself to the right, and then with her left hand to the left; and sometimes she leans forward as though she were being dragged violently, as thieves and murderers are dragged and hauled violently along by other men's hands, representing our Lord Jesus's words when he said to them, *Are ye come out, as it were against a thief, with swords and clubs?* [Lk 22:52]. And immediately after that she stretches out her right arm and clenches her fist, and, looking fierce, she makes dreadful signs and gestures with her eyes and her hands, like someone who is angry and hostile. And after that she immediately strikes herself on the cheek so hard that her whole body sways down towards the ground with the force of the stroke; then she strikes herself on the back of her head—between her shoulders—on her neck—and she falls face-down, bending her body in an amazing way and dashing her head on the ground. At another time, too, she violently grabs her hair, which around her forehead is quite short, and strikes the ground with her head, swinging her body down in an amazing way without moving her feet. And she also takes herself by the hair, on both the right and left sides, pulling and bending herself in different directions by yanking with her hands in a way that can be neither told nor heard. Having already beaten her cheeks again and again both with the flat of her hand and with her fists, now she also grabs them in her fingers as if she were going to pull them off. And again, she bends her arm and, folding the others back into her hand, sticks out her index finger and attacks her eyes with it again and again, now one and now the other, as if she wanted to dig them out or stab them in. And she does all this often and at great length. So it seems that in a new and unheard of manner she enacts in herself both the part of the suffering Christ and the part of the tormenting enemy; she represents the person of our Lord while she suffers, and of the enemy while she pulls, drags, strikes, or threatens.

When these and other similar actions have been performed repeatedly and indescribably for the first Nocturn of Matins, she throws herself down to the ground on her back in a very seemly and decent way, as though to rest from the burden of her great labour; and then she has no bodily strength, but sighs for heavenly and spiritual solace, and she goes to God in spirit.

And after what is usually a long time of half-conscious rest she stands up again strengthened and refreshed, ready to celebrate the second Nocturn of Matins in the way described before. And instead of psalms, this new timbrel-player uses her flesh for a harp, and her cheeks for a timbrel, and her eyes for a psaltery,[6] and her hands and fingers for a plectrum (which is a means of making music), and so with this new manner of singing she follows the watches of the second Nocturn, performing again the likeness, manner, and outward signs of the beginning of our Lord's Passion, as I have described before. After that, when the sufferings come to an end, she rests from that unbearable labour as much as she can, as though she is completely overcome and reduced to nothing. And a little after that she begins to sob and sigh occasionally, like a dying person. Then, as though she is giving up the ghost, she loses consciousness and her whole body rests from pain and labour. And now she is usually in this state of ecstasy for a long time; what one sees is rigid limbs, a pale and bloodless face and an absence of feeling, movement, or breath, like a dead body. Eventually our Lord, the taker and giver of life, brings bright weather after the tempest and restores her to life again. And with a marvellous seemliness and modest gladness of bearing which is caused by her spiritual joy, she does not think of any sorrow or complain about God's rod; her face shows no sign of agitation or tribulation, the gracious brightness of her outer appearance rather affirms and proves the inner mirth of her mind.

Next, a wooden panel on which a picture of our crucified Lord has been skilfully painted is given to her, and holding it open and unwrapped[7] with both hands, she looks devoutly at our Lord, and she says the following words again and again: "*zouche here, zouche here*," which in English means, "sweet Lord, sweet Lord," and with her pure virgin lips she kisses the feet of our Lord's image sweetly and often, pausing now and again to heave deep sighs—long, joyful, and amorous—from the bottom of her heart, with her breast and throat clearly moving and a sweet whispering-sound coming from her lips. After that she looks calmly at the same image with all the force of her mind. And a little later, when she has tasted, as it is believed, the unspeakable sweetness of his Passion, she once more goes into her accustomed state of ecstasy and becomes completely rigid, holding the picture as she did before; and meanwhile her lips are pressed to the feet of Christ, and her neck and her head slightly raised from the ground, as is appropriate for a kiss—and so she remains, rigid and unmoving, with all the rest of her body flat on the floor. And sometimes the picture is leant against her breast, and sometimes held near her face, according to its position when she goes into her ecstasy. And in the intervals of those ecstasies, her fingers hold the picture so tightly that if anyone shakes, moves, or pulls it, as though to take it away by force, it cannot be separated from her, but her whole body is moved with the movement of the picture. Then her soul, returning from the country of spiritual joys, brings her body back to life, gladdens her mind, and lights up her face, making it shine with a gracious brightness. And she remains like this for some time, and those who have seen just what happens say that the more she looks at the picture the more delight she feels and the more signs of her devotion she gives, as I have said before. But indeed, while she is feeling these joys the virgin's attitude does not change—her face is turned to gaze steadfastly at the image so that she sees nobody and nothing except the picture, nor does she speak to anybody or answer anybody who speaks to her; she thinks only of our Lord.

When all this has taken place, much more solemnly and marvellously than I could ever write it down, she closes and covers the picture and hands it to someone beside her. Then she holds her arms out to her mother and her younger sisters, who are her attendants, and they take her and lift her from the ground and, carrying her, they lay her down in her bed. And for them she has a bright expression, a loving heart and a cheerful mind, with words of spiritual sweetness. However, she says very few words that are spoken aloud, but those she does say are made delightful with a mild and ready joyfulness and maidenly modesty. And so, when the Nocturns, Matins, and Lauds have wonderfully ended, she spends the rest of the time until the Hour of Prime in joy and mirth and in thanking and praising our Lord, without forgetting the country she frequents in spirit, in which, as Isaiah says, *Joy and gladness shall be found . . . , thanksgiving and the voice of praise* [51:3].

WHAT SHE DOES FOR THE HOUR OF PRIME

From now on the other Hours will be described more briefly, for many things which have already been explained apply to the Hours which follow, so there is no need to go through them in such detail every time, but, when necessary, what has been said before can be referred to. At Prime, after her ecstasy, she arises with marvellous quickness, and then stands upright and, putting both hands behind her back, she joins her arms together, so that she is holding her right elbow with the fingers of her left hand and her left elbow with the fingers of her right hand. And she walks in her chamber with her arms joined together behind her back, like a thief who has been publicly arrested and led with bound hands to the courtroom or the gallows. For the whole of that Hour she represents how our Lord Jesus was led from Annas to Caiaphas,[8] then to Pilate, from Pilate to Herod, then back to Pilate again, with his hands bound behind him in a shameful and humiliating way. But indeed, my memory cannot hold or my brain enumerate all the signs of violence and enactment of insults which the virgin, with her hands bound in this way, represents in her own person.

After she has walked like this in her chamber for quite some time, with a wonderful bending of her body, and always with her hands joined and held against her back, she lays herself down on the ground with a decent and easy movement, holding her arms joined beneath her, and she remains like this for a long while, quite rigid, in an ecstasy. And then she pulls her hands out from behind her back and beats her own breast with such hard and frequent strokes of her flat hands that everyone who sees it marvels greatly and judges that it is beyond the strength of man for one person both to strike and to suffer such swift and heavy blows, even if he were flourishing in nature, age, health, and constitution. I do not know which is more amazing in such a feeble and frail creature, giving the blows or receiving them. However, I believe that all is to be attributed to God, to whom nothing is difficult or impossible; especially as the same virgin, as I said before, lacks bodily strength when she comes to herself or is left to herself.

Then truly, after such marvellous and miserable self-mortification, she immediately stands upright with amazing nimbleness and without the help of her own hands or of anyone else's; and then she walks up and down in her chamber as she did before, with her arms and hands joined behind her back, and she also stands very straight, as rigid as a statue. And that is how she celebrates the Hour of Prime, either walking or standing or lying, or else hitting herself, inciting prayer; after this there follows anguish, aching, and sorrow, and then she goes into ecstasy, and after the ecstasy she takes the picture and gazes at it, and after that comes comfort, joy, and mirth, and again, ecstasies, and thus she is carried to bed. And thus the Hour of Prime comes to an end, as I have described before with the Hour of Matins.

WHAT SHE DOES FOR THE HOUR OF TERCE

Truly, at the Hour of Terce and the Hours which follow, she begins, continues, and concludes as she did before, except that for Terce by sitting on the ground and by standing she signifies and shows how our Lord was tied to a pillar. She joins her arms before her breast with her fingers under her elbows, and in this position she holds her joined arms away from her breast, as though there were an empty space for a pillar between her arms and her breast; and thus she shows as best she can how the pillar was embraced by the tightly bound arms of our most sweet Lord Jesus. And everything else which is done in the rites of this Hour concludes as I have described before.

WHAT SHE DOES FOR THE HOURS OF SEXT, NONE, AND EVENSONG

Indeed, at the Hours of Sext, of None, and of Evensong she follows the same rites in the disposition of her body, except for the times when she is lying in the manner described above and beating herself. But so that this may be understood more fully, I shall set it out more plainly. At each of these three Hours, immediately after the ecstasy which always comes before the Hour, she rises swiftly from her bed and puts one foot under the other, twisting them together, and stands upright in this way, and stretching out her arms and hands in the form of a cross, she remains like that for some time, with her eyes open, neither seeing nor feeling. And if at any time the little finger of her right hand is touched, the fingers of her other hand and her whole body move in just the same way. After she has stood so lovingly with her feet and body in the same position for a long time, without swaying or putting her hands out, she does not fall down, but she bends her body backwards so that she is lying on the ground, and she lies there in a swoon as though she were on a cross. A little after that, as I said before, she beats her breast for a long time, fiercely and rapidly; and those who went nearer were able to tell, from counting and estimating, that she beat her breast a hundred times, sometimes with double and continuous blows from both hands.

After this, because she cannot walk while one foot is over the other and she is lying with them twisted together, she changes her position, turning herself on her breast, back, and sides in a way which I cannot describe; and then she rises up nimbly with no help from her other foot or her hands and she stands upright on the one foot which is touching the ground—and no one who reads this can understand how amazingly it is done. Then she stretches herself out again in the shape of a cross. And at other times, it is said, she bends down to the ground while standing on only one foot and leans her whole body towards the ground, inclining to one side; and the maiden stands like this for a long time, leaning right over, bent to one side; and it seems beyond the strength of man that she manages to support her leaning body on one wounded foot. And she does this, I remember, near the end of the Hours in which she represents the shape of the cross; and then she seems to enact the taking down of our Lord from the cross. Furthermore, after many kinds of representation of our Lord's cross and much suffering for the tormented virgin, there follow the very devout prayers of an indescribable kind which I have told you about before, not as well as I wish, but as best I can. But I know well that my power and my skill are less than my desire. After her last enactment of our Lord Jesus on the cross has signified his end, she is all pale and bloodless, and bends her head now forwards, now to the right, then to the left, as if she were expounding what is written in the Gospel, *Filius hominis non habet ubi caput suum reclinet,* that is to say, *The Son of man hath not where to lay his head* [Mt 8:20, Lk 9:58]. And a little after that, sobbing and lamenting indescribably as though she is about to give up the ghost, she lays her head down on her right shoulder. Then, after a short time, she lies down on the ground as she usually does.

But I will repeat now what I have said before, that she truly lies down, moves, bends over, and performs other similar actions; I can assert that human eyes can see her do this; but it is believed that she does not do it with her own strength, but with some other power known only to God. After this come the sorrows, anguish, consolations, and gladness and other things which are enacted at Matins. Indeed, these holy signs of the cross are shown in the body and limbs of the innocent virgin during the three offices in which it is believed that our Lord Jesus hung on the cross—that is to say Sext, None, and Evensong.

WHAT SHE DOES AT THE HOUR OF COMPLINE
At the Hour of Compline she holds and bears her body, whether sitting or standing, so that she is representing the burying of our Lord, except for the times when she is striking the extremities of her body, reaching across with her arms. And she continues like this and ends the Hour with beating of hands, ecstasies, prayers, and the other things that I have described before.

However, to explain further what I have said before, it should be known that it is marvellous how this maiden is moved to arise at the Hour of Matins and at the other Hours by an infallible and unknown clock.[9] And sometimes she represents our Lord's Passion with symbolic actions of her limbs, and at other times she shows her own compassion of both heart and body in her lamentations and suffering; and after this her behaviour and expression show how much she rejoices in the Resurrection and the fruit of the Passion; and though it rarely happens, nevertheless she will sometimes speak of the delights of her heart in very joyful and serious words.

And I and my companions, both abbots and monks, at midnight and at some of the other Hours too, saw blood coming out of her eyes, and it dropped down and stained her linen over-garment. And at noon on a Friday we also saw blood flow from the wounds on her hands and feet and out of her side. Through a hole in her tunic we saw blood, which was not completely red but looked as though it were mixed with water, running out over her breast, and the woollen cloth which lay against her flesh was stained with the same blood, and so was part of her side near the wound. And we saw that not only was the cloth itself which touched the maiden's flesh—that is to say, her hands, feet, and side—sprinkled and dyed with blood, but her breasts were also all stained with the blood which was running from her eyes. And also at times blood ran out at the ends of her fingers between the nails and the flesh, perhaps enacting what our Lord Jesus suffered from the anguish and painful binding of his arms and hands.

Furthermore, on the same Friday, she represented for us how our blessed Lady, Christ's mother, stood beside the cross; she put her left hand under her left cheek and bent her head and her neck to the same side, holding her right hand under her right breast. And then in another representation she showed blessed St John the Evangelist; bending her head down, with folded fingers she clasped her hands together and held them down on her left side.[10]

And it must also be known that in all the bodily movement and bearing of this virgin nothing appears unseemly or offensive. As she walks in her chamber, even though she cannot see and her clothes are trailing on the ground, she never trips, stumbles, or staggers; and when she flings herself to the ground or lies down or rises up, with her limbs moving in all directions, her clothes always cover her, there is nothing which appears unseemly or immodest.

That is enough description of the Hours for the present, though much that also occurred has been left out because of my imperfect memory and the inadequacy of my feeble pen when dealing with such a difficult subject. Before we go on to other matters, however, and in case those who hear this do not believe the marvels for which we abbots and monks went to see this virgin and remained with her for so many hours, it must be known that long ago the bishop of that diocese arranged for the virgin to be kept and looked after by a very respectable and religious man; his way of life is holy and honourable, his opinions sound, and his authority great. He was abbot of Sint-Truiden, of the Benedictine order, and the maiden was his cousin and lived near him. He, like another St John the Evangelist, undertook to care for the virgin,[11] and he had a fair chamber built for her with a suitable holy chapel, and arranged everything so that God could be properly worshipped there; so that the chapel is separated from the chamber by a small screen of lattice, and in that screen there is a door which opens into the chapel, and the altar can be seen from the maiden's bed. This reverend abbot, our most dear friend in Christ, was with us during everything which I have described and was our informant and reliable expounder of the virgin's words.

WHAT SHE DOES AT THE TIME OF MASS

Let us now go to Mass, which this virgin hears most gladly when a priest is available for her; she listens to him with marvellously devout concentration, sighing and longing with her whole heart for the sight of our Lord's body. And indeed, as soon as she sees the elevation of the consecrated host, the very moment that she perceives it, she leans over with an amazing movement of her whole body along the bed, stretching her arms out on both sides and taking on the form of a cross, and she remains like this, as rigid as a post, in a swoon of ecstasy, so that her arms, head and neck, and part of her shoulders are out of the bed; and that part of her body is suspended in the air without moving as long as the Mass continues, and the virgin's face is always somewhat stretched up towards the altar, as if she were constantly gazing at the host through the middle of the door; and the rest of her body, from the hips to the soles of her feet, is still as it was before and stretched out along the length of the bed. Then when the Mass is over and the priest has taken off his chasuble, the virgin comes to herself again and is returned to her usual position, so that she lies in her bed just as she lay before she went into an ecstasy.

However, if she is going to receive the sacrament, she turns towards the altar again and her mother and sisters lift her up and put bedclothes or two pillows behind her, and so she remains like that, neither sitting nor lying but between the two, holding her hands together, sometimes with sighs of devotion and spiritual eagerness, sometimes weeping and waiting meekly for the arrival of her Saviour and spouse. And when the priest, wearing an alb, offers her the sacrament, she meets our Lord with her entire soul and at the very moment when she opens her mouth and receives the host she goes immediately into an ecstasy, so that she closes her mouth and puts her lips together and remains as still as a stone; nor can it be seen that she holds the sacrament in her mouth—there is no sign of saliva or of swallowing, she does not disclose it in her mouth, nor does she move her teeth, her lips, or her cheeks. And she remains like this, rigid and in ecstasy, for a good while. And when the pillows are taken away, or the other bedclothes, which held her up before, she nevertheless remains motionless with her body and limbs in the same position as when she received the sacrament.

Afterwards she comes to herself again and leans her head back where it was before. And her expression appears more bright, lovely, and gracious than I can write or say; and she is then delighting in the heavenly and spiritual sweetness of our Lord; and it seems that she rejects bodily sight and pays no attention to people speaking; and as far as possible she modestly refuses to be seen. . . .

The abbot [her cousin] told me and my companions that on Good Friday in the year of our Lord 1266 this virgin's head began to ache in an interval between two of the Hours, while she was resting from her efforts as usual, and there was no way that she could hold her head still on the pillow, but she kept rolling it to and fro. And when her mother and her sisters saw this, they lighted candles and they looked more closely at her, carefully examining the maiden's head. And they saw, and showed to other people who were there, puncture-marks as of thorns round the virgin's head like a garland, all red with bloody drops, betokening the crown of thorns of our Lord. . . .

Furthermore, let it be known to those who want to know, the outward purity of this virgin Elizabeth bears witness and gives clear evidence of her inner purity. For those who live with her all assert that she keeps her tongue from evil and her lips from speaking guile [Ps 33:14], so that no spittle or moisture of any kind[12] comes from her mouth or uncleanness from her nose. As far as her food and drink is concerned, I write what I am certain of. Once at a suitable time, I think I remember it was between Sext and None, her mother brought her a little milk in a little dish, and then our companion, the abbot of Clairvaux, put a spoonful of it to her mouth, and she sipped three sips of it with apparent difficulty, and then she began to gag at it, as if she were being given food which she loathed. And then she was offered her drink, wine mixed with water, and when she had tasted it she would not drink it. And I dare say with a good conscience that a dove would have drunk more well-water in one sip than the maiden did from that cup. And it is truly believed that she only eats and drinks because other people want her to, not because she needs or wishes to herself. And at other times, if fruit, meat, or fish is held to her mouth she sucks in some of its subtle substance, receiving none of the gross matter.

Furthermore, it is to be noted that neither her father nor her mother nor any of her household can be persuaded to receive any gift or any kind of present; they say that they have enough, and are satisfied with what God has given them. Indeed, they are marvellously straightforward and innocent, as we learned from our own observation and the accounts of other reliable men.

So this virgin, whose whole life is a miracle, who is indeed herself all miracle, as the preceding account shows, enacts and displays in her own body, not just Christ but Christ crucified, and also the symbolic body of Christ, which is Holy Church. See how she represents Holy Church's ritual in the separate Hours ordained by God, as David says, *Seven times a day I have given praise to thee* [Ps 118:164]. In her wounds and sufferings she affirms the truth of the Passion, in her joy and mirth after suffering the gladness of the Resurrection; in her ecstasy the Ascension; in the glow of her revelations and spiritual life she symbolizes the sending of the Holy Ghost and the sacrament of the altar and that of confession, and then desire for the salvation of all men and sorrow at the unkindness and damnation of mankind. What is written above reveals openly enough that you, man, are beyond excuse if such living arguments and open reproofs do not stir you to strength of faith, desire of love, and devotion. Much is still to be written of this matter, but pressing tasks and weakness of body make me lay down my pen.

Here ends the life of St Elizabeth of Spaalbeek, who passed to Christ in the year of our Lord 1266.

Marguerite Porete

EXTRACTS FROM *THE MIRROR OF SIMPLE SOULS*

CHAPTER I

. . . Now listen humbly at the beginning to a brief exemplum of
worldly love and understand its application to divine love. Long
ago there was a lady, a king's daughter, who was of great distinction
and of noble nature, and who lived in a foreign land. It so happened
that word came to this lady of the great courtesy and great generosity of King Alexander, and she fell in love with him for his noble
graciousness and his great renown. But this lady was so far from the
great lord on whom she had set her love that she could neither possess him nor see him; and so she was very often miserable, because
no love but this would satisfy her. And when she saw that this distant love, so near to her, was so far from her,[1] she thought to comfort herself by imagining some figure that would bear the likeness
of the one she loved and for whom she felt her heart so often
wounded. And then she had an image painted, that represented as
closely as possible the appearance of the king whom she loved so
much. And by looking at this image, along with other observances,
she was relieved; and thus she comforted herself with the representation of her love, so that she was raised from misery.

Truly, says the Soul who had this book written, I am saying this
about myself: this is how it is with me. Word comes to me of a king
of great power, who for courtesy and great generosity is a noble
Alexander. But he is so far from me and I from him, says this Soul,
that I can find no comfort in myself. And to summon me he gave
me this book, which represents some of his observances of love.
But, though I have his image, that does not mean that I live in the
freedom of peace; but I am in a foreign land, far from the peace in
which the noble lovers of this lord live, perfect and pure and made
free by the gift of the lord with whom they live.[2] . . .

CHAPTER III

. . . This book says truly of the Soul, in saying that she has six wings, as the Seraphim have. With two she covers the face of our Lord; that is, the more knowledge the Soul has of God's goodness, the more she knows that she does not know the smallest speck of his goodness, which is not understood except by himself. And with two she covers his feet; that is, the more knowledge the Soul has of the suffering that Jesus Christ endured for us, the more perfectly she knows that she knows nothing in comparison with what he did suffer for us, which is not known except by himself. And with two she flies and thus remains both hovering and resting; that is, all that she desires and loves and praises comes from God's goodness. These are the wings she flies with, and so remains hovering, because she is always in God's sight, and resting, because she always dwells in God's will. What should the Soul fear, even though she is in the world? And even if it could be that the world, the flesh, and that enemy the Devil, and the four elements, the birds of the air, and the beasts of the earth tormented her and despised her and devoured her, what could she lose if God dwells with her? Oh, is he not all powerful? Yes, without doubt, he is all power, all wisdom, and all goodness; our father, our brother, and our true friend. He is without beginning and shall be without ending. He is beyond comprehension except by himself, and is, was, and shall be without end three Persons and one single God. Such is the beloved of our souls, says the Soul.

Through such love, says Love himself, the Soul may say to the Virtues, "I take leave of you"—and the Soul has been a servant to those Virtues for many a day.

I agree, Lady Love, says the Soul, that is how it was then; but now it is like this: your courtesy has removed me from their dominion. Therefore I say: Virtues, I take leave of you for evermore. Now my heart will be freer and more at peace than it has been. Indeed I know well that your service is too burdensome. Once I pledged my heart to you without separation: you know this well. I was obedient to you in all things. Oh, I was then your servant, but now I am liberated from servitude to you. I know well, I set my heart on you completely, and so I put up with great servitude for a long time, suffering many grievous torments and enduring many pains. It is a wonder that I have escaped with my life. But now I do not care, because it has come about that I have left your dominion, in which I have been many nights and days, so that I was never free. But now I have departed from you, and so I dwell in peace.³

The Soul, says Love, does not care for shame or for honour, for poverty or riches, for comfort or discomfort, for hell or for paradise.

For God's sake, O Love, says Reason, what is the meaning of what you have said?

What is its meaning? says Love. It is known to those to whom God has given understanding and to no others, for no writing teaches it, and human wisdom cannot grasp it, and no creature can attain it either by effort or by desert. But it is a gift given by the Most High, in whom this creature is lost through abundance of knowledge, and has become nothing in her understanding.⁴ . . . And the Soul has become nothing, [she wishes for everything and wishes for nothing,] she knows everything and knows nothing.

Ah, how can it be, Lady Love, says Reason, that the Soul may wish as this writing says, when it has previously said that she has no will?

O Reason, says Love, what she wishes with is not her will, but all that she inwardly wills is the will of God. For the Soul does not dwell in Love, which might make her will this through some desire, but Love dwells in her, and has taken her will, and does his will with her. Love now works in her without her help, so that no trouble can remain with her. The Soul, says Love, can no longer speak of God, for she is deprived of all outward desires and all inward longings, so that what the Soul does, she does in keeping with some good observance, or by command of Holy Church, without any desire, for the will that gave desire to her is dead.

Ah Love, says Reason (who leaps to conclusions and neglects the sweet kernel of meaning), what wonder is it if the Soul is too dull to feel grace or inward desire, since she has taken leave of the Virtues that teach manners to all good souls? Without them no one can be saved or achieve the life of perfection, and anyone who has them may not be deceived, and the Soul has taken leave of them! Is she out of her mind to speak like this?

Oh, certainly not, says Love, for this Soul possesses the Virtues more fully and has more of them than any other creature. But she does not follow their observances, for she is not in their service as she used to be. No, says Love, if God wills, she has been servant long enough now to become free from this time forward.

Well, Love, says Reason, when was she a servant?

When she dwelt in Love and was under obedience to you and to the other Virtues, says Love. The souls that are of this kind have dwelt so long in Love and under obedience to the Virtues that they have become free.

And when are these souls free? says Reason.

When Love dwells in them and guides them, and the Virtues serve them without any resistance or effort on the souls' part.

Truly, Love, says Reason, the souls that become free in this way have known for many a day what dominion can do. And if someone should ask them what is the greatest torment a creature can suffer, they would say it is to dwell in Love and under obedience to the Virtues. For they are obliged to give the Virtues all that they demand, at whatever cost to nature; and they demand honour, possessions, heart, body, and life. They say to the Soul that has given them all this, and has nothing left with which to comfort nature, that *the just man shall scarcely be saved* [I Pet 4:18]; and then, made sorrowful by this, she would willingly be tormented in hell until the day of judgement on condition that she might then be certain to be saved.

It is true, says Love, that those over whom the Virtues have power live in such bondage. But the souls I speak of have gained the advantage over the Virtues; for they do nothing for the Virtues, but the Virtues do all that the souls wish, without haughtiness or resistance, for the souls are mistresses over them. If anyone asks these free souls, secure and at peace, if they would wish to be in purgatory, they say no; if they would be certain of their salvation while alive, they say no; if they would be in paradise, they say no. Well, what would they wish? They have no will at all to wish for these things, and if they wished anything they would descend from Love. For he who is,[5] who possesses their wills, knows what is good for them, and that is sufficient for them without knowledge or certainty. These souls, says Love, live by knowing and praising Love. That is their continual observance, without cessation, for knowledge and love and praise dwell in them. The souls of this kind cannot identify good or evil, and have no knowledge of their own to judge whether they are converted or perverted.

So as to speak more easily of these souls, says Love, let us take one to stand for all. This Soul does not desire contempt or poverty or tribulation or discomfort or Masses or sermons or fasting or prayers, and she gives to nature all that it demands without reluctance of conscience.[6]. . . She has no concern about anything she lacks, except at the moment of need; and no one but an innocent can be without this pressing concern.

Ah, for God's sake, says Reason, what does this mean?

I have answered you before now, says Love, and I say again, that none of the teachers of natural wisdom, and none of the teachers of written learning, and none of those who dwell in Love and under obedience to the Virtues, understand it, but only those alone who practise Perfect Love[7]––and you can be sure of this. If such souls could be found, they could tell the truth if they wished; but I cannot guarantee that it would be understood except by those alone who practise Perfect Love. This gift is sometimes given, says Love, in a single instant, and let him who has it guard it, for it is the most perfect gift that God gives to a creature. This Soul is a student of theology. She sits in the valley of humility and on the plain of truth, and she rests on the mountain of love. . . .

[Love has explained that God wishes the Soul set free to wish to have the divine will, which she cannot have.]

. . . Ah, Love, says Reason, . . . I pray you to make clear and explain to ordinary people these double words that are hard for their understandings to grasp, so that some of them may perhaps achieve this state of being; and thus this book may reveal to all the true light of truth and the perfection of charity of those who are specially called and chosen by God and supremely loved by him.

Reason, says Love, I will answer for the benefit of those on whose behalf you make this compassionate request. Reason, says Love, where are these double words that you beg me to explain for this book's listeners, who dwell in will and desire—this book which we call *The Mirror of Simple Souls*?

My reply to this, Lady Love, says Reason, is that this book says amazing things about the Soul. It says that she does not care for shame or for honour, for poverty or for riches, for comfort or for discomfort, for love or for hate, for hell or for paradise. It says too that the Soul has everything and has nothing, she knows everything and knows nothing, she wills everything and wills nothing. And, says Reason, she does not desire contempt or poverty or martyrdom, tribulation or sermons or fasts or prayers. And she gives Nature all that it demands, without reluctance of conscience. It is certain, Love, says Reason, that no one can understand this according to my way of understanding unless they learn it from being taught by you; for my advice, the best advice I can give, is that people should desire contempt and poverty and all kinds of tribulation, Masses, sermons, fasts, and prayers; and that people should fear all kinds of love, whatever they may be, because of the dangers they may lead to; and that people should desire paradise above all things, and also fear going to hell; and that they should reject all kinds of honour and all temporal things and all comforts, denying Nature all that it demands except for that without which they could not survive, following the example of suffering set by our lord Jesus Christ. This is the best advice I can give, says Reason, to those who live in obedience to me. And so I say that no one will understand this book by my way of understanding, unless they understand it by virtue of Faith and by the power of Love, who are my mistresses, for I obey them in all things. And yet, says Reason, I say this much, that he who has these two strings in his heart, the light of Faith and the power of Love, has permission to do what pleases him, by witness of God himself, who says to the Soul, "Love Love, and do what you will."[8]

Reason, says Love, you are very wise in all matters that concern you, you who want answers to what was said earlier and who ask what it means. These are good questions, and I am willing to answer all that you have asked. Reason, says Love, I assure you that the souls who are guided by Perfect Love would as soon have shame as honour and honour as shame, poverty as riches and riches as poverty, and torment from God and his creatures as consolation from God and his creatures, and would as soon be hated as loved and loved as hated, and have hell as paradise and paradise as hell, and low rank as high and high rank as low. This means, indeed, that they neither wish nor do not wish any form of prosperity or any form of adversity, for these souls have no will except what God wills in them; and God's will does not trouble these lofty creatures with such afflictions as we have been describing. I have said previously, says Love, that these souls would as soon have all kinds of adversity of heart, in body and in soul, as prosperity, and all kinds of prosperity as adversity. This is so, says Love, because their will is not the cause when such things come to them. These souls do not know what the end may be, or for what purpose God wishes to provide for their salvation or the salvation of their fellow Christians, or for what reason God wishes to be just or merciful, or for

what purpose God wishes to give the soul the lofty gifts of goodness or of his divine nobility; and for this reason the free Soul has
no will to will or not to will, but only to will the will of God, and
endure his divine ordinance in peace.

Love, says Reason, I still have something to ask, for the book
says that the Soul has everything and has nothing.

It is true, says Love, for the Soul has God in her by divine grace,
and she who has God has everything. And it says that she has nothing, because all that the Soul has of God in her by gift of divine
grace seems nothing to her, nor is it any more than nothing in comparison with what she loves, which is in God himself and which
he gives to none but himself. And in this sense the Soul has everything and she has nothing, she knows everything and she knows
nothing. . . .

. . . [The Soul, says Love,] feels no unhappiness for any sin she ever
committed, or for the suffering that Christ Jesus endured for her, or
for any sin or unhappiness of her fellow Christians.

Ah, God, says Reason, what does this mean? Love, you have resolved my other questions, teach me how to interpret this.

It means, says Love, that this is outside her and she cannot feel it,
because her thought is fixed in the realm of peace, that is, in the
Trinity. She cannot move from there or feel unhappiness as long as
her beloved is at ease, regardless of whether anyone should fall into
sin, or on account of any sin that has ever been committed. This is
displeasing to her will in so far as it is to God; it is his own displeasure that gives such displeasure to the Soul. Truly, says Love, if
the Trinity is not troubled by such displeasure, no more is the Soul
that is fixed in him and led by him. But if the Soul that is fixed so
high were able to help any of her fellow Christians, she would help
them in their need with all her power. But the thoughts of such
souls are so divine that they do not rest sufficiently on transient or
created things to conceive any inward unhappiness for them, since
God is good beyond comprehension. . . .

. . . Ah, Holy Trinity, say Faith, Hope, and Charity, where are these
lofty souls who are such as this book describes? Who are they, and
what do they do? Teach us, for the sake of Love that knows all
things, and so we shall comfort those who are dismayed or aston-

ished to hear this book—for all Holy Church would wonder if she heard it, say these three divine Virtues.

I believe it, says Faith himself.

That is true, says Love, of Holy Church the Little that is governed by Reason, but not of Holy Church the Great that is ours and is governed by us.[9] . . .

CHAPTER IV

O Love, says Reason, I beg you to accept yet another question, for this book says that the Soul has taken leave of the Virtues for evermore, and you say that the Virtues are always with such souls, and more perfectly with them than with others. These are two contradictory statements, as it seems to me, says Reason: I cannot understand them.

I will satisfy you, says Love. It is true that the Soul has taken leave of the Virtues, so far as concerns their observances and all the desires they demand, but the Virtues have not taken leave of such souls, for they are always with them and perfectly obedient to them. And in this sense the Soul takes leave of them, and yet they are always with such souls. Let me give an illustration: if a man serves a master, he is with him[10] whom he serves, but the master is not with the servant. And if it happens that the servant earns so much from his master and learns so well that he becomes richer and wiser than the master and is considered better and nobler than he, then he who was master sees for certain that he who was servant is worth more and knows more in every way than he does, and he dwells with him to obey him in all things. This is just how you ought to understand these souls and the Virtues, for in the beginning the Soul did all that she could in heart and body, all that she was taught by Reason, who was at that time mistress and always told her that she must do all that the Virtues wished, without resistance, to the point of death. Thus Reason and the other Virtues were ladies and mistresses over the Soul, and the Soul was truly obedient to everything they chose to command. That is what a soul must do at first when she is a beginner, if she wants to live the life of the spirit. Now the Soul has earned and learned so much from the Virtues that she is above them, for such souls have in them all that the Virtues can teach, and beyond comparison much more. For the Soul has within her the mistress of Virtues who is called Divine

Love, and he has changed her entirely into himself and made her one with him, so that she is not with herself or with the Virtues.[11]

With whom is she then? says Reason, who wishes to learn by asking questions.

She is at my will, Reason, says Love: I have turned her entirely into myself.

And who are you, Love? says Reason. Are you not a Virtue along with us, but are above us?

I am God, says Love, for Love is God and God is Love, and the Soul is God by its condition of Love, and I am God by my divine nature. And this comes to her through Love's justice; so that this precious loved one is taught by me and guided by me without herself, for she is changed into me within me; and such a goal is gained by nurture.[12] . . .

. . . This Soul, says Love, swims in the sea of joy, that is, in the sea of delights that stream from divine influences. She feels no joy, for she herself is joy. She swims and drowns in joy, for she dwells in joy without feeling any joy. Joy is in her such a way that she herself is joy, by the power of joy that has changed her into itself. Now the will of the beloved and the will of the Soul are turned into one, like fire and flame, for Love has changed the Soul entirely into himself.

Ah, sweetest pure divine Love, says the Soul, what a sweet union this is, that has changed me into the thing that I love more than myself! I who can love so little have lost my own name for the sake of Love. Thus I am changed into the thing that I love more than myself, that is, into Love, for Love is all I love. . . .

. . . Ah, sweetest Love, says the bewildered Soul, for God's sake, tell me why he thought to create me and to redeem and restore me, to give me so little when he has so much to give?—but we dare not speak of what God wills to do. I know nothing, says the Soul, but if I had anything to give, I would not give such a small share—I who am nothing, while he is everything. Certainly I would not be able to hold anything back, but I would give him everything, if I had anything to give. And what little I have of any value I have not held back from him, but I have completely given him body, heart, and soul: he knows that. Now I have given him everything, so that I have nothing left to give; and from this it can easily be seen that if I had anything to give, I would gladly give it to him. And he who has taken all that I have of value, he gave it to me and now he keeps it all to himself. O Love, for God's sake, is that how Love behaves?

Ah, sweet Soul, says Love, you know better than you say. For if you have given him everything, that is the best that can happen to you, because you have given him nothing but what was his before you gave it to him. Now consider what you are doing for him.

Sweet Love, says the Soul, you speak the truth. I cannot and will not deny it.

O sweetest Soul, says Love, what would you wish him to give you? Are you not his creation? Do you wish to have from your beloved what is not fitting for him to give or for you to receive? Calm yourself, Lady Soul, if you believe me, because there is truly nothing for you other than to receive a creature's gift, such as is fitting for you to have.

Ah, Lady Love, says the Soul, you did not tell me this when I first knew you. You told me that in the companionship of the beloved and the lover there is no lordship or mastery, but there is. I can easily see this, since one has everything and the other has nothing in comparison with his everything. But if I could amend this, I would amend it, because if I had the power he has I would love him as much as you are worthy to be loved.[13]

Ah, sweetest Soul, says Love, you can say no more than this. Now be calm, for your will is enough for your beloved, and he sends this message to you by me, that you should be certain of what I am about to say: he will love nothing without you, and you shall love nothing without him. This is a very great privilege, and this will satisfy you, sweet Soul, if you believe me. . . .

CHAPTER V

. . . O lord God, says the Soul, no one except you can know my sins in this world in their own repulsive shape. But those in heaven, all those who will be there, will have knowledge of them, not to my shame but my great glory, for this reason, my sweet God: through those sins by which I have angered you, your mercy shall be known and your great generosity, full of courtesy, shall be felt.[14]. . .

. . . such souls,[15] says Love, are properly called Holy Church, because they sustain and teach and nourish all Holy Church—not by themselves, says Love, but the whole Trinity working through them. This is true, says Love; of this there is no doubt. Now, Holy-

Church-below-this-Holy-Church, says Love, what do you wish to say of those who are thus set above you as your betters, you who are accustomed to follow the advice of Reason in all things?

We wish to say, says Holy Church the Less, that these souls are above us in their way of life, for Love dwells in them, and Reason dwells in us. Love guides them, and Reason guides us. But this does not oppose us, says Holy Church the Little, rather we praise them in the glosses of our writings.[16]. . .

. . . O most well born, says Love to this precious Margaret,[17] it is right for you to be graciously dwelling only where no one enters unless he is of your lineage without illegitimacy. The Soul, says Love, has entered into the floods or waves of divine love—not, says Love, by attaining divine knowledge, for it is not possible for any understanding to be so greatly illuminated that it can attain to any of the outpourings of divine love; but the Soul's love is conjoined, clothed, and adorned in the more[18] of this surpassing divine love; not by attaining understanding of Love, but by achieving and attaining the more of truly surpassing love that is hers. The Soul, says Love, is so adorned with the clothing of the surpassing peace in which she lives and dwells, and was and is and shall be, without any being of her own! For, says Love, just as iron is clad in fire and loses its own appearance to the greater strength of what has changed it into itself, so the Soul, for love of this more, without knowing anything of what is less, is clad in the more and is entirely transformed and changed into it, and is always in the more of heavenly beloved peace without respite. The Soul, says Love, lives in the sweet country of surpassing peace, and there is nothing that can either help or trouble those who live there, neither created being, nor anything given, nor anything that God promises. . . .

[The Soul and Love speak obscurely of the Soul's state in "the sweet country of surpassing peace," and Reason asks for explanation of their "dark words."] Reason, says the Soul, you hear what is said to you but you never understand it. And so your questions have ruined this book. There are things that cannot be spoken except in plain and hasty words, but your questions have made them long, because that is what is needed for yourself and those you nourish, for the sake of your company who have the hearts of insects.

You have written it, says Love, so that Reason and all his stu-

dents, whatever their understanding may be, cannot oppose it because it does not seem to them well said. That is true, says the Soul,
but only those who are taught by Perfect Love understand it, and
they alone know what the book means. But he who is to understand it perfectly needs to be dead and mortified by all deaths, says
the Soul, for no one tastes this life unless he has died every death.

CHAPTER VI

Ah, treasurer Soul, says Reason, for God's sake tell us how many
deaths you need to die before you can perfectly understand this
book.

Ask that of Love, says the Soul, for she knows the truth.

Ah, Lady Love, says Reason, please tell us—not for me or those
I nourish, but for those who have taken leave of me, so that this
book may bring light, if God wishes.

Reason, says Love, those taught by you can well deal with two
deaths that the Soul has died, but the third death is understood by
no one alive except those of the mountain.

O Lady Love, says Reason, tell us, who are these people of the
mountain? They do not have shame or honour or fear for anything
that may happen in this life, says Love.

Well, says Reason, Lady Love, for God's sake answer our questions before you say anything further, because I am astonished to
hear of the life of these souls.

Reason, says Love, those who see this book and have achieved
this way of life understand it well, except that they need to explain
the glosses. But I will explain something of what you ask. There are,
says Love, two kinds of people who live a life of perfection in spiritual feeling by means of virtuous works. There is the life of those
who mortify the body in all things, performing works of charity;
and they take such pleasure in their works that they have no knowledge that there is any better existence than that of works of virtue
and deaths by martyrdom, and they desire to persevere in this existence with the aid of meditations full of prayers, always increasing
in good will. And the opinion these people hold, that this is the best
of all possible ways of life, means, says Love, that they are blinded,
and so they perish in their works. Because of the satisfaction they
take in their actions, says Love, these people are called kings. But
this is a way of life in which all are blinded, and those that have two
eyes unfailingly consider them as servants. But that is unknown to

them: they are like the crow, which believes there are no birds in the wood as beautiful as crows.

And I tell you, says the Soul, it is the same with those who always live in desire: they consider that there is no way of life comparable to that of desire, in which they always live, and in which they wish to remain always because they cannot believe that any other is so good.[19] And so those who take such satisfaction in what desire and will give them perish on the way. . . .

CHAPTER VII

. . . [Love and the Soul describe those who gain salvation by avoiding sin and excess, but who do not aim at perfection.] Oh, without doubt, says our lord Jesus Christ, they are discourteous. They have forgotten that I was not satisfied with anything I did for them unless I had done all that my Humanity could bear, to the point of death.

Ah, sweetest lord Jesus Christ, says the Soul, do not care about them or be displeased with them, for these souls are so concerned with and for themselves that they forget you because of their own littleness, and are satisfied with that.

Oh, says Love, without doubt it is great churlishness.

These people, says the Soul, are tradesmen, and are called thralls in the world, because they *are* thralls, for it is not fitting for any gentleman to know how to meddle with trade or to be one of them. But I shall tell you, says the Soul, how I make my peace with these people: Lady Love, it is because they are excluded from the court of your secret friends, just as a churl is from a court of nobles sitting in judgement in Paris, for no one can be present there unless he is of noble descent, and that is especially true of the king's court. And I content myself with this, says the Soul, for in the same way they are expelled from the court of your secret friends, to which those others are called who never forget the works of your sweet courtesy— that is, the scorn and poverty and the unbearable torments that you have suffered for us. They never forget the gift of your sufferings, which always serve them as a mirror and an example.

All things necessary, says Love, are prepared for these people, for so God promises them in the Gospel.[20] They are far more courteous, says Love, than the others just mentioned; yet all the same, says Love, they are little, so little by comparison with the greatness of those who are dead to the life of the spirit and exist in the life of glory that no one can express it. . . .

CHAPTER IX

. . . A bondman needs to have four quarterings[21] before he can be free and be called a gentleman, [says Love,] and it is just the same when applied to spiritual activity.

The first quartering belonging to the Soul that is free is that she is not at all reproved by conscience even though she does not perform the works of the Virtues. Ah, for God's sake, understand this if you can, you who hear it! How could Love's observance be the works of the Virtues, since work ceases when Love follows its observances?

The second quartering is that she has no will at all, no more than the dead have in their graves, except only for the divine will of God. The Soul has no care or concern for justice or mercy. She roots everything solely in the will of him who turns her into himself; and this is the second quartering by which the Soul is made free.

The third quartering is that she considers that there never was, nor is, nor ever shall be any creature worse[22] to him or better loved by him according to what she is—and do not misunderstand this!

The fourth quartering is that she believes that no more than it is possible for God to will anything but good is it possible for her to will anything but his divine will. Love has so adorned her with him that it makes her believe this of [him], who, of his goodness, has by his goodness turned her into this goodness; who, of his love, has by love turned her into this love; and who, of his will, has by his divine will completely changed her into this will. She is thus guided by him, in him, for him, and this is her belief; otherwise, she would not be free in all her quarterings.

Hearers of this book, understand the gloss, in which is found the stream or river that dissolves thought. This is when she is in the state of being in which God makes her have being, the state in which she has given up her will, so that she can only will the will of him who has, of himself and for himself, turned her into his goodness. And she who is thus free in all her quarterings lives in sovereignty, and there she loses her name and is dissolved, and in this dissolution is left by him, in him, for him. So she loses her name, just like a river named Oise or Meuse that comes from the sea, and when it re-enters the sea loses its name and the channel in which it ran through many countries carrying out its work, and comes to an end in the sea. There it rests and gives up its labour; and so it is, truly, with the Soul. For the moment this provides you with a sufficient illustration to interpret the meaning of how the Soul comes [out of] the sea and does her work, and how she comes to an end in the sea, where she gives up her labour and her name. She has no name but the name of him into whom she is completely changed—that is, Love. This is the release into freedom of her whose thought is changed into him. Then she is he that is; and this seems miraculous to her, and she is full of wonder, and Love that delights her is her pleasure.

Now the Soul has no name but the name of the oneness into which Love transforms her, just as the waters we have mentioned have the name of the sea; for as soon as water enters the sea it is sea, for then the nature of the ground does not affect it to the contrary; and nothing material makes it and the sea anything but one thing—not two things, but one. And it is just so with her we have mentioned, for Love has drawn all her nature into himself, so that Love and the Soul are entirely one—not two, for that would be discord, but only one, and so there is concord. . . .

. . .[Those who are free] do nothing unless it pleases them; and if they do, they deprive themselves of peace, freedom, and nobility. For the Soul is not fully perfected until she does what pleases her and is relieved of doing the opposite of her pleasure. This is true, says Love, because her will is ours. She has crossed the Red Sea, and her enemies are lost in it.[23] Her pleasures are our will, through the pure unity of the will of the Deity in which we have enclosed her. Her will is ours, because she has fallen from grace into the perfection of the works of the Virtues, and from the Virtues into Love, and from Love into nothingness, and from nothingness into the enlightenment of God, who sees this with the eyes of his majesty. At this level he has enlightened her with himself, and she is so lost in him that she sees neither him nor herself. If she saw herself in this divine goodness, she would exist for herself, but it is he who sees this goodness in her, having known this of her before she existed.[24] When he gave her his goodness, he made her mistress, and this was of his free will, of which he cannot deprive the Soul without the Soul's agreement. Now he has it [again], without any objection, in just the same way that he had it before she was mistress over it. Now nothing but he exists, no one but he is loved, for no one is but he. He calls her alone, he creates her all alone, and in the total soleness of his own being grants her that state which is the noblest existence that any creature can have in this perfect way of life. Below this there are five states in which people must live, each according to his vocation, before the Soul can gain this sixth state, which is the most beneficial and the best and the most noble and distinguished of all. And the seventh, which is made perfect without any fault, is in paradise. And thus God of his goodness performs his divine works in his creatures. *The Spirit breatheth where he will* [Jn 3:8] and performs marvels in his creatures. . . .

CHAPTER XIII

. . . [The Soul makes two requests.] The first is that, if she sees anything, she may always see what she was when God made everything out of nothing, and that she may be in complete certainty that, in so far as concerns herself, she is nothing but that and never shall be. Without this, she can never grasp the goodness of God.

The second is that she may see what she has done with the free will that God has given her. Then she will see that she has deprived God of his will in a single moment of consent to sin. This means that God knows all things, and whoever consents to sin deprives God of his will. This is true, because he does what God does not wish and is opposed to his divine goodness. . . .

. . . [The speaker is the Soul, now "the high exalted Spirit who is no longer in Reason's dominion."] God has nowhere to put his goodness, she says, unless he puts it in me. . . . And by this means I am the salvation of creatures and the glory of God. I will tell you how and why and in what this is so. It is because I am the height and the sum of all evils. For as I derive what is evil from my own nature, I am all evils; and he who derives all goodness from himself in his own nature is the height of all goodness. Now I am all evils, and he is all goodness, and alms ought to be given to the person who is poorer, or he is deprived of what is justly his. And God can do no wrong, or he would differ from himself. Then his goodness is mine, on account of my necessity and the just nature of his pure goodness. Now since I am all evils and he is all goodness, I need to have all his goodness before my evil can be quenched, nor can my poverty be relieved by anything less. And since he has so much of value, his goodness cannot endure that I should remain a beggar. And since I am all wickedness, I am compelled to be a beggar unless he gives me all his goodness, for nothing less than the complete plenitude of his goodness can satisfy my need or fill up the depth of my own wickedness. In this way, of his sheer goodness, by goodness, I have his divine goodness, and have had it without beginning, and shall have it without end; for I have always been known to his divine wisdom, by the will of his divine goodness, by the act of his divine power. If it were otherwise in practice, it would be a mere fable for me to say as I have said, that I am the salvation of all creatures and the glory of God.[25] Just as Christ is the redeemer of his people by his death and the praise of God the Father, so I, because of my wickedness, am the salvation of mankind and the glory of God the Father, for God the Father has given all his goodness to his Son, and that goodness of God is made known to mankind by the death of Jesus Christ his Son, who is everlastingly the magnificence of the Father and the redeemer of mankind.

Just so, says the Soul, I tell you that the Father has poured out and given forth all his goodness in me, and that goodness of God is given to mankind to be known by my wickedness. Thus I am everlastingly the praise of God and the salvation of mankind, for the salvation of all creatures is nothing but knowledge of God's goodness. And since by me all shall have knowledge of God's goodness— the goodness of God who, of his goodness, does me this goodness—God's goodness shall be known through me, and that goodness would never have been known were it not for my wickedness. And since God and his divine goodness are made known by my wickedness, and their salvation is nothing but knowledge of the divine goodness, I am the cause of the salvation of all creatures, for God's goodness is made known through me. And since God's goodness is known through me, I am his glory and his praise, his glory and his praise are nothing but knowledge of his divine goodness. And I am the cause of that, because the goodness of his pure nature is known by the wickedness of my cruel nature. I have no greater claim to have his goodness than because of my wickedness; and I can nevermore be without goodness because I cannot lose my wickedness; and in this respect he has assured me of his pure goodness beyond doubt. The nature of my wickedness alone is what has further adorned me with this gift. No work of goodness that I have ever done or ever might do gives me either hope or comfort, but only my wickedness, for it is by that that I have this certainty.

You have heard in this present writing how I have all his goodness. Thus I am salvation through being made one with the love that is God, for the stronger turns the weaker into itself. This making one is most delightful; those who have experienced it know this. The pupil of the eye does not shrink so fastidiously if you put into it iron or lint or stone, which are its death, as divine love does if you act against it. Its being is always in perfect accordance with its will.

Now you can understand how my wickedness causes me to have his goodness, on account of my necessity. For at times God permits evil to be done, so that greater good will arise afterwards; for all those who have been planted by the Father and come into this world have descended from perfection into imperfection so as to achieve greater perfection. And then the wound is opened, so that those who were hurt without knowing it can be healed; these people have been humbled by God himself. . . .

Chapter XV
[The seven states through which those who love God ascend towards him.] In the first state, the Soul is touched by God's grace and is separated from sin as far as she has power, intending to keep the commandments established by God as his law on pain of death. And the Soul considers with great fear the fact that God has commanded her to love him with all her heart and to love her fellow Christians as herself.[26] To the Soul this seems labour enough if she were to live a thousand years, to keep the commandments as well as she is able.

I found myself on this level, says the free Soul: I once saw such a day.

Now do not be dismayed, you who are in this state, at the thought of ascending higher, if you have within you a noble heart full of excellent courage. But little hearts dare not undertake great things or climb high, for lack of love. Such people are cowards—oh, how strange it is that they should dwell in fear, not permitting God to work in them!

Chapter XVI
In the second state, the Soul attends to the counsels God gives to those who specially love him, beyond what he commands. And he

who does not conduct himself in such a way as to fulfil all that he
knows might best please his beloved is no good lover. And then this
Soul sees herself above all that men advise, performing deeds that
mortify nature, and despising riches, pleasures, and honours, so as
to fulfil completely the counsels of perfection exemplified by Christ
Jesus.[27] And in doing so she feels no bitterness, and from it she can
have no dullness or weakness of body; for when her beloved has no
dullness, bitterness, or weakness, no more can the Soul that is
drawn upwards by him.

CHAPTER XVII
In the third state the Soul considers the love of works of perfection,
in which her spirit is sharpened by its desires, taking the love as a
means of multiplying such works in herself.[28] And the subtlety of
her thought in understanding her Lord's feelings makes it appear
that the only offering she can make to her beloved that would please
h[im] would be something that he loves, for in love no other gift is
of value than the thing that is most loved by the beloved. And the
will of this creature, inflamed by grace, loves only works of goodness, and she undertakes all such labours by which she may nourish
her spirit. Then, as a matter of true justice, it seems to her, loving
only works of goodness, that she does not know what to give Love
except to make a sacrifice of this, for no death could be so great a
martyrdom to her as to give up these works that she loves, for this is
the pleasure in which she delights and the life of the will that is fed in
her by this. Accordingly, she renounces the works in which she takes
this pleasure, and puts to death the will that receives life from them,
and obliges herself to martyr her will, obeying the will of another in
abstaining from the works of her own will, fulfilling the will of another so as to destroy her own will. And this is very hard, incomparably harder than the two previous states; for it is harder to conquer
the works willed by the spirit than it is to conquer the will of the
body in order to do the will of the spirit. Thus she needs to take the
lead in breaking herself, so as to enlarge the place where Love wishes
to have his being, and to burden herself with many states of being, so
as to unburden herself to achieve her own being.

CHAPTER XVIII
In the fourth state the Soul is drawn by the exaltation of love into
delight in the thoughts that arise in meditation, and through this ex-

altation of love she abstains from all outward labours and from obedience to others in favour of contemplation. Then the Soul is fastidious, noble, and delicate, so that she cannot endure anything to touch her, except for the sheer delight of Love's touches; in these she is extraordinarily glad and light-hearted, and they make her proud of the abundance of her love. Then she reveals the secrets of her heart, which make her grow tender and melt in love's sweetness, in the harmony of the union by which she comes into possession of these delights. Then the Soul believes that there is no higher life to be had than this of which she has lordship, for Love has fed her so fully with his delights that she does not know that God has any greater gift at hand to give to a soul than this love that Love for love has scattered within her. . . . Here she is deceived, for in fact there are two higher states than this in this life. . . .

CHAPTER XIX
In the fifth state the Soul considers what God is: it is he through whom all things exist, and not she; and in regard to their existence she is nothing. And this consideration brings her extreme shame, to see that he who is all goodness has put free will in her who is nothing but all wickedness. Divine goodness, out of sheer divine goodness, has put free will in her who consists only of evils, so that it is enclosed in all wickedness; and God wishes that what has no being should receive being by this gift from him. And divine goodness pours out before this will an ecstatic movement of divine light, which is spread by light within the Soul, and which reveals to the Soul's will the justice of that which is. . . .

[By this light the Soul sees the need to return her will to God.] Now the Soul is not, for by the abundance of divine knowledge she sees her nothingness, and this now makes her set herself at nothing. And she knows everything, for she sees by the depth of her knowledge of her nothingness, and she sees it to be so great that she can find in it neither beginning, measure, nor end, only a profound darkness without ground or bottom. . . .

CHAPTER XX
Now the Soul has fallen from love into nothingness; and without this nothingness she cannot be all; and if she has fallen rightly she has fallen so completely that she cannot rise up out of this depth,

nor ought she to do so. She ought to remain within it; and there the Soul loses pride and freedom. . . . For the will that made her often love at the height of contemplation and in the fourth state made her proud and fastidious has departed from her. But the fifth state has driven her from this to a condition that reveals her to herself. Now she lives in the knowledge of divine goodness, and this knowledge of divine goodness makes her renounce herself. And then the Soul is released from all forms of servitude and is put in possession of free being, which by its excellent nobility gives her repose from all things.

CHAPTER XXI

In the sixth state the Soul does not see her nothingness in the depth of her humility or God in his exalted goodness, but God sees himself in her in his divine majesty, which so illuminates her that she sees that nothing is but God himself, from whom all things have being; and what is, is God himself. And the Soul sees only God himself, for whoever sees in this way sees nothing but God, who sees this in himself. And then the Soul in the sixth state is freed from all things, pure, and illuminated—not glorified, for glorification comes in the seventh state, which will be ours in the glory of which no one can speak. But, pure and illuminated, she sees neither God nor herself, but God sees this of himself in her, for her, without her, and God shows her that there is none but he. She knows only him, she loves only him, she praises only him, for there is only he. What is belongs to his goodness. So she loves his goodness, which, by his goodness, he has given her. This goodness that God has given is in himself, and God cannot be separated from his goodness so that it ceases to remain with him. And therefore he is what belongs to his goodness, and his goodness is what God is. Thus through his exalted goodness, she sees goodness by divine light in the sixth state, and by beholding this the Soul is illuminated. There is only he who is, and she sees the being of his divine majesty by love's transformation of the goodness poured forth and returned to him. She sees this in him, of him who is the uncreated creator who has appropriated nothing from the creature. All belongs to his very own being, and his own self-being is the sixth state of being . . . of which we have promised to tell our listeners. And Love, of his high nobility, has fulfilled what was promised.

Chapter XXII

And he guards the seventh state within himself to give to us in ever-lasting glory. If we do not know it now, we shall know it when our soul leaves the body.

Chapter XXVII

. . . [The Soul speaks.] Lord, how much do I comprehend of your power, of your wisdom, and of your goodness? As much as I com-prehend of my weakness, of my foolishness, and of my wickedness.

Lord God, how much do I comprehend of my weakness, of my foolishness, and of my wickedness? As much as I comprehend of your power, of your wisdom, and of your goodness. And if I could comprehend one of these two, I should comprehend both. For if I could comprehend your goodness, I should comprehend my wickedness. And if I could comprehend my wickedness, I should comprehend your goodness. This is the means of judging.

And in as much as I know nothing of my wickedness in relation to what it is, I know nothing of your goodness in relation to what it is. And yet what little I know of my wickedness has given me what knowledge I have of your goodness.

O lord God, truly it is little, so little that it cannot be told, for it is nothing in relation to what I do not know. . . .

And then I considered this: what with my wickedness and what with his goodness, what could I do to make peace with him? . . .

And then I said that if it could be that I had never existed, on con-dition that I had never sinned against his will, if that pleased him it would be my pleasure.

And then I said to him that if it could be that he would afflict me with the greatest torments that lay within his power, so as to avenge himself on my sins, if that pleased him it would be my pleasure.

And then after that I said to him that if it could be that I were just as he is and were without imperfection, but that I should suffer as much poverty and scorn and torment as he has goodness, wis-dom, and power, so long as I had never acted against his will, if that pleased him it would be my pleasure.

And then I said to him that if it could be that I were turned to nothing, just as I came from nothing, so that he could take vengeance on me, if that pleased him it would be my pleasure.

And then I said to him that if it could be that I had of myself as much excellence as he has of himself, in such a way that it could not be taken from me or diminished unless I myself wished it, I would bestow all this on him and become nothing, rather than keep back anything that did not come to me from him; and, even if it could be that I might have all that I have mentioned,[29] I would not be able to do so if it meant keeping anything that did not come to me from him.

And then I said that if I had what I have mentioned of my own intrinsic nature, I would better love and sooner choose that it turned to nothing beyond recovery than that I should have it if it did not come from him. And if I had as much torment as he has power to inflict, I would love this torment better if it came from him than I would love everlasting glory that did not come from him.

And then I said to him that, rather than that I should henceforward do anything that displeased him, I would sooner choose that his Manhood should suffer on the cross as much torment again as he has suffered for me, if it could be that I could choose this rather than that I should do anything that displeased him.

And then I told him that if I knew and it were the case that everything that he has made of nothing—meaning myself and all other things—must become nothing unless I sinned against his will, my choice would be for it to become nothing rather than that I should sin.

And then I told him that if I knew that I would have as much unending torment as he has goodness unless I sinned against his will, I would choose to suffer those pains everlastingly rather than do anything that I knew would displease his will.

And then I told him that if it were possible that he could and would willingly give me everlastingly as much goodness as he has excellence, I would not love it except for him. And if I lost it, I would not care about it except for him. And if he gave it back to me after this loss, I would not accept it except for him. And if it were possible that it could please him better that I should become nothing and have no being than that I should accept this gift from him, I would prefer to become nothing.

And if it could be that I had what he has in him as well as he has it of himself, and that, if I wished, it would never fail, and I knew that it would please him better that I suffered as much torment from him as he has goodness in him, I would prefer that to remaining in this glory.

And even if I knew that the sweet Manhood of Christ Jesus, and the Virgin Mary, and all the court of heaven, could not endure that I should have this everlasting torment, but wished me to have back the state of being I had come from, and God saw (if it were possible) this pity and this desire of theirs, and said to me, "If you wish, I will willingly give you back the state you have come from, simply because my friends in my court wish it; but if they did not wish it, you should not have it. And so I offer you this gift if you will accept it," it would be my choice to remain in torment without end rather than accept it, since I did not have it from his will alone. So I would refuse it, coming from the prayers of Christ's Humanity, and of the saints, and of the Virgin Mary; I would not be able to endure it unless I had it from the pure love that he has for me, for my own sake, out of his pure goodness, and from his will alone, and the love that the beloved has for the lover.

And then I said to him that if I knew it could please him more that I loved someone else more than him—
Here my mind fails me: what happens is that I feel neither power nor will to concede this, but I answered that I must take advice.

And then I said that if it were possible that he loved someone else more than me—
Here my mind fails me: I do not know how to answer, or wish, or concede.

And I said to him that if it were possible that he could wish someone else to love me more than he loves me—
Here too my mind fails me: I do not know how to answer, any more than before. But I kept on saying that I must take advice about all these things; and so I did. I consulted him himself, and told him that these three matters were very hard, for if it were possible that I loved someone else more than him, and that he loved someone else more than me, and that someone else loved me more than he—
Here my mind failed me, for I could not wish or concede any of these three possibilities. And he kept on pressing me for an answer, and I so much loved to be with him that there was no way I could answer politely, and so I was in distress, and I could not easily get away. No one knows what this is like if he has not experienced it. And I could never have peace unless I answered these questions. . . .

Now I will tell you my answer. I told him that he wanted me to be tested by him in all ways. Alas, what have I said? I shall not speak another word. My heart alone confronted him in this battle. What shall I answer, in mortal anguish?—that he should thus wish to part from his lover, whom he had treated so well that I thought it could have lasted? But if it were possible, and if it were the case that, for the sake of change, he could wish for this, and that he willed it with his whole will, I answered him as follows:

O Lord, if it were possible that this change could endure everlastingly in reality, as in these questions: I love you of yourself for yourself; and so I would un-will that on your behalf;[30] and if, with the created nature you have given me, I had exactly what you have, and could do my will just as I can do with the will that you have given me, and if also I were allowed to be equal to you except that I could change my will for someone other than myself, you would not do this, because you would will it without any of your goodness. These three things are very painful to concede; but if I knew without doubt that this was what your will willed, with no diminishment of your divine goodness, I would will it without willing anything further. In saying this, my will meets its end. And so my will is martyred, and my love is martyred: you have brought them to martyrdom. What they had believed submits entirely: my heart once believed it would always live in love, through the desire of a good will. Now these two things[31] have come to an end in me, and their end has made me leave my childhood behind.

And there the country of freedom was revealed to me.

Bridget of Sweden

EXTRACTS FROM THE *LIBER CELESTIS*

EXTRACTS ON BRIDGET AS VISIONARY

(A) BOOK II, CHAPTER 16
[Christ speaks to Bridget:] "There are many marvels that I speak of with you and not with others who have served me for a long time and lived better lives than you have. I will answer them with this example: there is a lord who has many vines planted in many different places, and the wine from each vine tastes and has the character of the earth the vine grows on. After the grapes have been pressed, the lord will sometimes drink the wine made from the lower ones, sometimes that of the higher and better ones. If the lord is asked why he does this he will answer that he likes the lesser wine and that it appeals to him at that moment; however, this will not make him reject and despise his better and greater wines. He will store them away and keep them to be useful and to do him credit at suitable moments.

"This is what I am doing with you. I have many friends whose lives are sweeter to me than honey, who give me more delight than any wine and who shine more brightly than the sun in my sight. Nevertheless, as I told you at first, I have chosen you in my spirit because it pleases me to do so, and not because you are better or holier than others, or worthy to be compared to them in merit; I have chosen you solely because I wish to do so, just as I make fools wise men and sinners righteous according to my will. And do not judge that because I show you this grace I must therefore despise others, for I want you to know that I am storing them away and keeping them to do me more honour when I feel the moment has come. Therefore, humble yourself in every way and do not be troubled by anything except your sins. Love everyone, even those who seem to hate you and speak evil of you, for they give you an opportunity to grow in grace.

"I bid you to do three things, and I forbid you three. I allow you to do three things, and I advise you to do three. First, I bid you to desire nothing but your God; second, do away with all pride and boasting; third, hate all pleasures of the flesh. I forbid three things: all empty, filthy, and shameful words; all excessive and extravagant food and all superfluity of other things; all worldly joys and amusements. I allow you to do three things: to sleep sufficiently for bodily health; to be awake long enough for bodily exercise; to eat sufficiently for strength and physical well-being. I advise you to do three things: to fast and do other good deeds for which the kingdom of heaven is promised; to dispose of your possessions in the way which most honours God; and also to think of two things continually in your heart: first, what I suffered for you in my Passion and death; second, my justice and the judgement which is to come. These two will stir your heart to fear and dread. There is also one thing which I bid, command, advise, and allow: that you be obedient according to your obligation. I both bid and command that, because I am your God. I will allow you to do that because I am your bridegroom and your husband. And I advise you to do that because I am your friend."

(B) BOOK II, CHAPTER 18
[Christ speaks:] "I have done three marvellous things for you. You see with your spiritual eyes, and you hear with your spiritual ears, and with your bodily hand you feel my spirit move in your living breast. What you see you do not see as it really is, for if you saw the beauty of angels and holy souls your body could not bear the sight—it would burst asunder like a corrupt and rotten vessel with the joy your soul would feel. And indeed, if you saw devils as they really are you would either live with unbearable sorrow or die instantly at the fearful sight. And because of this, spiritual things are visible to you and shown in bodily likeness: angels in the likeness of men who have life and soul (for angels live in their spirits); devils are shown to you in the likeness of mortality, as beasts and other creatures without immortal souls (for when the flesh dies, the spirit dies, but in truth, devils are ever-dying and ever-living); spiritual ideas are conveyed to you through inner pictures, for the spirit could not otherwise apprehend them. And yet, among all these

other things, the greatest marvel of all is that you feel my spirit
moving in your heart."

Then she answered: "Oh, my Lord, son of the Virgin, why do
you condescend to harbour such a poor widow as I am? For I am
poor in all good works, and I have little understanding of inward
knowledge, and have long been consumed and wasted by sin." To
which he answered: "There are three things I can do. First, I can
make a poor man rich, and I can give the fool of little wit sufficient
understanding and knowledge. I can also make an old man young,
just as the bird called the phoenix brings dry sticks into a valley,
some of them a kind of stick which is by nature dry without and
hot within; heat from the sun's beams first penetrates these sticks,
setting them on fire, and from that all the other sticks are soon
burning. So it behoves you to gather virtues together, by means of
which you may be reborn free from sin. Among your bundle of
virtues you must have one branch which is dry without and hot
within, that is to say, a heart which without is clean and dry, free
from all worldly delights, and within is full of love, desiring nothing
but me. Then the fire of my love will penetrate that branch first,
setting all the virtues on fire; and in these flames you will be burned
and purged of your sins. You will rise like a bird made new, with
the skin of all vicious and wicked pleasures consumed in ashes."

(c) BOOK V, PROLOGUE

. . . Once it happened that as she was riding towards a castle of
hers,[1] honourably accompanied by a retinue of attendants and servants, her mind was lifted up to God almighty in prayer so that her
soul went into a state of ravishment, as though separated from her
bodily wits, suspended in an ecstasy of spiritual contemplation.
During this time she saw in the spirit a ladder fastened to the earth
and with its top touching heaven. And at the highest point of the
ladder she saw Jesus Christ sitting in judgement on a marvellous
throne, with the Virgin Mary at his feet; and around the throne
there was an infinite host of angels and a vast multitude of saints.
And halfway up the ladder the aforementioned Bridget saw a certain cleric whom she knew well and who was still living then, a man
who was very learned in divinity, but was nevertheless full of the
Devil's own deceit and wickedness. This man had a very impatient,
troubled manner, so he seemed more like a fiend than a humble
monk.

At that moment Lady Bridget saw all the inner passions of this cleric and all the secrets of his heart, and how he revealed his schemes to Christ the judge on his throne by the way he asked small-minded questions in a restless, unbecoming fashion. Then she heard and saw in the spirit how Christ the judge answered every question mildly, comprehensively, and fittingly. The Virgin Mary sometimes said a few words to Lady Bridget between his replies, as will be told later. The lady's ravishment lasted until she reached her castle at Vadstena, and she bore this book in mind all the time. And when her servants took her horse by the bridle and shook her to awaken her from her trance, she came to herself again and was sad to lose the pleasure she had been enjoying. However, this book of questions remained in her mind as though carved in marble, and she soon wrote it down in her own language and her confessor translated it into Latin.

(D) BOOK VI, CHAPTER 52

The bride said to Christ, "Oh, my dearest God, what you do to me is a wonderful thing, for you make my body slumber and lift up my soul to see, hear, and feel spiritual things whenever you wish to do so. Your words are wonderfully sweet to my soul and more delicious to me than any food. They enter my soul and leave me both satisfied and hungry. I am satisfied because I have no taste for anything else, but I crave them with holy hunger. Therefore, Lord, help me to do your will." Then Christ said, "I am acting like a king who sends wine to his servants and tells them to drink it because it is wholesome, it will heal sickness, and make the sorrowful glad and the healthy stronger. And the vessel in which it is sent is unsullied. In the same way I am sending my words by you, a suitable vessel; you must therefore speak them boldly where and when my spirit bids you." Then the bride said, "Lord, I am a sinful creature and ignorant of such work." Christ answered, "Who would be surprised if a lord took some of his money or precious metal and made some of it into a crown, some into cups, some into rings for his own use? It is not surprising if I do the same thing with my servants and use them to make myself more respected and revered, in spite of the fact that by nature one has a better understanding than another. Therefore, hold yourself ready to do my will."

Then the Mother[2] said, "You proud women of the kingdom of Sweden, who say, "Our ancestors left us extensive property and fine manors. Why should we lower ourselves to anything humbler? And our mothers were richly dressed, respected, and revered. Why should we not follow them and teach our children to do the same?" These women do not pay attention to the fact that my son, who was Lord of all, wore such modest and simple clothing. They do not look at his face, covered in blood as he hung on the cross, and how he was put to death among thieves. Those proud women are like something which is full of hot fire and burns all it touches. So the pride of these women, by the bad example it sets, burns all who see it. I am like a mother who shows her rod to her children and servants. The children are afraid of grieving their mother, and the servants are afraid of being beaten. Thus they all behave virtuously and avoid harm and wickedness. So I, the Mother of mercy, will show you and others the wages of sin, so those who are good will love God more deeply, and those who are wicked will flee from sin because they fear punishment. Thus I show mercy to both the good and the wicked.". . .

(E) BOOK VI, CHAPTER 88
It happened that an eminent monk said to Father Matthew that it was inconsistent with the Scriptures that Christ would ignore those who had renounced the world and reveal his secrets to such an aristocratic woman. And when the bride heard this, she prayed to God to reveal the truth. Then she heard Christ say, "That jangling cleric is too proud of his learning to want me. But I shall give him a clout and he will really know that I am God." And shortly after that he died of the palsy.

EXTRACTS ON THE LIVES OF CHRIST
AND THE VIRGIN MARY

(A) BOOK II, CHAPTER 21
Mary spoke and said, "My daughter, there are five things for you to think of: first, that all the limbs of my son's body went cold when he died, and the blood, which during his Passion had flowed from his wounds and adhered to all his limbs, ran together. Think also that his heart was stabbed so grievously and so unmercifully that the knight[3] did not stop until the spear had pierced both parts of his heart and reached his ribs.

And think how he was taken down from the cross. Those that took him down set up three ladders, one to his feet, another to his shoulders, and a third to the middle of his body. The first man went up and held him in the middle. The second went up another ladder and first pulled the nail out of one hand; then he moved the ladder and pulled the nail from the other hand; and these nails went right through the cross and showed on the other side. When the man who was supporting the body had come down, another went up and pulled the nails from the feet, and when he had nearly reached the ground again, one man held the body by the head, another by the feet, and I—his mother—held the middle of his body, and so we three bore him to a stone which I had covered with a clean linen cloth in which we wrapped the body. And I did not want to sew up the linen cloth, for I was certain that he would not rot in the grave. After this, Mary Magdalene and other holy women came, and many angels—as many as there are motes in a sunbeam—to offer and give service to their Maker.

"There is no man that can tell the sorrow I felt then. I was like a woman in childbed whose body is trembling so much all over after the birth of her baby that she can hardly breathe,[4] yet she is also as full of inner joy as can be because she knows that her baby has been born and will never return to its previous wretched state. So it was with me; for though I was overwhelmingly sad at the death of my son, yet my soul rejoiced greatly because I knew he would never die again but would live everlastingly; mirth and mourning were mingled. I can truly say that when my son was buried it was as though two hearts lay in the one grave. Is it not written that *Where thy treasure is, there is thy heart also* [Mt 6:21]? So my thoughts and my heart were forever in the sepulchre with my son." . . .

(B) BOOK IV, CHAPTER 70
The Mother said, "At the time of his Passion there were tears in my son's eyes and his whole body was sweating with fear of the pain. Then he was taken away from me, and I did not see him again until he was brought out to be scourged. And then he was violently thrown to the ground and his head struck the ground so hard that his teeth knocked together. And they struck him so pitilessly on the face and neck that although I was not standing close I could hear it. Then they made him take his clothes off, and he approached the pillar willingly and put his arms round it. They bound him to it, beat-

ing him so severely with scourges with sharp thorns in them that the flesh of his whole body was raked with wounds. The first blow struck my heart so painfully that I fainted. When I came to myself again I saw that his body was torn all over. Then one of them said, 'We will kill him without waiting for a death sentence.' And he went to the pillar and untied him and picked up his clothes, but they did not give him time to get dressed again; they dragged him away so that I could follow his bloody footsteps from the place where he was scourged to the place where he was crucified. And then he wiped his blood-covered face with his tunic.

"There were a hammer and four nails ready, and his whole body was stripped again except for a small loincloth to cover his private parts. The cross had been put together, but there was nothing at all for him to rest his head on, wounded as it was. Then he turned his back to the cross and first he spread out his right arm, which was immediately nailed down. Then they pulled up the other arm, stretching it to reach the other hole until the sinews were all torn. Then they pulled at his feet and laid them on the cross, fastening them with two nails through the hard bone. But at the first blow I fell down in a swoon, and when I woke again I saw my son hanging high above me and heard men talking to each other, 'This man, was he a thief or a robber or a liar?' Some replied and said, 'A liar.' Then they took a crown of thorns and put it tightly on his head, pulling it down to the middle of his forehead. The blood ran down and filled his ears, his eyes, and his beard, so that almost nothing could be seen of him but blood; nor could he see me standing close by the cross until the blood had been wiped from his brows.

"Then he commended me to John in a voice which came from deep in his chest. And he lifted up his head, with his eyes full of blood and tears, and said, *My God, my God, why hast thou forsaken me?* [Mt 27:46, Mk 15:34]. And as long as I lived on this earth, I could never forget that voice, for he was speaking more out of compassion for me than because of his own suffering. Then the colour of death came over him; his cheeks hung down over his teeth and people could count every rib in his side; his belly stuck to his back and his whole body trembled. I felt so faint that I fell to the ground. And his mouth was open so that people could see his teeth and his tongue. His chin had fallen to his breast, his eyes were open, and his body hanging loosely. His knees were bent to one side and his feet to the other. Then some of those who were standing around said,

'Ah, Mary, now your son is dead.' And others said, 'Lady, now your son's suffering is over and his bliss has begun.'

"And after a little while they opened his side with a spear. And when the spear was pulled out the head was the colour of blood, all dark so that I could see that it was his heart's blood: a sight which pierced my own heart so painfully that it was astonishing that it did not break. I waited while they took down his body, and I was very glad that I could touch his body and see his wounds and wipe the blood away. I kissed his mouth and his eyes. His arms were so stiff that I could not bend them to put them on his breast, only on his belly. His knees could not be pulled down.

"Before, he had been so fair that everyone who saw him was glad, and if they had any sorrows they were comforted. And furthermore, good men felt a spiritual warmth towards him. And those who were bad were less unhappy while they could see him and were comforted, so much so that they used to say, 'Let's go and see Mary's son so that we can feel better while we are with him.' When he was twenty years old he was a grown man in size and strength. He was big, not fleshy but lean. His eyebrows and his beard were auburn-coloured and his beard was a palm long. His forehead was straight and of medium size, and his nose neither too big nor too small. His eyes were so bright that even his enemies liked to look at him. His lips were full enough and reddish. His chin was not too long. His cheeks were reasonably full. His skin was white mixed with red. He walked very upright. There was no flaw on his whole body, as those who saw him bound naked at the pillar can bear witness. His skin was free from lice, scaliness, or any other impurity."

(C) BOOK VI, CHAPTERS 58–59
The Mother said to the bride, "I have told you of my sorrows, but it was not the least of my sorrows when I fled with my son into Egypt, and heard of the slaying of the Holy Innocents and how Herod pursued my son. You may ask what my son did all the time until his preaching and his Passion. My answer is that as the Gospels say, he was subject to his father and mother.[5] And yet he performed miracles in his youth, for kings sought him out, and on his coming into Egypt, the idols and false gods fell down and were destroyed.[6] Angels showed themselves to him and served him. He never got dirty and his hair was never untidy. As he grew, he went to the temple in Jerusalem with us on feast days; and later, when he

was older, he did work with his hands—respectable and suitable work—and he often said comforting things to us, so that we loved to hear him speak. We lived in poverty and discomfort, and he brought us no gold, but he always gave us patience. And sometimes we earned what we needed by our work, sometimes we had to put up with things patiently. He sometimes had discussions with men learned in the law, too, and argued with them openly, so that they marvelled greatly at his knowledge. It happened once that I was thinking of his coming Passion and was full of sorrow; and then he said to me, 'Mother, do you not know that I am with my Father and my Father is with me? It is my Father's will and my will that I should suffer death so that mankind may be brought to bliss.' And we often saw a marvellous light around him and Joseph and I heard angels singing with him. And no evil spirit could abide his presence."

The Mother said to the bride that she had felt wonderful things and stirrings within herself from the moment she had conceived Christ, and that the child [John the Baptist] rejoiced greatly in Elizabeth's womb when they met each other beside a well. And Joseph had thought himself unworthy to serve her from the moment when she conceived, before the time when the angel told him that she had conceived by the Holy Ghost and that it was the Son of God she bore within her. And from the moment when she conceived, she had devoted herself continually to prayer, vigils, and reading, except for a certain amount of time when she did her household tasks. And anything left over after they had eaten what they needed they gave to the poor. "And," she said, "Joseph took true care of me and preserved my maidenhead. He wished for nothing but heavenly things, and besought God that he should never die until the time when he saw God's will fulfilled in me, his wife. And because his obedience to God's will was so wonderful, he now enjoys wonderful bliss in heaven."

(D) BOOK VI, CHAPTER 62

The Mother said, "One day, some years after my son's ascension, I felt great inner sorrow because I so longed to go to my son. And a bright angel appeared and told me that my son said the time had come when I should go bodily to join him and receive the crown that was ordained for me. I asked him, 'Do you know the day and the hour of my passing?' The angel said, 'Your son's friends shall come and bury your body.' Then the angel went away, and I prepared myself for my journey and went about as usual. It happened one day that my soul was lifted up in such joyful contemplation that it could hardly contain itself, and in this joy and gladness it departed from my body. But you shall not know how it was honoured and what it saw until the time when your own soul departs from your body. Then my son's friends came and buried me in the valley of Jehoshaphat with a multitude of angels as great as the motes in a sunbeam. But the Devil did not dare come near. And my body lay buried in the earth for fifteen days, after which it was taken up into heaven by a multitude of angels.

"And this number is not without a great mystery, for in the seventh hour there shall be a general resurrection of bodies, and in the eighth hour the bliss of both souls and bodies shall be fulfilled. The first hour lasted from the beginning of the world until the Law of Moses began. The second hour was from Moses until the Incarnation. The third was when my son ordained baptism and tempered the harshness of the Old Law. The fourth was when he preached. The fifth was when he died and rose again and gave proof of his Resurrection. The sixth was when he went up to heaven and sent down the Holy Ghost. The seventh shall be when he sits in Judgement. And in the eighth, all prophecies shall be fulfilled, those who have lived well shall enjoy perfect bliss and God shall be seen as he is in heaven."[7]

(E) BOOK VII, CHAPTER 16

On Mount Calvary[8] Christ showed the bride, weeping and grieving, how he died on the cross. He told her to pay attention to a hole which was cut into the stone of the hillside, for that was where the foot of his cross was fastened at the time of his Passion, so that it would not fall. Then there were two planks fastened to the cross like steps, below the place where his feet would stand, so that those who were to crucify him might climb up and stand more easily. Then they climbed up the steps and dragged Jesus up with them very scornfully and shamefully, and he followed them *as a sheep to the slaughter* [Is 53:7]. And when he reached the highest plank he willingly stretched out his arm and opened his right hand, and they drove the nail through and into the cross at the point where the bone is most solid. Then they dragged his left arm with a rope as hard as they could and fastened it to the cross in the same way. Then they dragged his body down by the feet as hard as they could and put one foot over the other, fastening them down with two nails, and they dragged his body so hard that all the veins and sinews seemed as if they were torn. They put the crown of thorns on his head, thrusting it down so hard that the blood ran down and filled his eyes, and his ears and his beard were crimson with blood. Then those who had crucified him took away the planks, and He hung there on the cross.

And then the bride looked to one side, and she saw his sorrowful mother lying on the ground, trembling as though she was dying, and John and her sisters were beside her and comforting her. ('But then a new sorrow for that sorrowful mother penetrated me, so that I felt as though I was being pierced by a sword of bitterness.'⁹) And when that sorrowful mother, near death, looked at her son, she was pierced by the sword of sorrow. And when her son saw her and his other friends sorrowing and weeping so bitterly, with a weeping voice he entrusted his mother to John, so that men knew by his voice that his heart was full of sorrow.

Then his eyes, which had been so bright, seemed to go dead, and his mouth was open and full of blood, and his face all pale with blood scattered over it. His body was livid and wan for lack of blood. His flesh was so tender that at the lightest touch of the scourges the blood had run out, leaving it all blue. He shrivelled on the cross in his bitter pain and then the torment of his wounds reached his heart and death coursed through every part of his body.

Then he cried to the Father in a loud voice, weeping, *My God, My God, why hast thou forsaken me?* [Mt 27:46, Mk 15:34]. His lips were pale and his tongue bloody; his belly clung so closely to his back that it seemed he had no bowels within him.¹⁰ And then he cried out a second time in a loud voice, *Father, into thy hands I commend my spirit* [Lk 23:46], and his head rose for a moment, then fell again, and he gave up the ghost.

And when his mother saw this she trembled with grief, and would have fallen to the ground if the other women had not held her up. And the weight of Christ's body loosened his hands a little from the nails, so that the nails in the feet were bearing his whole weight. His hands and his fingers and his backbone were so stiff that they would not bend.

Then those wicked tormentors jeered at his mother, and one of them came like a madman and thrust a spear into his right side so pitilessly that it pierced his breast almost to the other side, and when he drew it out, a great stream of blood followed it, covering the iron point and some of the shaft with blood. And when his mother saw that, she fainted.

And when this was over, and the people had left, some of his friends came and took him down from the cross, and his mother took him in her arms and sat down with him, and laid him on her lap, all torn and wounded. And with the tears from her eyes and those of others she washed his wounds and she dried them with a linen cloth, and she closed his eyes and kissed them and wrapped him in a winding sheet of fine, clean linen. And they laid him sorrowfully in the grave.

(F) BOOK VI, CHAPTER 22

The bride said, "When I was in Bethlehem I saw a maiden who was with child, the fairest I ever saw, dressed in a simple kirtle and wrapped in a white cloak; and there was a pleasant-looking old man with her, and an ox and an ass with them. And he tethered the ox and the ass to the stall and went and lit a candle for the maiden, fastening it to the wall. Then he went out, for it was nearly time for her child to be delivered. She took off her cloak and took the kerchief from her head and stood there in nothing but her kirtle, and her hair hung down around her shoulders as fair as gold. She took two clean pieces of linen and two of woollen cloth which she had brought with her to wrap her child in when he was born, and she laid them down beside her ready for when they were needed.

"And when she had prepared everything, she knelt down with great reverence and prayed, and putting her back to the crib she turned her face to the east and raised her hands and her eyes to heaven, and she was exalted in contemplation so sweet that it is indescribable. Then I saw something moving in her womb and all at once she bore her son. And the place was filled with such light and radiance that it was brighter than the sun and the light from the candle which Joseph had placed there could not be seen. And the bearing of the child was so swift that I could not see it being born, but I saw the blessed child lying naked on the ground, and he had the fairest skin I have ever seen, unblemished. I also saw the afterbirth, that is the caul the child was born in, lying all white on the

ground. Then I heard the song of angels, wonderfully delightful and
sweet.

"And when the maiden felt that she had borne her child, she
bowed her head, held up her hands and worshipped the child, and
said to him, 'Welcome, my God, my Lord and my Son!'

"And the child, weeping and shivering with cold and the hardness of the floor, stretched out looking for nourishment. Then his
mother took him in her arms, and clasped him to her breast, and
with her cheek and her breast she warmed him with great joy and
delight.[11] She sat down on the ground and laid her child on her
knee, and took him and laid him first in a linen cloth and then in a
woollen one, and bound his body, his arms, and his legs with a
swaddling band; she also wrapped two small linen cloths which she
had brought with her around his head.

"And then Joseph came in and fell to his knees and worshipped
him, weeping for joy. The Mother had not changed colour, nor was
she at all sick or weak, and her belly was as slender as before she
had conceived. She rose, and Joseph helped her lay the child in the
crib, and they both knelt down and worshipped him."

EXTRACTS ON THE CORRUPTION OF
THE CHURCH

(A) BOOK III, CHAPTER 27

The bride said to the Mother, "Oh, Mary, I beseech you to help me;
I pray for the most excellent city of Rome. I can see with my own
eyes that there are many churches where the bodies of many blessed
saints lie at rest; some of the buildings have been enlarged, but the
hearts of those who occupy them and administer them are far from
God. Give them the gift of charity. For I have gathered from writings that there are seven thousand martyrs for every day of the year.
And even if their souls do not enjoy less bliss in heaven because
their deeds are disregarded on earth, I pray nevertheless that your
saints and their relics should be more honoured, that people should
worship them more devoutly." The Mother answered and said, "If
you measured out a piece of earth a hundred feet wide and a hundred feet long and sowed it full of wheat, and if the wheat grew so
densely that a fingernail could not be put between one stalk and another, and if each ear of wheat bore a hundred grains—there would

still be more martyrs and confessors[12] in Rome from the time when Peter arrived there humbly until the time when Pope Celestine[13] gave up his proud throne and returned to his solitary life.

"I am speaking of those martyrs and confessors who preached the true faith in opposition to erroneous belief, true humility in opposition to pride, and who were true to their faith in death, or who were willing to die for their faith. Peter and others burned with such love that they would gladly have died for every man if they could have done so; nor could they be reproached by those they preached to, because they cared more for the salvation of souls than for their own lives or renown. Therefore they were judicious and went out cautiously and secretly to win more souls. And yet not all those between Peter and Celestine were good, nor were all evil; there were three different levels: good, better, and best.

"At the first level there were those who thought thus: 'We believe everything that Holy Church tells us to believe. We will cheat no one, and if we have deceived anyone we will put it right. And we wish with our whole hearts to serve God.' Comparable to these were founders of Rome at the time of Romulus who thought according to their own faith: 'We understand and know from the created world that there is one God, maker of all things. We will love him above all else.' And many others thought thus: 'We have heard from the Hebrews that the true God revealed himself to them by evident miracles; therefore, if we knew in whom we could base our faith, we would gladly do the best thing and serve God.' All these people were at the first level. (And those who have received the faith, and live in it in wedlock and other good ways of life as Holy Church has ordained, they are at the good level.)

"But those who give up their own will and their worldly goods for God's sake, and have shown a good example to others by words and works, and who value nothing so much as they do Christ, they were at the better level. And those who gave their bodies up to death were at the best and highest level. But where shall we find the most fervent charity at any of these levels now? It is true that knights, doctors [of divinity], and monks are considered to be at the better and the best levels, for no way of life is stricter than that of a knight if it is lived according to its original ordinance, for if a monk must wear a cowl, a knight must wear a coat of mail, which is much harder. A monk must fight against his own flesh, but a knight must fight against armed enemies, and though a monk may live a life of abstinence, a knight lives in continual fear of death. Therefore, knighthood was not ordained for Christian men to encourage worldly honours and avarice, but to strengthen righteousness and spread the true faith abroad, so knighthood and monastic orders should be at the levels of better and best. But now those at every level have betrayed the state originally ordained for them and charity has turned into avarice. If a man offered them a florin for holding their tongues, they would rather let truth perish than lose the florin."

Then the bride said, "I saw many orchards and gardens on the earth, and many roses and lilies among them. And in a wide place I saw a field which was a hundred paces long and as many wide. Corn had been sown in that field and each grain had multiplied a hundredfold. Then I heard a voice say, 'Rome, Rome, your walls are broken, your gates are unguarded, your sacred vessels have been sold, your wine, your sacrifices, your incense have all been burnt, so no sweet savour comes from your holy place.'"

Then Christ said to his bride, "The earth which you saw symbolizes every place where the Christian faith now exists. The gardens symbolize the places where holy saints gained their crowns, though many which you have not been shown were chosen for God among the pagans and in Jerusalem. The field a hundred paces wide symbolizes Rome; as many were martyred in Rome as in most of the world afterwards, for that place is specially chosen for the love of God. The wheat you saw symbolizes those who gained heaven by punishing their flesh or living an innocent and contrite life; the roses symbolize martyrs, red with the blood they have shed; the lilies symbolize confessors who held and taught the faith.

"But now I can speak to Rome as the prophet once spoke to Jerusalem, which once lived in righteousness and whose princes once loved peace. But now it has turned the colour of rust and its princes are murderers. Would to God, Rome, that you knew how your days are numbered, then you would mourn and not rejoice. Once Rome was bright with the red blood of martyrs and strongly built with the bones of saints; now the gates of Rome are deserted, for those who guarded them have all been led astray by avarice. The walls have been razed, because they pay no heed when the souls of men perish: the clergy and the people, who are the walls, are scattered by lust and bodily pleasures. The holy vessels, that is to say, the sacraments, are now despised and disregarded, for they are given in exchange for worldly favour and riches. The altars are deserted because they who should occupy them lack charity, and even if they are holding God in their hands, their hearts and their love are not for Him, for they are full of avarice. And the holy place, which betokens longing for the sight of God and his bliss, has now turned into the desire of pleasure and worldly vanity.

"And so Rome is now as you have seen it; the altars are deserted because money which should have been spent on the poor and on the worship of God is spent in the taverns. However, you must know that from the time of Peter, who was so humble, until Boniface[14] stepped up onto the proud throne, innumerable souls went to heaven, and there are still some in Rome who love God, and if someone helped them they would cry out to God and he would have mercy on them."

(B) BOOK IV, CHAPTER 22

The Son said to the bride, "If anything could trouble me, I would now say that I regret that I made man. For now man runs of his own will like a beast into the net because he gives in to all his appetites. Nor can the Fiend be blamed nowadays, for man is quicker to sin than the Fiend is to tempt him. Just as coupled hounds run ahead of their leader when they see their prey because they have become accustomed to doing so, so men who have become accustomed to sin run after it faster than the Fiend runs to test and tempt them. This is not surprising, for it is a very long time since the Church of Rome, the highest authority in the world, pleased God by its holiness and its virtuous and exemplary life as it once did. And because of the state of the head, all the other parts are weak; men do not notice how God, richest of all, became poor to teach us that we should despise worldly things and love and long for heavenly things.

"Everyone wishes to follow the example of someone from a poor family who becomes rich with false riches, but few want to imitate the poverty of Christ. But there shall come a ploughman who will not be concerned with the earth or with bodily beauty, nor will he fear the threats of man nor pay any attention to people's importance. He will throw the body down for the worms and send the soul to its rightful place. You must therefore warn my friends to be vigilant and careful, for this will not happen when the world ends—it will happen in these days, and many of those now living will see it. Wives will be widows, children fatherless, and men shall lose all pleasure.

"Nevertheless I will receive anyone who turns humbly to me, and anyone who does the work of righteousness shall gain me. For it is right that the house which the king will enter should be cleaned, and a glass cleaned so that the drink will show through it; the more quickly wheat is separated from chaff the sooner the bread will be made. And then, just as summer follows winter, so I shall send comfort after tribulation to those who are humble and long for heavenly things. And I shall treat some according to the proverb: 'Smite him on the neck and he will run,' for tribulation will make a man exert himself. And I shall treat some according to the saying: 'Open your mouth and I will fill it.' And to some I shall say, 'Come, you simple laymen, and I will give you such words and such wisdom that the greatest speakers will not be able to stand up to you.' And I have done thus in these days. And great men have suddenly passed away because they would not do my bidding."

(C) BOOK IV, CHAPTER 33

The bride complained of the city of Rome in this way: "Ah, Lord, how wretched in body and soul is this city now, which was once so worthy and blessed in both ways. They who should defend it are robbing it, so the house which was once honoured by glorious miracles and the bones of holy saints is now desolate. The temples have been ruined and stripped of their walls, so buildings which were once used by men are now open to cattle and dogs. It has also been ruined spiritually; many good decrees made by holy popes under the inspiration of the Holy Ghost for the glory of God and the salvation of men's souls have been done away with, and many abuses have been put in their place through the prompting of the Fiend. It was ordained by Holy Church that anyone who took holy orders and was given advancement in the Church should live a pure life, be devoted to the service of God, and give a good example both by his own life and by his teaching of others. But now the system is being abused, prebends are given to men who although they are not married are not decent, and live with their concubines in their houses. Priests, deacons, and subdeacons once had a horror of living in corruption, but now some of them are happy to see their mistresses walking around pregnant in public and do not feel ashamed. They can better be called the Fiend's lions than clerks of Holy Church.

"Also, St Benedict and other holy fathers laid down rules, with the permission of popes, and built abbeys where abbots and monks were to serve God day and night. And it was a joy to hear them night and day; many sinners were reformed and turned to a virtuous life through their prayers and good teaching, and souls in purgatory were released from torment by their prayers. And he who best followed the rule was the most esteemed. A monk could be recognised by his habit in those days. But now abbots do not live with their brothers in their abbeys, but round about in castles and manor houses. Therefore religion has perished among them, and their abbeys fall, and the service of God is debased; good men do not delight in them, and they do not reform the weak, and it is not likely that they are much help to the souls in purgatory. And in this city there are some who greet their children with words which acknowledge that they are theirs. It is almost impossible to know them from their habits, for they wear short kirtles and narrow sleeves and have swords hanging at their sides; some even wear armour under their kirtles so that they can pursue their pleasures more boldly.

"Once there were also holy men who gave up great riches for the love of poverty, and they laid down rules for giving up personal possessions. They shunned all kinds of pride and dressed in poor clothing. They shunned the pleasures of the flesh, and they and their brothers were called mendicants; popes confirmed their rules and valued the friars greatly. But now they have turned away from the intentions of Augustine, Dominic, and Francis, who laid down their rules through the inspiration of the Holy Ghost.[15] There are many men who are considered rich who do not have so much money or so many jewels as they have, so people say. Some of them break their rules by having personal possessions, setting no store by poverty. Their habits are as fine as if they were bishops. And St Gregory and others built places where women were enclosed so that they could hardly be seen, but now their gates stand open to priests and lay people alike, sometimes even at night, if the sisters wish. It was also decreed that there should be no payment for hearing confession, but nowadays rich men pay what they like while poor men will not be heard until they have made a bargain with the confessor.

"It was also decreed that lay people should confess, be absolved, and receive communion at least once a year, and monks and those in holy orders more often. A second decree was that those who could not live a chaste life should marry. A third, that all Christian people should fast during Lent, on Ember Days,[16] and on vigils, unless they were excused because of sickness or infirmity. Fourthly, men should rest on holy days. Fifthly, Christians should have nothing to do with lending money at interest. But now, contrary to the first decree, many have died full of years in Rome without ever having been absolved or given communion. Contrary to the second, men leave their wives and take mistresses—some have both wife and mistress at the same time. Contrary to the third, healthy people eat meat in Lent, and few fast at any meal. Fourthly, they do not observe holy days. Contrary to the fifth, Christians are now greedier usurers than Jews. Excommunication was decreed as the remedy for all this, but now men do not care any more about being cursed than they do about being blessed because the priests let them into church even when they are excommunicated, and neither the priests nor other men anywhere avoid being with them as they should do. It is therefore no wonder that I call Rome an unhappy city, for there are many other abuses practised within it, and if they are not remedied, there is no doubt that the Christian faith will perish, unless someone comes who loves God above all else, loves his neighbour as himself, and does away with all these abuses."

(D) BOOK VII, CHAPTER 21

Christ said to the bride, "There was a man called Francis, who turned away from all worldly pride and avarice and lust of the flesh and other vices; his one great longing was to reform his life. This is what he said: 'There is nothing in the world that I would not gladly leave for the love and worship of my lord Jesus Christ, and I will work hard to bring as many people as I can to the same way of life.' This rule begun by Francis was not of man's making, nor did it come from man's wisdom: it was of my own making, according to my own will. Every single word which is written in it was inspired by my spirit, and so were the other rules which my friends began, lived by themselves, and inspired others to live by.

"For a long time Francis's brothers, called Friars Minor, followed this rule devoutly and spiritually according to my intention, and that made the Fiend very resentful. At last, after he had tried hard for a long time to trouble the brothers, he found a cleric who thought as follows: 'I would love to be in a position where people looked up to me, where I had bodily ease, and where I should want for nothing and could save up some money. I shall enter the order of St Francis, and I shall pretend to be very humble and meek and obedient.' And so he entered the Franciscan order, and through his falsehood the Fiend entered him. And then the Fiend thought: 'Just as many were led by Francis to renounce the world and gain heavenly bliss, so shall this bro-ther Enemy, for that shall be what he is called, lead many from humility to pride, from voluntary poverty to avarice, from obedience to self-will and physical indulgence'; so he became enemy of Francis's rule.

"Then the enemy brother thought: 'When others are fasting I shall eat secretly, and when others are silent I shall get a party together and make merry without it being known, but when I can be seen I shall behave humbly so that I am considered holy. Then, according to the rule I must not handle gold and silver or own it, so I shall find a special friend who will keep my gold and silver secretly for me, ready for when I want it. I shall also go to university and study so that lay people and those in my order will revere me, and I shall have horses, silver dishes, precious hangings, and handsome clothes. If anyone asks me why I am doing this, I shall say that I am doing it for the prestige of my order; I shall nevertheless try hard to get a bishopric, and then I would be in a very comfortable position, for I would be my own man and could indulge in all bodily pleasures.'

"Listen to what the Fiend has done to Francis's order; there are many followers of brother Enemy and they mingle with the Franciscan friars. Nevertheless, after their death I shall separate them; Francis's friars I shall judge fit to join him in the bliss of heaven, the others shall go to torment unless they change their lives a great deal before they die. And those friars must understand, and others in religious orders who have property although it is forbidden by their rule, that even if they gave me some of it, their gift would be abominable to me and deserve no thanks. I am better pleased when they keep the vows of poverty of their orders than if they made me a present of all the gold and silver in the world.

"And you must know that you would not have seen and heard this vision if it had not been for that Franciscan friar who loved me and prayed so fervently that he might be given some counsel which would benefit his soul."

MISCELLANEOUS EXTRACTS

(A) BOOK II, CHAPTER 29

John the Baptist said to the bride, "The Lord Jesus has called you
from darkness to light, from filth to purity, from confinement to
freedom; all this obliges you to give great thanks to God. There is a
bird called the magpie which loves her nestlings because the eggs
came out of her own body. She makes herself a nest out of old
things for three reasons: to rest on, for protection from the rain and
to keep dry, and also to care for her nestlings and feed them. When
the young birds are fledged she coaxes them to fly, first with food,
then with her voice, then by flying herself as an example. At first
the fledglings fly after their mother a little above the nest because
they love her; then they fly further according to their strength; finally, with skill and practice, they can fly perfectly.

"This bird represents God, who brings forth every soul like a
mother. There is a nest appointed for every soul, for it is closely
joined to a portion of earth in which God feeds it with good feelings and protects it from evil thoughts, providing a dry shelter from
the rain of evil influences. But the soul should rule the body, set it
easy tasks, and provide reasonably for them; God, like a good
mother, teaches the soul to profit from good works; flying a little
above his nest, he can diligently learn through good and heavenly
thoughts how vile his nest (that is, his body) really is, how fair and
bright are heavenly things.

"Then God cries out thus in a loud voice: 'Whoever follows me
shall have everlasting life, and he that loves me shall not die.' This
voice leads to heaven. And truly he who does not hear this voice is
either ungrateful to God or deaf. The bird, God, teaches man's soul
to fly, setting him an example in his manhood. God's manhood had
two wings: a pure life and good works; man should strive for these
with all his might. But when the fledglings begin to fly they must
beware that ravening beasts do not come near them on earth, for a
bird is not as strong as a beast. They must also beware of birds of
prey, for the fledglings are not as strong as they are, so it is safest for
them to live a secluded life until they are full-grown. They must
also beware of desiring prey themselves, for fear of traps and snares.

"The most dangerous beasts are avarice and worldly pleasures;
the bird, man's soul, must beware of these for they are accustomed

to capture their prey quickly, when a man thinks he has them under control they slip away, and then his will is attacked by a very sharp craving. Beware of the birds of prey, too—that is, pride and the desire for worldly honour; this makes a man long to rise higher and higher, to fly above everyone else and hate those who fly beneath him. The bird must beware of this, choose to live in a humble and secluded place and think that others are as good as he is himself. Thirdly, he must beware of the trap that is worldly joy, for that is indeed a trap. Foolish joy and pleasure make a man unstable of heart, leading to sorrow either before or after death. Therefore, daughter, let your longing for bliss take you out of your nest, and beware of the beasts of avarice, the birds of pride and of foolish joy."

(B) BOOK III, CHAPTER 26

... Then Christ said to the bride, "Now I may complain, for people do not consider me; they are eagerly pursuing their own desires instead of doing my will. You must be constant and meek and not let your heart swell with pride if I reveal to you the dangers faced by others. Nor must you say who they are unless you are told to do so, for I am not telling you about them so that others may judge them, but so that they may improve and change their way of life. I shall reveal the risks they are running so that they may know the righteousness and the mercy of God. Nor should they flee as though they had already been judged: if the worst man who is alive today were to turn to me with contrition and a desire for amendment, I am ready to forgive him. Then he whom I called the worst man yesterday, if he amends I will call him my friend today, and he will be so much my friend that if his contrition is lasting I will not only forgive him his sin, but also the punishment his sin deserved, as I shall explain in the following example. If there were two large drops of quicksilver and they were about to run together, even if there were only a minute space between them, God is so powerful that He could keep them apart. In the same way, if a man were so deeply enmeshed in the works of the Fiend that he were about to perish and lose his immortal soul, even then, if he were contrite and wished to amend his life he would receive my mercy and forgiveness.

"You may ask why, since I am so merciful, I show no mercy to Jews and pagans, some of whom would die for my sake if they were taught my Faith. My answer to this is that I show mercy to all people, Jews and pagans; anyone who hears that their faith is not the true one . . . , or anyone who steadfastly believes that their faith is best and never hears another taught or preached without trying as hard as possible to reach a knowledge of the truth—such men shall receive a more merciful judgement.

"For there are two manners of judgement, one for those who shall be saved, one for those who shall be damned. Judgement on the Christian who shall be damned is merciless; his suffering will last forever, he will dwell in darkness, with his evil will firmly and obstinately set against God. Christians who are saved will enjoy bliss and happiness in the sight of God, joined to Him in love forever. Faithless Christians, Jews, and pagans shall be excluded from their company, however. For even if they did not have the true Faith, they nevertheless had a conscience which showed them that there was one God and only one whom they should have worshipped, and whom they grieved and offended. And those who wished to behave virtuously and who avoided sin shall have less torment than evil Christians. However, they will never enjoy the comfort of heavenly bliss nor the sight of God, for they were never baptised" (because something held them back, something which is hidden from us and only known to God's secret judgement). "But those who have sincerely sought God, not giving up or being stopped by any suffering or fear, or by any loss of wealth or worldly honour, if the difficulties they faced were more than could have been overcome by human weakness, I shall reward them according to their faith and good will, as I did Cornelius and the centurion.[17]

However, there is one kind of ignorance that is associated with wickedness, another with piety and the difficulty of finding the true faith. There are also three baptisms: one of water, one of blood, and one of perfect intent. And God, who knows all hearts and rewards each man according to his desert, pays attention to all these. Not even the smallest good deed goes unrewarded, for I, who was born and brought forth of the Father without beginning and eventually was born into the world of time, know what every being deserves and give to each according to their worth. You are under a great obligation to God that you were born to Christian people and in the time of grace. For there are many who would have wished to have and to see what is offered to those who are Christians, but they did not do so."

(C) BOOK IV, CHAPTER 51

The bride said, "I thought I saw a soul brought to judgement by a knight and a black Ethiopian. And I was told, 'What you see happened to the soul at the moment when it left the body.' This soul stood up above, sorrowful and naked, and it seemed to me that everything which it said was answered from a book. Then the armed man spoke as follows: 'Judge,[18] it is not right that those sins that have been cleansed by confession and absolution should be shamefully recited.' Then it was answered from the book of righteousness, 'There followed neither contrition nor amendment as he had promised and been told to perform; and because he would not when he might, he is now punished.' Then the soul began to weep as though it were going to fall to pieces. But no sound was heard, although the tears could be seen. Then the Judge said, 'Now your conscience makes known the sins which were not amended.' At this the soul cried out loudly, 'Alas that I have not kept God's commandments as I was taught, and that I did not fear God's judgement.' And it was answered from the book, 'Therefore you shall now fear the Fiend.'

"Then the soul, all trembling and quaking, said, 'Because I did not love God, I did little good.' And again he was answered from the book, 'Therefore you shall now be near the Fiend, for he drew you near to him with temptations.' Then the soul said, 'I understand now that everything I did was at the Fiend's instigation.' To which the answer from the book was, 'The Fiend shall reward you with trouble and sorrow.' Then the soul said, 'I clothed my body from head to heel with pride and wore many vain and magnificent garments; some of these I chose for myself, and some were those usually worn by my countrymen. I washed my hands and face not only to make them clean, but so that others should admire me.' And the answer from the book was, 'It is the nature of the Fiend to reward you with torment.' Then the soul said, 'I was ready to speak dishonestly in order to please people, and I desired everything that would not bring me worldly shame.' And the answer from the book was, 'Therefore your tongue will be torn out, your teeth bent, and you shall feel nothing that is pleasing.' Then the soul said, 'It gave me great pleasure that I was followed by many and that they imitated what I did.' And the answer from the book was, 'All those who followed you in sin shall be punished with you, and for each one who followed you, you will suffer a new torture.'

"Then it seemed to me that a band was bound so tightly round his head that his forehead and the back of his head were squashed together, his eyeballs hung down his cheeks, his ears looked as though they were on fire, and his brains burst out of his nostrils and ears; his tongue was hanging out and his teeth clamped together, the bones in his arms were broken and twisted like a rope; the skin was pulled from his head and tied around his neck; his breast and his belly were so dragged together and his ribs so badly broken that one could see his heart and bowels; his shoulders were broken and hung down by his sides, and the broken bones were drawn out like threads from a linen cloth.

"And then the black Ethiopian said, 'Now the sins of this soul are partly punished. And therefore put us together for evermore.' Then the armed knight said, 'O righteous Judge, this soul thought thus at the end of his earthly life: "If God would give me enough time, I would gladly amend my trespasses and never sin again but serve God truly all the days of my life." ' Then it was answered from the book, 'Those who think such thoughts at the end are not doomed to hell. And therefore,' the Judge said, 'through my Passion he shall be saved and attain heaven after he has been purged in purgatory.' "

(D) BOOK IV, CHAPTER 63

The Fiend appeared to the bride with a long belly, and said, "I advise you to stop believing such things as your understanding cannot encompass and to believe those things which your understanding shows you clearly. For you see with your eyes and hear with your bodily ears the breaking of the material bread of the host. You have seen it taken from the place where it was reserved and thrown away, you have seen it being improperly handled and falling to the ground, which I would not allow to happen to myself. Still less will God tolerate such irreverent treatment of himself."[19]

Then the bride said to Christ in his human nature, "Ah, Lord Jesus Christ, I thank you for all your goodness, and for three things especially. First, you pierce my soul with penance and contrition, and with these you clear away my grievous sins. Second, you feed my soul with your love and with thought of your Passion. Third, you comfort all who call on you. Therefore, Lord, have mercy on me and keep me firm in sound faith, for although I deserve to be beguiled, yet I trust that the Fiend will do no more than you will allow him to do, and what you allow is always bearable."

Then Christ said to the Fiend, "I command you to say, so that this bride may hear and understand—when Thomas touched my body after the Resurrection, was it a body or a spirit? If it was a body, how did I come to the disciples when the gates were shut and locked? And if it were as a spirit, how could I be seen and felt?[20] The Fiend answered, "After the Resurrection you were both a body and a spirit, for your body was exalted and you could therefore enter and be wherever you wished." Then Christ said to the Fiend, "When Moses' rod was turned into a serpent,[21] was it a real serpent within and without, or was it only the likeness of a serpent? And the twelve baskets of fragments,[22] were they bread or the likeness of bread?" Then the Fiend said, "The rod became a real serpent and the baskets were filled with real bread; and that was only through your might and your power."

Then Christ said, "Since I am now as mighty as I was then, why may I now not place my real body in the hands of priests, since one needs no more labour or skill from my godhead than the other? And now, father of lies, just as your evil is the greatest of all, so my charity is the highest of all. Therefore if someone through his wickedness burned this sacrament or another defiled it under his feet, neither of them would defile me, who ordain everything as I wish. Therefore, daughter, believe that I am Christ, restorer of life, very truth and endless power. And indeed, if you have complete trust and steadfastly believe that I am truly in the hands of the priest after he has said the words which I ordained, you partake of my real body, true God and true Man, in the form and likeness of bread."

(E) BOOK VI, CHAPTER 31

The bride was shown two fiends, alike in every way, standing before the judgement seat. Their mouths were open as though they were wolves, their eyes burned like fire, their ears hung down like those of hounds; they had long bellies and their hands were like a griffon's feet. There were no joints in their thighs and their feet were cut off in the middle. Then one of them said, "Judge, judge this soul for me, for it is now like me, although you made it like yourself. So judge him to be mine, for we have the same inclinations and the same desires." The Judge said, "How is he like you?" and the fiend answered, "Just as we are alike in our outer appearance, so we are alike in our deeds. We have eyes, but we do not see what is good, we have ears, but we do not hear your praise. Our mouths open to speak words which will grieve you. His hands are like a griffon because he held on to all his profits until his death, and would have held on longer if he had lived longer. His belly is hanging down because his covetousness and his desires were never satisfied. His breast is cold because he does not love you. His thighs have no joints because he did not incline towards you, and neither did I. Our feet are cut off because our love turned away from you to the world and the pleasures of the flesh. Our tastes were alike, for we did not want your sweetness, nor would we taste your goodness. Now, since we are so alike, judge that we should live together."

Then an angel said, "Lord God, I have watched carefully over this soul, and it would not obey me. I therefore left it like a sack which is empty and useless. This soul thought that your words were nothing but lies and your judgement a delusion; he did not think your mercy was worth having. He kept his marriage vows, not for love of you, but for the sensual love he felt for his wife. He also heard Mass and served God, not because he was devout, but for the sake of public opinion, and so that you would give him bodily health and worldly riches and honour and preserve him from misfortune. But, Lord, his rewards in this world were much greater than he ever deserved. You gave him fair children and bodily health and riches, and preserved him from misfortune. Therefore I now believe that his soul is void of all goodness."

Then the fiend said, "Judge, since you have rewarded this soul a hundredfold more than it deserved of you, I ask that it should be judged mine, for he and I have but one mind and one opinion." Then the Judge said, "Let the soul say what it desires." Then the soul said to the Judge, "You are so odious to me that I would rather be in everlasting torment in hell than please you by being in heaven." The fiend said, "That is just what I wish for." The Judge said to the soul, "Your will is your judge and you shall have that judgement."

But then Christ said to me, "This soul is worse than that of the thief;[23] the voices of men cry for vengeance, the angels turn away, and the saints fly from it." The fiend said, "Your sentence must therefore be that we are to dwell together." The Judge said, "If this soul in his dying moments had asked forgiveness with the intention of amendment, he would not have fallen into your hands. But he was evil until the end, so now he shall go with you. Nevertheless if he did any good you must restrain your malice, not punishing him as sorely as you would like to do." And then the fiend rejoiced greatly, and the Judge said to him, "Say, so that this bride may understand, why you are rejoicing so much." The fiend replied, "The more that I punish this soul, the more I am punished. But because you bought it with your blood and sacrificed yourself for it, and because I have enticed it to follow me and to leave you, who loved it so dearly, that is why I am rejoicing."

The Judge said, "Your wickedness is great, but look around you and see." And there was a soul going up to heaven, as bright as a star. And then Christ said to the fiend, "What would you give to have that soul at your mercy?" The fiend answered, "All the souls that are in hell. And yet if there were a pillar made of the points of swords going up from earth to heaven, I would climb to the top of it if I could get that soul in my power." Then Christ said, "Your wickedness is great; however, if it were possible, I would still die again for the sake of one soul." And then Christ said to that soul, "Come, my love, to the bliss for which you have longed. I shall give you myself, who am all goodness."

(f) BOOK VI, CHAPTERS 84–85
A priest was singing his first Mass in an abbey one Whit Sunday[24] and at the moment of the elevation the bride saw a fire descending from heaven onto the altar, and in the priest's hands she saw a lamb with the face of a man and all burning. And a voice said to her, "This is how the Holy Ghost descended to the apostles." And again she saw in the priest's hand a wonderfully beautiful child, which said, "Blessed are all of you who believe in the true Faith, and I shall come to judge those who do not."

It happened that the bride was sitting at table with a bishop and other great lords, and she smelled an amazing stench, like rotten fish, which none could smell but she. And a man came in who was excommunicated, but because he was a great man he took no notice. Then Christ said to the bride, "This is the stench of a man who has been cursed, and it is as perilous to a man's soul as stinking fish is to the body. You must therefore tell the bishop to punish such men, so that they do not defile others."

(G) BOOK VII, CHAPTER 14

The Mother showed the bride in bodily likeness what was done to the soul of her son.[25] She saw in her spirit a fair field, and there she saw Jesus sitting on a throne, like a crowned king, and on every side of him there was a great company of saints and angels, and the Mother of mercy was standing near and listening to his judgement. And there was a soul standing before the Judge, trembling with fear and as naked as a new-born child. It was also blind (but it had a very clear inward understanding of what was said in the judgement). To the right of the soul there stood an angel, and to the left a fiend, but neither of them was next to it.

Then the fiend cried out to the Judge, "Almighty, I want to lodge a complaint against your Mother, Lady of us all, that she has wronged me over this soul; for she would not let me come near it, and by rights I should have presented it." Then the Mother said, "You fiend, this soul was not yours, but mine, and I therefore present it to the Judge. For when this soul was in the body it loved me so well that no worldly pleasure could interfere with the gladness he felt in his heart that I was the mother of God; and because God gave me that grace, he loved God with all his heart. Because of this love for me and my Son, my Son promised me as a favour that neither you nor any other fiend should come near his soul at his passing." Then the fiend said, "I have written down his sins, for as soon as he reached years of discretion and understood sin, he yielded to worldly pride and the desires of the flesh." Then the angel answered and said, "As soon as his mother saw that he was inclined to sin, she urged him to works of mercy, and prayed most earnestly that God should have mercy on him and should never let his soul be lost. And so, through his mother's prayers, he began to fear God, so that as often as he fell into sin, he rose again by confession and absolution."

Then the fiend said, "I will repeat his sins." And he looked for his petition, and it had gone. And then the fiend cried, "Alas, I can neither find the sins nor remember the time when he sinned." Then the angel said, "It is his mother's prayers and her tears and her deep sorrow for this sin that have done this, because they gave him contrition for his sins and grace to obtain absolution for them: and that is why you have forgotten them."

Then the fiend said, "Nevertheless, there are many reasons why he should be mine: he was slain in God's service and did not live to do the good he might have done." Then the fiend looked and it had all vanished, and he cried, "Alas"—it was all lost. Then the angel said, "His mother's tears have done this."

The fiend said, "I still have all his venial sins," and the angel replied, "He asked leave and left his country on pilgrimage, and has completed his undertaking, and he left his friends and endured great hardship. So he was given indulgence and pardon when he visited holy places, and he tried hard to make amends to God for his sin. And this was through the prayers of his mother, who laboured in prayer a great deal for him."

Then the fiend said, "There is still one thing: he profited from wrongdoing." The angel said, "His mother has atoned for that by giving alms; and he, too, sought throughout the city to make amends to all he had harmed. And his heirs will make amends for anything which remains undone."

Then the fiend said, "He should still be punished, however, for he did not do so much good in his life as he might have done." The angel replied, "It is written that *to him who asks it shall be given, and to him that knocks it shall be opened;*[26] for more than thirty years his mother has begged and prayed with many tears to God for him, asking that he should be given grace to serve Him truly. And this knight had such an ardent love of God that the only life he wanted was to serve God and to please him, and this God granted him. And this fulfilled all that was needed for him to go to heaven. And because of the great desire that he had to go on pilgrimage to Jerusalem, and because he was very anxious to help bring the Holy Land into the hands of Christian men so that the Holy Sepulchre should be honoured—with the help of the Mother of mercy, this has made up for all the virtue he lacked, and suffices to bring him to bliss. Therefore you, fiend, have no right to him." Then the fiend said, "May the old woman who wept so many tears be cursed."

And then the Judge, Christ himself, said, "Go hence, you fiend!" And then he said to the knight, "Come to me, my loved one." Then the bride said, "God be blessed." And the angel said to her, "This revelation is not only for you, but so that God's friends may know how much he loves them, and what he will do for the tears and prayers of his friends. And you must know that your son would not have been granted this grace if you had not taught him early to love God."

Julian of Norwich

EXTRACTS FROM *REVELATIONS OF DIVINE LOVE* (SHORT TEXT)

This is a vision shown, through God's goodness, to a devout woman, and her name is Julian, and she is a recluse at Norwich and is still alive in the year of our Lord 1413; in this vision there are many comforting and very moving words for all those who wish to be lovers of Christ.

(A) CHAPTER 1

I asked for three graces of God's gift. The first was vivid perception of Christ's Passion, the second was bodily sickness, and the third was for God to give me three wounds. I thought of the first as I was meditating: it seemed to me that I could feel the Passion of Christ strongly, but yet I longed by God's grace to feel it more intensely. I thought how I wished I had been there at the crucifixion with Mary Magdalene and with others who were Christ's dear friends, that I might have seen in the flesh the Passion of our Lord which he suffered for me, so that I could have suffered with him as others did who loved him. Nevertheless, I firmly believed in all the torments of Christ as Holy Church reveals and teaches them, and also in the paintings of crucifixes that are made by God's grace in the likeness of Christ's Passion, according to the teaching of Holy Church, as far as human imagination can reach.

In spite of all this true faith, I longed to be shown him in the flesh so that I might have more knowledge of our Lord and Saviour's bodily suffering and of our Lady's fellow-suffering and that of all his true friends who have believed in his pain then and since; I wanted to be one of them and suffer with him. I never wished for any other sight or showing of God until my soul left my body, for I faithfully trusted that I would be saved, and my intention was this:

that afterwards, because of the showing, I would have a truer perception of Christ's Passion.

As for the second gift, there came to me with contrition, freely, without any effort on my part, a strong wish to have of God's gift a bodily sickness. And I wanted this bodily sickness to be to the death, so that I might in that sickness receive all the rites of Holy Church, that I might myself believe I was dying and that everyone who saw me might believe the same, for I wanted no hopes of fleshly or earthly life. I longed to have in this sickness every kind of suffering both of body and soul that I would experience if I died, with all the terror and turmoil of the fiends,[1] and all other kinds of torment, except for actually giving up the ghost, because I hoped that it might be to my benefit when I died, for I longed to be soon with my God.

I longed for these two things—the Passion and the sickness—with one reservation, for it seemed to me that they went beyond the common course of prayers; and therefore I said, "Lord, you know what I would have. If it is your will that I should have it, grant it to me. And if it is not your will, good Lord, do not be displeased, for I only want what you want." I asked for this sickness in my youth, to have it when I was thirty years old.

As for the third gift, I heard a man of Holy Church tell the story of St Cecilia; from his description I understood that she received three sword wounds in the neck from which she slowly and painfully died.[2] Moved by this I conceived a great longing, praying our Lord God that he would grant me three wounds in my lifetime: that is to say, the wound of contrition, the wound of compassion, and the wound of an earnest longing for God. Just as I asked for the other two with a reservation, so I asked for the third with no reservation. The first two of the longings just mentioned passed from my mind, and the third stayed with me continually.

CHAPTER 2

And when I was thirty and a half years old, God sent me a bodily sickness in which I lay for three days and three nights; and on the fourth night I received all the rites of Holy Church and did not believe that I would live until morning. And after this I lingered on for two days and two nights. And on the third night I often thought that I was dying, and so did those who were with me. But at this time I was very sorry and reluctant to die, not because there was anything on earth that I wanted to live for, nor because I feared anything, for I trusted in God, but because I wanted to live so as to love God better and for longer, so that through the grace of longer life I might know and love God better in the bliss of heaven. For it seemed to me that all the short time I could live here was as nothing compared with that heavenly bliss. So I thought, "My good Lord, may my ceasing to live be to your glory!" And I was answered in my reason, and by the pains I felt, that I was dying. And I fully accepted the will of God with all the will of my heart.

So I endured till day, and by then my body was dead to all sensation from the waist down. Then I felt I wanted to be in a sitting position, leaning with my head back against the bedding, so that my heart could be more freely at God's disposition, and so that I could think of God while I was still alive; and those who were with me sent for the parson, my parish priest, to be present at my death. He came, and a boy with him, and brought a cross, and by the time he came my eyes were fixed and I could not speak. The parson set the cross before my face and said, "Daughter, I have brought you the image of your Saviour. Look upon it and be comforted, in reverence to him that died for you and me." It seemed to me that I was well as I was, for my eyes were looking fixedly upwards into heaven, where I trusted that I was going. But nevertheless I consented to fix my eyes on the face of the crucifix if I could, so as to be able to do so for longer until the moment of my death; because I thought that I might be able to bear looking straight ahead for longer than I could manage to look upwards. After this my sight began to fail and the room was dim all around me, as dark as if it had been night, except that in the image of the cross an ordinary, household light remained—I could not understand how. Everything except the cross was ugly to me, as if crowded with fiends. After this I felt as if the upper part of my body was beginning to die. My hands fell down on either side, and my head settled down sideways for weakness. The greatest pain that I felt was shortness of breath and failing of life. Then I truly believed that I was at the point of death. And at this moment all my suffering suddenly left me, and I was as completely well, especially in the upper part of my body, as ever I was before or after. I marvelled at this change, for it seemed to me a mysterious work of God, not a natural one. And yet, although I felt comfortable, I still did not expect to live, nor did feeling more comfortable comfort me entirely, for I felt that I would rather have been released from this world, for in my heart I was willing to die.

CHAPTER 3

And it suddenly occurred to me that I should entreat our Lord graciously to give me the second wound, so that he would fill my whole body with remembrance of the feeling of his blessed Passion, as I had prayed before; for I wanted his pains to be my pains, with compassion, and then longing for God. Yet in this I never asked for a bodily sight or any kind of showing of God, but for fellow-suffering, such as it seemed to me a naturally kind soul might feel for our Lord Jesus, who was willing to become a mortal man for love. I wanted to suffer with him, while living in my mortal body, as God would give me grace.

And I suddenly saw the red blood trickling down from under the crown of thorns, all hot, freshly, plentifully, and vividly, just as I imagined it was at the moment when the crown of thorns was thrust onto his blessed head—he who was both God and man, the same who suffered for me. I believed truly and strongly that it was he himself who showed me this, without any intermediary, and then I said, *Benedicite dominus!*[3] Because I meant this with such deep veneration, I said it in a very loud voice; and I was astounded, feeling wonder and admiration that he was willing to be so familiar with a sinful being living in this wretched flesh. I supposed at that time that our Lord Jesus of his courteous love would show me comfort before the time of my temptation. For I thought it might well be, by God's permission and under his protection, that I would be tempted by fiends before I died. With this sight of the blessed Passion, along with the Godhead that I saw in my mind, I saw that I, yes, and every creature living that would be saved, could have strength to resist all the fiends of hell and all spiritual enemies.

CHAPTER 4

And at the same time that I saw this bodily sight, our Lord showed me a spiritual vision of his familiar love. I saw that for us he is everything that is good and comforting and helpful. He is our clothing, wrapping and enveloping us for love, embracing us and guiding us in all things, hanging about us in tender love, so that he can never leave us. And so in this vision, as I understand it, I saw truly that he is everything that is good for us.

And in this vision he showed me a little thing, the size of a hazel nut, lying in the palm of my hand, and to my mind's eye it was as round as any ball. I looked at it and thought, "What can this be?" And the answer came to me, "It is all that is made." I wondered how it could last, for it was so small I thought it might suddenly disappear. And the answer in my mind was, "It lasts and will last for ever because God loves it; and in the same way everything exists through the love of God." In this little thing I saw three attributes: the first is that God made it, the second is that he loves it, the third is that God cares for it. But what does that mean to me? Truly, the maker, the lover, the carer; for until I become one substance with him, I can never have love, rest or true bliss; that is to say, until I am so bound to him that there may be no created thing between my God and me. And who shall do this deed? Truly, himself, by his mercy and his grace, for he has made me and blessedly restored me to that end.

Then God brought our Lady into my mind. I saw her spiritually in bodily likeness, a meek and simple maid, young of age, in the same bodily form as when she conceived. God also showed me part of the wisdom and truth of her soul so that I understood with what reverence she beheld her God who is her maker, and how reverently she marvelled that he chose to be born of her, a simple creature of his own making. For what made her marvel was that he who was her Maker chose to be born of the creature he had made. And the wisdom of her faithfulness, and knowledge of the greatness of her Maker and the littleness of her who was made, moved her to say very humbly to the angel Gabriel, *Behold, the handmaid of the Lord* [Lk 1:38]. With this sight I really understood that she is greater in worthiness and fullness of grace than all that God made below her; for nothing that is made is above her except the blessed Manhood of Christ. This little thing that is made that is below our Lady St Mary, God showed it to me as small as if it had been a hazel nut. It was so small I thought it might have disappeared.

In this blessed revelation God showed me three nothings.[4] Of these nothings this was the first I was shown, and all men and women who wish to lead the contemplative life need to have knowledge of it: they should choose to set at nothing everything that is made so as to have the love of God who is unmade. This is why those who choose to occupy themselves with earthly business and are always pursuing worldly success have nothing here of God in their hearts and souls: because they love and seek their rest in this little thing where there is no rest, and know nothing of God, who is almighty, all wise and all good, for he is true rest. God wishes to be known, and is pleased that we should rest in him; for all that is below him does nothing to satisfy us. And this is why, until all that is made seems as nothing, no soul can be at rest. When a soul sets all at nothing for love, to have him who is everything that is good, then it is able to receive spiritual rest.

CHAPTER 5

And during the time that our Lord was showing in spiritual sight what I have just described, the bodily sight of the plentiful bleeding from Christ's head remained, and as long as I could see this sight I kept saying, *Benedicite dominus*. In this first showing from our Lord I saw six things in my understanding: the first is the signs of Christ's blessed Passion and the plentiful shedding of his precious blood; the second is the Maiden who is his beloved mother; the third is the blessed Godhead that ever was, is, and ever shall be, almighty, all wisdom and all love. The fourth is all that he has made; it is vast and wide, fair and good, but it looked so small to me because I saw it in the presence of him that is Maker of all things; to a soul that sees the Maker of all, all that is made seems very small. The fifth thing I understood is that he made everything that is made for love; and the same love sustains everything, and shall do so for ever, as has been said before. The sixth is that God is everything that is good, and the goodness that is in everything is God. And all these our Lord showed me in the first vision, and gave me time and space to contemplate it. And when the bodily vision stopped, the spiritual vision remained in my understanding. And I waited with reverent fear, rejoicing in what I saw, and longing, as far as I dared, to see more if it was his will, or else to see the same vision for longer.

CHAPTER 6

All that I saw concerning myself, I mean to be applied to all my fellow Christians, for I am taught by our Lord's spiritual showing that this is what he means. And therefore I beg you all for God's sake and advise you all for your own advantage that you stop paying attention to the poor, worldly, sinful creature to whom this vision was shown, and eagerly, attentively, lovingly and humbly contemplate God, who in his gracious love and in his eternal goodness wanted the vision to be generally known to comfort us all. And you who hear and see this vision and this teaching, which come from Jesus Christ to edify your souls, it is God's will and my desire that you should receive it with joy and pleasure as great as if Jesus had shown it to you as he did to me.

I am not good because of the showing, unless I love God better, and so may and should everyone that sees it and hears it with good will and true intention; and so my desire is that it should bring everyone the same advantage that I desired for myself, and this is how God moved me the first time I saw it. For it is universal and addressed to all because we are all one, and I am sure I saw it for the advantage of many others. Indeed it was not shown to me because God loved me better than the lowest soul that is in a state of grace, for I am sure that there are very many who never had a showing or vision, but only the normal teaching of Holy Church, and who love God better than I do. For if I look solely at myself, I am really nothing; but as one of mankind in general, I am in oneness of love with all my fellow Christians; for upon this oneness of love depends the life of all who shall be saved; for God is all that is good, and God has made all that is made, and God loves all that he has made.

And if any man or woman ceases to love any of his fellow Christians, then he loves none, for he does not love all; and so at that moment he is not saved, for he is not at peace; and he who loves all his fellow Christians loves all that is; for in those who shall be saved, all is included: that is all that is made and the Maker of all; for in man is God, and so in man is all. And he who loves all his fellow Christians in this way, he loves all; and he who loves in this way is saved. And thus I wish to love, and thus I love, and thus I am saved. (I am speaking in the person of my fellow Christians.) And the more I love with this kind of love while I am here, the more like I am to the bliss that I shall have in heaven without end, which is God, who in his endless love was willing to become our brother and suffer for us. And I am sure that whoever looks at it in this way will be truly taught and greatly comforted if he needs comfort.

But God forbid that you should say or assume that I am a teacher, for that is not what I mean, nor did I ever mean it; for I am a woman, ignorant, weak, and frail. But I know well that I have received what I say from him who is the supreme teacher. But in truth, I am moved to tell you about it by love, for I wish God to be known and my fellow Christians helped, as I wish to be helped myself, so that sin shall be more hated and God more loved. Just because I am a woman, must I therefore believe that I must not tell you about the goodness of God, when I saw at the same time both his goodness and his wish that it should be known? And you will see that clearly in the chapters which follow, if they are well and truly understood. Then you must quickly forget me, a paltry creature, you must not let me hinder you, but look directly at Jesus, who is teacher of all. I speak of those who will be saved, for at this time God showed me no others. But in all things I believe what Holy Church teaches, for in all things I saw this blessed showing of our Lord as one who is in the presence of God, and I never perceived anything in it that bewilders me or keeps me from the true teaching of Holy Church.

CHAPTER 7

All this blessed teaching of our Lord God was shown me in three parts: that is, by bodily sight, and by words formed in my understanding, and by spiritual sight. But I neither can nor may show you the spiritual vision as openly or as fully as I would like to. But I trust that our Lord God almighty will, out of his own goodness and love for you, make you receive it more spiritually and more sweetly than I can or may tell you; and so may it be, for we are all one in love. And in all this I was much moved with love for my fellow Christians, wishing that they might see and know what I was seeing; I wanted it to comfort them all as it did me, for the vision was shown for everyone and not for any one particular person. And what comforted me most in the vision was that our Lord is so familiar and courteous. And this was what gave me most happiness and the strongest sense of spiritual safety. Then I said to the people who were with me, "For me, today is the Day of Judgment." And I said this because I thought I was dying; for on the day that someone dies, he receives his eternal judgment. I said this because I wanted them to love God better and set a lower value on the vanity of the world, to remind them that life is short, as they might see by my example; for all this time I thought I was dying.

EXTRACTS FROM *REVELATIONS OF DIVINE LOVE* (LONG TEXT)

(B) *CHAPTER 10: THE THIRD REVELATION IS OF THE DISCOLOURING OF CHRIST'S FACE, OF OUR REDEMPTION, AND THE DISCOLOURING OF THE VERNICLE;[5] AND HOW GOD WANTS US TO SEEK HIM EAGERLY, RESTING IN HIM STEADFASTLY AND TRUSTING HIM GREATLY.*

And after this I saw with my bodily sight in the face of Christ on the crucifix which hung before me, which I was looking at continuously, a part of his Passion: contempt and spitting, dirt and blows, and many lingering pains, more than I can tell, and frequent changes of colour. And once I saw how half his face, beginning at the ear, was covered in dry blood until it reached the middle of his face, and after that the other half was covered in the same way, and meanwhile the first part was as before. I saw this bodily, in distress and darkness, and I wished for better bodily sight to see it more clearly. And I was answered in my reason, "If God wants to show you more, he will be your light. You need no light but him." For I saw him and sought him; for we are now so blind and so unwise that we never seek God until out of his goodness he shows himself to us, and if he graciously lets us see something of himself, then we are moved by the same grace to seek with a great longing to see him more fully; and thus I saw him and I sought him, I had him and I wanted him. And it seems to me that this is, or should be, our usual way of proceeding.

At one moment my consciousness was taken down on to the sea bed, and there I saw green hills and valleys, looking as though they were covered in moss, with seaweed and sand.[6] Then I understood this: that if a man or a woman were under the wide waters, if he could see God (and God is constantly with us) he would be safe, body and soul, and be unharmed, and furthermore, he would have more joy and comfort than words can say. For God wants us to believe that we can see him constantly, even though we think we see very little of him, and if we believe this he makes us grow in grace continually; for he wants to be seen and he wants to be sought; he wants to be waited for and he wants to be trusted.

This second showing was so humble and so small and so simple that my spirits were greatly troubled as I saw it, grieving and fearing and longing; and I doubted for some time whether it was a showing. And then several times our good Lord let me see more clearly so that I truly understood that it was indeed a showing. It was the form and likeness of the foul, dead covering which our fair, bright, blessed Lord bore when he took on human flesh for our sins. It made me think of the holy vernicle at Rome, on which he printed his own sacred face during his cruel Passion, willingly going to his death, and often changing colour. Many marvel how it may be, the brownness and blackness, the pitifulness and the leanness of this image, considering that he printed it with his sacred face, which is the fairness of heaven, the flower of earth, and fruit of the Virgin's womb. Then how could this image be so discoloured and so far from fair? I would like to say how, by the grace of God, I understand this. We know through our faith, and believe by the preaching and teaching of Holy Church, that the Holy Trinity made mankind in his image and in his likeness. In the same way we know that when man fell so deeply and so wretchedly through sin, the only help through whom man could be restored was he who made man. And he who made man for love, by that same love would restore man to the same blessed state, or to one more blessed. And just as we were made like the Trinity when we were first made, our Maker wanted us to be like Jesus Christ our Saviour, in heaven without end, by the miracle of our re-making. Then between these two he wanted, loving and honouring man, to make himself as much like man in this mortal life, in our vileness and our wretchedness, as a man without guilt might be. So this means what was said before: it was the image and likeness of our vile, black, mortal covering which hid our fair, bright, blessed Lord.

But I can boldly say with great confidence, and we ought to believe, that never was man so fair as he until the time his fair colour was changed by his trouble and sorrow and his suffering and final agony. This is spoken of in the eighth revelation, where more is said about the same image. And when I mentioned the vernicle in Rome, I mean that it moves with various changes of colour and expression, sometimes looking more cheerful and animated, sometimes more wretched and deathly, as may be seen in the eighth revelation.

And this vision instructed my understanding that it pleases God a great deal if the soul never ceases to search; for the soul can do no more than seek, suffer and trust, and souls that do this are moved by the Holy Ghost; and the splendour of having found God comes by his special grace when it is his will. Seeking with faith, hope and

love pleases our Lord, and finding pleases the soul and fills it with
joy. And thus my understanding was taught that seeking is as good
as finding for the time that our soul is allowed to labour. It is God's
wish that we seek to behold him, for then he will graciously show
himself to us when he wills. And God himself will teach how a soul
may behold him, and that most honours him and benefits you, leading you to receive the greatest humility and strength by means of
the grace and guidance of the Holy Ghost; for if a soul attaches
itself solely to God with true trust, either by seeking him or by
beholding him, it is honouring him as much as possible, it seems
to me.

There are two actions that may be seen in this vision: one is seeking, the other is beholding. The seeking is within everyone's reach;
everyone *may* have it by God's grace, and *ought* to have it by the
Church's wisdom and teaching. It is God's wish that we should observe three things in our seeking: the first is that our search should
be committed and diligent, with no laziness, as it may be through
his grace, glad and cheerful without unreasonable depression and
unprofitable misery. The second is that for his love we await him
steadfastly, without grumbling and struggling against him, until our
life's end, for life lasts only a short while. The third is that we
should trust him utterly with sure and certain faith, for that is what
he wishes. We know that he will appear suddenly and joyfully to all
those that love him; for he works secretly, and he wishes to be perceived, and his appearance will be very sudden; and he wants us
to trust him, for he is most kind and approachable—blessed may
he be! . . .

(C) *CHAPTER 26: THE TWELFTH REVELATION IS THAT THE
LORD OUR GOD IS SUPREME BEING.*
And after this our Lord showed himself in even greater glory, it
seemed to me, than when I saw him before, and from this revelation
I learned that our soul will never rest until it comes to him knowing
that he is the fullness of joy, of everyday and princely blessedness
and the only true life. Our Lord Jesus said repeatedly, "It is I, it is I;
it is I who am highest; it is I you love; it is I who delight you; it is I
you serve; it is I you long for; it is I you desire; it is I who am your
purpose; it is I who am all; it is I that Holy Church preaches and
teaches you; it is I who showed myself to you here." The number of
these utterances went beyond my wit and all my understanding and

all my powers, and it is supreme, it seems to me, for there is included within it—I cannot tell how much; but the joy that I perceived as they were revealed surpasses all that the heart may wish and the soul may desire; and therefore the utterances are not fully explained here, but, according to the powers of understanding and loving which are given by the grace of God, may everyone receive them as our Lord intended.

CHAPTER 27: THE THIRTEENTH REVELATION IS THAT OUR LORD GOD WISHES US TO HOLD IN HIGH ACCOUNT ALL THAT HE HAS DONE IN MAKING ALL THINGS WITH SUCH NOBILITY; AND OF OTHER THINGS; AND HOW SIN CAN ONLY BE RECOGNIZED BY SUFFERING.

After this, our Lord reminded me of the longing I had had for him;[7] and I saw that nothing kept me from him but sin, and I saw that this is so with all of us. And I thought that if sin had never existed, we should all have been pure and like himself, as God made us; and so I had often wondered before now in my folly why, in his great foreseeing wisdom, God had not prevented the beginning of sin; for then, I thought, all would have been well. I ought certainly to have abandoned these thoughts, but nevertheless I grieved and sorrowed over the question with no reason or judgment. But Jesus, who in this vision informed me of all that I needed to know, answered with this assurance: "Sin is befitting, but all shall be well, and all shall be well, and all manner of things shall be well."

With this bare word "sin" our Lord brought to my mind the whole extent of all that is not good, and the shameful scorn and the utter humiliation that he bore for us in this life, and his dying, and all the pains and sufferings of all his creatures, both in body and spirit—for we are all to some extent brought to nothing and shall be brought to nothing as our master Jesus was, until we are fully purged: that is to say until our mortal flesh is brought completely to nothing, and all those of our inward feelings which are not truly good. He gave me insight into these things, along with all pains that ever were and ever shall be; and compared with these I realize that Christ's Passion was the greatest pain and went beyond them all. And all this was shown in a flash, and quickly changed into comfort; for our good Lord did not want the soul to be afraid of this ugly sight.

But I did not see sin; for I believe it has no sort of substance nor portion of being, nor could it be recognized were it not for the suffering which it causes. And this suffering seems to me to be something transient, for it purges us and makes us know ourselves and pray for mercy; for the Passion of our Lord supports us against all this, and that is his blessed will. And because of the tender love which our good Lord feels for all who shall be saved, he supports us willingly and sweetly, meaning this: "It is true that sin is the cause of all this suffering, but all shall be well, and all shall be well, and all manner of things shall be well." These words were said very tenderly, with no suggestion that I or anyone who will be saved was being blamed. It would therefore be very strange to blame or wonder at God because of my sin, since he does not blame me for sinning.

And in these same words I saw a marvellous great mystery hidden in God, a mystery which he will make openly known to us in heaven; in which knowledge we shall truly see the reason why he allowed sin to exist; and seeing this we shall rejoice eternally in our Lord God.

CHAPTER 28: *HOW THE CHILDREN OF SALVATION SHALL BE SHAKEN BY SORROWS, BUT CHRIST REJOICES IN COMPASSION; AND A REMEDY FOR TRIBULATION.*

Thus I saw how Christ feels compassion for us because of sin. And just as I was earlier filled with suffering and compassion at the Passion of Christ, so was I now also partly filled with compassion for all my fellow Christians, for those well-beloved people who shall be saved; that is to say, God's servants, Holy Church, will be shaken in sorrows and anguish and tribulation in this world, as men shake a cloth in the wind. And to this God answered as follows: "I shall make some great thing out of this in heaven, something eternally worthy and everlastingly joyful."

Yes, I saw as far as this—that our Lord rejoices in the tribulations of his servants with pity and compassion; in order to bring to bliss each person that he loves he lays on each of them something which in his sight is no cause of blame, something for which they are blamed and despised in this world, scorned, violently treated and cast out; and this he does to prevent the damage that would be done to them by the pomp and vainglory of this wretched life, and to prepare their path to heaven, and to raise them to his bliss which lasts without end; for he says, "I shall shatter you for your vain passions and your vicious pride; and after that I shall gather you together and make you humble and meek, pure and holy, by uniting you with me." And then I saw that whenever a man feels kind compassion with love for his fellow Christian, it is Christ within him.

That same humiliation which was revealed in his Passion was revealed again here in this compassion, in which there were two ways of understanding our Lord's meaning: one was the bliss to which we are bought and in which he will rejoice, the other is for strength in our suffering; for he wants us to know that it will all be turned into glory and profit by virtue of his Passion, and to know we do not suffer alone, but with him, recognizing that we are grounded in him, and he wants us to see that his pain and his humiliation go so far beyond all that we may suffer that it cannot be fully conceived. And consideration of this will save us from grumbling and despair as we experience suffering; and if we truly see that our sin deserves it, his love will nevertheless excuse us, and in his great kindness he takes away all our blame and watches over us with compassion and pity, like children, not hateful but innocent.

CHAPTER 29: ADAM'S SIN WAS THE GREATEST OF ALL, BUT THE ATONEMENT FOR IT IS MORE PLEASING TO GOD THAN THE SIN WAS EVER HARMFUL.

But I paused at this, contemplating these things in general, sad and grieving, and in my thought I said to our Lord with great reverence, "Ah, my good Lord, how could all be well, given the great harm that has been done to humankind by sin?" And here I prayed, as much as I dared, for some clearer explanation to ease my mind over this. And our blessed Lord answered most compassionately and in a very friendly way, and showed that Adam's sin was the greatest harm that ever was done, or ever shall be, until the end of the world; and he also showed that this is publicly acknowledged through all Holy Church on earth. Furthermore he taught that I should consider the glorious atonement; for this atonement is incomparably more pleasing to God and more glorious in saving mankind than Adam's sin was ever harmful.

So what our blessed Lord's teaching means is that we should take heed of the following: "Since I have turned the greatest possible harm into good, it is my will that you should know from this that I shall turn all lesser evil into good." . . .

*(D) Chapter 32: How everything shall be well, and
Scripture fulfilled; and we must remain steadfast in
the faith of Holy Church, as Christ desires.*

At one time our good Lord said, "All manner of things shall be
well"; and at another time he said, "You shall see for yourself that
all manner of things shall be well"; and the soul understood these
two sayings differently. On the one hand he wants us to know that
he does not only concern himself with great and noble things, but
also with small, humble and simple things, with both one and the
other; and this is what he means when he says, "All manner of
things shall be well"; for he wants us to know that the smallest
thing shall not be forgotten. But another thing understood is this:
deeds are done which appear so evil to us and people suffer such
terrible evils that it does not seem as though any good will ever
come of them; and we consider this, sorrowing and grieving over it
so that we cannot find peace in the blessed contemplation of God as
we should do; and this is why: our reasoning powers are so blind
now, so humble and so simple, that we cannot know the high, marvellous wisdom, the might and the goodness of the Holy Trinity.
And this is what he means where he says, "You shall see for yourself that all manner of things shall be well," as if he said, "Pay attention to this now, faithfully and confidently, and at the end of time
you will truly see it in the fullness of joy." And thus I understand
the five sayings mentioned above—"I may make all things well,"
etc.—as a powerful and comforting pledge for all the works of our
Lord God which are to come.

It appears to me that there is a deed which the Holy Trinity shall
do on the last day, and when that deed shall be done and how it
shall be done is unknown to all creatures under Christ, and shall be
until it has been done. And he wants us to know this because he
wants us to feel more ease in our souls and more at peace in love,
rejoicing in him and no longer considering all the tumults which
might keep us from the truth. This is the great deed ordained by our
Lord God from eternity, treasured up and hidden in his blessed
breast, only known to himself, and by this deed he shall make all
things well; for just as the Holy Trinity made all things from nothing, so the Holy Trinity shall make all well that is not well.

And I wondered greatly at this revelation, and considered our
faith, wondering as follows: our faith is grounded in God's word,

and it is part of our faith that we should believe that God's word will be kept in all things; and one point of our faith is that many shall be damned—like the angels who fell out of heaven from pride, who are now fiends, and men on earth who die outside the faith of Holy Church, that is, those who are heathens, and also any man who has received Christianity and lives an unChristian life and so dies excluded from the love of God. Holy Church teaches me to believe that all these shall be condemned everlastingly to hell. And given all this, I thought it impossible that all manner of things should be well, as our Lord revealed at this time. And I received no other answer in showing from our Lord God but this: "What is impossible to you is not impossible to me. I shall keep my word in all things and I shall make all things well."

Thus I was taught by the grace of God that I should steadfastly remain in the faith, as I had previously understood, and at the same time that I should firmly believe that all things should be well as our Lord God revealed on the same occasion. For this is the great deed that our Lord shall do, the deed by which he will keep his word in all things and shall make all well that is not well. And how the deed shall be done there is no creature under Christ that knows or shall know until it is done, so far as I understood our Lord's meaning at this time.

CHAPTER 33: ALL DAMNED SOULS ARE CONDEMNED LIKE THE DEVIL IN THE SIGHT OF GOD; AND THESE REVELATIONS DO NOT CANCEL OUT THE FAITH OF HOLY CHURCH, BUT STRENGTHEN IT; AND THE MORE ANXIOUS WE ARE TO KNOW GOD'S MYSTERIES, THE LESS WE KNOW.

And yet in all this I desired, as far as I dared, to have a complete vision of hell and purgatory. But it was not my intention to put to the test anything which belongs to our faith—for I firmly believed that hell and purgatory have the purpose taught by Holy Church—but my idea was that I might have seen them so that I could learn everything belonging to my faith that could help me to live to the greater glory of God and to my greater spiritual profit. But as for this desire, I could learn nothing about it, except what I have previously said in the fifth showing, where I saw that the Devil is scorned by God and endlessly damned; and, seeing this, I understood that all beings who live their lives in a state of sin, like the Devil, and who die in this state, are never again mentioned before God and all his holy ones any more than the Devil is mentioned, even though they are human beings, whether or not they have been christened.

For though my revelation was of goodness, and there was little mention of evil, yet I was not drawn by it from a single detail of the faith which Holy Church teaches us to believe.[8] I saw the Passion of Christ in several different showings—in the first, in the second, in the fifth and in the eighth—as I have said before, and although I felt some of the sorrow of our Lady and of the true friends who saw him suffer, yet I did not see the Jews who did him to death specified individually, although I knew by my faith that they were cursed and damned for ever except for those who are converted through grace.[9] And I was taught and instructed to observe every detail of the faith with no exceptions, in every respect as I had previously understood it, hoping that I was observing the faith with God's mercy and grace, and begging and praying inwardly that I might continue in it until the end of my life.

And it is God's will that we should pay attention to all the deeds he has done, for he wants us to know from them all that he will do, but we must always stop ourselves from considering what the great deed will be. And we must pray to be like our brothers and sisters who are saints in heaven and who only want what God wants, then all our joy will be in God and we shall be content both with what is hidden and with what is shown; for I saw our Lord's purpose quite clearly: the more anxious we are to discover his secret knowledge about this or anything else, the further we shall be from knowing it. . . .

(E) CHAPTER 50: HOW THE CHOSEN SOUL WAS NEVER DEAD IN THE SIGHT OF GOD, AND HOW SHE WONDERED ABOUT THIS; AND THREE THINGS WHICH EMBOLDENED HER TO ASK GOD TO EXPLAIN IT TO HER.

And in this mortal life mercy and forgiveness are our path and keep leading us on to grace. And through the distress and sorrow that we ourselves fall into, the earthly judgment of men often considers us dead, but in the sight of God, the soul that shall be saved was never dead, nor ever shall be. But yet at this point I was amazed and marvelled most earnestly in my soul, thinking as follows: "My good Lord, I see that you are truth itself and I know for certain that we sin grievously every day and deserve to be bitterly blamed; and I can neither give up the knowledge of this truth, nor can I see that you show us any kind of blame. How can this be?" For I knew through the universal teaching of Holy Church and through my own experience that the guilt of our sin weighs us down continually, from Adam, the first man, until the time when we come up into heaven; then this was what amazed me, that I saw our Lord God blaming us no more than if we were as pure and as holy as angels in heaven. And between these two contraries my reason was greatly tormented by my blindness, and could not rest for fear that God's blessed presence should pass from my sight and I should be left not knowing how he regards us in our sin; for either I needed to see in God that sin was all done away with, or else I needed to see in God how he sees it, so that I might truly know how it befits me to see sin and what sort of blame is ours.

My longing endured as I looked continually towards him, and yet my trouble and perplexity were so great that I could not be patient, thinking, "If I suppose that we are not sinners nor do we deserve blame, my good Lord, how can it then be that I cannot see this certainty in you, who are my God, my Maker, in whom I long to see all truths? Three reasons give me the courage to ask this: the first is because it is such a humble thing, for if it were exalted I should be afraid; the second is that it is so universal, for if it were special and secret, that would also make me afraid; the third is that it seems to me that I need to know it if I am to live here, in order to recognize good and evil, so that I may through reason and through grace distinguish between them more clearly, and love goodness and hate evil, as Holy Church teaches." I cried inwardly with all my might, beseeching God for help, thinking as follows: "Ah! Lord Jesus, king of bliss, how can I be helped? Who can show me and tell me what I need to know if I cannot see it now in you?"

CHAPTER 51: THE ANSWER TO THE PREVIOUS DOUBT
THROUGH A MARVELLOUS PARABLE OF A LORD AND A
SERVANT; AND HOW GOD WISHES US TO WAIT FOR HIM,
FOR IT WAS NEARLY TWENTY YEARS LATER BEFORE SHE
UNDERSTOOD THIS EXAMPLE FULLY; AND HOW IT IS
UNDERSTOOD THAT CHRIST SITS AT THE RIGHT HAND
OF THE FATHER.

And then our kind Lord answered by showing in very mysterious images a wonderful parable of a lord who has a servant, and he gave me sight to aid my understanding of both. And this sight was shown twofold in the lord and twofold in the servant: on the one hand it was shown spiritually in bodily likeness, on the other it was shown more spiritually with no bodily likeness.

The first kind of vision was this: the bodily likeness of two people, a lord and a servant, and with this God gave me spiritual understanding. The lord sits with dignity, in rest and peace: the servant stands, waiting reverently in front of his lord, ready to do his will. The lord looks at his servant lovingly and kindly, and he gently sends him to a certain place to do his will. The servant does not just walk, but leaps forward and runs in great haste, in loving anxiety to do his lord's will. And he falls immediately into a slough and is very badly hurt. And then he groans and moans and wails and writhes, but he cannot get up or help himself in any way. And in all this I saw that his greatest trouble was lack of help; for he could not turn his face to look at his loving lord, who was very close to him, and who is the source of all help; but, like a man who was weak and foolish for the time being, he paid attention to his own senses, and his misery continued, and in this misery he suffered seven great torments. The first was the grievous bruising which he received when he fell, which was a torment he could feel. The second was the weight of his body. The third was the weakness caused by these two. The fourth that his reason was blinded and his mind stunned to such an extent that he had almost forgotten his own love for the lord. The fifth was that he could not rise. The sixth was the most astonishing to me, and it was that he lay alone; I looked hard all round, and far and near, high and low, I could see no one to help him. The seventh torment was that the place where he lay was long, hard and full of difficulties. I marvelled at how this servant could humbly suffer all that misery. And I watched carefully to see if I could perceive any fault in him, or if the lord would blame him at all; and in truth there was no fault to be seen, for his good will and his great longing were the only cause of his fall; and he was as willing and inwardly good as when he stood before his lord ready to do his will.

And this is how his loving lord tenderly continued to consider him, and now in two ways. Outwardly he regarded him gently and kindly, with great sorrow and pity, and this was the first way; the second was more inward, more spiritual, and this was shown when my understanding was led into the lord. I saw him rejoicing greatly because of the honourable rest and nobility to which he would and must bring his servant through his plentiful grace. This was the second kind of showing; and now my understanding took me back to the first, while keeping both in my mind. Then this kind lord said within himself, "Look, look at my beloved servant, what injury and distress he has received in my service for love of me, yes, and all because his will was good! Is it not reasonable that I should compensate him for his terror and his dread, his hurt and his injury and all his misery? And not only this, but would it not be proper for me to give a gift that would be better for him and give him more glory than if he had never been injured? Otherwise it seems to me that I would do him no favour." And then an inward, spiritual explanation of the lord's purpose penetrated my soul. I saw that, given his own greatness and glory, it needs must be that his dear servant whom he loved so much should be truly and blissfully rewarded for ever, more than he would have been if he had not fallen; yes, and to such an extent that his fall and the misery it caused him should be transformed into great and surpassing glory and eternal bliss.

And at this point the showing of the parable vanished, and our good Lord guided my understanding as to the appearance and meaning of the revelation to the end. But in spite of this guidance, I never lost my sense of wonder at the parable. It seemed that it was given me as an answer to my longing, and yet at that time I could not grasp it fully to my own satisfaction; for in the servant who represented Adam, as I shall explain, I saw many different properties which could in no way be attributed just to Adam. And so for the moment I was in a state of great bewilderment; for a full understanding of this marvellous parable was not given to me at that time.

In this mysterious parable, three aspects of the revelation remain largely hidden; yet I saw and understood that each of the showings is full of mysteries, and so I ought now to enumerate these three aspects and the limited progress I have made in understanding them. The first is the early stage of teaching which I understood from it while it was being shown to me; the second is the inner learning which I have come to understand from it since then; the third is the whole revelation from beginning to end, as set out in this book, which our Lord God in his goodness often shows freely to the eyes of my mind. And these three are so united in my mind that I neither can nor may separate them.[10]

And through these three, united as one, I have been taught how I ought to believe and trust in our Lord God: that just as he showed it out of his goodness and for his own purpose, so out of the same goodness and for the same purpose he will explain the vision to us when he so wishes. Because twenty years after the time of the showing, all but three months, I received inner teaching, as follows: "You need to pay attention to all the properties and conditions of what you were shown in the parable, though they may seem mysterious and insignificant in your eyes." I accepted this willingly and with great eagerness, looking inwardly with great care at all the details and properties which were shown at the time of the vision, so far as my wit and understanding would serve. I began by looking at the lord and the servant, and the way the lord was sitting, and the place where he sat, and then the colour of his clothing and the way it was shaped, and his outward appearance, and the nobility and goodness within; I looked at the way the servant stood and where and how, at the sort of clothing he wore, its colour and shape, at his outward behaviour and at his inner goodness and his readiness.

The lord who sat with dignity, in rest and peace, I understood to be God. The servant who stood in front of the lord, I understood that he represented Adam—that is to say, that one man and his fall were shown in that vision to make it understood how God considers any man and his fall; for in the sight of God, all men are one. This man's strength was broken and enfeebled; and his understanding was numbed, for he turned away from looking at his lord. But in the sight of God his purpose remained undiminished; for I saw our Lord commend and approve his purpose, but the man himself was obstructed and blind to the knowledge of this purpose, and this causes him great sorrow and grievous misery; for neither can he clearly see his loving lord, who is most gentle and kind to him, nor can he see truly how he himself appears to his loving lord. And I am quite certain that if we really and truly see these two things, then we shall attain rest and peace partially here on earth and the full bliss of heaven, through his plentiful grace. And this was the beginning of the teaching revealed to me at this same time, through which I might come to know God's attitude to us in our sin. And then I saw that only suffering blames and punishes, and our kind Lord comforts and grieves; he always considers the soul cheerfully, loving and longing to bring us to bliss.

The place where our Lord sat was humble, on the barren earth, deserted, alone in a wilderness. His clothing was full and ample, as befits a lord; the cloth was as blue as azure, most sober and comely.

His expression was merciful, the colour of his face a comely brown with pronounced features; his eyes were black, most comely and handsome, appearing full of tender pity; and within him there was a great refuge, long and wide and all full of endless heavens. And his tender expression as he kept looking at his servant, especially when he fell, I thought it could melt our hearts with love and break them in two with joy. The comely expression showed a handsome mixture which was wonderful to look at: it was partly sorrow and pity, partly joy and bliss. The joy and bliss are as far beyond sorrow and pity as heaven is above earth. The pity was earthly and the bliss was heavenly. The sorrow in the Father's pity was for the fall of Adam, his most loved creature; the joy and bliss was for his beloved Son, who is equal to the Father. The merciful gaze of his tender expression filled the whole earth and went down with Adam into hell, and this unending pity kept Adam from everlasting death. And this mercy and pity remain with mankind until the time we come up into heaven. But man is blind in this life, and therefore we cannot see our father, God, as he is. And when, out of his goodness, he wants to show himself to man, he shows himself in a familiar way, like a man; nevertheless I saw truly that we should know and believe that the Father is not a man. But his sitting on the barren earth in a deserted place means this: he made man's soul to be his own city and his dwelling place, the most pleasing to him of all his works; and once man had fallen into sorrow and pain he was not fit to serve that noble purpose, and therefore our kind Father would prepare no other place for himself but sit upon the earth waiting for mankind, who is mixed with earth, until the time when, through his grace, his beloved Son had bought back his city and restored its noble beauty with his hard labour.

The blue of his clothing signifies his steadfastness. The brown of his fair face with the handsome blackness of the eyes was most suited to showing his holy gravity. The fullness of his clothing, which was fair, glowing brightly about him, signifies that he has enclosed within him all the heavens and all joy and bliss. And a glimpse of this was given where I said, "My understanding was led into the lord," when I saw him rejoicing greatly because of the glorious Resurrection to which he wills to bring and shall bring his servant through his plentiful grace.

And yet I marvelled as I considered the lord and the aforementioned servant. I saw the lord sitting with dignity, and the servant standing reverently in front of his lord; and there is a double meaning in this servant, one without and another within. Outwardly, he was simply dressed, as a labourer might be who was ready to work, and he stood very near the lord, not right in front of him, but a little to one side, on the left. His clothing was a white tunic, unlined, old and all spoilt, stained with the sweat of his body, tight-fitting and short on him, only reaching about a hand's breadth below the knee, threadbare, looking as if it would soon be worn out—in rags and tatters. And I was very surprised about this, thinking, "Now this is unsuitable clothing for such a well-loved servant to wear in front of such an honourable lord."

Love was shown deep within him, and this love which he had for the lord was just like the love which the lord had for him. His servant's wisdom saw inwardly that there was one thing he could do which would be to the lord's honour. And the servant for love, with no regard for himself or for anything that might happen to him, leapt quickly forward and ran at his lord's command to perform his will and serve his glory. For it looked from his outer clothing as if he had been a labourer continuously for a long time; yet from the inward sight that I had of both the lord and the servant, it seemed that he was a new one—that is to say, newly beginning to labour, a servant who had never been sent out before. There was a treasure in the earth which the lord loved. I marvelled and wondered what it could be. And I was answered in my understanding, "It is a food which is sweet and pleasing to the lord." For I saw the lord sit like a man, and I saw neither food nor drink to serve him; this was one marvel. Another marvel was that this dignified lord had only the one servant, and him he sent out. I watched, wondering what kind of labour it could be that the servant should do. And then I understood that he would do the greatest labour and the hardest toil of all—he would be a gardener, digging and ditching, toiling and sweating, and turning the earth upside down, and delving deeply and watering the plants at the right time. And this would continue to be his work, and he would make fresh water flow, and noble and plentiful fruits spring up, which he would bring before the lord and serve him as he wished. And he should never turn back until he had prepared this food all ready as he knew it pleased the lord, and then he should take this food, with the drink as part of it, and carry it very reverently to the lord. And all this time the lord would sit in the same place, waiting for the servant whom he had sent out.

And yet I wondered where the servant came from; for I saw that the lord has within himself eternal life and every kind of goodness, except for the treasure which was in the earth—and that had its origin in the lord in wonderful depths of endless love—but it was not entirely to his glory until this servant had prepared it nobly in this way, and brought it to him, into his own presence; and without the lord there was nothing but a wilderness. And I did not understand all that this parable meant, and that was why I wondered where the servant came from.

In the servant is comprehended the second person of the Trinity, and in the servant is comprehended Adam—that is to say, all men. And therefore when I say "the Son," it means the Godhead, which is equal with the Father, and when I say "the servant," it means Christ's Humanity, which is truly Adam. The servant's nearness represents the Son, and his standing on the left side represents Adam. The lord is the Father, God; the servant is the Son, Christ Jesus. The Holy Ghost is the equal love which is in both of them. When Adam fell, God's son fell; because of the true union made in heaven, God's son could not leave Adam, for by Adam I understand all men. Adam fell from life to death into the valley of this wretched world, and after that into hell. God's son fell with Adam into the valley of the Virgin's womb (and she was the fairest daughter of Adam), in order to free Adam from guilt in heaven and in earth; and with his great power he fetched him out of hell.

The wisdom and goodness in the servant represent God's son. That he was poorly dressed as a labourer and standing near the left-hand side represents Christ's Humanity and Adam, with all the consequent trouble and weakness; for in this parable our good Lord showed his own son and Adam as but one man. The strength and the goodness which we have come from Jesus Christ, the weakness and the blindness which we have come from Adam, and these two were represented in the servant.

And thus our good Lord Jesus has taken upon himself all our guilt; and therefore our Father neither may nor will assign us any more guilt than he does to his own son, dearly-loved Christ. Thus the Son was the servant before he came to earth, standing ready before the Father, waiting until the time when he would send him to do that glorious deed by which mankind was brought back to heaven; that is to say that in spite of the fact that he is God, equal with the Father as regards the Godhead, yet because of his providential purpose to become man to save man in fulfilment of his Father's will, he stood in front of his Father like a servant, willingly taking all our burden upon himself. And then he leapt forward eagerly at the Father's will and immediately he fell low into the Virgin's womb, with no regard to himself or to his harsh suffering. The white tunic is the flesh; the single thickness shows that there was nothing at all between the Godhead and the Humanity; the tightness shows poverty; it was old because Adam wore it; it was sweat-stained from Adam's toil; it was short to show the servant must labour.

And this is how I saw the Son standing, and what he said inwardly was, "Look, my dear Father, I am standing before you in Adam's tunic, all ready to leap forward and to run. It is my wish to be on earth to work for your glory whenever it is your wish to send me. How long must I linger?" The Son knew very well when it would be his Father's will and how long he had to linger, that is to say, in so far as he is the Godhead, for he is the Wisdom of the Father. Therefore what was conveyed was in respect of the Manhood of Christ; for all mankind who shall be saved by Christ's precious Incarnation and blessed Passion, all are Christ's Manhood. He is the head and we are his limbs; and these limbs do not know the day and the time when every passing grief and sorrow will come to an end, and everlasting joy and bliss will be accomplished, the day and time which all the company of heaven longs to see. And all those under heaven who shall come there shall do so by longing and wishing; and this wish and longing was shown in the servant standing in front of the lord, or, to put it differently, in the Son standing in front of the Father in Adam's tunic; for the wish and the craving of all mankind that shall be saved appeared in Jesus; for Jesus is all who shall be saved and all who shall be saved are Jesus; and all through God's love, along with the obedience, humility and patience, and other virtues which pertain to us.

Also this wonderful parable gives me some teaching, as if it were the beginning of an ABC, through which I may have some understanding of our Lord's purpose, for the mysteries of the revelation are hidden in it, though indeed all the showings are full of mysteries. That the Father was sitting signifies his Godhead, in that it shows rest and peace; for there may be no labour in the Godhead. And that he showed himself as lord has meaning in relation to our humanity. That the servant was standing signifies labour; that he

was to one side and on the left signifies that he was not quite worthy to stand right in front of the lord. His leaping up belonged to
the Godhead and his running to Christ's Manhood; for the Godhead leapt from the Father into the Virgin's womb, falling when he
took on our nature; and in this fall he was grievously hurt; the hurt
he received was our flesh in which he soon felt deathly pain. That
he stood in awe before the lord but not quite in front of him signifies that his clothing was not respectable enough to stand right before the lord; nor could or should that be his duty while he was a
labourer; neither could he sit in rest and peace with the lord until he
had justly earned his peace with his hard labour; that he was on the
left side shows that the Father deliberately left his own Son in human form to suffer all man's pains without sparing him. By the fact
that his tunic would soon be in rags and tatters is understood the
blows and the scourging, the thorns and the nails, the pulling and
the dragging, tearing his tender flesh; as I saw in part, the flesh was
torn from the skull, falling in shreds until the bleeding stopped; and
then it began to dry again, clinging to the bone. And by the tossing
and turning, groaning and moaning, it is understood that he could
never rise again in his full power from the time that he fell into the
Virgin's womb until his body was slain and he died, yielding his
soul into the Father's hands with all mankind for whom he was
sent. And at this point he first began to show his power; for he went
into hell, and when he was there he raised up out of the deep depths
the great root[11] of those who were truly united with him in high
heaven. The body was in the grave until Easter morning, and from
that time he lay down no more; for then was truly ended the tossing
and turning, the groaning and moaning; and our foul mortal flesh
which God's son took upon himself, which was Adam's old tunic,
tight, bare and short, was then made by our Saviour newly beautiful, white and bright and eternally pure, full and ample, fairer and
richer than the clothing which I saw on the Father, for that clothing
was blue, and Christ's clothing is now of a comely, handsome mixture which is so wonderful that I cannot describe it; for it is all
glory. Now the lord does not sit in a wilderness on earth, but sits in
the noblest seat in heaven, which he made to his own liking. Now
the Son does not stand in awe in front of the Father like a servant,
plainly dressed and partly naked, but he stands immediately before
the Father, richly dressed in holy munificence, with a crown of inestimable richness on his head; for it was shown that we are his

crown, and that this crown is the Father's joy, the Son's glory, the Holy Ghost's delight, and unending and wonderful bliss to all who are in heaven. Now the Son does not stand before the Father on his left, like a labourer, but he sits at his Father's right hand in eternal rest and peace. This does not mean that the Son sits on the Father's right hand, side by side with him, as one person sits by another in this world; for as I see it there is no such sitting in the Trinity; but he sits on his Father's right hand, which is to say in the highest rank of the Father's joys. Now the spouse, God's son, is at peace with his beloved bride, who is the fair Virgin of eternal joy.[12] Now the Son sits, true God and man, in his city in rest and peace, which his Father has eternally held in preparation for him; and the Father in the Son, and the Holy Ghost in the Father and in the Son. . . .

FROM CHAPTER 57

. . . Thus our Lady is our mother in whom we are all enclosed and we are born from her in Christ; for she who is mother of our Saviour is mother of all who will be saved in our Saviour. And our Saviour is our true mother in whom we are eternally born and by whom we shall always be enclosed. This was shown abundantly, fully and sweetly; and it is spoken of in the first showing where he says that we are all enclosed in him and he is enclosed in us; and it is spoken of in the sixteenth showing, where it says that he sits in our soul; for it is his pleasure to reign blissfully in our understanding, and to sit restfully in our soul, and to dwell endlessly in our soul, working us all into himself; and in this working he wants us to help him, giving him all our attention, learning what he teaches, keeping his laws, desiring that everything he does should be done, faithfully trusting in him; for I saw truly that our essential being is in God. . . .

CHAPTER 60: HOW WE ARE REDEEMED AND ENLARGED BY THE MERCY AND GRACE OF OUR SWEET, KIND AND EVER-LOVING MOTHER JESUS; AND OF THE PROPERTIES OF MOTHERHOOD; BUT JESUS IS OUR TRUE MOTHER, FEEDING US NOT WITH MILK, BUT WITH HIMSELF, OPENING HIS SIDE FOR US AND CLAIMING ALL OUR LOVE.

But now it is necessary to say a little more about this enlargement, as I understand it in our Lord's meaning, how we are redeemed by the motherhood of mercy and grace and brought back into our natural dwelling where we were made by the motherhood of natural love; a natural love which never leaves us. Our natural Mother, our gracious Mother (for he wanted to become our mother completely in every way), undertook to begin his work very humbly and very gently in the Virgin's womb. And he showed this in the first revelation, where he brought that humble maiden before my mind's eye in the girlish form she had when she conceived; that is to say, our great God, the most sovereign wisdom of all, was raised in this humble place and dressed himself in our poor flesh to do the service and duties of motherhood in every way. The mother's service is the closest, the most helpful and the most sure, for it is the most faithful. No one ever might, nor could, nor has performed this service fully but he alone. We know that our mothers only bring us into the world to suffer and die, but our true mother, Jesus, he who is all love, bears us into joy and eternal life; blessed may he be! So he sustains us within himself in love and was in labour for the full time until he suffered the sharpest pangs and the most grievous sufferings that ever were or shall be, and at the last he died. And when it was finished and he had born us to bliss, even this could not fully satisfy his marvellous love; and that he showed in these high surpassing words of love, "If I could suffer more, I would suffer more."

He could not die any more, but he would not stop working. So next he had to feed us, for a mother's dear love has made him our debtor. The mother can give her child her milk to suck, but our dear mother Jesus can feed us with himself, and he does so most generously and most tenderly with the holy sacrament which is the precious food of life itself. And with all the sweet sacraments he sustains us most mercifully and most graciously. And this is what he meant in those blessed words when he said, "It is I that Holy Church preaches and teaches to you,"[13] that is to say, "All the health and life of the sacraments, all the power and grace of my word, all the goodness which is ordained in Holy Church for you, it is I."

The mother can lay the child tenderly to her breast, but our tender mother Jesus, he can familiarly lead us into his blessed breast through his sweet open side, and show within part of the Godhead and the joys of heaven, with spiritual certainty of endless bliss; and that was shown in the tenth revelation, giving the same understanding in the sweet words where he says, "Look how I love you," looking into his side and rejoicing. This fair, lovely word "mother," it is so sweet and so tender in itself that it cannot truly be said of any but of him, and of her who is the true mother of him and of everyone. To the nature of motherhood belong tender love, wisdom and knowledge, and it is good, for although the birth of our body is only low, humble and modest compared with the birth of our soul, yet it is he who does it in the beings by whom it is done. The kind, loving mother who knows and recognizes the need of her child, she watches over it most tenderly, as the nature and condition of motherhood demands. And as it grows in age her actions change, although her love does not. And as it grows older still, she allows it to be beaten to break down vices so that the child may gain in virtue and grace. These actions, with all that is fair and good, our Lord performs them through those by whom they are done. Thus he is our natural mother through the work of grace in the lower part, for love of the higher part. And he wants us to know it; for he wants all our love to be bound to him. And in this I saw that all the debt we owe, at God's bidding, for his fatherhood and motherhood, is fulfilled by loving God truly; a blessed love which Christ arouses in us. And this was shown in everything, and especially in the great, generous words where he says, "It is I that you love."

CHAPTER 61: JESUS BEHAVES MORE TENDERLY IN GIVING US SPIRITUAL BIRTH; THOUGH HE ALLOWS US TO FALL SO THAT WE MAY RECOGNIZE OUR SINFULNESS, HE QUICKLY RAISES US, NOT WITHDRAWING HIS LOVE BECAUSE OF OUR TRANSGRESSION, FOR HE CANNOT ALLOW HIS CHILD TO PERISH; HE WANTS US TO HAVE THE NATURE OF A CHILD, ALWAYS RUSHING TO HIM IN OUR NEED.

And in our spiritual birth he behaves with incomparably more tenderness, in as much as our soul is of greater value in his eyes. He fires our understanding, he directs our ways, he eases our conscience, he comforts our soul, he enlightens our heart and gives us some degree of knowledge and love of his blessed Godhead, with awareness through grace of his precious Manhood and his blessed Passion, and with courteous wonder at his great and surpassing goodness; and he makes us love all that he loves, for his love's sake, and makes us take pleasure in him and all his works. If we fall, he quickly raises us by calling us tenderly and touching us with grace. And when we have been strengthened like this by his dear actions, then we choose him willingly, through his precious grace, we choose to serve him and to love him for ever and ever. And after this he allows some of us to fall harder and more painfully than we ever did before, or so it seems to us. And those of us who are not very wise think that all our earlier effort has gone for nothing. But it is not so; for we need to fall, and we need to be aware of it; for if we did not fall, we should not know how weak and wretched we are of ourselves, nor should we know our Maker's marvellous love so fully; for in heaven we shall see truly and everlastingly that we have sinned grievously in this life, and we shall see that in spite of this his love for us remained unharmed, and we were never less valuable to him. And by experiencing this failure, we shall gain a great and marvellous knowledge of love in God for all eternity; for that love which cannot and will not be broken by sin is strong and marvellous. And this is one aspect of the benefit we gain. Another is the humility and gentleness we shall gain from seeing our fall; for by this we shall be raised up high in heaven, a rise which we might never have known without that humility. And therefore we need to see it, and if we do not see it, though we should fall, it would not profit us. Usually, we fall first, then we see it, and both through the mercy of God. The mother may allow the child to fall sometimes and to be hurt for its own benefit, but her love does not allow the child ever to be in any real danger. And though our earthly mother may allow her child to perish, our heavenly mother Jesus cannot allow us who are his children to perish; for he and none but he is almighty, all wisdom and all love. Blessed may he be!

But often when our falling and our wretched sin is shown to us, we are so terrified and so very ashamed that we hardly know where to put ourselves. But then our kind Mother does not want us to run from him, there is nothing he wants less. But he wants us to behave like a child; for when it is hurt or frightened it runs to its mother for help as fast as it can; and he wants us to do the same, like a humble child, saying, "My kind Mother, my gracious Mother, my dearest Mother, take pity on me. I have made myself dirty and unlike you and I neither may nor can remedy this without your special help and grace." And if we do not feel that we are immediately given help, we can be sure that he is behaving like a wise mother, for if he sees that it would be more beneficial for us to grieve and weep, with sorrow and pity he allows it to continue until the right moment, and all for love. So then he wants us to take on the nature of a child which always naturally trusts the love of its mother in weal and woe.

And he wants us to cling strongly to the faith of Holy Church and find our dearest Mother there in the comfort of true understanding with the whole blessed community; for a single person may often feel broken, but the whole body of Holy Church has never been broken, nor ever shall be, for all eternity. And therefore it is a safe, good and gracious thing to wish humbly and strongly to be supported by and united to our mother, Holy Church—that is Christ Jesus; for there is plenty of the food of mercy which is his dearest blood and precious water to make us clean and pure. The blessed wounds of our Saviour are open and rejoice to heal us; the sweet, gracious hands of our Mother are ready and carefully surround us; for in all this he does the work of a kind nurse who has nothing to do but occupy herself with the salvation of her child. His task is to save us, and it is his glory to do so, and it is his wish that we know it; for he wants us to love him tenderly, and trust him humbly and strongly. And he showed this in these gracious words, "I hold you quite safely.". . .

CHAPTER 86: THE GOOD LORD SHOWED THAT THIS BOOK SHOULD BE COMPLETED DIFFERENTLY FROM THE WAY IT WAS FIRST WRITTEN; AND THIS IS THE WAY HE WANTS US TO PRAY TO HIM FOR HIS WORK, THANKING, TRUSTING, AND REJOICING IN HIM; AND HOW HE REVEALED THIS SHOWING BECAUSE HE WANTS TO MAKE IT KNOWN, IN WHICH KNOWLEDGE HE WILL GIVE US GRACE TO LOVE HIM; FOR FIFTEEN YEARS LATER CAME THE ANSWER THAT THE CAUSE OF ALL THIS SHOWING WAS LOVE, WHICH MAY JESUS GRANT US. AMEN.

This book was begun by God's gift and his grace, but it seems to me that it is not yet completed. With God's inspiration let us all pray to him for charity, thanking, trusting and rejoicing; for this is how our good Lord wants us to pray to him, as I understood from all that he conveyed, and from the sweet words where he says very cheeringly, "I am the foundation of your prayers"; for I truly saw and understood in what our Lord conveyed that he showed this because he wants to have it better known than it is. Through this knowledge he will give us grace to love and cling to him; for he feels such great love for his heavenly treasure on earth that he wants to give us clearer and more comforting sight of heavenly joy as he draws our hearts to him, because of the sorrow and darkness which we are in.

And from the time that this was shown, I often longed to know what our Lord meant. And fifteen years and more later my spiritual understanding received an answer, which was this: "Do you want to know what your Lord meant? Know well that love was what he meant. Who showed you this? Love. What did he show? Love. Why did he show it to you? For love. Hold fast to this and you will know and understand more of the same; but you will never understand or know from it anything else for all eternity." This is how I was taught that our Lord's meaning was love. And I saw quite certainly in this and in everything that God loved us before he made us; and his love has never diminished and never shall. And all his works were done in this love; and in this love he has made everything for our profit; and in this love our life is everlasting. We had our beginning when we were made; but the love in which he made us was in him since before time began; and in this love we have our beginning. And all this shall be seen in God without end, which may Jesus grant us. Amen.

Anonymous

A REVELATION OF PURGATORY

The praise for any undertaking which serves the purpose of benefitting human souls is to be given to God alone and to our Lady St Mary and to no other earthly man or woman.

Dear brothers and sisters and all other true Christian friends who read this treatise, listen and hear how a woman was afflicted in her sleep by a spirit from purgatory[1] and how she recounted her suffering to her spiritual father and spoke as follows:

Father, I want to tell you how terribly I was afflicted in my sleep on the night of the feast of St Lawrence,[2] in the year of our Lord 1422.

I went to bed at eight o'clock[3] and I fell asleep. And then between nine and ten it seemed to me that I was seized and carried away into purgatory, and I immediately saw all the torments which had often been shown to me before, as you know well, father, from my confessions and the accounts I have given you. But, dear sir, on this St Lawrence's night there was no spirit to show them to me, but all of a sudden it seemed to me that I saw them; and indeed, dear father, I have never woken from a vision of the torments in such a state of wretched terror as I did then, and that was because I was not led by any spirit I had seen before who might have comforted me.

And in this vision of purgatory it seemed I saw three great fires, and it seemed each fire was in a different place; but, sir, they were not separate, each was joined to another. And these three fires were wonderful and horrible, most especially the largest of them, which was in the middle. For that fire was so horrible and so foul-smelling that all the creatures in the world could never describe how abominably it stank; for there was pitch and tar, lead and brimstone and oil, and everything that could burn, and every torment that one could imagine, and every kind of Christian man and woman who had lived here in this world in whatever social position. But among all the torments of all the men and women that I saw, it seemed that priests who had led lecherous lives and their women with them, whether or not they were members of religious orders—in that revelation it seemed that men and women belonging to religious orders suffered the greatest torment.

And in that great fire it seemed I saw the spirit of a woman I knew, a woman who had been a sister in a religious house[4] when she was alive and had been called Margaret. I thought I saw her in this horrible fire, and she was suffering such torment that I could not describe it for fear. And I woke up in dreadful terror and by that time it was just striking ten. And I was terrified and dreaded going to sleep again, so I got up, and a little girl[5] got up with me and the two of us said the Seven Psalms and the Litany. And by the time we had finished saying the *Agnus dei*[6] I was so sleepy that I could not go on, but told the child to go back to bed and did the same myself. And by then it was striking eleven o'clock and by the time I had counted the last stroke I fell asleep.

And immediately it seemed that the spirit of this woman Margaret that I had seen in torment before came to me. And it seemed to me as though she was covered in strange wounds, as though she had been torn with iron combs, that was how she seemed to be wounded and ripped, but at her heart especially it seemed I saw a grievous and horrible wound, and from that wound came a flame of fire. And she said, "May you be accursed and may woe betide you if you do not hasten to help me." And by the time she had said that I felt such terror that I could not speak; but in my heart I kept thinking, "May Jesus's Passion help me," and that comforted my soul. And then it seemed she was going to cast fire upon me and leap towards me and kill me; but I realised that it was beyond her power, for God's Passion strengthened me. However, she was such a grisly sight that she terrified me. And it seemed she was being followed by a little dog and a little cat, all on fire. And then it seemed I said to her, "What are you, in the name of God, afflicting me so sorely like this? And I conjure you in the name of the Father and the Son and the Holy Ghost, three persons and one God in Trinity, that you tell me what you are, afflicting me like this, and whether you are a spirit from purgatory wanting my help or a spirit from hell to overcome and harm me." And then she said, "No, I am a spirit from purgatory wanting your help, and not a spirit from hell to vex you; and if you want to know what spirit I am that suffers such great torment in purgatory for my sins, I am the spirit of Margaret who was a sister in a nunnery which you knew well, and you knew me when I lived there, too. And I ask for your help in the name of God."

And then I asked her what I should do. And then she said, "You shall have thirteen Masses said for me, in the way I shall tell you." And then she named a good man who is my confessor, "and ask him to say a requiem Mass[7] for me. And he shall say the whole of the psalm *Miserere mei deus*[8] every day for five days. And when he begins to say '*Miserere mei*,' he is to say that verse to the end five times, looking up with his heart and his eyes towards God," for the more devoutly he said it, the more her torments would be lessened and the greater would be his reward. "And when he has said this verse five times, let him say the whole psalm to the end. And tell him," she said, "to say the hymn *Veni creator spiritus*[9] right through to the end for five days. Go as well to your confessor Father John and ask him to say three Masses of the Trinity[10] for me, and the *Miserere* on five days with the hymn *Veni creator spiritus*, in the way just described. And also send a message to your holy father who is a recluse at Westminster[11] and ask him to sing two Masses of St Peter for me, and say the *Miserere* and the *Veni creator* in the way described for five days. And ask him to ask Master Piers Cowme[12] to say two Masses of the Holy Ghost for me, and say the *Miserere* and the *Veni creator* in the way described for three days. Also ask Father Richard Bowne[13] to say three Masses of our Lady for me and say the *Miserere* and the *Veni creator* in the way described for three days. Also ask Master John Percy[14] to say two Masses of All Saints for me with the office *Gaudiamus omnes in domino* and three commemorations[15] of the Trinity, and to say the *Miserere* and the *Veni creator* in the way described for three days."

And then I asked her why she wanted to have these Masses said like this. And she said that no other prayer could help her as much. And I asked her why she wanted the *Miserere* said for her so often. And she said so that God would have mercy on her and pity her, for, she said, whenever that psalm with the hymn she had mentioned was said for her, she would at that moment be released from some part of her torment. "And also," she said, "any man or woman who is in the habit of saying the psalm and the hymn as described before, if he is in danger of sinning or in despair of his faith or of God's mercy, he will through the power of God have true knowledge of his faults and through the mercy of God be delivered from temptation on that occasion. And also if a man or a woman is tempted by any of the Seven Deadly Sins[16] in the form of theft, manslaughter, slander, backbiting or any kind of cursed lechery, let him say the *Miserere* and the *Veni creator spiritus* right through with sincere feeling, and the wicked spirits which are afflicting him with that temptation will depart for the time being."

And then I asked how it benefited a soul to say more Masses of the Trinity and of our Lady and of St Peter than to say requiem Masses. And she said, "Yes, really nothing does a soul more good, if it were possible to do it, than to have said for that soul a hundred Masses of the Trinity and a hundred of our Lady and fifty of St Peter and fifty of requiem, and three hundred times with all these Masses to say the *Miserere* and the *Veni creator spiritus;* and whatever kind of sin he has done in his life, there is no kind of torment in purgatory from which he will not be quickly delivered, and many other souls delivered for his sake. However, if these Masses are said for any soul that is damned, the help and the benefit will go to his next of kin in purgatory, from which it will quickly free them; for purgatory is nothing but a merciful place where man's sin is cleansed. And they shall soon be shown such great mercy that through the power and the mercy of God and the virtue of these holy Masses they shall quickly be released from their torment and be led to the earthly paradise where Adam first lived, and there they shall be washed in the well of grace with the water of purification and be anointed with the oil of mercy. I cannot yet tell you anything more about heavenly bliss, for until now I have only known torment. And therefore let any man or woman that is in a position[17] to do so have these holy Masses said for him, and, even if he were suffering the greatest torments of purgatory, he would soon be delivered from them and from all others if these Masses were said in the way I have described to you, with other good deeds and almsgiving according to the will of the dead person. And if a man or woman is not in a position to have these Masses said for him in the way I have told you, let him have thirteen said for him like that, followed by the *Miserere* and the *Veni creator spiritus*. But the Masses of our Lady should be *Salve sancta parens*. And when these Masses have been said, the soul will soon be out of torment."

And, father, I had all this revelation on the first night. And then, father, when she had said all this, the little dog and the cat which had brought her to me took her back to her torment again. And yet before she left me she said I would see her the following night in all her torments before she came to me again, and that seven devils would torment her, and that the little dog and the cat would always be with her in the fire to increase her suffering, and how the worm of conscience would always be gnawing her inwardly—and she said that this worm was the greatest torment of all in purgatory or in hell, for, she said, during the torments that gnawing never stopped. And then I asked the spirit, "What do you know of the pains of hell since you have never been there? How do you know any more about them than you do about the joys of heaven?" And then she said, "Oh yes, I know well from God's justice and by human reason that the worm of conscience causes the greatest suffering both here and there, but I can tell you no more of hell, for, like others who have appeared to you before, I am not allowed to do so. And as for heaven, I told you before how when I was out of purgatory I would be led to the earthly paradise and be washed in the well of grace and made clean, and be anointed with the oil of mercy, and I told you that I could not say any more about heaven, for as yet I had not been there. And therefore," she said, "I can tell you something of heaven and something of hell." And with that she said farewell to me, calling me by my name, and asking me to pay great attention to her torments on the following night, for I would see both hers and those of others. And with that she went away with a strange shriek and a great cry, and I thought she also said, "Oh dear Lady, help me!"

And soon after that, my dear father, I woke up. And by then it was striking one o'clock in the morning, and it was striking eleven when I fell asleep. And when I rose in the morning I went to Master Forest,[18] my spiritual father, and told him what he was to do for her, and he agreed at once. And then I went to Father John Wynburne,[19] my other spiritual father, and told him what he was to do for her, and he agreed too. And so did all the priests she had wanted to say Masses for her.

Now, father, the next night following that, I went to bed and fell asleep, and was immediately shown the torments of Margaret and of many others in purgatory. But, father, neither she nor any other spirit led me there, but, father, when I was asleep I thought I saw them at once without any guide. And I immediately thought I saw Margaret in her worst clothes, as she appeared on earth, and in the greatest of the fires which I had seen before in purgatory; and I thought I saw seven devils around her, and one of them put a long gown on her, with a long train behind, and it was lined with sharp hooks, and it seemed as though the gown and the hooks were all fiery-red and burning. And then the same devil took serpents and pitch and tar and made curls and put them on her head, and he took a great long adder and wound it round her head, and it seemed to me that it hissed on her head like burning-hot iron in cold water; and it seemed to me that when she was dressed up like that she cried out so loudly that the whole world might have heard her; and the little dog and the cat were gnawing and tearing her legs and arms. And then the devil that had dressed her up like this said, "You must suffer this because of your foul, stinking pride and the way you used to boast, offending against meekness, when you were on earth; and this dog and this cat[20] shall always gnaw at you while you are here, because you loved them so beyond reason when you were alive. For I am the devil of Pride, and therefore I shall do my job and torture you to repay you for serving me on earth." And it seemed to me that there were many devils with him.

And then it seemed that two more devils appeared, and one pulled out her tongue, and the other pulled out her heart, and it seemed to me that they raked it with iron rakes. "And this," they said, "you shall have for your anger and your envy, and for swearing false oaths and for backbiting and slandering, for you did all this when you were alive; and we are the devils of Wrath and Envy, and all these adders and snakes which you can see with us shall torture you for the wicked vices which you practised on earth, without having done penance before you came here." And then it seemed to me that two other devils appeared, one of them with sharp razors, and he went up to her as though he was going to cut her flesh, and so he did while I was watching, and it seemed to me that he pared away all her lips; and he took a great iron hook and thrust it through her heart. And the other devil melted lead and brimstone and every kind of stinking poison which anyone could imagine; and he also prepared for her the likeness of every kind of food and drink which is delicious in this world and which she used to have, rousing herself to sin rather than virtue. And it seemed to me that the food was all adders and snakes, and they made her eat them against her will, and they also made her drink every kind of damnable poison, and they said, "Eat and drink this for your accursed gluttony and mis-spending, wasting and taking too much while you were alive." And then it seemed to me that this devil and the other devil cut away her flesh and her lips and thrust the hook into her heart. And then they dragged her into a great black pool, and the water seemed as cold as ice, and much of it looked frozen to me; and they threw her into it and pushed her up and down, and said, "Take this bath for your sloth and your gluttony." And then they took her out of the water and threw her into a great fire, and they left her there, and that, they said, would be her bed because she had so loved taking her slothful ease while she was on earth, and did not attend God's holy services[21] when she might have done. And there they left her with many serpents around her.

And then it seemed to me that two other devils appeared, and one of them brought a lot of gold and silver which was melted and poured it down her throat, and it ran out of her stomach, and the devil said, "Take this for your accursed and wicked covetousness, and for the way you spent money wastefully when you had it and because you did not want to help others who were in need, and you misused gold and silver." And then it seemed to me that the other devil led her up to a great brass vat, and in the vat there was every kind of stinking thing and every kind of poison and serpents both large and small; and he put her in the vat amidst the foul poison and tore her apart limb from limb, and he said, "Take this bath for your vile, stinking lechery." And, father, it seemed to me that she cried out horribly and said, "Let everybody take warning from me, and do their penance before they die and stop taking pleasure in their wicked sins," and she said, "These two devils that are torturing me here are the devils of covetousness and lechery."

And so it seemed to me, my dear father, that she was afflicted by these torments for some time, for the duration of half an hour. And in all that time it seemed to me that I did not see her, but I heard her crying out horribly, and I often seemed to hear her say, "Dear Lady, help me!"

And it seemed to me that I was standing by myself and I was watching her torments and those of many men and women, both secular and religious, and married men and women, and single men and women. And it seemed to me that I saw from the torments and sufferings which sin a man or woman had committed most often in their lives and which of the Seven Sins they loved best, each person in their station. However, among all the torments and among all the Christian people, it seemed to me that lechery was most severely punished, and especially when the sinners were of Holy Church, whether or not they belonged to religious orders.

It seemed to me, father, that I saw priests and their women suffering torment, and most of them were bound together by iron chains. However, there were some priests who had women who were not bound to them as the others were, and though it seemed to me that their outward suffering was almost as great, their inward suffering seemed less. These were the torments of most of the priests and their women: it seemed to me that they were flung into dark pits full of fierce fire, and every kind of thing which could melt to increase their suffering was thrown in to them. And it seemed to me that the pit was full of adders and snakes and all evil serpents; and it seemed to me that they were so tormented there that all the creatures in the world could not number their sufferings. And then it seemed to me, my dear father, that they were taken out of the pit and cast into an extremely deep pool of water, and it seemed to me that much of it was frozen, for it looked as cold as any ice. And there it seemed to me that the devil tore their flesh apart with strong hooks.

And then, father, it seemed to me that there were also a number of tall gibbets hanging over the water—like those used to let a bucket down into a well to draw water—and it seemed to me as though these gibbets were full of sharp razors and they were bent as though they were hooks. And it seemed to me that these razors were put into the priests' throats and came out through their mouths. And it seemed to me that the priests were plunged up and down in that stinking water like buckets plunged into a well; and when they had been tortured for a long time, they were taken down and brought out of the water. And immediately they were thrown into fierce fires. And these devils threw oil and grease at them and blew hard with powerful bellows so that I could see nothing of them. And then soon after that it seemed to me that the devils laid the priests on anvils as blacksmiths do red-hot iron and beat them with hammers—all those priests, but not their women, for it seemed to me that they were separated from them. And then it seemed to me that they cried out so horribly that the whole world could not make such a horrible noise or cry out so hideously. And then it seemed to me that the devils took burning metal like red gold, and they put it all hot into the priests' mouths, and the burning ran through their bodies. And then a devil said, "Take this delicious drink for your wrongful mis-spending of God's gifts in waste, in cursed lechery, and to feed your gluttony and wicked pride."

Also, father, these devils took out the priests' tongues, and it seemed to me that they cut them up. And then it seemed to me that these devils said, "Take this torture of your tongues for the false and foul slanderous, lecherous words which you spoke with them, enticing many women to commit that sin and abandon their good lives—nuns, wives, anchoresses, single women and maidens, and many women who never would have committed that sin. You with your deceptive gold and your persuasive words led them to sin, and so they are being tormented here with you for the pleasure they took in it and their longing for your gold and their failure to do penance before they died; therefore they shall pay very dearly for it here."

Then it seemed to me that the devils had many sharp razors in their hands, and they carved off the crowns[22] of some of the priests' heads—and it looked like their fingers and their lips too—and said, "Take this for your misuse of them; and also because you heads and prelates of Holy Church should have chastised sin in yourselves and your households and in your agents and those of people under you, and you did not; and because you went along with their love of gold and of flattering words so that they would be more likely to let you have your own way." And then it seemed to me that the devils took burning adders and put them through the priests' ears and said, "Take this because you were prelates of Holy Church and you would never listen to the truth when you did wrong, but destroyed utterly anyone who told you anything you did not want to hear."

And then it seemed to me that the devils took out their hearts, and in their hearts there was a fierce worm, which was biting their heartstrings to pieces and all their internal organs. And then the devils said, "Take this worm of conscience which will never stop gnawing and biting within you till all your sins are forgiven; and that is because you would not give up your sin, nor do penance for it before you died. Also at Communion you often received your God unworthily and handled the host when you were in a very impure state, and that was because of your stinking sin of lechery and all the other sins against your conscience. That is why the crowns of your heads and your fingers have been carved off, and you are debased here for the misuse of your priesthood."

And then it seemed that I saw many devils running around them and tearing the private parts of both the priests and their women. However, it seemed to me that men and women belonging to religious orders had a hundred times more torture than those who were secular—that is, secular priests and women who did not belong to religious orders—for the former were thrown on great wheels and turned around with fierce fire. And adders and snakes and devils surrounded them constantly. And the devils turned the wheels so fast that I could not see them, but they cried out horribly, as though everyone in the world had cried out at once. And this torture, father, was given to men and women in religious orders and prelates of Holy Church more than to secular priests or secular women. But priests of all kinds were thrown into deep pits, and their women with them. And they all cried out together in the most horrible way, and this is what they cried: "Woe to pride, covetousness, and lechery and the wicked pleasures of the world, and woe to the wicked desires of those who would never do penance while they lived in this wretched world. And therefore we must pay dearly for it here, and let every Christian man and woman take warning from us and forsake sin and do penance while they are alive." And this, my dear father, is how it seemed to me that I saw priests punished in purgatory.

And then, father, it seemed to me that I immediately saw the torment of monks and nuns living in solitude and of all other religious women living unaccompanied by a man whatever their status on earth. And, father, it seemed to me that their torment was to be burnt over a fierce fire, and the devils were continuously raking their flesh with strong hooks, as women draw wool with combs, I think. And they put every kind of foul poison on them, and some took great long adders and serpents and thrust them, burning, through their heads. And some bound their foreheads tightly with garlands of adders, and they seemed to me to hiss on their heads like burning-hot iron in cold water. And it seemed to me that the devils took out their hearts and tore them to pieces with hooks. And then the devils said to them, "Take these adders with which your heads are pierced for the pleasure you took in listening to the wrong things, idle words which encouraged you to sin rather than good words which might have encouraged in you the virtue suitable for your way of life. Take also these adders that are binding your foreheads for the way you constricted them so tightly while you were alive to increase your lustful pleasure."

Also, father, it seemed to me that the devils slit the nuns' lips, and the devils told them to take that for the lecherous kisses with which they had kissed men and led many to sin who would not otherwise have done so. Also, it seemed to me that the devils threw veils of fire upon their heads which came down to their brows, and then the devils said, "Take these veils for the way you showed your faces when you were alive—against the rules of your order—encouraging sin both in yourselves and in others." Then it seemed to me the devils took out their tongues and put adders on them and toads, and then the devils said, "Take this for your wicked lechery and foul words and foul behaviour and backbiting and slander." And then it seemed to me that those devils came down and tore apart their hearts and all their limbs. And then the devils said, "Take this for your wicked sloth and your fantasies and your foul behavior and for the wicked thoughts you enjoyed as you lay there." And then it seemed to me that they and the devils roared so loudly that if the whole world had heard it while awake, as I did in my sleep, everyone would have been terrified. And thus much, father, I saw of the torture of religious women.

And then soon after that I thought I saw the torture of married men and women, and this was their torture: they were put in great barrels full of adders and snakes and every kind of stinking thing, and it seemed to me that the barrels were immediately closed at both ends, and they were sealed into them; and then it seemed to me that those devils took long iron spikes, all burning hot, and thrust them through the barrels, and as fast as they could they turned the barrels round, as men do when cleaning armour.[23] And then it seemed to me that the barrels broke, and so much smoke gushed out that everyone around was covered in it. And then it seemed to me that those devils took pitch and melted it and poured it down their throats; but, father, it did not run out of them but remained inside them. And then it seemed to me that the devils tore them apart, bone from bone. And then the devils said to them, "Take this bitter bath that you had in the barrel for the wicked and sinful way that you lay in your foul beds of lechery, and also for breaking your marriage promises, contrary to the will of God, and failing to be faithful to your wives and your husbands as the law of God demands. And take also this bitter pitch for the sweet food and drink which you used gluttonously to swallow to satisfy your cravings. And take also this bitter tearing of your bodies for the soft beds and soft clothes in which you sinned, and also for the wicked deeds you did against the will of God and your own consciences." And this, my dear father, is how I thought I saw the torments of married men and women.

And then, father, after these I saw the torments of single men and women; and it seemed to me that these were put on spits and roasted; and also many adders and snakes and toads and newts and a swarm of foul poisonous creatures as dense as possible was set on them to suck them and gnaw them. And then they were taken off the spits and those devils dragged them right through the fires with hard, sharp hooks, both single men and women, and they tore out their hearts and their most private parts. And then the devils said to them, "Take this torture because you misused your body with the foul lust of lechery and with all other sins, against God's will and your own conscience, and because you misused your body unnecessarily with the sin of lechery when you might have made a free choice of wedlock which was permitted by God; and under the law of God marriage was open and available to every man and woman who was not in a religious order and was permitted to marry by God's law, and you might have married and avoided lechery. And because you refused to do so and because you despised the institution of marriage, and because you were afraid that if you married, other men would take your wives—for this foul suspicion and foul misuse of your bodies, take this bitter torment in purgatory, and these adders and these snakes to gnaw you continuously until the sin which bound you has been worn away and God has shown you his mercy. For know well that this is not hell, but this is an instrument of God's justice to purge you of your sins in purgatory, because you were unwilling to do penance while you were alive and before you came here." And that is what those devils there seemed to say; and this much, father, I saw of the torment of single men and women.

And it seemed to me that I saw all this from the time when Margaret's spirit left me until she returned. And soon after that Margaret came to me again, and then she said to me, "Now you have seen my bitter torments that I suffered in these great fires of purgatory." And then, father, it seemed to me that straightaway she came out of the great vat, and came to me; and then she said, "You may know by the devils who were my torturers and by the tortures they gave me what sin I have committed; and they will never torture me for it again. God reward you for it and all those who have helped to free me from my torments." And then I asked her why she cried so piteously, "Sweet Lady, help me!" and why she cried out more to our Lady than she did to God almighty or any of the other saints. And then she said, "Well, yes, because she is the chief of all the saints except God himself, and because she is the well of mercy, I cried out to her in my great sorrow, and also because her entreaty and prayers would be more likely to deliver me, and also while I was alive I fasted her fast."[24] And the spirit told me again that any-one who had fasted our Lady's fast while they were alive would never lack her help when they entered purgatory. And then I asked her why she cried out so dismally when she was in that great vat, and why I could not see her. And then she said, "If you had seen my torment you would have been so terrified that your body could not have contained your spirit without great disturbance of your wits, or else serious sickness, for my torment was so intense, and that is why I cried out so horribly." And then I asked her why that flame of fire came out of her mouth, and why so many fiery sparks came from her heart, and why her heart was so wounded, and why the little dog and the cat followed her; and what good was done her by those Masses and those prayers which she asked to have said for her. And then she said that as far as the fiery flame at her mouth was concerned, that was because she had sworn great oaths while she was alive; and as for the wound in her heart and its sparkling fire, that was because she had often sworn by our Lord's heart, and that was why the fiery sparks came from her heart—and that, she said, was one of the worst torments that she had; and as for the little dog and the cat, they were her pets when she was alive, and she had given too much love to such foul creatures, "and therefore they fol-low me to increase my suffering until the bonds of sin are worn away and break apart. And as for the Masses and the prayers that were said for me, they have released me from my torment more quickly, and also from now on I shall not be tortured by any devils, except one, and that will be my wicked angel, and he will take me through these other two fires of purgatory; and if any dregs of sin remain, I shall be purified there; and the dog and the cat will follow me no more." And then she said, "Farewell," and called me by my name, and she said she would only afflict me with the sight of torments for one more night. And then it seemed to me that she left me, but she did not cry out in the way she did before. And then, father, I awoke from my sleep; and then I felt very weary and very badly frightened. And, father, it seemed to me that I saw this much on that night.

And then, my dear father, it seemed to me that she came to me the following night. And then, dear father, she seemed to me to be as black as coal, but she had no fiery flame in her mouth as she had before, and the wound in her heart had closed, too, and all the wounds which she had seemed to have on her body had closed up. And then she seemed to say to me, "Watch carefully how I shall now be delivered from my torment and enter the bliss of paradise." And then it seemed to me that she went away from me, and immediately a devil took her and threw her into the middle fire, and there it seemed to me that he had bellows in his hand and blew hard, and it seemed to me that she lay there frying in the fire like a fish in hot oil. And then it seemed to me that he took her up again and led her through that middle fire, and as she went, the blackness fell away as if it had been the tallow of a candle when it runs down in the heat; and by the time she had come to the end of that great fire, it seemed to me that she had turned all red and brightly-coloured, like blood-red meat. And then it seemed to me that she went into the third fire, and that fire seemed to me as clear as any amber, and the devil took her right into it, and as she went further and further into that fire she became clearer and clearer. And it seemed to me that she did not linger in that fire; it seemed that she passed quickly through it until she came out at the other side, and by the time she came out, she had become wonderfully white and fair. And then it seemed to me that she said, "Blessed be God and our Lady St Mary that I am here now, and God reward you and all that have helped me achieve it so quickly; and if I had not received the favour of help, I should have been punished in purgatory for three more years; and if I had not appeared to you and been helped by you I would have received even harsher torture."

And then she said, "There are three kinds of purgatory. One is the great fire of purgatory that you saw me in first, and that is just like the torments of hell, except that we shall be saved and they shall not. And these other two fires count as a second." And then I asked her if all who died would go to the first fire—that is, to the great fire. And she said, "No, Jews and Saracens and other heathen people die and they shall never go there, but shall go straight to the torments of hell, for they shall never be saved; and all those who enter the great fire of purgatory shall be saved, whatever torments they suffer." And then I said to her, "I meant, do all Christian people go there before going to the other two fires?" And then she said, "No, sister, God forbid! For many thousands go to the middle fire that do not go to the great fire, and their punishment is lesser or greater to the extent that by grace they have felt contrition and made satisfaction and done penance for their sins. For," she said, "the greatest fire is the chief agent of God's justice in purgatory. For," she said, "all the deadly sins which men and women have committed in the world for which they have been shriven and for which they have not done penance before dying, for these they will be punished in the torments of purgatory. And so will many men and women that will not give up their sin before they are unexpectedly taken by death. And also many men and women hold many cursed opinions, for they will say that so long as they can speak three words before their death they are not worried, and that is a very dangerous view; but still God in his great mercy grants these words to many when they lie on their deathbed, for he is very reluctant to lose what he bought dearly.[25] And because his mind is going, and because he feels so ill, the dying man confesses as well as he can and puts himself at God's mercy—everyone like that shall go into this fire until the bonds of sin are burnt away, some for a longer time, some for a shorter, and all according to whether they have friends on earth to help, and all according to whether they have done good on earth before they died, and according to whether they have patiently suffered sickness and tribulations here on earth before they died—for," she said, "a day of sickness and tribulation on earth shall stand for a year in purgatory. And that shall be in the great fire. But all that enter the greatest fire shall come through the middle fire, and then through the clear fire, and so pass through the pains of purgatory." And, she said, "Many shall pass through the middle fire and not enter the great fire, and they are those who have committed many venial sins,[26] and have only been shriven for them in a general way, and some of the sins should have been individually shriven before they died. And there are many cases of forgotten sins that are not recalled, or of over-lenient penance, or of penance enjoined but too little or too negligently performed, or insufficient repentance, or penance enjoined but not completed before they died—all these people will be purified and will complete their penance in the middle fire of purgatory, and so come out of it and go to the third fire of purification, as I am doing now. And many go to the clear fire as soon as they are dead, and go neither to the great fire, nor yet to the middle fire, but go straight to the clear fire and then immediately into bliss; and those who do that are innocents and devout men and women in religious orders and anchorites and anchoresses, and all holy people living an enclosed life, and all holy martyrs and confessors.[27] And God himself showed his blessed Mother the pains of purgatory, though they did not touch her. All manner of Christian men and women in the world, whatsoever sin they may have committed, if they have completed their penance before dying, through the mercy of God and the great trust they have in God and in his mercy and the contrition they felt for their sin, as soon as they die they shall enter the third fire of mercy and so pass on to the bliss of heaven with very little punishment or delay."

And then, father, I thought she said next, "I have explained to you these bitter torments of purgatory, and I would like to explain to you two more purgatories, but I can remain here no longer. But this is the general purgatory for all that are christened. And the second purgatory exists for those who suffer sickness and great affliction in this world, and in accordance with their contrition, and with the pardon which they have earned for themselves while they were not in a state of deadly sin—for they may earn themselves enough pardon in this world to do away with all the pains of purgatory and bring them quickly to the bliss of heaven; and this second purgatory is that of mercy. The third purgatory is that of grace: when a man or woman has most continued to sin and sinned most, he will be punished there if God gives him grace, and not suffer the general pains of purgatory; and that is called the purgatory of grace—but their pains will be very great until God has mercy on them. And many such spirits and also those from the general purgatory appear to men waking in this world, and they both come to men and tell them what can help them, and so they are released from their sufferings. Also many appear to men and women in the world in their sleep, as I did to you, and say what can help themselves and their friends. And all this is the purgatory of grace. So I have described three purgatories to you: one is the purgatory of justice, which is the general purgatory that you have already seen; the second is the purgatory of mercy; and the third is the purgatory of grace, as I have told you. But every man or woman that has these Masses said for him, and the psalm *Miserere mei deus* with the hymn *Veni creator spiritus* in the way I have described already—and if someone is not in a position to have these Masses said for him, let him have the thirteen Masses said with the prayers following as I said before—through his mercy, God will deliver them from their torment. And if there is any priest who will do the same for himself before he dies, that will release him from all his torments in purgatory when he gets there as quickly as if they were said for him immediately after his death; and he will receive a great reward and great thanks from God for his trouble; and if he would do it for any friend of his, it would be better than if it were done by any other man, and they shall be the more speedily delivered from their torment because of his goodwill and his true labour.

And then she said, "Every educated man and woman that is feeling any temptation as I described before, let him say this hymn *Veni creator spiritus* and the devil and that temptation shall soon leave him, and let him then thank his God and ask for his mercy and say *Miserere mei deus* and greet our Lady with five *Aves*."[28] And then she said, "Now I have told you everything according to God's will, and come to the end of purgatory; pay great attention to what you see me do now; and if you had not gone to Southwick,[29] on pilgrimage for me in honour of God and of our Lady—for I had vowed to go there and could not do so, and you did it for me—otherwise I should have been horribly held back in my journey when I had been weighed and released from this torment, and you will soon see this."

And soon after that it seemed to me that a fair lady came, and a fair young man with her, about twenty years old; and he was carrying a pair of scales in his hand, and he was clad all in white clothes; and it seemed to me that the lady was clad in white interwoven with gold and her garment was decorated with gold stars, and she had a golden royal crown on her head, and a sceptre in her hand, and at the end of the sceptre there was a small cross. And then she spoke to the man in white: "Son," she said, "take this woman and let her be weighed." And then Margaret was immediately in one pan of the scales, and the devil was in the other, and a great long worm with him; and twice the scales dropped down more heavily on his side, and the devil enumerated all the sins for which she had been suffering torment. And then the man in white said, "Her sins are forgiven, for she has already done penance for them, and she is now given to the fount of mercy who is here, the queen of heaven and earth, empress of hell and of purgatory, and the blessed mother of God—she is given to her. What can you say to this woman?" And then it seemed to me that the devil took out that great worm and said, "Here is the worm of conscience which shall still work in her for a thing which remains, and that is that she made a vow to go on a pilgrimage and did not fulfil it." And then it seemed to me that the fair lady said, "There is someone who has done it for her, and my Son and I have had mercy on this woman. And fie on you, foul Satan! You and the worm of conscience shall never harm her more." And at these words it seemed to me that the scale dropped down on the fair lady's side. And it seemed to me that the devil and the worm gave a great cry and disappeared immediately. And then the fair lady took a white cloth and wrapped it all round her, and then this lady said, "Come with me, my daughter, and you shall receive the oil of mercy and your conscience shall be made pure. And all those who have helped you out of your torment so quickly shall be richly rewarded, and when they come to purgatory they will quickly find the great mercy of almighty God, and they shall pass more quickly out of torment for your sake."

And then this fair lady led her to a strong bridge, and at the end of the bridge was a fair white chapel, and it seemed to me that a great multitude of people came out of it to greet her with a fair procession and a joyful song. And then this fair lady and this procession led her to a fair well, and there her whole body was washed. And suddenly a white chapel appeared beside the well, and the lady and the procession led Margaret into it. And then thirteen men came in and one of them sang a Mass, and it seemed to me that the fair lady presented Margaret to them, and all at once it seemed to me that a crown was placed on her head, and a sceptre in her hand; and then the man who was singing the Mass said, "Daughter, receive here the crown of grace and mercy, and this sceptre of victory, for you have overcome all your enemies." And it seemed to me that this man sang the remainder of the Mass, and when the Mass was over they all went out of the chapel; and the man who had sung the

Mass took Margaret with him and led her to a golden gate, and the procession went with him. And he said to Margaret, "Daughter, go in at this gate and receive the bliss of paradise and heaven which Adam was in and which is your natural inheritance." And at once, father, I woke and everything had vanished. That is all for this time, father; but may God bring us to his kingdom, Amen.

Margery Kempe

EXTRACTS FROM *THE BOOK OF MARGERY KEMPE*
(BOOK I)

CHAPTER 11

It happened one Friday, Midsummer Eve,[1] in very hot weather—as this creature was coming from York carrying a bottle of beer in her hand, and her husband a cake tucked inside his clothes against his chest—that her husband asked his wife this question: "Margery, if there came a man with a sword who would strike off my head unless I made love with you as I used to do before, tell me on your conscience—for you say you will not lie—whether you would allow my head to be cut off, or else allow me to make love with you again, as I did at one time?"

"Alas, sir," she said, "why are you raising this matter, when we have been chaste for these past eight weeks?"

"Because I want to know the truth of your heart."

And then she said with great sorrow, "Truly, I would rather see you being killed, than that we should turn back to our uncleanness."

And he replied, "You are no good wife."

And then she asked her husband what was the reason that he had not made love to her for the last eight weeks, since she lay with him every night in his bed. And he said that he was made so afraid when he would have touched her, that he dared do no more.

"Now, good sir, mend your ways and ask God's mercy, for I told you nearly three years ago that you[r desire for sex] would suddenly be slain—and this is now the third year, and I hope yet that I shall have my wish. Good sir, I pray you to grant what I shall ask, and I shall pray for you to be saved through the mercy of our Lord Jesus Christ, and you shall have more reward in heaven than if you wore a hair-shirt or wore a coat of mail as a penance. I pray you, allow me to make a vow of chastity at whichever bishop's hand that God wills."

"No," he said, "I won't allow you to do that, because now I can make love to you without mortal sin, and then I wouldn't be able to."

Then she replied, "If it be the will of the Holy Ghost to fulfil what I have said, I pray God that you may consent to this; and if it be not the will of the Holy Ghost, I pray God that you never consent."

Then they went on towards Bridlington and the weather was extremely hot, this creature all the time having great sorrow and great fear for her chastity. And as they came by a cross her husband sat down under the cross, calling his wife to him and saying these words to her: "Margery, grant me my desire, and I shall grant you your desire. My first desire is that we shall still lie together in one bed as we have done before; the second, that you shall pay my debts before you go to Jerusalem;[2] and the third, that you shall eat and drink with me on Fridays as you used to do."

"No, sir," she said. "I will never agree to break my Friday fast as long as I live."

"Well," he said, "then I'm going to have sex with you again."

She begged him to allow her to say her prayers, and he kindly allowed it. Then she knelt down beside a cross in the field and prayed in this way, with a great abundance of tears: "Lord God, you know all things. You know what sorrow I have had to be chaste for you in my body all these three years, and now I might have my will and dare not, for love of you. For if I were to break that custom of fasting from meat and drink on Fridays which you commanded me, I should now have my desire. But, blessed Lord, you know I will not go against your will, and great is my sorrow now unless I find comfort in you. Now, blessed Jesus, make your will known to my unworthy self, so that I may afterwards follow and fulfil it with all my might."

And then our Lord Jesus Christ with great sweetness spoke to this creature, commanding her to go again to her husband and pray him to grant her what she desired: "And he shall have what he desires. For, my beloved daughter, this was the reason why I ordered you to fast, so that you should the sooner obtain your desire, and now it is granted to you. I no longer wish you to fast, and therefore

I command you in the name of Jesus to eat and drink as your husband does."

Then this creature thanked our Lord Jesus Christ for his grace and his goodness, and afterwards got up and went to her husband, saying to him, "Sir, if you please, you shall grant me my desire, and you shall have your desire. Grant me that you will not come into my bed, and I grant you that I will pay your debts before I go to Jerusalem. And make my body free to God, so that you never make any claim on me requesting any conjugal debt after this day as long as you live—and I shall eat and drink on Fridays at your bidding."

Then her husband replied to her, "May your body be as freely available to God as it has been to me."

This creature thanked God greatly, rejoicing that she had her desire, praying her husband that they should say three paternosters in worship of the Trinity for the great grace that had been granted them. And so they did, kneeling under a cross, and afterwards they ate and drank together in great gladness of spirit. This was on a Friday, on Midsummer's Eve.

Then they went on to Bridlington and also to many other places, and spoke with God's servants, both anchorites and recluses, and many other of our Lord's lovers, with many worthy clerics, doctors and bachelors of divinity as well, in many different places. And to various people amongst them this creature revealed her feelings and her contemplations, as she was commanded to do, to find out if there was any deception in her feelings.

CHAPTER 17

... Then she made her way to Norwich, and came into his church on a Thursday a little before noon. And the Vicar[3] was walking up and down with another priest who was his confessor, and who was still alive when this book was written. And this creature was dressed in black clothing at that time.

She greeted the Vicar, asking him if she could—in the afternoon, when he had eaten—speak with him for an hour or two of the love of God. He, lifting up his hands and blessing himself, said, "Bless us! How could a woman occupy one or two hours with the love of our Lord? I shan't eat a thing till I find out what you can say of our Lord God in the space of an hour."

Then he sat himself down in the church. She, sitting a little to one side, told him all the words which God had revealed to her in

her soul. Afterwards she told him the whole manner of her life from
her childhood, as closely as it would come to mind—how unkind
and unnatural she had been towards our Lord Jesus Christ; how
proud and vain she had been in her bearing; how obstinate against
the laws of God, and how envious towards her fellow Christians;
how she was chastised (later when it pleased our Lord Christ Jesus)
with many tribulations and horrible temptations, and how afterwards she was fed and comforted with holy meditations, and specially in the memory of our Lord's Passion.

And, while she conversed on the Passion of our Lord Jesus
Christ, she heard so terrible a melody that she could not bear it.
Then this creature fell down, as if she had lost her bodily strength,
and lay still for a long while, desiring to put it aside, and she could
not. Then she knew indeed by her faith that there was great joy in
heaven, where the least point of bliss surpasses without any comparison all the joy that ever might be thought or felt in this life. She
was greatly strengthened in her faith and the more bold to tell the
Vicar her feelings, which she had by revelations about both the living and the dead, and about his own self.

She told him how sometimes the Father of Heaven conversed
with her soul as plainly and as certainly as one friend speaks to another through bodily speech. Sometimes the Second Person in Trinity, sometimes all Three Persons in Trinity and one substance in
Godhead, spoke to her soul, and informed her in her faith and in his
love—how she should love him, worship him and dread him—so
excellently that she never heard any book, neither Hilton's book,
nor Bride's book, nor *Stimulus Amoris*, nor *Incendium Amoris*, nor
any other book that she ever heard read,[4] that spoke so exaltedly of
the love of God as she felt highly working in her soul, if she could
have communicated what she felt.

Sometimes our Lady spoke to her mind; sometimes St Peter,
sometimes St Paul, sometimes St Katherine,[5] or whatever saint in
heaven she was devoted to, appeared to her soul and taught her how
she should love our Lord and how she should please him. These
conversations were so sweet, so holy and so devout, that often this
creature could not bear it, but fell down and twisted and wrenched
her body about, and made remarkable faces and gestures, with vehement sobbing and great abundance of tears, sometimes saying
"Jesus mercy," and sometimes, "I die."

And therefore many people slandered her, not believing that it was the work of God, but that some evil spirit tormented her in her body or else that she had some bodily sickness. . . .

CHAPTER 18

. . . And then she was commanded by our Lord to go to an anchoress in the same city who was called Dame Julian. And so she did, and told her about the grace, that God had put into her soul, of compunction, contrition, sweetness and devotion, compassion with holy meditation and high contemplation, and very many holy speeches and converse that our Lord spoke to her soul, and also many wonderful revelations, which she described to the anchoress to find out if there were any deception in them, for the anchoress was expert in such things and could give good advice.

The anchoress, hearing the marvellous goodness of our Lord, highly thanked God with all her heart for his visitation, advising this creature to be obedient to the will of our Lord and fulfil with all her might whatever he put into her soul, if it were not against the worship of God and the profit of her fellow Christians. For if it were, then it were not the influence of a good spirit, but rather of an evil spirit. "The Holy Ghost never urges a thing against charity, and if he did, he would be contrary to his own self for he is all charity. Also he moves a soul to all chasteness, for chaste livers are called the temple of the Holy Ghost, and the Holy Ghost makes a soul stable and steadfast in the right faith and the right belief.

"And a double man in soul is always unstable and unsteadfast in all his ways. He that is forever doubting is like the wave of the sea which is moved and borne about with the wind, and that man is not likely to receive the gifts of God.

"Any creature that has these tokens may steadfastly believe that the Holy Ghost dwells in his soul. And much more, when God visits a creature with tears of contrition, devotion or compassion, he may and ought to believe that the Holy Ghost is in his soul. St Paul says that the Holy Ghost asks for us with mourning and weeping unspeakable; that is to say, he causes us to ask and pray with mourning and weeping so plentifully that the tears may not be numbered. No evil spirit may give these tokens, for St Jerome says that tears torment the devil more than do the pains of hell. God and the devil are always at odds, and they shall never dwell together in one place, and the devil has no power in a man's soul.

"Holy Writ says that the soul of a righteous man is the seat of

God, and so I trust, sister, that you are. I pray God grant you per-
severance. Set all your trust in God and do not fear the talk of the
world, for the more contempt, shame and reproof that you have in
this world, the more is your merit in the sight of God. Patience is
necessary for you, for in that shall you keep your soul."

Great was the holy conversation that the anchoress and this creature had through talking of the love of our Lord Jesus Christ for the
many days that they were together. . . .

Chapter 22

As this creature lay in contemplation, weeping bitterly in her spirit,
she said to our Lord Jesus Christ, "Ah, Lord, maidens are now
dancing merrily in heaven. Shall I not do so? Because I am no virgin, lack of virginity is now great sorrow to me. I think I wish I had
been killed as soon as I was taken from the font, so that I should
never have displeased you, and then, blessed Lord, you would have
had my virginity without end. Ah, dear God, I have not loved you
all the days of my life, and I keenly regret that; I have run away
from you, and you have run after me; I would fall into despair, and
you would not let me."

"Ah, daughter, how often have I told you that your sins are forgiven you and that we are united together [in love] without end? To
me you are a love unlike any other, daughter, and therefore I promise you that you shall have a singular grace in heaven, daughter, and
I promise you that I shall come to your end, at your dying, with my
blessed mother, and my holy angels and twelve apostles, St Katherine, St Margaret[6] and St Mary Magdalene, and many other saints
that are in heaven, who greatly worship me for the grace that I give
to you, your God, your Lord Jesus. You need fear no grievous
pains in dying for you shall have your desire, which is to have your
mind more on my Passion than on your own pain. You shall not
fear the devil of hell, for he has no power over you. He fears you
more than you do him. He is angry with you, because you torment
him more with your weeping than all the fire in hell does; you win
many souls from him with your weeping. And I have promised you
that you should have no other purgatory than the slanderous talk of
this world, for I have chastised you myself as I would, by many
great fears and torments that you have had with evil spirits, both
sleeping and waking, for many years. And therefore I shall preserve
you at your end through my mercy, so that they shall have no

power over you either in body or in soul. It is a great grace and miracle that you still have your wits, considering the vexation that you have had from them in the past.

"I have also, daughter, chastised you with the fear of my Godhead, and many times I have frightened you with great winds and storms, so that you thought vengeance would have fallen on you for sin. I have tested you by many tribulations, many great griefs and many grievous sicknesses, so that you have been anointed for death, and entirely through my grace you have escaped. Therefore don't be at all afraid, daughter, for with my own hands which were nailed to the cross I shall take your soul from your body with great joy and melody, with sweet smells and fragrances, and offer it to my father in heaven, where you shall see him face to face, dwelling with him without end.

"Daughter, you will be very welcome to my father, and to my mother, and to all my saints in heaven, for you have given them drink very many times with the tears of your eyes. All my holy saints shall rejoice at your coming home. You shall be fulfilled with every kind of love that you desire. Then you will bless the time that you were made and the body that has [dearly] redeemed you. He shall rejoice in you and you in him without end.

"Daughter, I promise you the same grace that I promised St Katherine, St Margaret, St Barbara[7] and St Paul, in that if any person on earth until the Day of Judgement asks any boon of you and believes that God loves you, he shall have his boon or else something better. Therefore those that believe that God loves you shall be blessed without end. The souls in purgatory shall rejoice at your coming home, for they well know that God loves you specially. And men on earth shall rejoice in God for you, for he shall work much grace for you and make all the world to know that God loves you. You have been despised for my love, and therefore you shall be honoured for my love.

"Daughter, when you are in heaven you will be able to ask what you wish, and I shall grant you all your desire. I have told you before that you are a singular lover of God, and therefore you shall have a singular love in heaven, a singular reward and a singular honour. And because you are a maiden in your soul, I shall take you by the one hand in heaven, and my mother by the other, and so you shall dance in heaven with other holy maidens and virgins, for I may call you dearly bought and my own beloved darling. I shall say to you, my own blessed spouse, 'Welcome to me, with every kind of joy and gladness, here to dwell with me and never to depart from me without end, but ever to dwell with me in joy and bliss, which no eye may see, nor ear hear, nor tongue tell, nor heart think, that I have ordained for you and for all my servants who desire to love and please me as you do.' "

CHAPTER 35

As this creature was in the church of the Holy Apostles at Rome[8] on St Lateran's Day,[9] the Father of Heaven said to her, "Daughter, I am well pleased with you, in as much as you believe in all the sacraments of Holy Church and in all faith involved in that, and especially because you believe in the manhood of my son, and because of the great compassion that you have for his bitter Passion."

The Father also said to this creature, "Daughter, I will have you wedded to my Godhead, because I shall show you my secrets and my counsels, for you shall live with me without end."

Then this creature kept silence in her soul and did not answer to this, because she was very much afraid of the Godhead; and she had no knowledge of the conversation of the Godhead, for all her love and affection were fixed on the manhood of Christ, and of that she did have knowledge and would not be parted from that for anything.

She had so much feeling for the manhood of Christ, that when she saw women in Rome carrying children in their arms, if she could discover that any were boys, she would cry, roar and weep as if she had seen Christ in his childhood. And if she could have had her way, she would often have taken the children out of their mothers' arms and kissed them instead of Christ. And if she saw a handsome man, she had great pain to look at him, lest she might see him who was both God and man. And therefore she cried many times and often when she met a handsome man, and wept and sobbed bitterly for the manhood of Christ as she went about the streets of Rome, so that those who saw her were greatly astonished at her, because they did not know the reason.

Therefore it was not surprising if she was still and did not answer the Father of Heaven, when he told her that she should be wedded to his Godhead. Then the Second Person, Christ Jesus, whose manhood she loved so much, said to her, "What do you say to my Father, Margery, daughter, about these words that he speaks to you? Are you well pleased that it should be so?"

And then she would not answer the Second Person, but wept amazingly much, desiring to have himself still, and in no way to be parted from him. Then the Second Person in Trinity answered his Father for her, and said, "Father, excuse her, for she is still only young and has not completely learned how she should answer."

And then the Father took her by the hand [spiritually] in her soul, before the Son and the Holy Ghost, and the mother of Jesus, and all the twelve apostles, and St Katherine and St Margaret and many other saints and holy virgins, with a great multitude of angels, saying to her soul, "I take you, Margery, for my wedded wife, for fairer, for fouler, for richer, for poorer, provided that you are humble and meek in doing what I command you to do. For, daughter, there was never a child so kind to its mother as I shall be to you, both in joy and sorrow, to help you and comfort you. And that I pledge to you."

And then the mother of God and all the saints that were present there in her soul prayed that they might have much joy together. Then this creature with high devotion, with great abundance of tears, thanked God for this spiritual comfort, holding herself in her own feeling very unworthy of any such grace as she felt, for she felt many great comforts, both spiritual comforts and bodily comforts. Sometimes she sensed sweet smells in her nose; they were sweeter, she thought, than any earthly sweet thing ever was that she smelled before, nor could she ever tell how sweet they were, for she thought she might have lived on them if they had lasted.

Sometimes she heard with her bodily ears such sounds and melodies that she could not hear what anyone said to her at that time unless he spoke louder. These sounds and melodies she had heard nearly every day for twenty-five years when this book was written, and especially when she was in devout prayer, also many times while she was at Rome, and in England too.

She saw with her bodily eyes many white things flying all about her on all sides, as thickly in a way as specks in a sunbeam; they were very delicate and comforting, and the brighter the sun shone, the better she could see them. She saw them at many different times and in many different places, both in church and in her chamber, at her meals and at her prayers, in the fields and in town, both walking and sitting. And many times she was afraid what they might be, for she saw them at night in darkness as well as in daylight. Then when she was afraid of them, our Lord said to her, "By this token, daughter, believe it is God who speaks in you, for wherever God is, heaven is, and where God is, there are many angels, and God is in you and you are in him. And therefore, don't be afraid, daughter, for these betoken that you have many angels around you, to keep you both day and night so that no devil shall have power over you, nor evil men harm you."

Then from that time forward she used to say when she saw them coming: "*Benedictus qui venit in nomine Domini.*"[10]

Our Lord also gave her another token which lasted about sixteen years, and increased ever more and more, and that was a flame of fire of love—marvelously hot and delectable and very comforting, never diminishing but ever increasing; for though the weather were never so cold she felt the heat burning in her breast and at her heart, as veritably as a man would feel the material fire if he put his hand or his finger into it.

When she first felt the fire of love burning in her breast she was afraid of it, and then our Lord answered in her mind and said, "Daughter, don't be afraid, because this heat is the heat of the Holy Ghost, which will burn away all your sins, for the fire of love quenches all sins. And you shall understand by this token that the Holy Ghost is in you, and you know very well that wherever the Holy Ghost is, there is the Father, and where the Father is, there is the Son, and so you have fully in your soul all of the Holy Trinity. Therefore you have great cause to love me well, and yet you shall have greater cause than you ever had to love me, for you shall hear what you never heard, and you shall see what you never saw, and you shall feel what you never felt.

"For, daughter, you are as sure of the love of God, as God is God. Your soul is more sure of the love of God than of your own body, for your soul will part from your body, but God shall never part from your soul, for they are united together without end. Therefore, daughter, you have as great reason to be merry as any lady in this world; and if you knew, daughter, how much you please me when you willingly allow me to speak in you, you would never do otherwise, for this is a holy life and the time is very well spent. For, daughter, this life pleases me more than wearing the coat of mail for penance, or the hair-shirt, or fasting on bread and water;

for if you said a thousand *paternosters* every day you would not please me as much as you do when you are in silence and allow me to speak in your soul."

CHAPTER 36

"Fasting, daughter, is good for young beginners, and discreet penance, especially what their confessor gives them or enjoins them to do. And to pray many beads is good for those who can do no better, yet it is not perfect. But it is a good way towards perfection. For I tell you, daughter, those who are great fasters and great doers of penance want it to be considered the best life; those also who give themselves over to saying many devotions would have that to be the best life; and those who give very generous alms would like that considered the best life.

"And I have often told you, daughter, that thinking, weeping, and high contemplation is the best life on earth. You shall have more merit in heaven for one year of thinking in your mind than for a hundred years of praying with your mouth; and yet you will not believe me, for you will pray many beads whether I wish it or not. And yet, daughter, I will not be displeased with you whether you think, say or speak, for I am always pleased with you.

"And if I were on earth as bodily as I was before I died on the cross, I would not be ashamed of you, as many other people are, for I would take you by the hand amongst the people and greet you warmly, so that they would certainly know that I loved you dearly.

"For it is appropriate for the wife to be on homely terms with her husband. Be he ever so great a lord and she ever so poor a woman when he weds her, yet they must lie together and rest together in joy and peace. Just so must it be between you and me, for I take no heed of what you have been but what you would be, and I have often told you that I have clean forgiven you all your sins.

"Therefore I must be intimate with you, and lie in your bed with you. Daughter, you greatly desire to see me, and you may boldly, when you are in bed, take me to you as your wedded husband, as your dear darling, and as your sweet son, for I want to be loved as a son should be loved by the mother, and I want you to love me, daughter, as a good wife ought to love her husband. Therefore you can boldly take me in the arms of your soul and kiss my mouth, my head, and my feet as sweetly as you want. And as often as you think of me or would do any good deed to me, you shall have the same reward in heaven as if you did it to my own precious body which is in heaven, for I ask no more of you but your heart, to love me who loves you, for my love is always ready for you."

Then she gave thanks and praise to our Lord Jesus Christ for the high grace and mercy that he showed to her, unworthy wretch.

This creature had various tokens in her hearing. One was a kind of sound as if it were a pair of bellows blowing in her ear. She—being dismayed at this—was warned in her soul to have no fear, for it was the sound of the Holy Ghost. And then our Lord turned that sound into the voice of a dove, and afterwards he turned it into the voice of a little bird which is called a redbreast, that often sang very merrily in her right ear. And then she would always have great grace after she heard such a token. She had been used to such tokens for about twenty-five years at the time of writing this book.

Then our Lord Jesus Christ said to his creature, "By these tokens you may well know that I love you, for you are to me a true mother and to all the world, because of that great charity which is in you; and yet I am cause of that charity myself, and you shall have great reward for it in heaven."

CHAPTER 57

Then it so happened that another monk came to Lynn at the time of removing—as was the custom amongst them—who had no love for the said creature, nor would allow her to come into their chapel, as she had done before he came there.

Then the Prior of Lynn, Dom Thomas Hevyngham, meeting the said creature and Master Robert Spryngolde, who was her confessor at that time, asked them to excuse him if she no longer received communion in his chapel; "for there has come," he said, "a new brother of mine who will not come into our chapel as long as she is in it. And therefore, please provide yourselves with another place."

Master Robert answered, "Sir, we must then give her communion in the church—we may not choose, for she has my Lord of Canterbury's letter and seal, in which we are commanded, by virtue of obedience, to hear her confession and administer the sacrament to her as often as we are required."[11]

Then after this time she received communion at the high altar in St Margaret's Church, and our Lord visited her with such great grace when she should receive communion that she cried so loudly that it could be heard all round the church, and outside as well, as if she would have died because of it, so that she could not receive the sacrament from the priest's hands, the priest turning back again to the altar with the precious sacrament until her crying had ceased. And then he, turning back to her, would minister to her as he ought to do. And thus it happened many times when she was to receive communion; and sometimes she would weep very softly and silently in receiving the precious sacrament without any violence, just as our Lord would visit her with his grace.

One Good Friday, as the said creature beheld priests kneeling and other worthy men with torches burning in their hands before the Easter Sepulchre, representing the lamentable death and doleful burying of our Lord Jesus Christ according to the good custom of Holy Church,[12] the memory of our Lady's sorrows, which she suffered when she beheld his precious body hanging on the cross and then buried before her eyes, suddenly filled the heart of this creature. Her mind was drawn wholly into the Passion of our Lord Christ Jesus, whom she beheld with her spiritual eye in the sight of her soul as truly as if she had seen his precious body beaten, scourged and crucified with her bodily eye, which sight and spiritual beholding worked by grace so fervently in her mind, wounding her with pity and compassion, so that she sobbed, roared and cried, and, spreading her arms out wide, said with a loud voice, "I die, I die," so that many people were astonished at her, and wondered what was the matter with her. And the more she tried to keep herself from crying, the louder she cried, for it was not in her power to take it or leave it, but as God would send it. Then a priest took her in his arms and carried her into the Prior's Cloister to let her get the air, supposing she would not otherwise have lasted, her affliction was so great. Then she turned all blue like lead, and sweated dreadfully.

And this manner of crying lasted for a period of ten years, as is written before. And every Good Friday in all these years she was weeping and sobbing five or six hours together, and also cried loudly many times, so that she could not restrain herself from doing so, which made her very weak and feeble in her bodily strength. Sometimes she wept for an hour on Good Friday for the sins of the people, having more sorrow for their sins than for her own, inasmuch as our Lord forgave her her own sins before she went to Jerusalem.

Nevertheless, she wept for her own sins most plentifully when it pleased our Lord to visit her with his grace. Sometimes she wept another hour for the souls in purgatory; another hour for those who were in misfortune, in poverty, or in any distress; another hour for Jews, Saracens, and all false heretics, that God out of his great goodness should set aside their blindness, so that they might through his grace be turned to the faith of Holy Church and be children of salvation.

Many times, when this creature would say her prayers, our Lord said to her, "Daughter, ask what you wish, and you shall have it."

She said, "I ask for absolutely nothing, Lord, except what you may well give me, and that is mercy, which I ask for the people's sins. Often during the year you say to me that you have forgiven me my sins. Therefore I now ask mercy for the sins of the people, as I would do for my own, for, Lord, you are all charity, and charity brought you into this wretched world and caused you to suffer hard pains for our sins. Why should I not then have charity for the people and desire forgiveness of their sins?

"Blessed Lord, I think you have shown very great charity to me, unworthy wretch that I am. You are as gracious to me as though I were as pure a maiden as any is in this world, and as though I had never sinned.

"Therefore, Lord, I wish I had a well of tears to constrain you with, so that you would not take utter vengeance on man's soul, to part him from you without end; for it is a hard thing, to think that any earthly man should ever do any sin through which he should be parted from your glorious face without end.[13]

"If I could, Lord, give the people contrition and weeping as good as that which you gave me for my own sins and other men's sins also, and as easily as I could give a penny out of my own purse, I should soon fill men's hearts with contrition so that they might cease from their sin. I wonder very much in my heart, Lord, that I—who have been so sinful a woman, and the most unworthy creature that you ever showed your mercy to in all this world—should have such great charity towards my fellow Christian souls. I think that, though they had ordained for me the most shameful death that any man or woman might ever suffer on earth, yet I would forgive them it for your love, Lord, and have their souls saved from everlasting damnation.

"And therefore, Lord, I shall not cease, when I may weep, to weep for them abundantly, prosper if I may. And if you wish, Lord, that I cease from weeping, I pray you, take me out of this world. What should I do there, unless I might profit? For though it were possible that all this world might be saved through the tears of my eyes, I would not be worthy of thanks. Therefore, all praising, all honour, all worship be to you, Lord. If it were your will, Lord, I would for your love, and for the magnifying of your name, be chopped up as small as meat for the pot."

CHAPTER 58

On one occasion, as the said creature was in her contemplation, she hungered very much for God's word, and said, "Alas, Lord! as many clerics as you have in this world, and you will not send me one of them who might fill my soul with your word and with reading of Holy Scripture, for all the clerics that preach may not satisfy me, for I think that my soul is always just as hungry. If I had money enough, I would give a noble every day to have a sermon, for your word is worth more to me than all the money in this world. And therefore, blessed Lord, take pity on me, for you have taken away from me the anchorite who was a singular solace and comfort to me, and many times refreshed me with your holy word."

Then our Lord Jesus Christ answered in her soul, saying, "There shall come someone from far away who shall fulfil your desire."

So, many days after this answer, there came a priest to Lynn who had never known her before and, when he saw her going along the streets, he was greatly moved to speak with her, and inquired of other people what sort of woman she was. They said they trusted to God that she was a very good woman.

Afterwards, the priest sent for her, asking her to come and speak with him and with his mother, for he had hired a room for his mother and for himself, and so they lived together. Then the creature came to learn his will, and she spoke with his mother and with him, and was very kindly received by them both.

Then the priest took a book and read in it how our Lord, seeing the city of Jerusalem, wept over her, rehearsing the misfortunes and sorrows that should come upon her, for she did not know the time of her visitation.[14] When the said creature heard it read how our Lord wept, then she wept bitterly and cried loudly, neither the priest nor his mother knowing any reason for her weeping. When her crying and her weeping were ceased, they rejoiced and were very merry in our Lord. Afterwards she took her leave and parted from them at that time.

When she was gone, the priest said to his mother, "I am amazed at why this woman weeps and cries so. Nevertheless, I think she is a good woman, and I greatly desire to speak more with her."

His mother was well pleased, and advised that he should do so. And afterwards this same priest loved her and trusted her greatly, and blessed the time that he ever knew her, for he found great spiritual comfort in her, and was caused to look up much good scripture, and many a good doctor, at which he would not have looked at that time, had it not been for her.

He read to her many a good book of high contemplation, and other books, such as the Bible with doctor's commentaries on it, St Bride's book, Hilton's book, Bonaventura's *Stimulus Amoris*, *Incendium Amoris*, and others similar. And then she knew it was a spirit sent from God which said to her these words, as is written a little before, when she complained of a lack of reading: "There shall come someone from far away who shall fulfil your desire." And thus she knew by experience that it was a very true spirit.

The said priest read books to her for the most part of seven or eight years, to the great increase of his knowledge and of his merit, and he suffered many an evil word for her love, inasmuch as he read her so many books, and supported her in her weeping and her crying. Afterwards he became beneficed and had a large cure of souls, and then he was very pleased that he had read so much before.

CHAPTER 59

Thus, through listening to holy books and through listening to holy sermons, she was always increasing in contemplation and holy meditation. It would be impossible to write all the holy thoughts, holy speeches, and high revelations which our Lord showed to her, both concerning herself and other men and women, and also concerning many souls, some to be saved and some to be damned.

This was a great punishment and a sharp chastisement to her. To know of those who would be saved she was very glad and joyful because she longed as much as she dared for all men to be saved and when our Lord revealed to her any who would be damned, she had great pain. She would not hear it, nor believe that it was God who showed her such things, and put it out of her mind as much as she could. Our Lord blamed her for this, and bade her believe that it was his high mercy and his goodness to reveal to her his secret counsels, saying to her mind, "Daughter, you must hear of the damned as well as of the saved."

She would give no credence to the counsel of God, but rather believed it was some evil spirit out to deceive her. Then for her forwardness and her unbelief, our Lord withdrew from her all good thoughts and all good recollections of holy speeches and conversation, and the high contemplation which she had been used to before, and allowed her to have as many evil thoughts as she previously had good thoughts. And this affliction lasted twelve days altogether, and just as previously she had four hours in the morning of holy speeches and confabulation with our Lord, so she now had as many hours of foul thoughts and foul recollections of lechery and all uncleanness, as though she would have prostituted herself with all manner of people.

And so the devil deluded her, dallying with her with accursed thoughts, just as our Lord dallied with her previously with holy thoughts. And just as before she had many glorious visions and high contemplation upon the manhood of our Lord, upon our Lady, and upon many other holy saints, even so now she had horrible and abominable visions—despite anything she could do—of seeing men's genitals, and other such abominations.

She saw, as she really thought, various men of religion, priests and many others, both heathen and Christian, coming before her eyes so that she could not avoid them or put them out of her sight, and showing her their naked genitals.

And with that the devil ordered her in her mind to choose which of them she would have first, and she must prostitute herself to them all.

And he said she liked one of them better than all the others. She thought he spoke the truth; she could not say no; and she had to do his bidding, and yet she would not have done it for all this world. But yet she thought it should be done and she thought that these horrible sights and accursed thoughts were delicious to her against her will. Wherever she went or whatever she did, these accursed thoughts remained with her. When she would see the sacrament, say her prayers, or do any other good deed, such abomination was always put into her mind. She was shriven and did all that she could, but she found no release, until she was nearly in despair. It cannot be written what pain she felt, and what sorrow she was in.

Then she said, "Alas, Lord, you have said before that you would never forsake me. Where is now the truthfulness of your word?"

And immediately afterwards her good angel came to her, saying. "Daughter, God has not forsaken you, nor ever shall forsake you, as he has promised you. But because you do not believe that it is the spirit of God that speaks in your soul and reveals to you his secret counsels, of some that shall be saved and some that shall be damned, therefore God chastises you in this way, and this chastising shall endure twelve days until you will believe that it is God who speaks to you and no devil."

Then she said to her angel, "Ah, I pray you, pray for me to my Lord Jesus Christ, that he will vouchsafe to take from me these accursed thoughts, and speak to me as he did before now, and I shall make a promise to God that I shall believe that it is God who has spoken to me before, for I may no longer endure this great pain."

Her angel said to her again, "Daughter, my Lord Jesus will not take it away from you until you have suffered it twelve days, for he wishes that you should know by that means whether it is better that God speak to you or the devil. And my Lord Christ Jesus is never the angrier with you, though he allow you to feel this pain."

So she suffered that pain until twelve days were passed, and then she had as holy thoughts, as holy reflections, and as holy desires, as holy speeches and conversation with our Lord Jesus Christ as she ever had before, our Lord saying to her, "Daughter, now believe indeed that I am no devil."

Then she was filled with joy, for she heard our Lord speaking to her as he used to do. Therefore she said, "I shall believe that every good thought is the speech of God. Blessed may you be, Lord, that you do not disdain to comfort me again. I would not, Lord, for all this world suffer such another pain as I suffered these twelve days, for I thought I was in hell—blessed may you be that it is past. Therefore, Lord, I will now lie still and be obedient to your will. I pray you, Lord, speak in me what is most pleasing to you.". . .

CHAPTER 62
Afterwards, on St James's Day, the good friar preached in St James's Chapel yard in Lynn—he was at that time neither bachelor nor doc-

tor of divinity—where there were many people and a great audience, for he had a holy name and great favour amongst the people, in so much that some men, if they knew that he would preach in the district, would go with him or else follow him from town to town, such great delight had they to hear him, and so—blessed may God be—he preached most holily and devoutly.

Nevertheless, on this day he preached a great deal against the said creature, not mentioning her name, but so conveying his thoughts that people well understood that he meant her. Then there was much protest amongst the people, for many men and many women trusted and loved her very much, and were very sad and sorry that he spoke so much against her as he did, wishing that they had not heard him that day.

When he heard the murmuring and grumbling of the people, and supposing he would be gainsaid another day by those who were her friends, he, striking his hand on the pulpit, said, "If I hear these matters repeated any more, I shall so strike the nail on the head," he said, "that it shall shame all her supporters."

And then many of those who pretended friendship to her hung back out of a little vain dread that they had of his words, and dared not very well speak with her. Among these people was the same priest who afterwards wrote down this book, and he was resolved never again to believe her feelings.

And yet our Lord drew him back in a short time—blessed may he be—so that he loved her more, and trusted more in her weeping and her crying than he ever did before. For afterwards he read of a woman called Mary of Oignies, and of her manner of life, of the wonderful sweetness that she had in hearing the word of God, of the wonderful compassion that she had in thinking of his Passion, of the abundant tears that she wept, which made her so weak and feeble that she could not endure to look upon the cross, nor hear our Lord's Passion repeated, without dissolving into tears of pity and compassion.

Of the plentiful grace of her tears, it treats especially in the book before mentioned, in the eighteenth chapter which begins *Bonus est, domine, sperantibus in te,*[15] and also in the nineteenth chapter, where it tells how she, at the request of a priest that he should not be troubled or disturbed at his Mass by her weeping and sobbing, went out at the church door, crying with a loud voice, such that she could not restrain herself.

And our Lord also visited the priest when at Mass with such grace and such devotion when he should read the Holy Gospel, that he wept amazingly, so that he wetted his vestments and the ornaments of the altar, and could not control his weeping or his sobbing, it was so abundant; nor could be restrain it, or very well stand at the altar because of it.

Then he well believed that the good woman, for whom he had previously had little affection, could not restrain her weeping, her sobbing, nor her crying, and that she felt much more abundance of grace than he ever did, beyond comparison. Then he well knew that God gave his grace to whom he would.

Then the priest who wrote this treatise, through the prompting of a worthy clerk, a bachelor of divinity, had seen and read the matter before written much more seriously and in greater detail than it is written in this present treatise. (For here is included only a little of the purpose of it, because he did not have a very clear memory of the said matter when he wrote this treatise, and therefore he wrote less about it.)

Then he drew towards and inclined more steadfastly to the said creature, whom he had fled and avoided because of the friar's preaching, as is written before. The same priest also read afterwards in a treatise which is called *The Prick of Love*,[16] the second chapter, that Bonaventura wrote these following words about himself: "Ah, Lord, what shall I more cry out and call? You delay and do not come, and I, weary and overcome with desire, begin to go mad, for love governs me, and not reason. I run with a hasty course wherever you wish. I submit, Lord. Those who see me are irked and have pity, not knowing me to be drunk with your love. 'Lord,' they say, 'see, that mad man cries out in the streets,' but they do not perceive how great is the desire of my heart."

He also read similar material about Richard of Hampole,[17] the hermit, in the *Incendium Amoris,* which prompted him to give credence to the said creature. Elizabeth of Hungary[18] also cried with a loud voice, as is written in her treatise.

And many others, who had forsaken her because of the friar's preaching, repented and turned to her once more by process of time, notwithstanding that the friar kept his opinion. He would always in his sermons have a part against her, whether she were there or not, and caused many people to think very badly of her for many long days.

For some said that she had a devil within her, and some said to her own face that the friar should have driven those devils out of her. Thus was she slandered, and eaten and gnawed by people's talk, because of the grace that God worked in her of contrition, of devotion, and of compassion, through the gift of which graces she wept, sobbed, and cried very bitterly against her will—she might not choose, for she would rather have wept softly and privately than openly, if it had been in her power. . . .

CHAPTER 76

It happened one time that the husband of the said creature—a man of great age, over sixty years old—would have come down from his chamber bare-foot and bare-legged, and he slithered, or else missed his footing, and fell to the ground from the stairs, with his head twisted underneath him, seriously broken and bruised, so much so that he had five linen plugs in the wounds in his head for many days while his head was healing.

And, as God willed, it was known to some of his neighbours how he had fallen down the stairs, perhaps through the din and the rushing of his falling. And so they came in to him and found him lying with his head twisted under himself, half alive, all streaked with blood, and never likely to have spoken with priest nor clerk, except through high grace and miracle.

Then the said creature, his wife, was sent for, and so she came to him. Then he was taken up and his head was sewn, and he was ill for a long time after, so that people thought he would die. And then people said, if he died, his wife deserved to be hanged for his death, for as much as she could have looked after him and did not. They did not live together, nor did they sleep together for—as it is written before—they both with one assent and with the free will of each other had made a vow to live chaste. And therefore, to avoid all risks, they lived in different places, where no suspicion could be had of their lack of chastity. For, at first, they lived together after they had made their vow, and then people slandered them, and said they enjoyed their lust and their pleasure as they did before the making of their vow. And when they went out on pilgrimage, or to see and speak with other spiritually-minded creatures, many evil folk whose tongues were their own hurt, lacking the fear and love of our Lord Jesus Christ, believed and said that they went rather to woods, groves or valleys, to enjoy the lust of their bodies, where people should not espy it or know it.

Knowing how prone people were to believe evil of them, and desiring to avoid all occasion as far as they properly could, by mutual good will and consent, they parted from each other as regards their board and lodging, and went to board in different places. And this was the reason that she was not with him, and also so that she should not be hindered from her contemplation. And therefore, when he had fallen and was seriously hurt, as is it said before, people said, if he died, it was proper that she should answer for his death. Then she prayed to our Lord that her husband might live a year, and she be delivered from slander, if it were his pleasure.

Our Lord said to her mind, "Daughter, you shall have your boon, for he shall live, and I have performed a great miracle for you that he was not dead. And I bid you take him home, and look after him for my love."

She said, "No, good Lord, for I shall then not attend to you as I do now."

"Yes, daughter," said our Lord, "you shall have as much reward for looking after him and helping him in his need at home, as if you were in church to say your prayers. And you have said many times that you would gladly look after me. I pray you now, look after him for love of me, for he has sometime fulfilled both your will and my will, and he has made your body freely available to me, so that you should serve me and live chaste and clean, and therefore I wish you to be available to help him in his need, in my name."

"Ah, Lord," said she, "for your mercy, grant me grace to obey your will, and fulfil your will, and never let my spiritual enemies have any power to hinder me from fulfilling your will."

Then she took her husband home with her and looked after him for years afterwards, as long as he lived. She had very much trouble with him, for in his last days he turned childish and lacked reason, so that he could not go to a stool to relieve himself, or else he would not, but like a child discharged his excrement into his linen clothes as he sat there by the fire or at the table—wherever it was, he would spare no place. And therefore her labour was all the greater, in washing and wringing, and so were her expenses for keeping a fire going. All this hindered her a very great deal from her contemplation, so that many times she would have disliked her work, except that she thought to herself how she in her young days had had very many delectable thoughts, physical lust, and inordinate love for his body. And therefore she was glad to be punished by means of the same body, and took it much the more easily, and served him and helped him, she thought, as she would have done Christ himself.

CHAPTER 85

One time, as the said creature was kneeling before an altar of the Cross and saying a prayer, her eyelids kept closing together, as though she would have slept. And in the end she couldn't choose; she fell into a little slumber, and at once there appeared truly to her sight an angel, all clothed in white, as if he were a little child, bearing a huge book before him. Then this creature said to the child, or else to the angel, "Ah," she said, "this is the Book of Life."

And she saw in the book the Trinity, and all in gold. Then she said to the child, "Where is my name?"

The child answered and said, "Here is your name, written at the Trinity's foot," and with that he was gone, she didn't know where.

And soon afterwards, our Lord Jesus Christ spoke to her and said, "Daughter, see that you are now true and steadfast, and have a good faith, for your name is written in heaven in the Book of Life, and this was an angel who gave you comfort. And therefore, daughter, you must be very merry, for I am very busy both morning and afternoon to draw your heart into my heart, for you should keep your mind altogether upon me, and you shall much increase your love towards God. For, daughter, if you will follow after God's counsel, you may not do amiss, for God's counsel is to be meek, patient in charity and in chastity."

Another time, as this creature lay in her contemplation in a chapel of our Lady, her mind was occupied in the Passion of our Lord Jesus Christ, and she thought truly that she saw our Lord appear to her spiritual sight in his manhood, with his wounds bleeding as freshly as though he had been scourged before her.

And then she wept and cried with all the strength of her body, for, if her sorrow were great before this spiritual sight, it was yet greater afterwards than it was before, and her love was more increased towards our Lord. And then she felt great wonder that our Lord would become man, and suffer such grievous pain for her, who was so unkind a creature to him.

Another time, as she was in a church of St Margaret, in the choir, being in great sweetness and devotion, with great abundance of tears, she asked our Lord Jesus Christ how she might best please him. And he answered her soul, saying, "Daughter, have mind of your wickedness, and think of my goodness."

Then she prayed these words many times and often, "Lord, for your great goodness, have mercy on all my wickedness, as surely as I was never so wicked as you are good, nor ever may be, even if I would, for you are so good that you may be no better. And therefore it is a great marvel that any man should ever be parted from you without end."

Then as she lay still in the choir, weeping and mourning for her sins, she was suddenly in a kind of sleep. And at once she saw, with her spiritual eye, our Lord's body lying before her, and his head, as she thought, close by her, with his blessed face turned upwards, the handsomest man that ever might be seen or imagined. And then, as she looked, there came someone with a dagger and cut that precious body all along the breast. And then she wept amazingly bitterly, having more thought, pity and compassion of the Passion of our Lord Jesus Christ than she had before. And so every day her thoughts and her love for our Lord increased, blessed may he be, and the more that her love increased, the more was her sorrow for the sins of the people.

Another time, the said creature being in a chapel of our Lady, weeping bitterly at the memory of our Lord's Passion, and such other graces and goodness as our Lord ministered to her mind, suddenly—she knew not how soon—she was in a kind of sleep.

And at once, in the sight of her soul, she saw our Lord standing right up over her, so near that she thought she took his toes in her hand and felt them, and to her feeling it was as if they had been really flesh and bones. And then she thanked God for everything, for through these spiritual sights her affection was entirely drawn into the manhood of Christ and into the memory of his Passion, until that time that it pleased our Lord to give her understanding of his incomprehensible Godhead.

As is written before, these kinds of visions and feelings she had soon after her conversion, when she was all set and fully intending to serve God with all her heart and strength, and had completely left the world, and stayed in church both morning and afternoon, and most especially in the time of Lent, when she with great insistence and much prayer had her husband's permission to live chaste and clean, and did great bodily penance before she went to Jeru-salem.

But afterwards, when her husband and she with one assent had made a vow of chastity, as is written before, and she had been to Rome and Jerusalem, and suffered much contempt and reproof for her weeping and her crying, our Lord, of his mercy, drew her affec-tion into his Godhead, and that was more fervent in love and desire, and more subtle in understanding, than was the manhood. And nevertheless, the fire of love increased in her, and her understanding was more enlightened and her devotion more fervent than it was before, while she had her meditation and her contemplation only in his manhood. Yet she did not have that manner of proceeding with crying as she had before, but it was more subtle and more soft, and easier for her spirit to bear, and as plentiful in tears, as it ever was before.

Another time, while this creature was in a house of the Preaching Friars, in a chapel of our Lady, standing at her prayers, her eyelids went a little together in a kind of sleep, and suddenly she saw, she thought, our Lady in the fairest vision that she ever saw, holding a fair white kerchief in her hand and saying to her, "Daughter, would you like to see my son?"

And with that she saw forthwith our Lady hold her blessed son in her hand, and swathe him very lightly in the white kerchief, so that she could see how she did it. This creature then had a new spir-itual joy and a new spiritual comfort, which was so marvellous that she could never tell of it as she felt it.

CHAPTER 86

On one occasion our Lord spoke to the said creature, when it pleased him, saying to her spiritual understanding, "Daughter, for as many times as you have received the blessed sacrament of the al-tar with many more holy thoughts than you can repeat, for as many times you shall be rewarded in heaven with new joys and new com-forts. And daughter, in heaven it shall be known to you how many days you have had of high contemplation through my gift on earth, and although they are my gifts and graces which I have given you, yet you shall have the same grace and reward in heaven as if they were of your own merits, for I have freely given them to you.

"But I thank you highly, daughter, that you have allowed me to work my will in you, and that you would let me be so homely with you. For in nothing, daughter, that you might do on earth might you any better please me than allow me to speak to you in your soul, for at that time you understand my will and I understand your will. And also, daughter, you call my mother to come into your soul, and take me in her arms, and lay me to her breasts and give me suck.

"Also, daughter, I know the holy thoughts and the good desires that you have when you receive me, and the good charity that you have towards me in the time that you receive my precious body into your soul, and also how you call Mary Magdalene into your soul to welcome me, for, daughter, I know well enough what you are thinking. You think that she is worthiest, in your soul, and you trust most in her prayers, next to my mother, and so you may indeed, daughter, for she is a very great mediator to me for you in the bliss of heaven. And sometimes, daughter, you think your soul so large and so wide that you call all the court of heaven into your soul to welcome me. I know very well, daughter, what you say: 'Come, all twelve apostles, who were so well beloved of God on earth, and receive your Lord in my soul.'

"You also pray Katherine, Margaret, and all holy virgins to welcome me in your soul. And then you pray my blessed mother, Mary Magdalene, all apostles, martyrs, confessors, Katherine, Margaret, and all holy virgins, that they should decorate the chamber of your soul with many fair flowers and with many sweet spices, so that I might rest there within.

"Furthermore, you sometimes imagine, daughter, that you have a cushion of gold, another of red velvet, the third of white silk, in your soul. And you think that my Father sits on the cushion of gold, for with him lies might and power. And you think that I, the Second Person of the Trinity, your love and your joy, sit on the red cushion of velvet, for upon me is all your thought, because I bought you so dearly, and you think that you can never requite me the love that I have shown you, though you were slain a thousand times a day, if it were possible, for my love. Thus you think, daughter, in your soul, that I am worthy to sit on a red cushion, in remembrance of the red blood that I shed for you. Moreover, you think that the Holy Ghost sits on a white cushion, for you think that he is full of love and purity, and therefore it is fitting for him to sit on a white cushion, for he is a giver of all holy thoughts and chastity.

"And yet I know well enough, daughter, that you think you may not worship the Father unless you worship the Son, and that you may not worship the Son unless you worship the Holy Ghost. And you also think sometimes, daughter, that the Father is almighty and all-knowing and all grace and goodness and you think the same of the Son, that he is almighty and all-knowing and all grace and goodness And you think that the Holy Ghost has the same properties, equal with the Father and the Son, and proceeding from them both.

"You also think that each of the three Persons in the Trinity has what the other has in their Godhead, and so you truly believe, daughter, in your soul, that there are three divers Persons and one God in substance, and that each knows what the others know, and each may do what the others may, and each wills what the others will. And, daughter, this is a true faith and a right faith, and this faith you have only of my gift.

"And therefore, daughter, if you will consider thoroughly, you have great cause to love me very well, and to give me your heart completely, so that I may fully rest within it, as I wish to myself. For if you allow me, daughter, to rest in your soul on earth, believe it indeed that you shall rest with me in heaven without end.

"And therefore, daughter, don't be surprised if you weep bitterly when you are given communion, and receive my blessed body in form of bread, for you pray to me before you receive communion, saying to me in your mind, 'As surely, Lord, as you love me, make me clean from all sin, and give me grace to receive your precious body worthily, with all manner of worship and reverence.'

"And, daughter, rest assured that I hear your prayer, for you may not say anything to please me better than 'as surely as I love you,' for then I fulfil my grace in you, and give you many a holy thought—it is impossible to tell them all.

"And because of the great homeliness that I show towards you at that time, you are much bolder to ask for grace for yourself, for your husband, for your children; and you make every Christian man and woman your child in your soul for the time, and would have as much grace for them as for your own children. You also ask for mercy for your husband, and you think you are much beholden to me, that I have given you the sort of man who would let you live chaste, he being alive and in good physical health. In truth, daughter, you think most truly, and therefore you have great cause to love me very well.

"Daughter, if you knew how many wives there are in this world, who would love me and serve me well and duly if they might be as free from their husbands as you are from yours, you would say that you were very much beholden to me. And yet they are thwarted from their will and suffer very great pain, and therefore they shall have great reward in heaven, for I receive every good will as a deed.

"Sometimes, daughter, I make you have great sorrow for your confessor's sins especially, so that he should have as full forgiveness for his sins as you would have for yours. And sometimes, when you receive the precious sacrament, I make you pray for your confessor in this way—that as many men and women might be turned by his preaching, as you wish were turned by the tears of your eyes, and that my holy words might settle as keenly in their hearts, as you wish they would settle in your heart. And you also ask the same grace for all good men who preach my word on earth, that they might bring profit to all reasonable creatures.

"And often, on the day that you receive my precious body, you ask for grace and mercy for all your friends, and for all your enemies who ever caused you shame or rebuke, either scorned you or jibed at you for the grace that I work in you, and for all this world, both young and old, bitterly weeping many tears and sobbing. You have suffered much shame and much reproof, and therefore you shall have very much bliss in heaven.

"Daughter, do not be ashamed to receive my grace when I will give it you, for I shall not be ashamed of you, so that you shall be received into the bliss of heaven—there to be rewarded for every good thought, for every good word, and for every good deed, and for every day of contemplation, and for all good desires that you have had here in this world—with me everlastingly as my beloved darling, as my blessed spouse, and as my holy wife.

"And therefore, do not be afraid, daughter, though people wonder why you weep so bitterly when you receive me, for, if they knew what grace I place in you at that time, they should rather wonder that your heart does not burst asunder. And so it should, if I did not control that grace myself; but you see for yourself, daughter, that when you have received me into your soul, you are in peace and quiet, and sob no longer. And at this people are greatly amazed, but it need be no surprise to you, for you know that I proceed like a husband who would wed a wife. At the time he weds her, he thinks he is sure enough of her, and that no man shall part them, for then, daughter, they may go to bed together without any shame or fear of other people, and sleep in rest and peace if they will. And things are like this between you and me, daughter, for you have every week, especially on Sunday, great fear and dread in your soul how you may best be sure of my love, and, with great reverence and holy dread, how you may best receive me to the salvation of your soul, with all manner of meekness, humility and charity, as any lady in this world is busy to receive her husband, when he comes home and has been long away from her.

"My beloved daughter, I thank you highly for all people whom you have looked after when ill in my name, and for all kindness and service that you have done them in any degree, for you shall have the same reward with me in heaven, as though you had looked after my own self while I was here on earth. Also, daughter, I thank you for as many times as you have bathed me, in your soul, at home in your chamber, as though I had been present there in my manhood, for I well know, daughter, all the holy thoughts that you have shown me in your mind. And also, daughter, I thank you for all the times that you have harboured me and my blessed mother in your bed.

"For these, and all other good thoughts and good deeds that you have thought in my name, and performed for my love, you shall have with me and with my mother, with my holy angels, with my apostles, with my martyrs, confessors and virgins, and with all my holy saints, all manner of joy and bliss, lasting without end."

NOTES

INTRODUCTION

1. *Liber Celestis*, Book VI, chapter 88: cf. Bridget Morris, *St Birgitta of Sweden* (Woodbridge: Boydell, 1999), p. 111.
2. See Elizabeth of Spaalbeek, p. 116.
3. See *Vita*, passage (a) below.
4. Morris, *St Birgitta*, pp. 3–4, n. 12.
5. *The Book of Margery Kempe*, translated by B.A. Windeatt (Harmondsworth: Penguin, 1985), pp. 208–209.
6. Janette Dillon, "Holy Women and Their Confessors or Confessors and Their Holy Women? Margery Kempe and the Continental Tradition," in *Prophets Abroad: The Reception of Continental Holy Women in Late-Medieval England*, Rosalynn Voaden, ed. (Cambridge: D.S Brewer, 1996).
7. See Christine the Astonishing, chapter XXIV.
8. Caroline Walker Bynum, *Fragmentation and Redemption: Essays on Gender and the Human Body in Medieval Religion* (New York: Zone, 1992), p. 186.
9. *Julian of Norwich: Revelations of Divine Love*, translated by Elizabeth Spearing (London: Penguin, 1998), pp. 17–18 and 69–74.
10. See passage (g).
11. Morris, *St Birgitta*, p. 54.
12. *Christina of Markyate: A Twelfth Century Recluse*, translated by C.H. Talbot (Oxford: Clarendon Press, 1959), p. 171.
13. Edmund Colledge and Romana Guarnieri, "The Glosses by 'M.N.' and Richard Methley to *The Mirror of Simple Souls*," *Archivo Italiano per la Storia della Pietà* 5 (1968), p. 359.
14. See Barbara Newman, "Possessed by the Spirit: Devout Women, Demoniacs, and the Apostolic Life in the Thirteenth Century," *Speculum* 73 (1998).
15. *lepers:* With their highly contagious and and then-incurable disease, lepers were social outcasts. Unlike Mary, Margery Kempe does not do anything as practical as caring for them, but piety does move her to kiss one.
16. See chapter 62.

17. Eileen Power, *Medieval English Nunneries c. 1275–1535* (Cambridge: Cambridge University Press, 1922), pp. 25–29.
18. Rudolph M. Bell, *Holy Anorexia* (Chicago: University of Chicago Press, 1985).
19. Morris, *St Birgitta*, p. 13.
20. See Book VI, Chapter 22.
21. F.P. Pickering, *Literature and Art in the Middle Ages* (London: Macmillan, 1970), p. 280.
22. Hildegard, *Vita*, passage (b); Hadewijch, Letter 18; Bridget, Book II, chapter 29.
23. Power, *Medieval English Nunneries*, p. 300.

ACKNOWLEDGMENTS AND A NOTE ON THE TEXTS

1. C.A. Robson, in *The Cambridge History of the Bible*, Vol. 2, G.W.H. Lampe, ed. (Cambridge: Cambridge University Press, 1969), p. 436.

HILDEGARD OF BINGEN

1. *magister:* Volmar, a monk and priest of the monastery of St. Disibod, where Hildegard had taken her vows in 1112. He had been her teacher and became her friend and secretary.
2. *woman . . . teacher:* probably Uda of Göllheim.
3. *Mainz Cathedral; . . . my writings . . . Trier:* Henry, Archbishop of Mainz, brought Hildegard's revelations before the synod of Trier (1147–1148), and Pope Eugene III gave his approval of her as yet incomplete *Scivias*.
4. *daughter . . . mentioned:* Richardis of Stade, a noblewoman who was Hildegard's most important patron and mother of one of her nuns, also called Richardis, who was particularly important to her as a much-loved friend and secretary.
5. *Guibert de Gembloux:* a French-speaking monk who became Hildegard's last secretary.
6. *rib:* i.e., woman. See Gen 2:22.

CHRISTINA OF MARKYATE

1. *Judith:* She achieved a holy victory when she beheaded the drunken Assyrian general Holofernes before he could sleep with her. (Judith 10–13, omitted from Protestant Bibles).
2. *these, . . . trials:* There is a gap in the manuscript at this point.
3. *foe . . . One:* There is a gap in the manuscript at this point.
4. *electuary:* a medicine in the form of a sweet paste or conserve.
5. *Marcigny . . . Fontevrault:* Two continental nunneries, the first founded

by St Hugh of Cluny in 1080, the second by Robert d'Arbrissel c. 1100. At that time, Western Europe was more culturally unified than at later periods with French as the language of the nobility in England as well as France, and political authority more fluid.

6. *Alban:* the first British martyr, probably martyred in the early third century; his shrine still exists in the cathedral at St. Albans (ancient Verulamium), near London.

7. *man . . . good works:* Geoffrey, abbot of St. Albans, Christina's closest friend and counsellor until his death in 1147.

8. *viaticum:* the Holy Communion given to those in immediate danger of death.

9. *Bermondsey:* a Cluniac monastery founded in 1082. Bermondsey is now an inner district of London.

10. *sacrist:* official in charge of the contents of a church, particularly those used in divine worship.

11. *Mary . . . Martha:* See Lk 10:38–42. Mary and Martha were generally taken as types of the contemplative and active lives, respectively.

12. *vigil:* A "vigil" was originally a prayer service held on the night before a major ecclesiastical feast, but it was eventually transferred to the whole day preceding the feast. *None:* See Elizabeth of Spaalbeek, note 3.

13. *Te Deum laudamus:* "We praise thee, O God," a Latin hymn to the Father and the Son in rhythmical prose, widely used in the liturgy.

14. *But whether . . . never knew:* This is an allusion to St Paul's similar statement about his visionary experience (2 Cor 12:1–5).

15. *we see . . . darkness:* See 1 Cor 13:12 and 2 Chr (Paralipomenon) 6:1.

HADEWIJCH

1. *sicut . . . terra, fiat . . . tua:* "On earth as it is in heaven" and "Thy will be done," from the Lord's Prayer; see Mt 6:10.

2. *certain person . . . living:* i.e., Hadewijch herself.

3. *these two:* i.e., Love and the lover.

4. *abysmal:* i.e., total, perfect.

5. *aliens:* outsiders.

6. *the broad . . . many:* Mt 7:13.

7. *"You . . . yours":* Song 2:16.

8. *totality:* the Divinity and Humanity in one.

9. *day . . . Assumption:* the day commemorating the bodily assumption of the Virgin Mary into heaven (August 15).

10. *eagle . . . Evangelist:* the "four living creatures" [Eze 1:5–6, Apoc 4:6–8] have been interpreted as symbols of the four Evangelists since the early days of the Christian Church (St Matthew, man; St Mark, lion; St Luke, ox; St John, eagle). The eagle also symbolizes the contemplative soul.

11. *feast . . . Epiphany:* the manifestation of Christ to the Gentiles in the persons of the Magi (January 6).
12. *Pentecost:* i.e., Whitsun, the day the Holy Ghost descended on the Apostles.
13. *ciborium:* a lidded vessel used to contain the sacramental bread of the Eucharist.
14. *his Body for the first time:* i.e., Jesus as he was at the Last Supper, on the eve of his Passion.

CHRISTINE THE ASTONISHING

1. *Sint-Truiden:* in the province of Limburg in what is now Belgium; developed around an abbey founded in the seventh century by St Trudo. Sometimes referred to as Saint-Trond, since French is also spoken locally.
2. *Agnus dei:* "Lamb of God [who takest away the sins of the world]" is recited by the priest during Mass, shortly before the Communion, and asks for mercy and peace.
3. *scapulary:* short cloak worn first by Benedictine monks and then by other religious orders as well.
4. *tilia:* i.e., lime tree.
5. *recluse:* someone who entered an enclosed, solitary life in a fixed place, in order to achieve greater spiritual perfection.

MARY OF OIGNIES

1. *compunction:* stinging of the heart; a stronger sense than in modern English.
2. *St Simeon:* c. 390–459; the first of the stylites or pillar ascetics. When a chain was removed from one of his ankles, maggots crawled out from underneath it.
3. *St Antony:* a fourth-century Egyptian hermit who lived in the desert, where he struggled with temptations. As a reminder that a vision of the flames of Hell overcame his fleshly desires, he was sometimes represented with flames under his feet.
4. *Holy Cross Day:* September 14; Mary was fasting during the worst and coldest weather.
5. *mortally . . . for ever:* at the second council of Clermont (1130), Pope Innocent II had declared that those slain in tournaments were to be denied Christian burial. Knights who took part in them were sometimes excommunicated, but tournaments remained very popular in spite of this and of the high incidence of injury and death.
6. *despair:* This included not just hopelessness but loss of faith in the possibility of salvation.

7. *suicide:* This would have meant burial in unconsecrated ground for her body and eternal damnation for her soul.

8. *relics:* Such relics were important in medieval religion; they often consisted of some bodily part so could be thought of as an embodiment of the whole saint. After her death, Jacques de Vitry wore a mummified finger from the body of Mary of Oignies in a reliquary around his neck.

9. *while . . . awake:* cf. Song 5:2, "I sleep, and my heart watcheth," a text frequently quoted to describe religious contemplation.

10. *presence of Christ:* i.e., Christ's body in the form of the consecrated host.

11. *Martinmas:* St. Martin's Day is November 11, so this period would include the coldest weather.

12. *long tails . . . tusks:* a reference to contemporary fashion in clothes and headdresses.

13. *her work:* As well as the spinning mentioned as accompanied by psalms, this work was probably clothmaking, important in the local economy and a way in which beguines frequently earned their living.

14. *follow . . . everything:* The Middle English has "follow Christ naked"; "naked to follow the naked Christ" was the watchword of some religious groups, such as the radical Franciscans.

15. *Joseph . . . Samaritan woman . . . St John:* Potiphar's wife makes advances to Joseph; one day, "she catching the skirt of his garment, said: Lie with me. But he leaving the garment in her hands, fled . . . " (Gen 39:12); after Jesus has revealed himself as the Messiah to a Samaritan woman at Jacob's well, the woman "left her water-pot" and summoned the men from the city to see the Christ (Jn 4:28–29); the reference to St. John the Evangelist may be a garbled allusion to Mk 14:51–52.

16. *Eve . . . Baptist:* June 23; the full statement of the date in the Middle English text is confused.

ELIZABETH OF SPAALBEEK

1. *Liège:* now capital city of province of same name in East Belgium, at the confluence of the Meuse and the Ourthe Rivers.

2. *Clairvaux:* famous and influential French Cistercian monastery, founded in 1115 by St. Bernard.

3. *Matins . . . Compline:* The exact time and the form of the seven offices have varied somewhat over the centuries and in different places and religious orders. Matins (followed by Lauds), the first office of the day, usually started at midnight or 1:00 A.M., Prime at about 6:00 A.M., Terce at the third hour after Prime, Sext at the sixth, and None at the ninth. Vespers or Evensong was said in the early evening, and Compline was

said before going to bed. These liturgical Hours were also associated with the stages of Christ's Passion; often the Agony in the Garden and the Betrayal with Matins and Lauds, then, in turn, Christ's appearance before Pilate, his flagellation, carrying the cross, the Crucifixion, the deposition, and the entombment. Elizabeth enacts these at the time of each office.

4. *Nocturn:* Nocturns were part of the night office and included psalms and lessons.
5. *timbrels:* This tambourine-like instrument and cymbals frequently accompany praise in the Old Testament.
6. *psaltery:* ancient stringed instrument played by plucking the strings with fingers or plectrum.
7. *unwrapped:* Such pictures sometimes had a second protective panel to fold over the painting and a fabric cover to wrap them in (cf. paintings of the Virgin reading a missal with similar fabric wrapping).
8. *Annas . . . Caiaphas:* the priests of the Jews before whom Jesus was arraigned when he was first arrested.
9. *clock:* Clocks were a relatively novel form of technology, even at the time when the Middle English version was made.
10. *Furthermore . . . left side:* Medieval pictures of the Crucifixion show the Virgin Mary on one side of the cross and St John on the other in the postures indicated here.
11. *St John . . . virgin:* "When Jesus therefore had seen his mother and the disciple standing, whom he loved, he saith to his mother: Woman, behold thy son./ After that, he saith to the disciple: Behold thy mother. And from that hour the disciple took her to his own" [Jn 19:26–27].
12. *spittle or moisture:* The imperfection of the female body was associated with its supposed moistness.

MARGUERITE PORETE

1. *so near . . . from her:* i.e., so near inwardly but so far outwardly.
2. *peace:* For both occurrences, the French has "palace."
3. *Virtues . . . in peace:* In French, this speech is in verse. In English it is followed by a lengthy gloss by the translator.
4. The translator adds a brief gloss. In the following sentence, the bracketed passage, missing from the Middle English but required by the sense, is taken from the French.
5. *he who is:* i.e., God.
6. Here the translator adds a lengthy gloss.
7. *Perfect Love* (Middle English *fyne love*): This is the *fine amour* or refined love of courtly poetry, experienced only by those of high rank and exquisite sensibility, here applied to the spiritual elite who are capable of achieving a special relationship with God in this life.

8. Augustine, *In epistolam Joannis ad Parthos,* tractatus 7, sect. 8.
9. *Holy Church the Little . . . Holy Church the Great:* The distinction, first drawn here, is between the Church as an earthly institution and what Marguerite sees as the true Church, consisting of Love's favoured servants. Cf. ch. IV.
10. *with him:* i.e., in his service.
11. *mistress . . . he . . . him:* The change of gender is in the Middle English, partly perhaps because *Amour* is grammatically masculine in French, partly because "Love" is usually personified as male in medieval allegories, and partly because of Love's self-identification with God a few lines later.
12. *nurture:* i.e., the Soul's upbringing in Love's court. Middle English *nurture* can mean both the material nourishment of a child and its training in good manners.
13. *I would love . . . to be loved:* The shift from *him* (the beloved, i.e., God) to *you* (Love) is in the Middle English. Cf. Love's statement above of her identity with God.
14. For this idea, that in heaven sins will be not shameful but glorious, cf. Julian of Norwich, Long Text, ch. 39.
15. *such souls:* the *Mirror*'s usual phrase to refer to those who have a special relationship with God.
16. *glosses:* interpretations revealing the hidden sense.
17. *Margaret:* The Middle English has "Daisy," translating the French *marguerite,* which also means "pearl"; a pun on the author's name. Similar puns on *marguerite* are found in French courtly poetry and are reflected in Chaucer's Prologue to *The Legend of Good Women.*
18. *the more:* i.e., that which is greater than itself.
19. *those who . . . so good:* This appears to be the way of life of the second of the "two kinds of people" mentioned above.
20. *All things . . . the Gospel:* cf. Mt 21:22: "And all things, whatsoever you shall ask in prayer, believing, you shall receive."
21. *quarterings:* the four quarters of the coat of arms that establishes the status of a gentleman or nobleman. The Middle English text reproduces the French word *costes,* which also means "sides."
22. *worse:* The Middle English word is *piere,* reproducing the French for "worse." The translator may not have understood this sentence.
23. *She has . . . lost in it:* The allusion is to the Israelites' crossing of the Red Sea, as they fled under the leadership of Moses from captivity in Egypt, while the pursuing Egyptians were drowned (see Ex 14:21–30).
24. The English makes poor sense, probably because the translator is reluctant to accept what seems to be Marguerite's meaning, that the Soul's separate existence limits God's existence, so that when she is completely dissolved into him he once more knows *himself* as he was before she existed.

25. *If it were . . . glory of God:* This is an attempt to make sense of a sentence that is not fully intelligible in the Middle English.
26. *And the Soul . . . as herself:* See Jesus's answer to the scribe in Mk 12:30–31: ". . . thou shalt love the Lord thy God with thy whole heart and with thy whole soul and with thy whole mind and with thy whole strength. This is the first commandment./ And the second is like to it: Thou shalt love thy neighbour as thyself. There is no other commandment greater than these."
27. *counsels of perfection:* Traditionally these are poverty, chastity, and obedience.
28. It is hard to make sense of this sentence in the Middle English.
29. *even if . . . have mentioned:* i.e., possess it unconditionally and forever.
30. *and so . . . behalf* (Middle English: *therfore that I unwolde for you):* The English translator seems to make a different sense out of his difficult French original; Marguerite expresses an anguished willingness to accept God's hypotheses, while the translator initially rejects them as being out of keeping with God's true nature.
31. *these two things:* i.e., my will and my love.

BRIDGET OF SWEDEN

1. Apparently a journey of about 25 miles (40 km) from Alvastra to Vadstena, and her revelation lasted about an hour (see Morris, *St Birgitta*, p. 87).
2. *the Mother:* the Virgin Mary
3. *knight:* i.e., the soldier mentioned in Jn 19:34. In medieval tradition his role was greatly expanded.
4. *I was . . . breathe:* Bridget herself bore eight children.
5. *Subject . . . mother:* See Lk 2:51.
6. *idols . . . destroyed:* the fulfilment of a prophecy attributed to Isaiah in apocryphal gospels, e.g., PseudoMatthew, ch. 23.
7. The idea that world history repeats the seven days of the Creation on a larger scale, followed by an eighth day of fulfilment, probably goes back to the final chapter of St. Augustine's *City of God.*
8. *Mount Calvary:* Bridget had visited the Holy Land.
9. *pierced . . . bitterness:* cf. Simeon's prophecy to Mary in Lk 2:35: "And thy own soul a sword shall pierce."
10. *His lips . . . within him:* This is thought to be the only detail in the description of the Passion that is completely original with Bridget.
11. *clasped him . . . and delight:* It appears that Bridget nursed her own children (Morris, *St Birgitta*, p. 52).
12. *Martyrs and confessors:* Martyrs are those who die for their faith; confessors were originally those who were persecuted for their faith with-

out suffering martyrdom, but later the word meant those whom the pope declared to be especially holy.

13. *Celestine:* St. Celestine V (c. 1215–1296) was elected to the papacy at a very advanced age and abdicated after only five months.

14. *Boniface:* Boniface VIII, who was pope from 1294 to 1303, asserted absolute papal power and supremacy over earthly rulers.

15. *Once ... Holy Ghost:* The order of Franciscan or Grey Friars, founded in 1209, originally forbade all money or property. There followed violent disagreement between moderate and strict followers; disputes between these and between Franciscans and Dominicans persisted during Bridget's lifetime, and friars became more lax and prosperous. Dominican (Black) and Augustinian or Austin friars also vowed both individual and corporate poverty.

16. *Ember Days:* four groups of three days which have been observed as days of fasting and abstinence.

17. *Cornelius ... centurion:* Cornelius is the religious gentile in Acts 10 who is told by an angel in a vision to seek St Peter and is received into the Church. The centurion is the soldier of Jn 19:34. According to medieval legend, Christ's blood opened his eyes and he was saved.

18. *Judge:* Most medieval churches depicted Christ sitting in judgement with souls being taken to heaven on one side and to hell on the other.

19. *The Fiend ... himself:* The Devil is tempting Bridget to doubt the bodily presence of Christ in the bread of the Eucharist. Belief in the real presence was the crucial test of Catholic orthodoxy in the late Middle Ages.

20. *Thomas ... felt:* Jn 20:19–29.

21. *Moses ... serpent:* Ex 4:1–5.

22. The miracle of the loaves and fishes; in Mk 8:19 and Lk 9:17 the fragments that remain after the multitude have been fed fill twelve baskets.

23. *thief:* the one crucified with Jesus who "blasphemed him, saying: If thou be Christ, save thyself and us" (Lk 23:39).

24. *Whit Sunday:* Pentecost, the day on which the Holy Ghost descended in tongues of fire upon the disciples (Acts 2:3).

25. *son:* Karl (late 1320s–1372), said to be his mother's favourite. A knight and a "lawman" (magistrate), his political activities led to exile in 1362; the *Book* and other sources suggest a rash, worldly, and self-indulgent man.

26. *To him ... opened:* See Mt 7:7 and Lk 11:10.

JULIAN OF NORWICH

1. *terror ... fiends:* Medieval pictures of deathbeds often show devils waiting eagerly to grasp the dying person's soul.

2. *St Cecilia . . . died:* The legend of St. Cecilia recounts that she was an aristocratic Christian girl in pagan Rome who, after converting her intended husband and his brother to Christianity, was sentenced to be beheaded. Three sword strokes failed to kill her immediately, but she died three days later. Chaucer retells the story as the *Second Nun's Tale*.

3. *'Benedicite dominus!':* "Blessed be thou, Lord!"

4. *three nothings:* The three nothings are probably all that is created, sin, and the Devil. Julian repeats various forms of the word *nought* throughout this paragraph, as indicated by the repetitions of "nothing" in the translation.

5. *vernicle:* The vernicle was the cloth, supposed to have belonged to St. Veronica, with which Christ's face was wiped as he was bearing the cross to Calvary; as Julian explains later, it was thought to have retained an impression of his face.

6. *sea bed . . . sand:* Here Julian's imagination may have been stimulated by the visions of divine protection beneath the sea in the Book of Jonah and in Psalm 68, usually associated with Jonah; but it is also worth bearing in mind how close the connections were between Norwich and the North Sea.

7. *the longing . . . him:* This is "the wound of an earnest longing for God" mentioned by Julian (see chapter 1 of the Short Text) as part of the third gift she had asked from God before she received her showings.

8. *For though . . . believe:* The absence of evil and of hell and purgatory from what Julian was shown puts her in danger of heresy; this is one of the places where she is most insistent on her full acceptance of the Church's teaching.

9. *yet . . . grace:* Theological antisemitism, directed against the Jews as (it was supposed) collectively responsible for Christ's death and subsequently antagonistic to all Christians, was a prominent feature of medieval Christianity. One manifestation that would have been familiar to Julian was the accusation that the twelfth-century child-martyr St. William of Norwich had been the victim of Jewish ritual murder. But she evidently accepted the condemnation of the Jews only because it was taught by the Church, not because it was part of her own religious vision.

10. *And these . . . separate them:* Julian's acknowledgment that she can no longer separate the vision as she originally saw and understood it, the deeper understanding that came subsequently, and the interpretation implied by the whole sequence of showings, helps to explain the difficulty of this chapter, and especially the frequent shifts of tense between past and present. They also reflect the way that the parable, revealed at a specific moment, has a meaning that stands outside time.

11. *root:* This image, appropriate to the gardening imagery of the whole

parable, may allude to the "root" of 2 (4) Kin 19:30, the "remnant" of those who would be saved even if disaster came upon Judah. The notion of the saved remnant reappears in Is 10:20–22, and from there St. Paul takes it up in Rom 9:27–29. But for Julian the "remnant" seems to have included all humanity, and the manuscript *grit rote* might also mean "great crowd."

12. *Now . . . joy:* an allusion to the Song of Songs (or Song of Solomon), which was read allegorically, with the spouse (*sponsus*) representing Christ and the bride (*sponsa*) the Blessed Virgin, the Church, or the human soul.

13. *It is I . . . to you:* chapter 26.

ANONYMOUS

1. *purgatory:* according to Roman Catholic teaching, a place of punishment where those who have died in the grace of God expiate their sins before admission to heaven.

2. *St Lawrence:* His feast day is August 10. It was believed that those who martyred him "laid him out on [an] iron grill, piled burning coals under it, and pressed heated iron pitchforks upon his body" [*The Golden Legend*]. Prayer and contemplation on his feast day might well lead to visions of purgatorial fires that night.

3. *eight o'clock:* This would have been after Compline, the last office of the day. The visionary is identifying herself as virtuous: there was much criticism of nuns staying up to drink and chat. Her visions are neatly fitted into the first period of a nun's sleep, between Compline and Matins.

4. *religious house:* Harley in her edition suggests the Benedictine abbey of St Mary's, Winchester, where there were several sisters called Margaret at this time.

5. *little girl:* It was common for bourgeois and aristocratic girls to be brought up in convents; they often slept in the same room as the nuns.

6. *Seven Psalms . . . Litany . . . Agnus dei:* The seven Penitential Psalms (nos 6, 31, 37, 50, 101, 129, and 142 in the Vulgate) tell the story of David's repentance. The Litany consists of a series of petitions; originally liturgical, it had become a popular form of private prayer. *Agnus dei qui tollis peccata mundi* . . . ("Lamb of God, who takest away the sins of the world . . .") is recited by the priest shortly before the Communion, and asks for mercy and peace.

7. *requiem Mass:* Mass for the repose of the soul of the dead.

8. *Miserere mei deus:* Psalm 50; one of the Penitential Psalms, it begins, "Have mercy on me, Oh God. . . ."

9. *Veni creator spiritus:* a hymn to the Holy Ghost. A seventeenth-century version, "Come Holy Ghost, our souls inspire . . ." is still pop-

ular. This hymn and the *Miserere* are written on the manuscript at the end of the *Revelation*.

10. *Masses of the Trinity:* The Mass had special prayers according to the day on which it was celebrated, e.g., the feast of the Trinity, of St. Peter, of the Assumption.

11. *recluse at Westminster:* A recluse or anchorite (female: anchoress) entered an enclosed, solitary life in a fixed place, in order to achieve greater spiritual perfection. Two recluses lived at the Benedictine abbey of Westminster in 1422: John London and William Alnwick.

12. *Piers Cowme:* Peter Combe, priest at Westminster Abbey from 1363.

13. *Richard Bowne:* Bone, priest at St. Mary's Abbey, Winchester.

14. *John Percy:* Pery, monk at St. Swithun's Priory, Winchester; his ordination as priest, and that of Richard Bowne, appear in William of Wykeham's ordination records.

15. *Gaudiamus . . . commemorations: Gaudiamus omnes in domino* ("Let us all rejoice in the Lord") was included in the Mass for All Saints. When two feasts were celebrated on the same day, certain prayers of one feast would be followed by the corresponding prayers of the other—referred to as *memoris* ("commemorations").

16. *Seven Deadly Sins:* Pride, Covetousness, Lust, Envy, Gluttony, Anger, Sloth ("Accidie").

17. *in a position:* A Mass cost fourpence, about a day's wages for a master craftsman.

18. *Master Forest:* John Forest held many offices in and around Winchester, including the mastership of St. Cross Hospital.

19. *John Wynburne:* His career seems to have been unaffected by his participation in a "grievous rebellion" against the prior of Christchurch–Twynham (near Winchester): in 1422 he was prior there himself.

20. *this dog and this cat:*

> Of smale houndes hadde she that she fedde
> With rosted flessh, or milk and wastel-breed.
> But soore wepte she if oon of hem were deed,
> Or if men smoot it with a yerde smerte.
> (Chaucer, *General Prologue*, 146–149)

Accounts of visitations show that the Church had difficulty enforcing the rule against nuns keeping pets.

21. *holy services:* Between Compline at 7:00 or 8:00 P.M. and Prime at 6:00 or 7:00 A.M. nuns were supposed to attend Matins, followed by Lauds at about 1.00 A.M. Failure to do so was frequently criticized.

22. *crowns:* tonsures, the sign of their having received holy orders.

23. *armour:* Armour or metal equipment was cleaned by being revolved in a barrel with sand and vinegar.

24. *fasted her fast:* Devotees of the Virgin fasted on Saturday, the day of her votive Mass, as well as on Friday.

25. *bought dearly:* This refers to God's sacrifice of his Son on the cross which redeemed humanity (redemption means buying back).

26. *venial sins:* By contrast with the deadly or mortal sins, which, if not absolved, lead to damnation, venial sins are those which do not deprive the soul of sanctifying grace.

27. *confessors:* See Bridget of Sweden, note 12.

28. *Aves: Ave Maria, gratia plena* . . . ("Hail Mary, full of grace . . ."): The prayer beginning with Gabriel's greeting (Lk 1:28) has been the most popular prayer to the Virgin since the twelfth century.

29. *Southwick:* Southwick Priory was a house of the Austin or black canons (like John Wynburne's Christchurch–Twynham); it was well known for a shrine to the Virgin Mary.

MARGERY KEMPE

1. *one . . . Eve:* Probably 23 June 1413; it is likely that Margery and her husband had been to see the Mystery Plays performed at York.

2. *I will pay . . . Jerusalem:* Margery's father had recently died and she may have received a legacy.

3. *the Vicar:* Richard of Caister, vicar of St. Stephen's church (d. 1420).

4. *any book . . . read:* the *Scale of Perfection* of Walter Hilton, the *Revelations* of St Bridget of Sweden, the *Stimulus Amoris*, thought to be by St. Bonaventura but now known to be by James of Milan, and the *Incendium Amoris* of Richard Rolle. Margery here mentions the same books as those later read to her by the young priest (chapter 58).

5. *St Katherine:* St. Katherine of Alexandria, supposedly a fourth-century virgin martyr, whose cult was popular in the Middle Ages. Of noble birth, she refused to marry the emperor because she was the bride of Christ. More than fifty philosophers failed to persuade her of the errors of Christianity. She was tortured by being broken on the wheel that became her symbol, and then beheaded.

6. *St Margaret:* St. Margaret of Antioch was a legendary virgin martyr who rejected the advances of the governor of Antioch and was tortured, imprisoned, and tempted by a devil, whom she boldly trampled underfoot. Margery Kempe was named after her, and many Norfolk churches were dedicated to her, including the principal church of Lynn.

7. *St Barbara:* The cult of this legendary virgin martyr was popular in the later Middle Ages. Shut up in a tower by her father so that no man should see her, she became a Christian; her furious father was killed by lightning after he handed her over to a judge to be condemned. She was the patron of those in peril of sudden death.

8. *church . . . at Rome:* the Church of the Santi Apostoli, almost completely rebuilt in the eighteenth century.

9. *St Lateran's Day:* 9 November, the feast of the dedication of the church of St. John Lateran (on the site of an ancient palace which had belonged to the Laterani family and then became the official papal residence). Margery was probably there in 1414.

10. *Benedictus . . . Domini:* "Blessed is he that comes in the name of the Lord."

11. *Lord of Canterbury . . . required:* Margery had visited Archbishop Chichele at Canterbury, talked to him "until the stars appeared in the sky," and been given a letter granting her "authority to choose her confessor and to receive communion every Sunday . . . throughout all his province" (Windeatt, p. 72).

12. *Good Friday . . . Holy Church:* The crucifix was wrapped in silk and buried with the Host in a special tomb-chest (usually in the chancel wall), and a vigil was kept.

13. *Therefore . . . without end:* Like Julian of Norwich, Margery is wishing for universal salvation.

14. *our Lord . . . visitation:* Lk 19:41–44.

15. *Of the plentiful grace . . . sperantibus in te . . . :* All this episode is placed in chapter V of the Middle English version, where the Latin is rendered as, "Lorde, thou arte ful good to hem that tristen in the."

16. *The Prick of Love:* probably a Middle English version of the *Stimulus Amoris.*

17. *Richard of Hampole:* i.e., Richard Rolle.

18. *Elizabeth of Hungary:* 1287–1331; she became a Franciscan tertiary, tending the poor and sick, after the death of her husband, the Landgrave of Thuringia. Her relics made Marburg a popular shrine.

FOR THE BEST IN PAPERBACKS, LOOK FOR THE 🐧

In every corner of the world, on every subject under the sun, Penguin represents quality and variety—the very best in publishing today.

For complete information about books available from Penguin—including Penguin Classics, Penguin Compass, and Puffins—and how to order them, write to us at the appropriate address below. Please note that for copyright reasons the selection of books varies from country to country.

In the United States: Please write to *Penguin Group (USA), P.O. Box 12289 Dept. B, Newark, New Jersey 07101-5289* or call 1-800-788-6262.

In the United Kingdom: Please write to *Dept. EP, Penguin Books Ltd, Bath Road, Harmondsworth, West Drayton, Middlesex UB7 0DA.*

In Canada: Please write to *Penguin Books Canada Ltd, 10 Alcorn Avenue, Suite 300, Toronto, Ontario M4V 3B2.*

In Australia: Please write to *Penguin Books Australia Ltd, P.O. Box 257, Ringwood, Victoria 3134.*

In New Zealand: Please write to *Penguin Books (NZ) Ltd, Private Bag 102902, North Shore Mail Centre, Auckland 10.*

In India: Please write to *Penguin Books India Pvt Ltd, 11 Panchsheel Shopping Centre, Panchsheel Park, New Delhi 110 017.*

In the Netherlands: Please write to *Penguin Books Netherlands bv, Postbus 3507, NL-1001 AH Amsterdam.*

In Germany: Please write to *Penguin Books Deutschland GmbH, Metzlerstrasse 26, 60594 Frankfurt am Main.*

In Spain: Please write to *Penguin Books S. A., Bravo Murillo 19, 1° B, 28015 Madrid.*

In Italy: Please write to *Penguin Italia s.r.l., Via Benedetto Croce 2, 20094 Corsico, Milano.*

In France: Please write to *Penguin France, Le Carré Wilson, 62 rue Benjamin Baillaud, 31500 Toulouse.*

In Japan: Please write to *Penguin Books Japan Ltd, Kaneko Building, 2-3-25 Koraku, Bunkyo-Ku, Tokyo 112.*

In South Africa: Please write to *Penguin Books South Africa (Pty) Ltd, Private Bag X14, Parkview, 2122 Johannesburg.*

Printed in the United States
by Baker & Taylor Publisher Services